ALSO BY MIKE STEWART

Sins of the Brother
Dog Island
*A Clean Kill**

*coming soon from Dell.

D0036880

A PERFECT LIFE

MIKE STEWART

A DELL BOOK

A PERFECT LIFE
A Dell Book / January 2005

Published by Bantam Dell
A division of Random House, Inc.
New York, New York

ISBN 0-440-24132-4

Manufactured in the United States of America
Published simultaneously in Canada

OPM 10 9 8 7 6 5 4 3 2 1

This book is dedicated—with affection, respect, and eternal gratitude—to my wonderful friend and agent, Sally McMillan. Her patience and support have no limits.

ACKNOWLEDGMENTS

First and foremost, I'd like to thank my wife, Amy, for listening, reading, consoling, and pushing during the writing of this story. She is always my best and toughest critic.

I'd also like to express my gratitude to my new editor, Kate Miciak, for her patience, understanding, and guidance. She's so good at what she does that it occasionally frightens me.

Finally, this novel would not have been possible without the extraordinary technological expertise of my friend Gary Warner. Gary confounds the stereotype of a computer expert through his humor and humanity while, at every turn, proving himself a thorough master of all things relating to the labyrinthine world of Internet security and modern identity theft. Any mistakes the story may contain in these areas are certainly mine and not his.

PRAISE FOR MIKE STEWART
AND HIS AWARD-WINNING THRILLERS

A CLEAN KILL

A 2002 *Publishers Weekly* Best Mystery of the Year
"The perfect summer read . . . a paranoia-inducing,
smart suspense novel. It's the best legal thriller of its
type since *The Firm*—but it's written better."
—*Flint Journal*

"Stewart's third mystery featuring attorney Tom
McInnes again combines the suspense, richly textured
plot, picturesque Alabama settings, double-crossing
characters and sparkling writing that set his first two
novels apart from the pack. . . . Stewart throws a
curveball in the surprising conclusion that will leave
mystery fans eagerly awaiting the fourth in the series."
—*Publishers Weekly* (starred review)

"Stewart knows how to build a solid case for his
sleuthing attorney." —*Pittsburgh Post-Gazette*

"A tense, nerve-wracking narrative, nonstop action, and
a tightly mortared plot keep the pages turning."
—*Library Journal*

"For fans of character-driven legal thrillers—such as
those written by Phillip Margolin, John Lescroart, and
Scott Turow—this one's a definite keeper."
—*Booklist*

SINS OF THE BROTHER

"A brilliantly plotted curve of rising suspense . . . An atmospheric setting, evocative family background, Chinese box of a plot, and a hero tough and clever enough to surprise you as much as the bad guys—it all makes for the most accomplished debut of the season, an obvious Edgar contender, and a serious threat for the title of Compleat Suspense Novel."
—*Kirkus Reviews* (starred review)

"[*Sins of the Brother*] will keep you on edge . . . with more twists than a country road."
—*Chicago Tribune*

"A novel of intelligence and authenticity [that will] please the most discriminating mystery reader."
—*Dallas Morning News*

"Intricate chess-game suspense . . . Attorney-turned-writer Mike Stewart makes a promising debut with *Sins of the Brother*."
—*Houston Chronicle*

"An impressive debut for a promising sleuth."
—*Booklist*

"As good as the characters and plot are, the writing is even better. [The] prose is so lean you could label it fat-free. . . . The tightness and the toughness of Stewart's prose are what Hemingway might write for today's market. *Sins of the Brother* exemplifies a trend in the best of today's novels, a story with tremendous

commercial appeal—watch for the movie—that is also a
beautifully crafted literary work.   Buy it; enjoy it;
tell your friends." —*First Draft*

"[A] slick, intelligent debut . . . [A] taut effort. The
brooding presence of the Alabama River provides ample
obligatory southern gothic ambiance, while the New
Orleans and Alabama settings lend pungent atmosphere
to a satisfyingly labyrinthine plot." —*Publishers Weekly*

"Familial conflicts, rural Southern characters, big-city-
lawyer tactics, and a slightly convoluted but intriguing
plot round out this debut mystery by a Birmingham
attorney." —*Library Journal*

"Most crime novelists trying to move in on John
Grisham's territory do so by upping the ante. . . . Mike
Stewart, in an impressive debut, has carved his own
niche by holding back. Stewart shows a gift for
economy of language and plot that is rare these days,
and a talent for evoking atmosphere that has all but
vanished from thriller novels. [He] finds heroism in
ordinary men placed in extraordinary circumstances
and evil in the seemingly banal, which makes *Sins of
the Brother* chillingly believable. He seems like the kind
of novelist whose career you'll want to follow, and this
is a good place to start." —*Washington Post*

"Good story...smart debut." —*New York Times*

DOG ISLAND

A Bird came down the Walk—
He did not know I saw—
He bit an Angleworm in halves
And he ate the fellow, raw

—Emily Dickinson

CHAPTER 1

Open country spread out beneath the night into distant, scribbled lines of pine and scrub brush. Freezing air whistled through invisible cracks in the hard convertible top; the whine of snow tires vibrated through rubber floor mats; and every whir, groan, and gear change poured into the Land Cruiser's interior as if amplified by a static-wracked sound system.

"Turn on the heater."

The two hitchhikers had been riding with Scott Thomas for only ten miles. He twisted a knob on the dash. "High as it'll go."

A male voice in back asked, "How old is this thing?"

"Old. It's a seventy-six."

"Freezing my ass off." The girl reached across from the passenger seat and put her hand on Scott's thigh. "Don't you wanna pull over somewhere?"

With her touch, he felt the weight of his decision to help these people settle over him. He gently lifted her hand and moved it away.

She tried to sound charming. "What's the hurry? Don't you like to have fun? Look at the shoulders on you. What are you, like a hockey player or something?"

Scott shook his head and breathed deeply to calm growing apprehension. He didn't tell the girl that he'd wrestled in college. Wrestlers—the real kind—learn to keep quiet about their sport around strangers. More than a few guys have something to prove, and winning a fight is only marginally less painful and undignified than losing one.

The guy in back said, "Strong-looking sonofabitch, all right. Not that big, though."

The girl giggled and touched Scott's shoulder. "Come on. Pull over. I can do things with my tongue that'll make that pretty curly hair stand on end."

Her boyfriend in the backseat—a tall kid with jelled hair—laughed. "Friendly, isn't she?"

Scott could feel things slipping. A palpable charge of confrontation was growing inside the Land Cruiser's cramped interior. The two kids were taking control—slowly asserting their aggression—without making any obvious move. He glanced at the girl. "What'd you say your name is?"

"Didn't." She giggled again and turned to look at the boy in back. "What's my name? I forget."

Scott sensed movement behind him and felt the boy's breath on the back of his neck. He jerked his foot off the gas, getting ready to slam the brake pedal to throw the guy off balance—to get some distance around him so he could do something to regain control. But the pinch of cold metal against the side of his throat stopped Scott's foot in midair. The old Land Cruiser slowed, and the sound of snow tires on pavement changed from high-pitched whine to a deep rumble.

The kid with the knife said, "Pull over. Now. Pull over, or I'll cut your throat and let my girl grab the wheel." Scott felt the moist, malodorous warmth of nervous breath roll across the skin between his hair and collar. Seconds passed. Scott's neck chilled as the boy inhaled deeply. "Go ahead and grab the steering wheel."

"What?"

"I'm not talking to you. Go ahead, baby. Take hold of the wheel. He tries to wreck us, I'm gonna cut him back to his neck bone."

Scott's mind raced. "Okay if I say something?"

The hitchhikers were quiet now. The only sound was the rumble of road and engine noise, softened by the rush of heated air blowing from somewhere beneath the dash.

"It took me two years to restore this thing, but it's not worth getting killed over." He tried to keep his voice calm, to sound reasonable. "Let me pull over. The car's yours."

The pinch of the knife edge lessened. "Pull over here."

Scott steered his four-wheel drive onto the shoulder and rolled to a stop. He put on the emergency brake and dropped the gearshift into neutral. He tried to be still inside his skin. "What now?"

The girl spoke. "Get the fuck out. What do you think?"

"He's still got the knife on my throat."

The crisp chill of the blade disappeared, leaving a shallow, stinging cut in its place. Scott popped his seat belt loose and pulled at the door release.

As his foot hit ground, he heard the girl say, "You got any money?" But by then he was already pumping his arms, kicking hard over yards of barren hayfield and angling away from the glare of headlights.

Scott sprinted into the dark, and time blurred. Distant trees remained distant as the field spun beneath his feet. Some time passed before he noticed that he heard no sounds outside the ones he made—only the hoarse rhythm of freezing air rushing into his lungs and the thumping of his boots pounding frozen earth. He stopped and turned. But no one was following. The road—a silver strand of reflected moonlight stretched tight across New

England countryside—was far away and empty. They were gone.

The strength flowed out of his legs. Scott lowered his backside onto frozen ground. He cussed. For a long time, he sat there and breathed.

A half hour passed before he ventured back onto the road. Low stone walls bracketed the right-of-way, bringing order to the landscape and quieting the pounding inside the chest of the young man who now walked there alone.

Scott Thomas was trying to work through his anger. The air was cold and sharp, the metallic scent of ozone overlaid with earthy aromas of decaying leaves and rich soil. Scott tried to imagine that he could smell the Atlantic, that he almost could feel its undulating movement against a shore that was still miles away. He was feeling his way along, using his feet to double-check the guesses his eyes were making about the ground ahead.

And, all the while, he watched for headlights and listened for the whir of snow tires on pavement.

The two kids had looked innocent enough when he'd picked them up. The girl had been a little skanky, but skank seemed to be in style. The boy had been friendly. They'd even paid for dinner at the truck stop—payment, they said, for the promised ride. Now Scott had been left to hike the edge of a lonely highway.

Snippets of music floated on the night air, and he paused to listen. Up ahead, he saw the glint of moonlight on a galvanized mailbox. Walking faster, he closed the distance and stopped at the mouth of a dirt road. Along with the music, he could now hear the soft din of people talking. He began to move toward the sounds, then hesitated. The sounds were wrong. Scott couldn't decide how—he could barely hear them.

Seconds passed. Cold winds from the Atlantic swept through barren treetops; something small clawed at the hard winter ground just out of sight; and Scott wondered why he could not move toward the sound of voices.

At the opposite end of the tire ruts where Scott Thomas waited—a quarter mile away, on the other side of a stand of wind-tortured pines and rambling brush—sat a classic New England vacation home. A house with weathered cedar shakes for siding; a house with long, wide porches and wooden framed windows painted pure white.

Parked to one side of the house sat a stolen Land Cruiser. Beside it, someone had parked a red Mercedes-Benz. Ancient monastic chants poured from a CD player in the Mercedes' dash. The boy and girl who had stolen Scott's ride lounged on wide wooden steps leading up to the porch. A pale man stood in front of them. He was in his late twenties, but dressed like a teenager. A gold ring pierced his left eyebrow.

"Any trouble?"

The knife boy laughed—a feminine, high-pitched sound. "Hell no. Boy almost shit himself."

The man with the pierced eyebrow was named Darryl Simmons, but the teenagers knew him only as Click. He held out his hand. "Give me the keys."

The girl put a hand on her boyfriend's arm. "Uh-uh, Click. That's five hundred you owe us."

Simmons stepped back and rolled his shoulders. "I've got a better idea. Give me the keys, and you're welcome to that little red Mercedes I picked up at the airport. Sell it. Whatever you want. Up to you." He smiled now. "Or"—he looked at the girl—"keep running your bitch mouth and maybe you won't be leaving here at all."

The boy handed over the keys. Click pulled five folded and gym-clipped twenties from his pocket and flipped them at the girl. The money fell. She went to a knee to grab it, then looked up. "What was this about, Click? Why'd you want that old four-wheeler from that guy?"

The girl needed a lesson. Click's right hand shot out and grabbed a handful of hair. She screamed. "Let go, you asshole!"

The pale skin on Click's knuckles turned white as he twisted the girl's face toward the ground. He held the boyfriend's eyes as he yanked the girl's head down and popped her hard in the face with his knee, then shoved her backward onto the steps.

Click nodded at the boyfriend. "You got a problem with this?"

The boy watched his sobbing girlfriend. "No. No problem."

"Too many questions. Right?"

The boy didn't answer.

"I said, too many questions, right?"

"Yeah, right, Click. Too many questions."

Click nodded at the boy. All he said was "Leave."

"We're gone, Click." The boy stood, yanked his girl up by one hand, and draped her arm over his shoulder to help her to the car. "Gone like we was never here."

Scott heard only bits of muted words and incongruous music—soft sounds that arrived sparse and indistinct and shaped by the wind. He stood very still at the mouth of the road and wondered why he could not move forward.

"Son?"

His heart popped hard in his chest. A car had stopped, and the passenger window of an ancient black Caddy was open. A man with elderly features and young eyes stared out.

The old man shook his head. "Wouldn't go up in there, I was you."

Scott hesitated for just a beat, then stepped toward the car. "Why? What's up there?"

"Just wouldn't, that's all." The old man paused to look Scott over. "You need a ride, son?"

Scott looked down the expanse of the empty road, then looked back at the driver. "I guess I do."

Long black fingers plucked at the passenger-door lock. Thick veins rolled beneath paper-thin skin on the backs of the old man's hands, and Scott noticed that the driver had fingernails like a woman or a guitar player. Pale half moons a quarter-inch long capped each bony digit.

Scott opened the door and swung his butt onto the seat. The driver dropped the transmission into drive and pulled away. Scott asked, "This highway one thirty-eight?"

The old man nodded. "Old one thirty-eight. They's a new one thirty-eight, too"—he pointed across Scott's nose—"over to the east, there. Not many folks use this one anymore."

"I was going to Boston when I lost my car. Picked up a couple of kids. One of them pulled a knife."

The old man didn't speak. He gripped the old-fashioned, oversized circle of steering wheel with both hands. Ten o'clock and two o'clock. The driver was precise. His spine was erect, almost arthritic, his black suit pressed and smooth as stovepipe.

Scott tried again. "Where are you heading tonight?"

"One thirty-eight go to Boston."

The driver didn't ask about the carjacking or how long Scott had been stranded on a lonely road in the middle of the night. He didn't even explain what it was about the dirt road that made it somewhere to avoid. But at least the old man had stopped. That was friendly enough.

Scott settled back against cloth upholstery—what

he had heard called a sofa on wheels—and watched winter fields spin past in the moonlight. Behind them, the faint drone of monastic chants dissipated into the night air.

As the Cadillac crested a hill and disappeared from sight, a woman who had watched Scott from the shadows turned and walked up the dirt road to join Click for the ride into Boston.

CHAPTER 2

Massachusetts is a wilderness. Tiny, million-dollar homes huddle along graveled beaches and saltwater marshes. Thoreau's woods rub up against the diesel stench of pock-marked interstates. Dangerous, hard-edged fishermen work and drink, fish and fight a short drive from Harvard professors and Back Bay bluebloods.

Scott Thomas loved it.

With his advisor's help, Scott had landed a one-bedroom garage apartment in Cambridge when he'd first arrived to begin doctoral studies at Harvard. It was the best neighborhood he'd ever lived in, unless you consider boarding school dormitories to be better. Scott did not. He'd spent too many Christmas vacations with the families of his teachers; he'd watched too many times as other students left for long weekends after he had refused mercy invitations to join them.

Scott had no family, not since he was ten years old. He had only himself, and he believed deeply that he had built himself—his beliefs, his character, his view of the world—from scratch. A trust fund scraped together from his father's investments had bought his education. Everything else, he had fought for all on his own.

Now his life was beginning. His life away from

school, away from paid nurturing, had started with his move to Cambridge.

The old man stopped in front of the big house on Welder Avenue and turned to Scott. "I guess you're rich."

Scott smiled. "I live over the garage."

"Student?"

Scott nodded, and so did the old man. It occurred to Scott that maybe his driver wanted money. "I appreciate the ride. I don't have much on me, but I could give you ten for gas money."

Creases formed around the driver's lips, and he may have been smiling. "You're a student. You need your money."

Scott nodded and popped open the door. When he did, the overhead light came on and Scott noticed the old man's fingernails again. "Are you a musician?"

"I'm down to the Blue Note on Bleeker next two weeks. Come by and you can buy me a whisky. Name's Walker." He nodded at the house. "Go on in. Call the po-lice 'bout your car."

Scott said, "I will. Thanks." The door shut with a satisfying sheet-metal thud, and the ancient black Caddy rolled into the night.

For the second time that evening, Scott stood alone on a cold strip of blacktop. He turned toward the house, and the crisp slush of his footsteps floated on wet winter air. Traces of snow hugged the curb, circled the trunk of a sugar maple, and lay in dirt-blackened chunks across the yard.

The main house was dark. The Ashtons had gone West to ski. But, as Scott walked across herringbone brick to the garage, he couldn't shake the feeling that he was being watched.

*   *   *

When Kate Billings stepped through the door of her apartment after midnight, she flicked on the television. Letterman had on some howling folk singer with kinky hair and an acoustic guitar. A musician or a band you've never heard of always means the end of the show. She kept walking into the bedroom, where she stripped off her clothes and stood in front of a full-length mirror.

Kate pinched imaginary pockets of fat on her hips and turned sideways to check out the side view of her butt. "Eight more pounds." She shook her head. "God." She turned back to face the mirror and examined the reflection of her breasts. Quietly she said, "Nice boobs, though." And they were. She thought so, and the men who'd had an up-close look seemed to think so, too. Of course, she thought, most men are just so happy to see a pair.

She smiled as she walked into her little bathroom and came out with an oversized towel, which she spread out in the center of the floor. Placing her toes on one end, Kate bent forward to position her hands on the far corners. She lowered her butt and began doing push-ups. Her elbows popped; they always did at first. Then the joints and muscles warmed, and her breathing grew deep. When she had counted thirty-five, she fought the impulse to stop on a multiple of five and trembled out three more. Now she collapsed and rolled onto her back. Two deep breaths, and she began her crunches.

Over the next thirty minutes, Kate Billings did isolation curls and triceps extensions with dumbbells, she pumped out military presses and shoulder shrugs, and she did leg work holding thirty-pound weights in each hand. Now she was ready for the barbell.

After she had returned the dumbbells to their spot beside the dresser, she carried the barbell to the center of the room and faced the mirror. She always worked out in the nude, and she always waited until the last two exercises—the ones with heavy weights—to watch herself in the mirror. By that point, she was pumped up. The muscles in her arms and legs were gorged with blood and tight beneath skin that glistened with sweat.

Kate began to watch herself at this point in the workout because, she believed, it gave her a view of what she would look like in just a few weeks. Perfection was, in her mind, *always* just a few weeks away. And that encouraged her to go on, to push harder every day to get there. But she also waited for the mirror until the last two exercises for another reason.

Watching her engorged muscles work and seeing the veins grow beneath wet skin, it was—well, she wondered if other women found it arousing to pump weights alone in their bedrooms. As she moved the heavy weights up and down, she wondered if her arousal was in anticipation of the way men would react when she *was* perfect, or was it some sort of self-worship, maybe even latent tendencies?

She smiled at herself in the mirror as she arched her back to curl the barbell up where cool steel pressed against the tops of her breasts. After setting the weights on the rug at her feet, she stretched out her lower back and straightened up. Her heart raced; her chest expanded, her breasts rising with each breath. She smiled and wondered if the young shrink at the hospital, if Dr. Scott Thomas, could explain why she enjoyed watching herself. Now that he was in her head, Kate imagined him lying on the bed watching her pump weights, imagined his eyes transfixed as her perfect breasts rose and fell with every breath. He was cute. Some of the other nurses had told her that Dr. Thomas had been some kind of almost Olympic-class wrestler in college.

Kate grabbed the beach towel off the floor and spread it carefully over her bedspread before lying down. She lightly touched the fingertips of her left hand to her collarbone, then traced a wandering path to her nipple. Now, as she concentrated on the last few seconds of her image in the mirror, she used her full hand to massage perspiration into her right breast. She closed her eyes and touched herself with her other hand. Seconds passed, then minutes. Kate hovered at the edge of release, but had begun to believe it wasn't going to come when the phone rang.

Kate glanced at her bedside clock. It was seventeen minutes past one in the morning, and suddenly each ring of the phone seemed to pour her full of everything she needed. Kate was usually quiet when she was alone, but now she began to whisper words and utter sounds as if encouraging a lover. On the eighth ring, Kate Billings filled to overflowing and gave herself over to the mixture of explosion and release that her imagination and her fingers had been seeking.

When her breathing had slowed, Kate leaned over and picked up the receiver. She punched in *69 and listened. She stood and walked over to stand in front of her mirror as she dialed the number recited by the operator's mechanical voice.

Her friend answered on the first ring. Classical music floated through the earpiece, and Kate smiled at her reflection.

Sirens squealed. The dark lawn tilted, and a mountain of bright flames morphed into a vinyl hospital sofa that melted into the rough shape of a Flexible Flyer. White tile flooring suddenly swept downward and curved out of sight like an enclosed roller coaster. The sled began to slip and swirl. Sirens wailed again from somewhere far away.

Scott needed it to stop.

The phone's ringing penetrated his sleep and pushed it aside. Scott reached over and fumbled among jumbled stacks of books and papers for the receiver. He knocked it off the cradle, and a tinny voice called his name from the carpet.

He called back, "Just a minute." The bedside lamp was easier to find. White light flooded the room and then faded into a single bulb. Sitting up now, he swung his feet onto the floor and found the receiver between his toes. He picked it up and breathed deeply to calm nerves worn jagged by the same half-remembered nightmare he'd been having for fifteen years.

When his breathing was normal, he said, "Hello?"

"Mr. Thomas?"

"Yes."

"You need to answer your door."

He massaged his eyes with thumb and forefinger, then reached up to run the fingers of his free hand through thick wavy hair that, no matter the effort, never looked quite tamed. Wire-rimmed glasses lay on the bedside table. He picked them up and looped a gold wire over each ear. "What's this about?" He glanced at red numbers on his clock radio. "It's two-thirty in the morning."

"Yes, two thirty-eight. This is the Cambridge police. You reported your car stolen earlier tonight. One of our officers has been outside your door for twenty minutes pressing the doorbell."

"I'm in back."

"What's that supposed to mean?" The dispatcher's pronunciation grew sharper, sliding her tone from condescending to confrontational.

"I live in an apartment over the garage. I don't even have a doorbell."

"Then you should have told us that when you called in your report."

Scott pushed again at his hair. It was a nervous habit. "I did."

"As a matter of fact, I have your report right here in front of me, and I can assure you that—"

"Please tell the officer to come around back. I'll meet him at the top of the steps."

"Right." The line went dead.

Scott shoved bare feet into untied leather sneakers and tugged at his zipper on the way to the door. Outside, the cop was already walking up painted wood steps that ran along the left side of the Ashtons' garage. Scott opened the door.

"Mr. Thomas?"

"Yes. Come in. I need to grab a shirt."

The cop chuckled as he followed Scott inside and pulled the door shut. "Don't wanna look like one of the perps on *Cops*?"

Scott went into the bedroom, got a sweatshirt from the dresser, and pulled it over his head. Back in his little living room, the patrolman waited by the front door. "That your Toyota?"

Scott stopped short. "What?"

The patrolman pulled a square of paper from his shirt pocket and unfolded it. "You reported the theft of a . . . a-ah, 1976 FJ40 Toyota Land Cruiser. Hard convertible top. Tan inside and out."

"Right." He blinked away sleep and tried to focus. "A guy and a girl—"

The cop pointed a thumb over his shoulder. "It's parked in your driveway."

CHAPTER 3

"What's the big deal?"

It was Friday morning, and Kate Billings leaned against the curved Formica top of the nurses' station, speaking to a plump redhead seated in front of a computer keyboard.

The plump nurse shrugged. "Her husband's rich. Something Hunter." She spun the wheel on her mouse to scroll down the computer screen. "*Charles* Hunter. He's the architect who designed the new children's wing. Supposed to be some kind of genius." She looked up at Kate. "Have you seen it? Guess I'm not *artistic* enough to appreciate it. Whole thing looks like a spaceship to me."

Kate smiled. "I think that was the idea. You know. Children's wing? Children? Spaceships? That kind of thing."

"Oh. Well, I guess that makes some kind of sense. Still looks stupid. Anyway, your new patient is Hunter's wife, Patricia."

"I've been taking care of her for two weeks. I know her name."

"I thought—"

"Mrs. Hunter has requested full-time nursing. That's what's new. Like I said, I've been taking her her meds and looking in for a couple of weeks, you know, whenever my rotation hit. I just meant what's the big deal about her that requires a full-time nurse. I didn't know her husband was the famous architect Hunter. I'd've been nicer to her."

The redhead smiled and stood and pushed her chair under the keyboard. "Oh. Okay. I just thought that because Dr. Reynolds asked for you specially. Course, I always wonder when a doctor does that." She paused to smooth white cotton fabric that had gathered around her ample waist. "Just watch yourself. You never know. I've seen Dr. Reynolds looking down my blouse a couple of times."

Kate grinned. "But you've got more to look at than I have."

The redhead stood a little straighter. "That's true, honey. A few extra pounds may pump up the back bumper, but what they do for the headlights makes up for it in spades." She winked. "Believe you me, honey. Believe you me."

Kate laughed as the redhead turned and walked away.

A deep voice came from behind her. "Nothing wrong with a healthy self-image."

Kate turned and came face to face with Dr. Phil Reynolds. She blushed. "We were just kidding around."

Reynolds was a tall, gaunt man with a white mane and twin cotton balls for eyebrows. And, as every student in psych rotation for twenty years had noticed, the snowy puffs above his eyes moved when he spoke. Even Dr. Reynolds's thoughts were often accompanied by much waggling of those famous eyebrows. Now they had moved apart to form quotes at the outside edges of his eyes. This was, Kate knew, a look of bemusement.

"We started out discussing my new patient, Patricia Hunter. I heard you asked for me to be assigned to her full time."

He nodded. "That's right."

Kate waited, but Reynolds had the therapist's habit of assessing when he should be speaking. Finally, she said, "May I ask why?"

"Why full time or why you?"

"Both, I guess."

"Full time because she can afford it and because her husband is important to this hospital. Not very pretty, but there it is." His pale eyes searched Kate's face. "Why you is a little harder to explain. Let's just call it a hunch."

"That clears that up."

The older man laughed. "Okay. Let's just say that Patricia Hunter is a strong woman. Wealthy. A little condescending. Unusually pretty." Reynolds pushed both hands into his hip pockets and looked at the floor. "I suppose I thought that she would be less likely to try to intimidate you and that you would be less likely than most of the nurses to be intimidated. You are . . ." The old shrink's cotton-ball eyebrows bunched beneath the weight of his discomfort.

Kate Billings was not analytical by nature, but she understood men. She always had. Now she interrupted to save him. "Can you tell me why Mrs. Hunter is here? I mean, I know depression. But I was wondering . . ."

Reynolds smiled with relief at not having to tell a beautiful young nurse that she was beautiful. It was a comment that hit too close to home for casual conversation in a busy hospital corridor. "Oh, ah. Her seventeen-year-old son, well, really, her stepson, Charles Hunter III, I think, died a few days before she checked herself in. The boy drowned somewhere down off the North Carolina coast. Mrs. Hunter is, as you said, experiencing depression." He lowered his voice. "Also, self-destructive thoughts. That kind of thing. She asked me for help."

"Do I need to do anything special?"

"No, no. Just be available to her at all times when you're on duty. I'd like you to switch to a noon-till-eight shift, though. Mrs. Hunter seems to be a late sleeper, and it'll make it easier for you to work with Dr. Thomas on this." The old man used the hospital courtesy of referring to doctoral students as "doctor," even though that title had yet to be earned. "You do know Scott, don't you? He's monitoring a number of patients for me."

Kate Billings flashed on her fantasy of Scott Thomas lying on her bed, his eyes transfixed on her breasts as she pumped weights, and her face colored. Dr. Reynolds said nothing, but his eyebrows floated higher on his forehead and a smile formed at the corners of his mouth.

"Yes, I know him. Not well. Just around the hospital."

"Yes, well, I'd like you to work with Scott. I'm not asking you to report to a graduate student. I'm just asking you to talk with him, to tell him any observations you may have about Mrs. Hunter. Dr. Thomas is in charge of coordinating her treatment." He paused. "That's about it. You'll start tomorrow at noon. Dr. Thomas will be in this afternoon after classes. Please touch base with him."

Kate knew that Patricia had asked for her by name. She smiled. "I will, Doctor."

As the old man walked away, Kate wondered how much Patricia had told him about their relationship. But, she thought, so far, so good.

CHAPTER 4

Scott Thomas hated hospitals.

He hated the long tubes of fluorescent light that made sick people look even sicker; he hated the depressing art—the waiting-room pastels and the picture-book landscapes that lined the hallways. He hated every cough, every gasp and wheeze that emanated from the patients' rooms, not because he lacked sympathy but because he seemed to feel every guttural response and plea in his own gut. Most of all, he hated the medicinal smells of disinfectant and managed death—smells whose stain had first seeped into his mind in a Birmingham waiting room when he was ten years old.

He pushed his glasses up to massage his eyes, then reached across the counter to pull a patient's chart from a stainless steel rack. Scanning the chart, he pulled a Palm Pilot out of a hip pocket and flipped open the metal case.

Behind him a child's voice said, "You're not supposed to do that."

He turned to see a little girl, seven or eight years old, standing outside the room of a newly admitted paranoid schizophrenic. Scott said, "I'm a doctor," which wasn't exactly true.

"You don't look like a doctor." She took a tentative

step forward and self-consciously tugged at the hem of a green sweatshirt that had *Limited Too* written in glitter across the chest. "Doctors wear white coats."

Earlier that afternoon, the girl's mother had been delivered to the psych floor in full-body restraints after a neighbor had discovered her cooking the family cat for lunch. Scott hadn't clocked in until four. He knew nothing of the girl or her mother. He smiled. "What do I look like?"

The girl didn't answer right away. She was studying his clothes. "I don't know what you look like. You dress like the boys in my class."

He smiled again because she was right. "What's your name?"

She crossed her arms. "Not supposed to tell."

Scott's eyes moved to the nurses' station and the corridors beyond. "Probably a good idea."

The little girl said, "I won't tell on you."

He said, "Thanks," but his eyes were scanning the hallways. He caught the eye of a plump, redheaded nurse leaving a patient's room. She paused, and Scott motioned for her to come.

He turned back to the little girl. "Are you here visiting?"

"My mommy's sick." The child's lip quivered slightly, but her guarded eyes never changed. It was the reaction of someone who is hurting but who is used to the sensation. This child was well versed in keeping the family secret. Scott had seen too many children of disturbed patients who wore that wounded expression. The truth was, he had seen it in the mirror.

He walked forward and squatted down to be level with her bright blue eyes. He pointed at the door behind her. "Is your daddy in there?"

She nodded, and her eyes left Scott to take in the nurse who was now standing beside him.

Scott looked up. The redhead looked irritated at

having been beckoned by a student shrink. Scott stood. "This beautiful little girl is visiting her mommy. She won't tell me her name, but she says I dress like I'm her age."

Understanding replaced irritation in the nurse's eyes. She knew as well as Scott that the psych floor was no place for a child. The only thing worse than seeing a parent in emotional trouble is seeing one strapped screaming to a hospital bed.

The nurse smiled. "Why, this is Mrs. Winton's little girl. How are you, honey?"

"My daddy told me to wait here."

The kid was no dummy. She sensed that the grown-ups were going to move her to a more convenient location, like a piece of awkward or misplaced furniture. Scott spoke to the nurse. "Why don't you step in and have a word with Mr. Winton while I stay here with Miss No-name?"

The nurse nodded, then she gently pushed by the child and into the room. Seconds later, a young father with old eyes and pale skin stepped into the hallway. He looked down at his daughter. "Time to go home."

"What about Mommy?"

The father's words caught in his throat.

Scott put his hand on the man's shoulder but spoke to the child. "We're going to take good care of her. Right now, your mother needs to rest. And you need to take your father home where he can get some rest, too." He turned to the nurse. "Why don't you take No-name—"

"My name's Savannah."

"Savannah, can you go with the nurse for just a minute? I'm sure she can find you a Coke or a Sprite. I need to speak with your father."

Winton told his daughter it was okay to go, and the plump nurse led her away.

When the child was out of earshot, Scott spoke quietly to the man whose wife had been losing her mind since the day they married. "I know this is hard."

Winton glared now. "You do? You know what this feels like?"

"Yes." Scott nodded, "I do. But, as tough as it is for you, it's a thousand times tougher for a child." The man started to interrupt, and Scott held up his hands. "I know you're doing the best you can. Just, please, find somewhere for your daughter besides these halls. It's a tough place for adults. For her . . ." His voice trailed off as he paused to examine the man's defeated face. "Look. My name's Scott Thomas. I'm here every weekday afternoon." He pulled a generic hospital card from his pocket and jotted his number on the back. "Call any time. Leave a message if I'm not here. I can find out more than you can. And"—he paused again—"see if you can get Savannah to talk to you about her mother. She's keeping too much inside, Mr. Winton. I know the look. She needs to know it's okay to talk with you about this."

The man nodded—the movement seemed to take all his strength—and left to collect his daughter.

Scott was standing at the nurses' station when father and child got on the elevator. The little girl held a soft drink in one hand. She caught Scott's eye, then she held up her free hand and made a squeezing, bye-bye motion. The wave was universal—something almost all little kids do—but it pulled hard at Scott's memory. The child's gesture echoing that of his own little brother years ago.

He mirrored her wave and smiled. But as he turned and navigated the spider web of hallways leading to room 1236, his smile faded.

Scott Thomas hated hospitals.

In the too-bright corridor, Scott paused to draw a deep breath before knocking on the door of his least favorite patient. A voice, muffled by the closed door, said, "Not now."

"Mrs. Hunter? It's Scott Thomas. I need to speak with you."

"I'm not dressed. Please come back later." It was something new each day. The first couple of times, Scott had fallen for it; then he had realized that Patricia Hunter would never have time for his questions.

"Cover up if you need to. I'm coming in." He pressed the lever on the door handle, but then hesitated a few seconds on the off chance she was telling the truth. When he stepped into the room, he found Mrs. Hunter lounging on her bed. She was dressed in cotton pajamas and a blue silk robe, and she leaned against half a dozen pillows. She was a beautiful woman—hospital pale and without a hint of makeup, but quite beautiful in that dark-haired, blue-eyed way that cameras love. Across her lap lay an open copy of *The Shining*.

He nodded at the book. "Are you a Stephen King fan?"

She smiled the way certain well-bred women do when they're irritated. "Is that psychologically significant?"

"Probably."

He glanced down at her chart. Patricia Hunter had checked herself in to Boston General two weeks earlier, complaining of depression and suicidal thoughts following the death of her stepson. After reviewing the notes from her counseling sessions and conducting nearly a dozen of these interviews, Scott had concluded that Mrs. Hunter suffered from nothing more serious than extraordinary and perverse self-involvement. It seemed that this woman had found in her stepson's death nothing so much as a bright lens to focus society's attention onto herself.

It was a harsh assessment, but this was a harsh woman. Truth be known, she was simply spoiled the way beautiful people often are throughout their lives—first by doting parents and teachers and then by the opposite sex. And Scott was still idealistic enough to resent the time and attention that Mrs. Hunter took away from the care of his other patients who wanted, and desperately needed, to get over real emotional harm. The psych ward nurses, who'd had the pleasure of her company twenty-four hours a day, had dubbed Mrs. Hunter a "carrier," meaning she didn't suffer from emotional harm so much as she inflicted it on others.

He looked up from her chart. "How are you feeling?"

"Peachy." She turned and gazed out the window. "Scotty?" Her boredom sounded forced. "You seem like a nice boy, but I do not want to be a part of your educational experience."

"Dr. Reynolds asked me to monitor the progress of—"

She transferred her gaze to the ceiling. "Where's the remote control?"

"On the bedside table. But, if you could wait a few minutes, we really need—" As Scott spoke, Patricia Hunter picked up the remote and clicked on the television. He raised his voice over the din. "We really need to talk about your progress." He glanced down at a list of questions on his clipboard. "Now, Dr. Reynolds isn't seeing your participation grow in your group sessions. We'd like to know if there's anything we can do to make you more comfortable."

"Go . . . away." She spaced out the words, pausing between them for emphasis.

"If you could just—"

She clicked off the television, settled into the pillows, then closed her beautiful blue eyes. "Turn off the light on your way out, Scotty."

Scott Thomas dropped the clipboard to his side and turned to leave. As he pulled open the door and reached to kill the lights, he said, "See you tomorrow, Mrs. Hunter."

Just before the door closed, he heard his patient say, "Fuck you, Scotty."

In the hallway he paused to jot a few notes on Mrs. Hunter's chart.

Patient P. Hunter remains hostile and uncoopera-
tive. Concur with Dr. Reynolds's assessment this
A.M. *Patient distrusts authority, suffers moderate*
paranoia and social disconnect. She is not, how-
ever, clinically depressed.

As he clipped the pen into his shirt pocket, Scott glanced at the closed door and spoke quietly to himself. "And fuck you, too, lady."

A voice sounded behind him. "That's not very professional."

Scott turned to see the smiling face of an attractive nurse only a couple of years older than he. "Oh. Hi, Kate." His face colored. "You surprised me."

Kate Billings wore a black trench coat over pure white scrubs. In one hand she held leather gloves that had puffs of rabbit fur lining the bottom edges. "Trouble with Mrs. Hunter?"

"Yeah." He motioned for Kate to follow him a few steps away from the door. "The woman's miserable. She's not clinically depressed, but she *is* miserable and wants everyone else to feel the same way. I'm afraid I just got enough of her. I think Dr. Reynolds has me come over here after classes just so he won't have to deal with her outside the group." He watched the nurse button her coat. "I hear you're stuck with her full time."

"She likes me. I bring her Xanax." Kate smiled. "Dr. Reynolds wanted you and me to get together this afternoon and kind of coordinate. I guess I need some guidance on what a full-time nurse is supposed to do. I keep picturing a lot of wasted time, sitting around waiting for her to ring a little bell or something."

Scott smiled back. Smiling at Kate Billings was easy.

"Unfortunately, I think you may have a pretty good handle on it. Basically, she's rich, she's spoiled, and she wants her backside kissed full time."

"Dr. Reynolds told me that one of the reasons he asked for me was because I wouldn't be intimidated."

"Patricia Hunter wanting her ass kissed isn't the same as us wanting you to kiss it."

"That's good." Kate held her purse under one arm while she pulled on gloves. "Is it true that her teenage stepson killed himself after she seduced him?"

"News to me, but I'm just her analyst." He added, "I know that sounds bad. But she's utilizing a bed here that could be occupied by someone who really needs it." He paused. "Seduced her own stepson, huh?"

"Probably gossip." She glanced in her purse to make sure her keys were there. "I hear you had your Jeep stolen."

"It's an old Land Cruiser. Looks a little like a Jeep Wrangler on steroids. I got it back."

"How'd that happen?"

"No one knows. Made me look like an idiot for reporting it. Pretty spooky, too. These two kids carjacked me at knifepoint out in the middle of nowhere, south of here, then just brought it to my apartment last night and left it."

"Probably got scared, found your address in the car somewhere, and brought it back."

"I guess."

"Anyway." Kate smiled that great smile again. "Gotta go. Hot date to get ready for."

"Good luck." It was something to say.

Kate glanced back over her shoulder as she headed for the elevators. "All I hope for now is a decent dinner and a movie without having to hear about his job or his ex. And, believe me, that takes some luck these days." She paused and turned back. "Dr. Thomas?"

"Yeah?"

"I was thinking. Why don't you take me out some night and see what kind of luck you have?"

Scott was still trying to think of a response when the elevator doors opened and Kate Billings disappeared inside.

CHAPTER 5

Scott's rhythmic breathing sent puffs of fog into the morning air. His apartment lay three hundred yards behind him now. His muscles were warm, his breathing deep and easy. Concrete—cracked and chipped by New England winters—spun beneath his feet. Frigid air burned his lungs, and his mind cleared. Other stocking-capped joggers moved stiffly in the morning air, and, as always, the movement and rhythm of running helped Scott to order his thoughts, to separate childhood demons from the pleasures of his work. After all, he was in the doctoral program in psychology at Harvard. He smiled and felt the hard, metallic taste of cold against his teeth.

Unbelievable.

Cutting through campus, he made his way to the Starbucks on Harvard Square, where he stood in line with the full weirdness of Harvard University, ordered a blueberry muffin top and a large cappuccino, and picked up a Saturday *New York Times* at the register. He ate standing until a stool opened up in front of the plate glass facing Church Street.

As Scott placed his purchases on the counter, a young man with a pierced eyebrow reached over and shoved at Scott's folded newspaper. "She's coming back."

Scott looked at the guy, then turned to see the

teenage girl who'd just vacated the stool push through the crowd and leave by the street door. "I don't think so." He sat on the stool.

"I said she's coming back."

Scott took a sip of his coffee. "Doesn't look like it."

The guy pushed to his feet. "Listen, asshole—"

Scott swiveled on the stool to meet the guy's eyes. "If your friend comes back, I'll be happy to give her my seat. Until she does, you really need to sit down and shut up."

The guy trembled. All he could get out was "Asshole."

Scott turned back to his newspaper. "Yeah, you said that."

A few seconds passed before the young man spun away from Scott and ran after his girl. When he'd gone, a woman in running shoes smiled at Scott from two seats away. She nodded at the departed irritant. "Nice guy."

Scott shrugged. "He had an argument with his girlfriend. Just needed to blow off some steam."

The woman's eyes narrowed. "How'd you know that? I listened to them bitch at each other for ten minutes before you came in."

"Lucky guess." He smiled. "Pretty obvious, if you think about it."

She gathered up her breakfast trash. "You should do this for a living."

"I do."

"Okay." She pointed out the window. "What do you make of *him*?"

Scott leaned forward to look down the sidewalk where a young man leaned against a lightpole. "What do you mean?"

"Sit back. Wait until I tell you to look."

The student shrink smiled, settled back onto his stool, and opened the newspaper.

"Okay, now."

Scott glanced up from the sports section and sighed.

But something in the woman's expression made him look again. When he leaned forward, his vision locked into a pair of extraordinarily dark and disturbing eyes, and something—something with the horrible familiarity of a half-forgotten nightmare—seized deep in his gut.

Scott fought the temptation to look away. The young man held his gaze for just a few seconds, then turned and trotted effortlessly across heavy midday traffic.

The woman leaned over to nudge Scott. "Well?"

"I don't know."

"What was wrong with his face? All shiny like that?"

"Scar tissue."

"Poor thing." She grimaced. "But what'd he have against you?"

"What are you talking about?"

"Well, *Mr.* I-do-this-for-a-living, that guy had been out there staring a hole in you since you walked in the front door."

"Maybe he thought he knew me from somewhere." Scott's thoughts stumbled for an explanation that would salve his own nerves. "I work at a hospital."

"Oh." The woman seemed satisfied. "That's probably it."

Fifteen minutes later, Scott was back on the sidewalk. Starbucks had been on the return side of his three-mile run. Now, a half mile from home, he walked and sipped coffee and scanned newspaper headlines. Israelis and Palestinians were killing each other; LAX had been evacuated again after a baggage checker fell asleep; identity theft was the fastest-growing crime in America. The end of history was turning out to be a real bear.

He jogged up open steps to the small porch outside the door to his apartment over the Ashtons' garage. He pulled a key from inside his shirt where it hung on a string around his neck. The metal was warm against his fingertips. He leaned down to fit it into the dead bolt.

Static electricity popped him hard on the ends of his fingers, and he let out a little yelp.

Smiling at the delicacy of his vocalization, he leaned back down and slid his key into the lock.

And a sound—a scraping noise—came from inside.

He tried the door. It wasn't locked. He pushed the door open and called out. "Hello?"

No one answered.

"Listen. There's a cheap stereo in the living room, and I keep my money in the bedside table. Already gave away a car this week."

He backed carefully down the steps and jogged out onto Welder Avenue. A block down, Scott ducked into a rose arbor that arched over a neighbor's front walk. He thought of finding a phone to call the cops. Instead he waited, realizing he was more curious than angry.

It's a fact of life. People break into apartments. It was almost sad that someone had chosen his. Scott only hoped they didn't want a three-year-old computer. He needed the computer.

Six minutes passed before the intruders walked casually out of the Ashtons' driveway and turned up Welder. One, a black teenage boy, wore an oversized denim jacket with matching jeans. A black stocking cap was pulled down below his eyebrows so that he couldn't blink without brushing wool with his eyelashes. His friend was white and dressed the same, and Scott noticed, not for the first time, that what looks streetwise on black kids just makes white kids look like they've been watching too much MTV.

Scott stepped out from the arch of dormant thorns to follow. There was, he thought, something extraordinarily satisfying about spying on people who had tried to do him wrong.

And it was amazingly easy. TV cop shows had led him to believe that criminals have some sixth sense about being followed. Not these. They were as stupid as most people who commit crimes for a living.

Only four blocks away, the pair in rapper duds climbed into a blue Lexus with tiny tires, chromed wheels, and a tag that Scott was able to memorize at a glance.

He watched them drive away. Back at his apartment, Scott checked every corner, closet, and drawer. His computer and stereo were just as he'd left them.

Nothing seemed to be missing.

He quickly jogged back outside, down the wooden steps, and across the yard to the main house. The Ashtons were on vacation, and he felt some sense of responsibility for the place. But every window and door was locked, and he could find no evidence of tampering.

Scott walked back out to the road and looked both ways. Seeing nothing out of the ordinary, he returned to his apartment and his newspaper.

Just after noon, Scott was finishing both the last of the Saturday newspaper and a pepperoni and banana-pepper pizza when his phone rang. A familiar voice said, "Scott?"

"Dr. Reynolds. How are you?"

"Fine. Fine. Enjoying your weekend, I hope."

Scott glanced at his Palm Pilot on the coffee table. He had jotted down the description and tag number of the blue Lexus on the touch screen when he returned home from his run. "It's one of the strangest weekends I've had in a while. You know I had my car stolen and returned within a few hours Thursday night?"

"I heard. I know it was distressing."

"Yeah. Well, this morning a couple of guys broke into my apartment."

"Are you all right?" Alarm colored the older man's voice.

"Oh, sure. I came back from running and found my door unlocked. So I backed off and waited out of sight. A few minutes later, two guys came walking out of the driveway."

"Did you call the police?"

"No. They didn't take anything. At least, as far as I can tell, they didn't. I already reported a stolen car that the cops found in my driveway. If I report this, too, they're going to think I'm some kind of nut."

"But—"

"I'll change out the lock before I go to bed tonight and keep an closer eye on the Ashtons' place for a while. They've got an alarm. I can't see where there's much else I can do."

"Right." Silence settled into the phone line. Reynolds was ready to move on, and he was struggling to transition from concern to disappointment. "I called to ask you to stop by the hospital this afternoon, Scott."

Saturday was supposed to be left free for keeping up with course work. That had been the deal. Scott asked, "Is something wrong?"

The old man hesitated again. "I've been looking over your patient notes this morning. And, uh, frankly, I think you're being a bit dismissive of Patricia Hunter's condition. I know she's difficult, Scott. But she lost a stepson. His name was Trey. He was a real person, Scott. Not just a name in a patient's history."

Scott felt his face flush. "Very few people can lecture me on loss, Dr. Reynolds." It was more than he should have said.

The older man sighed. "Be that as it may, you need to remember that lovable, well-adjusted people seldom need our kind of help."

Something deep in Scott's gut squirmed. This was the first time Reynolds had reprimanded him, and the younger man felt a surprisingly vivid clawing at his ego. Scott said, "Your patient notes aren't much different from mine, Doctor."

"We'll discuss this further at two o'clock. Please come by my office then."

Scott repeated, "Two o'clock," said good-bye, and hung up.

"A no-smoking blues club." Cannonball Walker shook his head. "What the hell they gonna do to us next?" The old bluesman had joined Scott between sets. The two men sat drinking bourbon. They were surrounded by a Pima-cotton sea of martini sippers. Recorded music floated through a dozen speakers.

Scott asked, "What's that they're playing now?"

The old musician sipped his bourbon, balancing the edge of the glass against a creased lower lip and tipping the whisky onto his tongue. "Clapton." His sharp features remained impassive. "Trying to sound black."

"Yeah, well, 'trying to sound black' is a pretty good description of most music these days, isn't it?"

"Lotsa good blues players, jazz, too, lots of 'em white. Most of 'em from the South, though. At least Chicago." Walker shook his head. "Guess I oughta be happy all these lawyers and stock brokers wanna . . . do whatever it is they're doin' here."

Scott sipped his bourbon. Fire rolled down his throat. The scent of woodsmoke saturated his sinuses. *Fire and smoke*. He'd only ordered the stuff because Walker had, but, sip by sip, it was definitely growing on him. "Anyway, I wanted to thank you again for picking me up the other night."

Walker kept his eyes on the tabletop as he nodded his head.

Scott decided to dive in. "Why'd you tell me not to

go up that dirt road where you found me? Have you been up there before?"

"I didn't tell you what to do. Just said I wouldn't go up in there if I was you. And, no, I ain't never been up that road." The old man paused to take a long pull at his drink. "Been up plenty of roads like it. Just not that one."

Walker's glass was empty. Scott pointed at it, and the old man nodded. The waitress was already there when he turned. She said, "Two more?"

Scott said, "At least," and she flashed the bright smile of one who works for tips. Scott turned back to Walker. "What do you mean, you've been up roads like it?"

Walker shook his head. All he said was "Plain old evil."

"What was evil?"

"You was standing in a *cloud* of evil. Why I stopped." Cannonball Walker moved his eyes over the younger man's face. "You think I'm full of shit, don't you?"

Scott shook his head and shifted in his chair. This was not a man he wanted to insult. "No, I don't. That's your belief system. I respect that. It's just . . ."

"A superstitious old man from down South don't understand that evil is some kinda boogeyman made up by people to explain the bad stuff life dumps on us?"

"Well . . ." Scott took a deep breath. "Yeah. I don't think evil exists. People are bundles of genetic and environmental influences. Every few months, some researcher ties one more form of aberrant behavior to a chemical or biological trigger." The waitress sat two thick glasses of Black Jack Daniel's on the table and took away Walker's empty. Scott looked from the waitress to Walker, whose young eyes seemed to have grown older, before going on. "All that stuff—hormones, brain chemicals, bad experiences—can, when they get messed up, work together to produce some bizarre behavior. People can do horrible things to each other. But, no, I don't believe in the concept of actual evil as a force or entity.

And, no disrespect intended, I don't see how anybody can feel the presence of—"

"Why didn't you walk up that road? Tell me that, Doc. I could hear voices and some kinda music when I rolled down my window." He paused to drink some bourbon. "You was out there all alone. Had your car stolen. 'Bout to freeze your nuts off. Tell me, what kept you from walkin' up that little road and joinin' the party?"

Scott rolled amber whisky around in his glass. A flickering flame, from the candle in the center of the table, played across the swirling surface. A chill ran along his spine. "I don't know."

"Uh-huh." The old man threw back his drink, and a wet cough pushed water into his eyes. "I don't know you, but . . . You're a shrink, right? Studyin' to be one?"

"Right."

"Well, how you gonna help people who are hurtin' if all you see is brain chemicals when you look at 'em? You're a good boy, but you're standin' back too far. Sometimes you gotta get up close and smell the hurt, breathe in the evil on a body before you can help 'em." He paused to scratch at salt-and-pepper hair with those long fingernails. "Too much talkin'."

"It might interest you to know that one of the most famous shrinks in the country, a man named Phil Reynolds, told me pretty much the same thing this afternoon while he was reaming me out about a pain-in-the-ass patient I've got."

"I'm givin' advice, but old men don't know everything."

Scott looked up from his drink. Candlelight fired Walker's black irises. "I know."

The old man said, "Maybe."

"And about you being from 'down South,' I was born in Birmingham. Lived there until I was ten."

Walker nodded. "Time for the next set." He stood. "You gonna stay around?"

"Someone's meeting me here."

"A woman?"

Scott smiled. "Yes. A woman. From the hospital."

The old bluesman grinned. "Well, at least you got that right. You do believe in pussy, don't you, boy?"

Scott colored a little, and Walker took the stage. The old man picked up a battered Les Paul and pulled the leather strap over his head. Some unseen hand turned a spot on him. White curls sparkled in his hair like the glitter that spelled out *Cannonball Walker* in vertical lettering on the black strap that ran from his shoulder to the neck of his Gibson.

Leaning into the mike, Walker said, "This one's called 'Don't Answer the Door.' B.B. King had some luck with it." He grinned at his audience. "But I do it better."

The old man's fingers sat flat on the strings, something like the way Thelonious Monk played piano, but the sound was rich and precise. He began, "Woman I don't want a soul, hanging around my house when I'm not at home."

A nearer voice said, "I couldn't find you," and Kate Billings pulled out the chair vacated by Cannonball Walker. "It's darker in here than out in the street." She wore jeans and some kind of shiny, clingy blouse. Her hairstyle was a little edgier than Scott had ever seen it at the hospital.

"Glad you could make it. You're early. I thought Patricia Hunter would have you there till four in the morning fluffing pillows. Maybe brewing herbal tea or something."

"No. Actually, I think I'm gonna like this personal nursing thing. I gave Mrs. Hunter her meds, waited thirty minutes, then asked if I could leave a little early."

She laughed. "Worked like a charm." She nodded at the stage. "Is this the man you told me about?"

"He's the one." Scott paused to listen to Walker pick out a heartbreaking bridge. "Great, isn't he?"

Kate wrinkled her nose. "If you say so. I'm kinda into eighties music right now."

"Knew there had to be something wrong with you."

Kate listened for a few seconds. "Sorry. I don't get it." The waitress appeared at Scott's elbow, and Kate ordered a "Blue Aztec."

Scott asked, "What's that?"

Disdain colored the waitress's smile. "It's a martini, sir."

Kate ignored her. "Scott? You're not a wannabe, are you? I dated a guy like that last year who drove me crazy. Nothing's more embarrassing than a white boy in a do-rag saying 'whack' every other sentence."

"No, no. I've been white my whole life. Had a lot of time to get used to it."

Kate seemed to understand that Scott had been kidding; so she showed her teeth.

Scott added, "You don't have to wanna be anything to appreciate classic American music."

She shrugged. "Whatever. Listen, what was going on with you and Dr. Reynolds today? You both looked like . . . Well, both of you looked pissed is how you looked. What was that about?"

Scott paused while the waitress set an oversized, fluorescent blue martini in front of Kate. He was glad for the interruption, since he had no intention of sharing the details of his humiliating meeting with Reynolds, and the pause gave him time to think. "It was," he said, "about a patient. No big deal."

Kate took in a mouthful of blue martini. "It was about my private patient, wasn't it?"

He nodded at her drink. "What the hell's in that thing?"

"You're trying to avoid my question."

"Do you think?"

"Okay, okay." She turned toward the stage. "Guess I'm going to have to listen to some 'classic American music,' whether I want to or not."

Kate made it through "The Thrill Is Gone," "Hummingbird," and a newer song called "Every Loser in Town Knows My Name."

That was all she could take. "I know you're enjoying this, Scott, but I came here by cab. Could you give me a ride home?"

He smiled. "Absolutely. I'm sorry tonight was a bust."

"Cute guy who likes geeky music beats the reverse every time. Let's just stick to movies or dinner in the future." She leaned closer. "That's my sneaky way of asking you to ask me out again, in case you didn't pick up on that."

"You're just so subtle."

"Yeah." She smiled and ran her tongue over her bottom lip. "That's me."

Scott stood, caught Cannonball Walker's eye, and mouthed the word *Sorry*. As he spoke, Scott moistened his thumb and forefinger in bourbon, then reached out to snuff out the candle on his table.

CHAPTER 6

Charles Hunter was used to getting what he wanted. At least he was nice about it. "Thank you for seeing me on Sunday afternoon, Doctor."

Reynolds nodded, and his white eyebrows bunched on either side of deep furrows above his nose. "I always think it's important to meet with family members whenever possible. Especially a spouse." The truth was that Charles Hunter could have requested a midnight hot-tub meeting with Phil Reynolds and he would have gotten it. The man had not only designed the new children's wing, he had kicked back his fees as a donation to the pediatric cancer center.

Nice begets courtesy. Nice with lots of money begets anything it wants.

Charles cut to the chase. "How's Patricia doing?"

Reynolds's eyebrows bunched harder, then floated apart. "Your wife is a difficult case. To be perfectly candid, Mrs. Hunter does not exhibit the classic signs of clinical depression. She has a good appetite, and we've noticed no problem with her sleeping. No insomnia, and she doesn't seem to use sleep as an escape."

"Well, then . . ."

Reynolds held up a palm. "If I may."

Charles nodded and settled back in his chair.

"Your wife is not clinically depressed. But she is exhibiting symptoms of mild paranoia, which manifest themselves in rather . . . This is an uncomfortable thing to tell you. But her relationship with the world is, let's say, stunted. She feels under siege." Reynolds tried to judge the effect his words were having on the architect. He couldn't.

Seconds passed before Charles Hunter spoke. "Has Patricia told you that I've asked for a divorce?"

"No. I'm very sorry to hear that."

Hunter nodded. "Doctor, what you just described are my wife's *good* traits. Patricia's a beautiful woman. I married her too soon after my first wife's death. Told myself it was for my daughter, Sarah. Trey, my son, was fourteen, but Sarah was only seven and needed a mother. My first wife, Jennie, and I didn't have any more children after Trey was born, not for a long time. I was working hard, and Jennie had gone back to school for her master's. Anyway, Sarah was born when I was thirty-six. Six years later, she'd lost her mother. I, of course, had lost my best friend—sappy as that may sound. Jennie and I met freshman year of college."

Reynolds didn't speak. He had been trained not to.

"Anyway, I'm just telling you this to explain that, when Jennie died, I hadn't been on a date with another woman since fall of my freshman year at the University of Chicago." He stopped talking, as if his point about Patricia had been made.

"It's tough for the living to compete with the dead. Maybe you could find a way to have a different kind of life than you had with Jennie. Maybe . . ."

"Damn it, Doctor!" Hunter snapped at Reynolds just as someone's fist bumped at the office door.

Reynolds said, "Yes?"

The door opened and a plump, redheaded nurse stuck

her head inside. "I'm sorry to bother you, Doctor. But Mr. Hunter has a phone call. They said it was urgent."

"Thank you, Sylvia." He turned to Hunter. "You can take it in here. I'll step outside."

As Reynolds rose and walked around the desk, his guest stood and touched his elbow. "I apologize for my tone a minute ago. This has been a difficult time. Patricia says she's here because *she* lost a stepson. She never seemed to notice that I lost a *son*, or that she'd left me alone to deal with that loss and to explain to my ten-year-old daughter why, after losing her mother, her brother had to die, too. And"—tears welled in his eyes—"explain to a little girl why her stepmother has suddenly deserted all of us. My son was my life, Doctor. More talented even than me at his age. Straight As since the first grade and a wonderful athlete. A track star. Still in high school, and my alma mater, the University of Chicago, had already offered him a scholarship to study art next summer in Rome." He paused to breathe deeply. "My son. Trey. A kid. A beautiful seventeen-year-old kid with the world at his feet."

Reynolds reached up to pat Hunter's shoulder. "I'll be outside." Hunter punched a blinking button and picked up the receiver. As the doctor closed his office door, he heard the architect clear the emotion from his voice before saying "It was stupid to call me here."

Reynolds moved away from the door. He had no wish to hear more.

Exactly one hour and thirty-five minutes after midnight, bright yellow light from the hallway cut a gash across Patricia Hunter's dark room. She stirred. A hand covered in latex pushed the door shut with a quiet thud, quickly followed by the click of the knob mechanism locking into place. There was no further movement, no other sound, until Patricia's breathing returned to a deep and even rhythm. A small, dry snore punctuated her every few breaths.

For long minutes, nothing happened. Then came the whispered friction of latex against cloth. A glowing green line began to radiate from the edges of a pocket at the intruder's side; then a latex-wrinkled hand emerged, holding the kind of chemical glow stick that tiny ghosts and goblins carry on Halloween night. Just the small, radiant ends of the stick protruded from a fist that seemed to float through the room without benefit of a supporting arm or body. It stopped at Patricia's bedside table and gently laid the light stick beside the remote control. Now, as the full length of the stick came uncovered, an eerie glow washed the room, and the shape of the intruder stood dark and motionless above Patricia's sleeping form.

In one swift movement, the dark presence leapt onto the bed, jammed a knee on either side of Patricia's blanketed arms, and snatched a hospital pillow from beneath her head. The sleeping woman started and gasped in air to scream, but the pillow had already sealed her mouth and nostrils and her muffled scream died inside polyester fill. The pillowcase scratched her lips and tongue; the faint yet bitter taste of laundry detergent flooded her mouth and licked at the back of her throat. She gagged and twisted against the covers, fighting and clawing against the dark form pinning her down. Tears flowed into the pillow along with her screams until she vomited and choked and vomited again. Patricia Hunter gagged once more and lost consciousness.

The murderer remained as still as the murdered— two human forms frozen in place as exactly 240 seconds were silently and methodically counted off inside the only conscious mind in the room. Finally, the latex-gloved fingers of one hand moved away from the pillow to press against Patricia's jugular. Her flesh felt warm but held no more life than butcher's meat.

The killer climbed down off of Patricia Hunter's corpse, lifted the covers, and fished out her left hand, which was then briefly placed inside a white plastic sleeve. After returning the plastic sleeve to a coat pocket, the murderer picked up the green light stick and quietly exited the room.

As the door clicked shut, the digital clock at the nurses' station read 1:41 A.M.

CHAPTER 7

Scott's phone rang at 3:00 A.M. He fumbled in the dark for the receiver, picked it up, and said, "Yes? Hello?"

"Patricia Hunter is dead. Murdered, we think. Come to the hospital as soon as possible."

"What?"

The caller said, "As soon as possible, Scott."

Scott managed to get out "Could you repeat . . ." before he heard a *click* and the line went dead. He lay in bed and thought of calling back but didn't even know who had called. He reached over to click on the bedside lamp. Fifteen minutes later, Scott Thomas cranked his Land Cruiser and pulled out onto Welder Avenue.

Four Boston Police cruisers were parked near the main entrance when he arrived at the hospital. He drove by and pulled into the parking deck.

Inside the hospital corridors, a couple of nurses called his name as he hurried to the psych floor without stopping. When the elevator opened on the twelfth floor, a plainclothes officer intercepted him. Three questions later, Scott was ushered to a doctors' conference room. As Scott stepped inside, Dr. Reynolds placed a phone into its cradle on the credenza and spoke to a second policeman. "She's not answering." Reynolds nodded at Scott without speaking.

The cop ignored Scott existence as he jotted something in a small notebook. "What time did . . ." He flipped back a page. "What time did Kate Billings get off work last night?"

Phil Reynolds scratched a thumbnail across a day's worth of white stubble on his jaw. "She works an overlapping shift. That, uh, means not a regular shift—you know eight, four, twelve. Kate's here five days a week from noon till eight P.M."

The cop kept writing. "What days?"

"It varies, I think. I could check for you, but I know she was here yesterday."

"That's okay. We're gonna need to talk to her tomorrow, though."

Dr. Reynolds nodded and turned his attention to Scott. The young psychologist's always tousled hair was now spread into a fanned turkey's tail at his crown, and his skin seemed drained of blood. Reynolds offered a weak smile. "Scott, why don't you step into the bathroom and comb your hair."

The officer with the notebook, a muscular Irish stereotype of a Boston cop, said, "We don't care about his hair, Doctor."

The elevator cop nodded at the Irish cop and motioned for him to step outside. Both detectives left the room.

Scott looked at Reynolds. "What happened?"

Reynolds shifted his weight from foot to foot. "Well, the police said not to say anything"—he paused—"but that's nonsense. The truth is that Mrs. Hunter has been . . . well, someone apparently crept into her room tonight and smothered her with a pillow."

Scott felt his stomach tighten in on itself. "Do they know who did it? I mean—"

The detectives came back into the room. "Let's all

have a seat and talk a little." He asked Scott and Dr. Reynolds to sit in a pair of chairs, while he propped one butt cheek on the conference table. Scott pointed discreetly at the cop, and Reynolds nodded.

The Irish cop asked, "What?"

Reynolds said, "Sorry?"

"What's Mr. Thomas pointin' at?"

The older shrink nodded to Scott, who explained. "You're establishing a position of superiority for the interview. You know, you're looking down on us. We're looking up to you." He paused to examine the policeman's passive face. "Sorry, this is what we do."

He seemed unimpressed. "I am Detective Tandy. That"—he pointed to the elevator cop, who looked vaguely Mediterranean—"is Lieutenant Cedris. We're just after a little preliminary information here. You don't have to talk with us, but things'll go a lot quicker if you're willing to cooperate."

Scott nodded, trying to project professional competence despite a hard fist of pain in his gut. "Sure. Absolutely."

"Doctor?"

Reynolds nodded. "Only we prefer to speak with you together."

Tandy turned to Scott. "Is that right?"

Scott's eyes moved around the room as he ran Reynolds's statement over in his mind. A few seconds passed before he simply said, "Yes."

"We would rather speak separately—"

Reynolds interrupted firmly. "No, Officer. I'm sorry, but hospital policy is never to let an employee submit to an interview without a hospital representative present. Here I guess Dr. Thomas and I can serve that purpose for each other. Unless you plan to arrest one of us."

The officer shook his head. "No. Not at this time."

He pointed at Scott. "Your boss just called you 'doctor.' Is that how I should address you?"

"No. I'm third year in the doctoral program. The title is more or less complimentary."

Tandy grinned. "Helps not to scare the patients."

"Something like that."

Tandy looked behind him before pushing back onto the tabletop and letting his feet dangle. "You don't know this, *Dr.* Thomas, because you just got here, but Dr. Reynolds here has been violating hospital policy for most of the last hour. Seems like *he* can talk all he wants without a representative present." He pulled out his little notebook and flipped it open. "Lemme see. I got about nine, maybe ten, pages here of Dr. Reynolds's statements that he made outside the presence of any kind of representative." He flipped the little book closed. "What's that tell an educated man like yourself, *Dr.* Thomas?"

"What are you getting at?" Scott ran his fingers though the turkey tail on his crown. "Look, I've had about three hours' sleep and just found out that one of my patients was murdered. So"—he searched for the right words—"stop talking in circles and ask what you want to know." He heard his voice rising in pitch and made a conscious effort to slow his breathing.

The officer shrugged. "I ain't talkin' in circles. Just pointin' out that Dr. Reynolds's bullshit hospital policy—"

Reynolds interrupted. "Now see here."

"That this alleged policy about havin' a *representative* present only applies to you." He paused, but Reynolds kept silent. "What I'm wondering is why you got your own little policy there. What is it makes you so special?"

Scott shook his head. "I'm not special."

"Where are you from, Dr. Thomas?"

"All over. I've been in school, boarding schools, since I was ten."

The cop leaned forward. "Mommy and Daddy didn't love you?"

"This interview is over," Reynolds said, raising his voice.

Scott placed his hand over the older man's forearm. "It's okay." He turned to face the Irish cop. "Mommy and Daddy loved me just fine until they both died in a house fire. After that, school was about the only place I had to go."

The dark cop, Cedris, stepped forward from the back of the room. "Detective Tandy, wait out in the hallway."

The Irish cop's cheeks glowed with broken capillaries. "You can't tell me what to do. Fine, the guy's parents died. Shit happens. Many's the time I wished my old man would drive off a cliff."

Lieutenant Cedris turned to Reynolds. "Am I correct in stating that this interview is over unless and until Detective Tandy leaves the room?"

Reynolds smiled. "Perfectly correct."

Tandy jumped down off the table, shoved his little notebook into a breast pocket, and slammed the door on the way out.

Scott said, "Good cop, bad cop?"

"Something like that. Different styles, anyhow." Cedris circled the table and pulled a chair around with the others. He looked at the older man. "This okay?"

Reynolds nodded.

Cedris sat. Then he asked Scott, "Do you prefer doctor or mister?"

"You can call me Scott."

"Okay, Scott. We're going to need you at the downtown precinct tomorrow for a full statement." He opened a notebook. "For now, please tell me the last time you saw Patricia Hunter."

Scott began with his arrival at the hospital Friday afternoon and told the officer everything he could remember about his brief meeting with Mrs. Hunter. He told about the inquisitive little girl; he detailed his brief conversation with Kate Billings; and he named when he could, and described when he couldn't, members of the cleaning staff who came around just after eight.

Toward the end of Scott's story, Detective Tandy opened the conference room door and stuck his head inside. The ruddy Irish cop looked full and satisfied. He shook his head at his partner and said two words: "Never happened." Then he left Scott alone with Dr. Reynolds and Lieutenant Cedris.

When, at the cop's instruction, Scott had repeated everything he knew a second time, Cedris asked the question he'd been waiting to ask. "One more thing. How'd you know to come here tonight?"

"What?"

"Just now. Why'd you show up at the hospital at three-thirty in the morning?"

"I thought you knew. I got a phone call."

"Yes." He flipped back a dozen pages in his little notebook. "You said someone called at three A.M., stating that Mrs. Hunter had been murdered and asking you to come to the hospital as soon as possible."

"Exactly."

Cedris smiled. "Okay. Fine. Who was it that called you, Scott?"

"I don't know."

"You don't know?"

"No, ah, it was just a quick message. Something like 'Patricia Hunter is dead. She's been murdered. Come to the hospital as soon as you can.' "

"Anything else?"

"I'm not sure. The phone woke me from a sound sleep."

"Of course it did. But no name?"

"No."

"Man or a woman?"

"I'm not sure. A woman, I think."

"You *think* it was a woman. No title? Nothing like that?"

Scott shook his head. Something was wrong.

"And it never occurred to you to call the hospital and verify some of this before you got dressed and drove down here in the middle of the night?"

"Am I some kind of suspect?"

Cedris asked, "Should you be?"

"No." Scott froze as the weight of the officer's inquiry sunk in. "I shouldn't."

"That's strange, Scott. That's very strange since my partner, Detective Tandy, has been searching the hospital for anyone who might have called you about the murder. And guess what?" Cedris paused, but neither Scott nor Dr. Reynolds spoke. " 'Never happened.' That's what he said. 'Never happened.' But you already knew that, didn't you, Scott? You know damn well that no one called you at—"

Reynolds blurted out, "That's it! No more questions until hospital counsel is present." The old man stood. "Come on, Scott. We're getting out of here."

Cedris blocked the two men's path. "Scott? Are you refusing to answer any more questions without a lawyer?"

"Yeah," Scott said, "I guess I am."

"You guess—"

"I refuse to answer any more questions until I confer with an attorney."

Cedris smiled and stepped aside. "That's all I wanted to know. Have a pleasant evening, Scott." He turned and nodded at the older man. "Dr. Reynolds."

The cops left around 5:00 A.M. Scott left a few minutes later, after receiving an awkward bear hug from Dr. Reynolds—a strange and unprecedented act that, more than anything else that happened that night, frightened Scott so deeply that the simple embrace sent waves of nausea rolling through the pit of his stomach.

CHAPTER 8

A tiny red light blinked in the dark of Kate Billings's bedroom. She stirred inside flannel sheets, glanced at the incoming-call light, and rolled onto her side. Kate had already turned off the phone's ringer, and she'd switched off her pager the minute she got home. She was off duty, she was exhausted, and whoever wanted her could damn well call back in the morning.

As sleep settled over her like a warm blanket, she realized that there was something wonderfully delicious about ignoring someone rude enough to interrupt her sleep.

Scott punched the OFF button and dropped the receiver on his bed. He spoke to the room. "You should've answered the phone, Kate." He shook his head at the bedspread. "You really should have."

Worry churned the hospital coffee in his stomach as he climbed back into bed a few minutes before sunrise. Finally, exhaustion overtook misery and he descended into the comparative comfort of a fitful sleep.

Less than an hour passed before Scott sensed some vague and whispered movement inside the room. Too exhausted to move—too tired to want to—he opened his eyes.

The morning sun cut through drawn miniblinds, slicing dark furniture and flooring into intersecting bands of light. A shadow flitted across drawn blinds. Scott's breathing came faster. He tried to concentrate, but the room was empty and he was just so tired. Sleep had begun to take him under again when floorboards creaked in the outer sitting room. Moving slowly—moving, he hoped, like a man turning in his sleep—Scott once again scanned the bedroom. Still he was alone. But the sound had been real.

He flipped the covers away, pivoted, and planted his feet on cold floorboards. Grabbing his glasses off the bedside table, he stepped to the closet and reached inside for the only weapon he owned. As his fingers closed around the leather grip of a softball bat, a hushed metallic sound sent something like an electric shock across his shoulders.

The bedroom doorknob was turning. The sleepy ex-wrestler sprang across the room and flattened against the wall before his mind had finished processing what was happening. He raised the bat overhead, but it occurred to him that bashing in a burglar's skull was more violence than he was willing to do. Shifting slightly to the right, Scott assumed a batter's stance, staying as close to the wall as possible. The old door popped and shuddered a little as it cleared the frame, and the white kid in rapper duds who'd broken into his apartment the day before stepped into the bedroom.

A jumble of thoughts tumbled through Scott's mind. He recognized the intruder; he understood that the second burglar from the day before was probably following the first into his room; he thought of what the second burglar might do if he pounded the first one with a bat. He swung hard at the intruder's stomach.

The kid twisted instinctively backward as the bat came around. Scott felt the soft thud of contact a split second before the tip of his bat slammed against the door frame. And he heard pain in the grunt that followed. Seconds passed. Only the soft rush of labored breathing came from the outer room.

Scott called out. "Who's there? Listen. The cops are on the way. I called 911. You'd better get the hell out of here."

"You wouldn't be lying to us, would you, jack?"

Scott could feel the soft thump of his heart in his neck and temples. "What?"

The same man's voice said, "You didn't call the damn cops." The speaker made a repeated humming sound, like an old lady disapproving of an unruly grandchild. "Kick the door shut. Go ahead, Scotty. Kick the mother."

Scott pushed the door shut with the thick end of his bat. "Are you leaving?"

"Soon." The man's voice was muffled now. "Go ahead. Call the cops. Whatever you want. We'll be gone before they get here." A loud crash came from the living room. "That's my partner. You pissed the boy off with that bat shit." A series of thumps and bangs echoed through the door. "Up to you, but I'm saying better make that call. You don't got the cops coming, hell, I may not be able to keep my boy out of there."

Scott glanced at the phone on the bedside table. If he moved to pick it up, he would be out in the open, unable to get the first shot with his bat at anyone coming through the doorway. His eyes scanned the room. "Okay. Send him in."

"You think you gonna Sammy Sosa his ass again? Shit won't work twice. Told you once, Scotty. Telling you again. Better jump on 911 before my boy here jump on you."

Scott's heel bumped the Gateway CPU on the floor next to his desk. Turning, he eased backward. Keeping his eyes on the closed door, he grabbed the mouse on the desk and double-clicked the telephone icon on his computer desktop. A number pad popped up on screen. He punched 911 on the keyboard and hit ENTER.

Two long rings buzzed through his computer speakers, and one of the intruders in the other room said, " 'Bout time."

"Emergency services." The voice sounded dangerously loud coming through his speakers.

Scott turned to speak into the little microphone stuck to the base of his monitor. He gave his name, phone number, and address. "Someone's in my apartment. Two burglars, I think."

"We'll send someone around." The operator paused. "Uh, sir, are you there, sir?"

"They're here *now*."

"I understand, sir. I'm having trouble hearing you."

"I said, they're here now."

"Yes, sir. I understand. Get out of the apartment if you can. Find a place of safety if you can't. A patrol car is on the way."

Scott reached back to click on the DONE button. As he did, the same burglar said, "I guess you're all safe now."

Scott stepped quickly back to the side of his door and readied the bat. "Kiss my ass."

The two men in his tiny living room were speaking quietly to each other—their indistinct words nothing but a low, unsteady rumble. Scott leaned against the door to listen, but couldn't make out what they were saying. He glanced back again at the computer, tried to remember how to record through the microphone onto the hard disk, and cussed in the dark. The soft rumble of voices ceased and started up again.

Scott reached back to feel for the microphone. It was shaped like a small disk and glued to the base of his monitor by one of those sticky foam-rubber things that came with the computer. He got his fingernails under it and ripped the plastic disk loose.

Pulling slowly, testing the length of the wire running from microphone to computer, Scott stretched the tiny mike to the base of the door. He leaned down and silently pushed the plastic disk under the corner of the door separating him from the burglars.

Scott glanced again at the keypad on the computer screen. He punched the first digit of his office phone number at the hospital, and the speaker let out a loud beep.

From the other room, "You callin' yo mama now?"

"Why don't you come in here and find out?"

"You keep talkin' tough, we might have to do that."

As the burglar spoke, Scott repeatedly punched the leftmost button at the top of keyboard. The green volume indicators on his screen retreated to nothing, and the speakers were off.

He punched in the remainder of his office number and waited. If the system was working right, if no one happened by his tiny cubicle and picked up the receiver, if the thing worked the way it usually did, the phone would ring four times, automated voice mail would answer, and the call would be recorded.

A lot of ifs, he thought, to record a lot of mumbling.

But then he heard the soft beep of numbers being dialed again, only this time the sounds emanated from the living room side of the door. When the beeping ended, Scott said, "*You* calling your mother now?"

"No, bitch. I'm callin' yo momma."

Scott was quiet. Listening. Louder mumbling was followed by the click of a flip phone snapping shut. Lower now, the mix of the two men's voices hummed through the wooden door. Scott was almost certain he made out the word "done" just before he heard the familiar, homey sound of his front door opening. A puff of frigid air rolled across the living room floor and brushed Scott's bare feet as it passed beneath the bedroom door.

"Got one more thing before we step out, Scotty." An unnatural pause lingered as cold air continued to wash over Scott's bare feet. "*We killed her*. We killed Patricia Hunter in her hospital room. Tell the police that."

The door slammed shut. Scott turned and reached for the mouse to click the DONE button on his telephone program.

Imagination wrung hours out of the next six minutes. Time slipped back into gear only when the faint swirling sounds of police sirens filled Scott's ears. But still he didn't move. He followed the dispatcher's instructions. He stayed in his place of safety until he heard a loud knock on the front door. "Police! We're coming in."

The front door banged against something. Scott called out. "I'm Scott Thomas. In the bedroom. I think they're gone."

A South Boston voice, filled with long vowels and sharp consonants, said, "Do you have a weapon?"

Scott hesitated to call out to someone on the other side of a closed door that he was unarmed. He had heard the siren, but . . .

"Sir! Are you armed? Do you have a weapon?"

"Uh, yes. I've got a softball bat."

Scott thought he heard soft laughter. "Please step through the door. It's safe. Whoever was here is gone now. You can keep the bat if it makes you feel better."

Scott opened the door.

Two uniformed cops stood side by side, blocking Scott's path to his front door. Each held an automatic pistol securely in both hands, the muzzles pointed at the floor three feet from their toes.

The smaller cop said, "Are you Mr. Thomas?"

Scott nodded. "Yes."

"We'd feel better if you put the bat down now, sir."

Scott turned and tossed his bat onto the sofa, but then stopped short. Two loaded firearms pointed in his direction had blocked out everything else until now.

White stuffing and yellow foam rubber spilled from ugly gashes in the sofa's cushions. Torn books and smashed videotapes were piled on the butchered sofa. Everything in the room—television, stereo, lamps, even a clay voodoo god from a trip to New Orleans—everything was smashed, torn, or broken.

The smaller cop spoke again, interrupting Scott's inspection of the mess. "We need to see some identification."

"I'm sorry? What?"

"I know this is upsetting, sir. But, if you don't mind, I'd like to step into your bedroom with you while you get your driver's license."

Scott was deep in sensory overload. "Sure. Right." He motioned with his hand. "Come on."

The short cop followed Scott into the bedroom. His partner brought up the rear. Both patrolmen, Scott noticed, kept their pistols drawn and at the ready position. While Scott fished his wallet out of a pair of jeans, the second patrolman, the one who never spoke, stepped into the bathroom and then the closet. When he was done, the larger officer said one word.

"Clear."

Both cops immediately holstered their weapons. Scott handed over his driver's license. The small cop took the license, squinted at it in the dim bedroom, and then pulled a black flashlight from his equipment belt.

Scott reached down and turned on the bedside lamp.

"Thank you, Mr. Thomas." He looked up. "My partner here will take your formal statement while I call this in."

Something prickled at Scott's shoulders. "What do you mean, call it in?"

The little cop's eyes glazed over. "Officer Jordan will take your statement." And he walked out.

* * *

The dispatcher's voice crackled through the box speaker in the patrol car. "Your vic is a suspect in a murder investigation."

Officer Marcus Tinelle felt a jolt of adrenaline. "You got a flag?"

"Got a 'must contact' from Boston PD for him. Just a second." Static hummed through the silence. "We'll radio your situation to Detectives Tandy and Cedris. Hold your position."

"Ten-four."

Only eight minutes passed before Marcus Tinelle's radio filled with the calm voice of Lieutenant Victor Cedris. "You got a cell phone, Tinelle?"

"Sure."

"Gimme the number."

Seconds later, Tinelle's phone vibrated in the palm of his hand.

Cedris asked, "What's happening?"

"The vic, Scott Thomas, called 911 at eight-thirty-three A.M. and reported two intruders inside his garage apartment on Welder Avenue. We arrived on the scene at eight-forty and entered the living room of a two-room apartment. The room had been trashed. Looked like maybe somebody was looking for something. Thomas was inside his bedroom, armed with a softball bat. He came out. My partner and I followed him back into the bedroom. There was no apparent damage to the bedroom. No one, other than Thomas, was present in the apartment." Tinelle hesitated. "I understand Thomas is a suspect in a murder investigation."

Cedris said, "But we don't care about that now, do we?"

"We don't?"

"You've got a burglary to solve, Tinelle. I'd consider it a personal favor if you'd pull out all the stops. Get a forensics team out there. Get fingerprints. Catalog everything in the apartment. You get my meaning here, Tinelle?"

Marcus Tinelle glanced at the steps leading up to Scott Thomas's apartment and grinned. "Got it."

The homicide detective's calm voice never changed. "I look forward to reading your report, Tinelle. And, remember, I owe you one."

An hour later, Cedris had just spread cream cheese on half a sesame seed bagel when the phone on his desk rang. He sighed and tossed the bagel on a wrinkled square of waxed paper. "Cedris. Homicide."

"This is Tinelle."

"Got something for me?"

"Well, yes and no. We're still here on Welder. Nothing's jumping out at us, but you're not gonna believe what Thomas is saying."

The patrolman paused for effect. Cedris was not impressed. "Am I supposed to guess?"

"Uh, no. Uh, well, the thing is that Thomas is claiming that these two burglars—who he never saw, by the way—had some kind of conversation with him through a closed door." The patrolman hesitated again. Cedris rubbed at his eyes with thumb and forefinger and sighed. Tinelle went on. "Thomas claims the burglars confessed to murdering the Hunter woman."

"What?"

Tinelle laughed. "Can you believe that?"

"No," Cedris said, "I can't."

"Graduate student at Harvard. Unbelievable. Guess they can't teach common sense."

"Even smart guys get punchy on three hours' sleep. We had the boy at the hospital until almost sunup. And, if Thomas did kill the Hunter woman, the boy's had a hell of a night. Best thing we can do is keep him talking. Don't wanna give him time to stop and think. We don't wanna give him a chance to get his shit together, if you see what I mean."

"Yeah. Right. He's also got some screwy story about using the microphone on his computer to record some of what the burglars were saying."

"Did you listen to what he had?"

"Nothing to listen to here. Claims he somehow used his computer to call voice mail where he works. Says if the mike picked up anything it'll be recorded as a voice message down at the hospital where he's some kind of student shrink." Tinelle hesitated again, and the thought flitted through Cedris's brain that there are worse traits than thinking before you speak. Tinelle said, "Thomas says he wants to talk to *you*."

It was Cedris's turn to think. He asked, "Is the forensics team on site?"

"Been here half an hour."

"Good. Didn't want it to look like I called 'em in. They know they're supposed to swarm over that place like ants at a picnic?"

"They know. Everything's set up."

"We need this perfect. Make sure you've got Scott Thomas's statement in writing and signed."

Tinelle grinned again. "Done."

"Good." Cedris picked up his bagel and folded it neatly inside the waxed paper. "I'm on my way."

CHAPTER 9

The hotel dining room went up more than out, giving its customers the experience of dining at the bottom of an ornate air shaft. For a height of three stories, a checkerboard of oil paintings stepped through gold-leafed plaster filigree, finally reaching an abrupt end at the foot of the mezzanine balcony. Above the balcony and centered over the dining room hung a tremendous gold chandelier, shimmering with hundreds of teardrop crystals.

Sitting at a table against the outside wall of this space, his coal-black fingers spread out on white linen like the sharp and flat keys on a piano, was an old bluesman named Cannonball Walker. His head was turned toward the plate glass next to his shoulder; his eyes scanned the sidewalks. People hurried along either side of moving traffic. Occasionally some brave and hurried soul broke loose from the throng to stutter-step through bumpers and blaring horns.

Only one dark form stood as still as death—a young man with shark's eyes and discolored skin that shone like wax in the cold winter light. Cannonball Walker sat and watched the young stranger watch him.

"Mr. Walker?"

Walker started slightly and turned to see Scott Thomas's lady friend standing beside his table.

"My name is Kate Billings. Scott Thomas is a friend of mine."

Walker rose to his feet and nodded. "Remember you from the club." He held out a hand toward the chair opposite his. "Have a seat." As they both sat, Walker said, "I was watching for you out the window. Didn't see you come up."

"I drove."

He nodded again and glanced out at the watcher. Walker's eyes dropped and scanned the tablecloth. "Well, Kate." He picked up a stemmed glass and took a sip of water. "What can I do for you? You want me to listen to a homemade CD shows you the next Billie Holiday? Or is it you know some big-busted lady of color who needs a date?"

Kate Billings picked up her napkin, folded it lengthwise from corner to corner, forming a perfect triangle, and draped it over her thigh. She began to straighten the stainless flatware as she spoke. "Mr. Walker . . ."

"Call me Canon."

She smiled. "Not Cannonball?"

The old man smiled back. "Street name. Canon's my Christian name."

"Okay, Canon. I came here to tell you that Scott's in trouble. Serious trouble." Something about the old man's expression made Kate stop short. "You already know about this, don't you?"

"No. Not really."

Kate knew the male animal. For better or worse, she'd been the beneficiary of an early education in the simpleminded sex-food-work agenda of the hairier gender. And this man, this old bluesman from down South, knew more than he was telling. She tried again. "But you're not surprised."

"No."

"Why not?"

Walker studied Kate's young face. "Can't say. Just thinkin' about the first time I saw the boy. That's all."

"What's that mean?"

Walker shrugged.

"Look, this is serious. Scott's mixed up in a murder at the hospital. You need to tell me what you know. If you call yourself Scott's friend . . ."

"I don't."

Kate sat up straight in her chair. "You don't what?"

"Don't call myself Scott's friend." The old man turned sideways in the chair and stretched his legs. "You know, he seems like a good boy. Smart. Tryin' to do right. I like him fine. But a *friend* ain't somebody you've met twice in your life. Not unless the friend is good lookin' and female. Men take a little longer."

"Then you're not interested in helping Scott?"

"Didn't say that, either. Just said he wasn't what I'd call a friend." He paused. "What's he need? Bail money? A lawyer? Somebody to get him out of town?"

This wasn't going the way Kate had planned. She needed time to think. She stood up from the table. "I'm not sure what Scott needs, Mr. Walker. But I'm afraid he's going to put too much trust in the police. Tell them everything he knows, thinking, you know, good guys always come out on top, or something equally idiotic. He needs advice from someone who's been around. I know he doesn't have any family. No one to help him. I thought maybe he could rely on you." As she spun to walk away, she added, "I guess I was wrong."

"Kate?"

She stopped and turned without answering.

"This boy on the street out there with the burned face? He a friend of yours?"

Kate's eyes drifted to the window and the street scene beyond. She shook her head. "I don't know what you're talking about."

As Kate Billings walked from the dining room, Cannonball Walker raised a hand at the waiter. The old man ordered a steak sandwich and iced tea.

The waiter jotted notes on a pad. "Anything else?"

"Yeah." He glanced out the window to find that his watcher had vanished. "But I don't think you got it."

The waiter smiled because he didn't know what else to do. Thirty minutes later, Walker stepped into the lobby and asked the bell captain to have his car brought around.

Needles of cold rain stung the back of Walker's neck and hands as he watched his black Caddy roll up the circular driveway. As the red-jacketed driver stepped out, Walker pressed three ones into his hand.

"Thank you, sir. Do you need any directions this afternoon?"

The old man shook his head and lowered his backside into the driver's seat. "Nope. Been there before."

The attendant closed the driver's door. Cannonball Walker buckled his seat belt and steered fourteen feet of black steel out into Boston's midday traffic.

Almost an hour later, Cannonball Walker pulled up next to the house on Welder Avenue. Two patrol cars were jammed into the driveway. An unmarked cruiser hugged the curb out front. Walker parked behind the cruiser and stepped out into the gray afternoon. Dark clouds had packed needles of cold rain into hard sleet. Each pellet felt like a fired BB against the old man's neck and cheeks.

No one was outside. Too damn cold. Walker mounted the wooden steps that cut a diagonal across the side of the garage and paused on the small porch to listen. He knocked, and the door opened.

A uniformed officer—kind of a munchkin—said, "May I help you?"

"Here to see Scott."

"There's been a break-in. Mr. Thomas is fine. No need to worry. But he can't be disturbed. He's talking with the detective."

Walker looked impassively at the tiny officer. "You gonna let me in outta this weather?"

"Uh, well . . ."

"Hell of a thing. Keep an old man standin' out in the sleet, freezin' to death. That the way you were raised, Officer?"

Patrolman Tinelle blinked and cleared his throat and stepped back one pace to let the old man step out of the sleet. "Sorry, sir. But you're going to have to come back later to see your friend." The expression on the officer's face changed. "But, as long as you're here, can I have your name?"

Walker had stepped into the demolished living room. He could see into the bedroom. Voices floated through the open doorway. The old man smiled and nodded at the patrolman; then he leaned past him and called out, "Scott!"

"Just a minute, sir. I told you—"

"Scott! It's me. Cannonball Walker. I need you out here *now*!"

The rumble of voices from the bedroom grew louder with protestations, and Scott Thomas walked into the living room. "Mr. Walker?"

Walker nodded at Tinelle. "This here mini-a-ture po-lice-man won't let me in outta the cold."

Scott stepped forward and glared at Tinelle. "What's wrong with you?" He turned to Walker. "Come on in. Please. I'm glad you came." He waved an impotent palm at the mess. "I'm in the middle of something here."

Tinelle shifted his eyes to Lieutenant Cedris, who

had entered the room behind Scott. The patrolman started to explain. "I *did* let him in out of the sleet. I just explained—"

Walker spoke over Tinelle's protestations. "Scott, if you don't mind, I need to speak with you in private for just a minute. It's important."

Scott glanced back. He'd already been through his story twice with the little cop and once with Cedris. The lieutenant could wait a few minutes for a fourth rendition. "Okay, why don't you step in here." Scott motioned toward the open bedroom door.

Walker shook his head. "Naw. I need to talk outside." The old man turned and stepped back out onto the porch. "Walk me out to the car."

Scott glanced at Cedris and then followed Walker. As the two men descended the iced steps, Scott started to warn the older man to be careful; then he noticed that Walker didn't much move like an old man. His step was light, almost graceful. The old bluesman moved like a dancer. Instead, Scott asked, "What is it? Is something wrong?"

Walker spoke over his shoulder. "Bet your ass it is." Then quietly, almost to himself: "Should've come faster."

"What?"

"That fine-lookin' little girl you brought to the club—what's her name? Kate? Kate came to my hotel to see me at lunch today. Said you got yourself messed up in some murder. That right?"

Scott wondered why in the world Kate Billings would have gone to see a man he barely knew about the murder of Patricia Hunter. "What'd she say?"

"Well, I'll tell you what she didn't say. She didn't say nothin' about somebody breakin' in and trashin' your apartment. What's goin' on?"

While the two men stood beneath a cascade of stinging sleet, Scott gave the abridged version of Patricia Hunter's murder and then explained to Cannonball Walker about the break-in.

The old man shook his head. "Did you really tell the cops that one of the burglars said he killed this woman, this patient of yours?"

"Well, yes. It's what he said, and I thought that the connection might help the police solve—"

"Shit."

Scott was surprised by Walker's irritation. "What's wrong?"

"Shit, shit, and shit. Get in the damn car." Scott opened the door and lowered his butt onto the cloth seat. Walker sat on the driver's side and slammed the door. "Ain't my business, but I'm suggestin' you go back up to your apartment there, invite all those cops to leave, and get you a good coat."

"I can't do that. It's a crime scene."

Walker chuckled. "How many cops you got up there?"

"Well, there's two patrolmen, a detective, and three nerdy-looking cops taking fingerprints and looking for fibers or clues or something."

"And you think they just be sendin' around six cops every time some poor student gets his crib tossed?"

"No. Like I said, there's a murder connected here. One of the burglars said . . ."

Walker's eyes flashed. "One of the burglars set your stupid white ass up to give the cops a free shot at your house." He shook his head. "Goddamn, Scott."

Scott flushed. "I don't have anything to hide."

"You don't, huh?"

"No." Scott was growing angry. "I don't. They can look all day. There's nothing to find. I haven't done anything wrong. And, and I may have recorded some of what the burglars said," he stammered.

"*May* have?"

"Well, yeah. I used a little computer mike and dialed my voice mail . . ."

Walker shook his head at the sleet-covered windshield. "Good God Almighty."

"What?"

"Did they take anything? The burglars, I mean. What'd they take?"

"No. It wasn't like that. They just trashed my place. Probably came there looking for . . ." He stopped midsentence.

"Those two boys just broke in not to steal anything, not to take anything 'cause there was nothin' to take, to *confess* to the murder, and then to tell *you* to call the cops."

Scott had been functioning on almost no sleep. The burglary, the destruction of his belongings, the arrival of the cops—everything had been moving too quickly to be processed. His mind felt sluggish, his thoughts bogged in a fog of sleeplessness. "Doesn't make much sense, does it?"

"No, Scott. No, it doesn't." When Walker spoke again, his voice had grown calm and quiet. "But I'll tell you what does make some sense. It makes some sense that maybe those two boys did have somethin' to do with this Hunter woman's death, that maybe they broke in, woke you up, and confessed to the murder in a way that nobody's gonna believe. Even if you got some of it on tape . . . there ain't no witnesses. Think about it: Who the hell's gonna believe you didn't stage the tape to support the rest of your story?" Walker leaned forward to look up at the garage. "Somebody wanted you to sound like you were makin' all this up, Scott."

Silence filled the interior of the Cadillac like frost in a meat locker. Seconds passed, and the logic of Cannonball's argument settled through the mush inside the young man's skull. "Oh, hell." Scott's words sounded weak, his voice deflated. "I was worrying about what they might've taken. Instead . . ." His voice trailed off.

Walker finished the thought. "Instead you should've been worryin' about is what those two boys left. If they didn't break in to take somethin', maybe they broke in to leave somethin' behind."

"Like . . . you mean to plant some evidence from Patricia Hunter's murder?"

"Yeah," Walker said, "that's what I mean."

Scott stepped back out into the winter storm and ran over frozen ground to his apartment.

CHAPTER 10

Scott was halfway up the steps before he realized he couldn't just rush in and order the police out of his home. The time for keeping the cops out of this was past. Cedris met him at the front door.

"What's the hurry?"

Scott pushed by him into the room. "Cold." He glanced back. "How about closing the door?"

Cedris pushed the door shut. "We were getting ready to go back over your statement. If you wouldn't mind stepping into . . ."

Scott's mind raced. If he kept quiet and just let them find some kind of planted evidence, he was screwed. If he spoke up and told Cedris that he suspected the burglars of planting evidence, he was screwed with an explanation. The latter sounded better than the former. Not much, but still better. "Detective? My friend wanted to know what happened. It occurred to him that the burglar told me to call the cops for a reason."

"Is that right?" Cedris smiled. "Well, did your friend have a theory? I'll take all the help I can get."

"The burglar knew about Patricia Hunter's murder, right?"

The man looked at Scott like he'd lost his mind. "Uh-huh."

"Guy even told me to call 911. So, my friend says, what if they came here to leave something, to hide something in all this mess they made? Doesn't that make some kind of sense? You know, maybe they planned to plant some kind of evidence to shift the blame to me or maybe just to shift it away from them. Then I woke up and popped one of them in the stomach with a bat. After that, they had to improvise, right?"

Cedris said nothing.

"I mean, the guy I hit went nuts and trashed my living room. And—"

"And the burglar you talked with through the door, he improvised admitting the murder of Patricia Hunter?"

Scott stopped short. "Hell, I don't know. Nothing about this makes sense."

The lieutenant scratched his jaw. "So you're changing your earlier statement."

"Hell, no. I'm just trying to help. I'm not changing anything. This just occurred to me, that's all."

Cedris flipped back a page in his little notebook. "I thought you said this occurred to your friend."

"Right."

"Well, which is it, Mr. Thomas? Was this new theory your idea or your friend's?"

"I'm trying to be helpful, and you keep twisting my words." Scott was beyond exhausted, and he could feel his face becoming flushed with anger and frustration. He pointed to the detective's notebook. "If you're writing in there that I've changed my story, then you're a liar."

Cedris straightened up and took a step toward Scott. "Be careful who you're calling a liar, Mr. Thomas. You're the one who seems to be making it up as you go. Now, I suggest you calm down and—"

"I'm ready for you to get out of my house."

"It's a pissant garage apartment, Scott. I don't think you could call this a house."

Even through the haze of his exhaustion, Scott understood that Cedris was pushing to get him to say something stupid. When he spoke again, his voice was just above a whisper. "Leave."

"One more thing. You said at the hospital last night that your parents died when you were a kid. Burned up in a house fire, I think you said. I was wondering. Did anyone else survive?"

Scott's breath caught up short. "What's that supposed to mean?"

"It's a simple question. Did anyone else in your family survive the fire that killed your parents? A sister? A brother? Maybe a pet poodle that didn't get barbecued?"

Scott's stomach felt as though it had folded in on itself. He breathed deeply to calm himself, and the earlier flush of anger faded to something colder and emptier. When he spoke, his words were quiet and spaced out. "I told you to leave."

Cedris locked eyes with Scott, then he glanced at a chubby cop wearing thick glasses and latex gloves. "We done?"

The chubby cop nodded, and Cedis said, "Let's go."

Cedris lingered by the front door as the forensics team filed out behind Officer Tinelle and his partner. When Cedris was alone with Scott, the detective said, "Last night at the hospital I'd pretty much decided you were just in the wrong place at the wrong time. But now. . . ." He sighed. "We got you reporting a stolen Land Cruiser that was found in your driveway. We got you showing up at the hospital following the murder of your patient, with no explanation as to why you knew all about a murder that no one had mentioned to you—"

Scott interrupted. "I told you. Someone from the hospital—"

"Yeah. I know. Some man-slash-woman with no

name and no title called to tell you about Patricia
Hunter's murder . . ."

"That's right. And whoever it was told me to come
down to the hospital as soon as possible."

Cedris opened the door. Freezing air pushed in. He
said, "In addition to everything else, we now got you al-
leging one unreported burglary from days ago where they
didn't take anything or, apparently, touch anything. And
we got this burglary here today where the same two guys
still didn't take anything. They just trashed your apartment, admitted to committing murder, and then taunted
you into calling the police while they were still here."
Cedris buttoned his coat. "You know what I'm starting to
think, Scott? I'm starting to think that I'm standing here
talking to a murderer. And a stupid one at that." Then he
walked out and closed the door behind him.

Five minutes passed before Scott heard a quiet
knock at his door and found Cannonball Walker standing on the stoop. Walker looked around. "Made a mess."

Scott nodded.

Walker walked through the room, pushing at debris
with the pointed toes of black dress shoes. "Po-lice do
any of this?"

"Nope. This is what the burglars did. The cops *took*
some stuff—evidence or . . . whatever—but the mess
was here when they got here."

Walker stopped in the middle of the room, and
Scott's eyes came to rest on the back of the old man's gray
topcoat. Melting sleet had painted the shoulders with a
black shawl that feathered down the outside of each arm.
A halo of sleet hovered at the edges of his salt-and-
pepper hair.

Scott asked, "Why'd you come?"

"That girl, Kate, she asked me . . ."

"I know. It's not the *who* I'm asking about. It's
the *why*."

The wet shoulders of the old man's topcoat rose a bit and resettled. "You don't trust me?"

Scott studied the man who stood in the ruin of his living room. "I trust you."

Walker turned. "Good," he said. "Let's you and me take a ride."

"Give me a minute." Scott walked into the bedroom, picked up the telephone, and punched in his number at the hospital. When the mechanical voice answered, he entered his voice mail code and listened to a recording of mumbling overlaid with static. He punched 3 to replay the message, then pressed the RECORD button on his answering machine.

"Scott?" Canon Walker had walked into the bedroom. "You 'bout ready?"

Scott held up a palm while the message played out. "Ready as I'm going to get."

Kate Billings was late to work. Something that never happened. Absolutely never. She had been expecting to face an inquisition—in her imagination, like some heavy-handed interrogation scene from *Law & Order*—the minute she appeared at the hospital, but nothing could have been further from the truth. Other than the high-pitched, palpable thrill of gossip that arced through the nurses' station, it was the same old psych ward where she'd worked as a nut nurse for almost three years. Murder, she thought, is shocking only to those it touches; the rest of the world just keeps humming along as if nothing out of the ordinary has happened . . . because it hasn't.

She lingered in the break room, thinking. At fifty-five minutes past noon—fifty-five minutes late—Kate clocked in and reported to the managing nurse. All Jill Meters wanted to know was "Are you okay?"

Kate nodded yes and learned that she had an appointment at police headquarters at three that afternoon. Jill smiled the way people do to make you feel better at a funeral. "Take a sick day. Nobody's going to care. It's not like you'd be letting anyone down, Kate. I mean, sorry to bring this up, but you're still on the schedule for private nursing duty, so it's not like anybody's going to have to take up your slack."

"I'd rather work, at least until I have to go in for my interview with the police." Kate hesitated. "But, Jill? I think maybe you should start looking for someone to come in and replace me. You know, for good."

The senior nurse frowned. Experienced nurses like Kate had the luxury of choosing where and even what hours they wanted to work. Title IX had forced the good old boys to open up the nation's med schools to qualified women, which had drastically thinned the ranks of more than a few nursing schools. Keeping good nurses happy and in place was one of the toughest parts of Jill's job, but now she simply asked, "Too much to handle?"

"Just time for a new city." Kate glanced out the window at a mix of snow and sleet swirling against the black-stained bricks of the cancer wing across the parking lot. "Somewhere *warm*." Kate turned back to hold Jill's eyes and smile, just a little. "I won't leave you in the lurch. Just start looking. When the police say it's okay to move on, I'm probably gone."

Jill reached out and squeezed Kate's shoulder. Kate placed her hand over Jill's and smiled more broadly.

Sleet and snow thickened throughout the afternoon into what now looked like a swirling sandstorm in the Caddy's headlights. Scott squirmed in his seat and reached up to adjust the blast of hot air coming from the dash.

The old bluesman asked, "Too hot?"

"I'm fine now."

Walker reached out with those long fingernails and worked a chromed lever in the center of the dashboard. The spray of hot air moved from the vents to the defroster. "Wasn't thinkin' about it." The old man flexed his hands on the steering wheel. A few seconds passed, and he nodded at the night as if making up his mind about something. He asked, "You're not on somethin', are you, Doc?"

"On something?"

Cannonball glanced over at Scott's dark profile. "You *seem* smart. Mostly. Go to Harvard and so on. But . . ." He paused. "You givin' them cops the run of your place like that." The old man's voice trailed off as he searched for a decent way to ask an insulting question.

Scott said, "Pretty stupid, huh?"

"And—no offense, Doc—but you're slurrin' your words like you're stoned or drunk."

The young shrink's eyes scanned the road ahead. "No sleep. Just, I guess, something like two or three hours last night—which would be okay, except that I spent the time when I'm usually sleeping being questioned by the cops about a murdered patient. Then there was the break-in. Waking up and hearing burglars in the next room. . . . Stress and no sleep is a bad combination."

"Uh-huh." Walker didn't sound convinced.

Scott needed this man's help. And, for reasons he didn't fully understand, he did not want Cannonball Walker to have a low opinion of him. He said, "Some researchers in Australia compared lost sleep to drinking. Their study showed that eighteen or twenty hours without sleep has about the same effect on your brain as a point one blood-alcohol level."

"Same as the drunk drivin' limit most places."

"Right. I don't know how much you know about stuff like this. But I'm slurring because the temporal lobe of my cerebral cortex is shutting down. It's where speech is processed in the brain. That part of the brain more or less flatlines after about eighteen hours of sleep deprivation. I can still talk because other parts of the brain take over. But I'm slurring because those other parts aren't as good at speech as the frontal lobe." Scott knew he was overexplaining, overcompensating for a perceived failing, but he couldn't stop the words from coming. "And, uh, you know, I'd probably have trouble doing a math problem right now."

Cannonball nodded, but he said, "You didn't seem to have any problem rememberin' all that stuff you just said."

"It's all old information. Stuff I memorized a long time ago. Spitting out facts isn't the same as critical thinking." Scott returned his eyes to the asphalt path before them. "I guess I could probably run a mile, too. Muscles and organs can repair themselves with simple rest. Speech and analysis require sleep. Neurons require sleep."

Cannonball took a few seconds to study his passenger before returning his gaze to the highway. "You know, you're kinda babblin'."

"Yeah." Scott pushed his glasses up to massage his eyes. "I know."

"Okay." The old man nodded. "But I'm not sure I wanna know that some part of my brain's up there floppin' around useless just because I stayed up all night with a woman instead of sleepin'." He sighed. "I guess everybody's different." Some time went by before he said, "That girl Kate? She a close friend, a girlfriend or what?"

Scott took a few beats to change gears. "Nothing really. I work with her at the hospital. She was the private nurse for the Hunter woman."

Oncoming headlights repeatedly magnified into blinding globes and then disappeared as cars heading toward Boston passed behind them. It was late afternoon, and outside it looked bright white and dark at the same time. Scott said, "Hard to see."

"Yeah." Walker reached up to turn down the heat coming through the defroster. "You're not screwin' her, are you? This Kate woman."

Scott shifted in his seat. "No. I'm not."

Walker shot a disbelieving sidelong glance. "You sure?"

Scott smiled. "I'm pretty sure I'd remember."

"Got that right." The old man moved his chin up and down. "Good lookin' woman."

Scott didn't say anything.

"You know, maybe she a, uh, Christian type goes around lookin' for folks to help. Is that what you think? Maybe some kind of saint."

Scott laughed. It felt good. "I'm not sure Kate Billings is a saint, Mr. Walker."

"Call me Canon. And, no. Kate didn't seem like no saint today at lunch when she asked me to help you out." They'd been outside of the traffic congestion surrounding Boston for over an hour. The men saw progressively fewer cars and more empty fields—a lot of nothing rolling endlessly across big frosted windows. Minutes passed before Canon Walker broke the silence again. "There's good people in the world. Good to their friends, good to their families. Even a few along the way who'll treat anybody they meet like he or she was God's own messenger sent down to find a perfect soul. But when somebody I don't know comes along askin' me for somethin' that don't seem to make sense—somethin' almost noble and smellin' of nonsense—well, I always figure I gotta ask myself, what's in it for them?

"And, somethin' else. . . ."

"What is it? What were you going to say?"

The bluesman cleared his throat. "Probably nothin'. Just . . . well, there was this man watchin' us—me and Kate, I mean—watchin' us through the restaurant window.

May've had nothin' to do with her. I don't know. But when Kate walked out, I turned around and this boy had disappeared."

"He was a boy?"

"He was . . . a little younger than you, I guess. Strange lookin'. Boy's face was shiny. Kind of like—"

"Like melted plastic?" Scott interrupted.

Walker looked over. "You know him?"

"No, I don't. But I've seen him outside a coffee shop window on Harvard Square."

"What was he doin'?"

Scott thought back. He shrugged. "Watching. Almost staring me down."

Walker focused on the ribbon of highway stretched out in front of his headlights.

Scott studied his face. "So you think Kate's up to something?"

"Your guess is good as mine. This boy—this watcher—may have nothin' to do with her. Lady may be a do-gooder, some kinda sweet angel. Or she's a lost soul with somethin' to prove. Could be she just thinks you got a nice ass on you. Wants you to slip her the high hard one."

Scott tried to think. Disjointed ideas and blurred images rolled around the mush inside his skull. Two days ago, he'd been smart. Now he felt slow and stupid, unable to make sense of the puzzle pieces sloshing around in his head. He asked, "You got any ideas?"

The old man nodded. "Just one. Goin' out to the road where I picked you up the other night. Figure we'll drive up that dirt road and see what's there. Far as I can tell, that's when this mess started."

"What are we supposed to be looking for?"

Walker flexed his hands on the steering wheel but didn't answer.

Scott looked up at the fabric underside of the car top. " 'Plain old evil.' Is that what you called it?"

Canon Walker shot a tired glance at his passenger. "Woman killed in her sick bed. Buncha punks fuckin' with your head, tryin' to ruin your life." He reached for the dashboard to turn the heat back up. "What would you call it?"

CHAPTER 11

The windows behind Charles Hunter's desk overlooked Boston Harbor. What was usually an extraordinary view had now been reduced to an abstract of wind, sleet, and snow. The swirling, late-afternoon storm wasn't much to look at, but he had been looking at it for most of an hour. He'd been sitting there watching the storm turn nasty. *Nasty.* It was, he thought, a word that described too much of his life. It was a word he'd never really used, never thought much about, until Jennie died. But it was a word that had come to describe the whole world after his son drowned. Drowned in the modern paradise Charles was creating.

Trey's death had sullied the project, dirtied the place in Charles's mind, until he decided the whole thing— the town, the architecture, even the gardens—would all be monuments to Trey. His own genius would be a monument to his son's.

Charles swiveled the black Aeron chair to face the glass walls of his office. Now he could see rows of drafting tables, each with a too-stylish twenty-something architect bent studiously over its angled top—each of them infinitely inferior, in Charles's mind, to the architect his son would have become.

A scattering of corkboards clung to the see-through

walls on suction-cup feet, cutting a series of rectangles out of his view of the bullpen. Detailed drawings of floor plans and building elevations were hung from the cork-boards and propped upright on half a dozen easels. In the center of the space—with architects it's always a space, never just a room—a seaside village had been built in miniature on a glass conference table that rested on stone trapezoids. The tiny, oddly traditional village was an oasis of warmth in Hunter's coldly modern office. At that moment, it was the only thing the architect had ever designed that he could bear to look at or think about.

His glass walls—with suction-cup coat hooks and display boards, with soft linen shades that could be lowered for temporary and minimal privacy—were now *too* open. The whole place was outdated. The see-through offices that he, along with everyone else, had promised would bring open communications and de-mocratize the workplace had instead placed everyone under a microscope. Managers watched workers and workers watched each other. No one ever felt free to daydream, to look out the window at that million-dollar view and imagine something wonderful. They were all too busy looking busy, too busy earning bonuses to dream and create.

But he had begun to change all that. He was build-ing a town of the future on the Carolina coast, a town that would embrace the town squares, front porches, and wide sidewalks of the past while bringing modern design principles to traditional forms. Charles stood and walked around his desk to examine the model village, and the tensions he'd been battling began to float away.

She was gone. Maybe with this, he thought as his eyes danced over the tiny village, life will be good again.

"Ready?"

Charles glanced up at Carol Petring, his junior

partner in the seaside development. He looked back down at the model and traced fingertips along a wavering line of cardboard seacoast before he replied. "Ready to get out of this mess?" Charles motioned at the storm outside his window.

"God, yes." Carol was twenty-five, tall and slender with auburn hair and a way of holding herself that was at once feminine and athletic. She was also the most gifted architect he'd ever known—except, of course, for himself.

Charles asked, "Can we take off in this?"

Carol nodded. "The pilot says yes. But if you'd rather wait till it clears . . ."

Charles walked to his desk and picked up a brushed aluminum briefcase. "No. I won't ask you to go, not if you're uncomfortable with the weather. But I'm ready to get the hell out of this city."

She turned to leave. "Just let me get my bag from the office." Over her shoulder, she added, "Meet you by the elevators."

Charles watched the young architect leave, then glanced down at his desktop. A pink message slip lay next to the phone. It was the message that had made him turn toward the window, that had made him spend most of an hour watching ice fall out of the sky.

He read the pink slip of paper for the ninth or tenth time that afternoon.

It was a Boston number. The URGENT box was checked. The message simply read *Call me*. The name of the caller was Kate Billings.

Winter evenings come early, and night had settled over the Massachusetts countryside by the time Scott Thomas and Canon Walker located the galvanized mailbox where they'd first met. Canon wheeled the old

Caddy onto thick layers of slush and slid to a stop, jolting Scott awake.

The ice storm had ended, and the sky had cleared into a deep black blanket scattered with hard points of light. The heater purred; the engine was running too quiet to hear. The old man didn't speak.

Scott broke the silence. "What is it?"

"What I told you." The old man peered into the darkness. "You feel it?"

Scott tried to feel something. Nothing came.

"I'm too tired to feel anything. I just want to go have a look at whatever's at the end of the road." He reached up to rub at his eyes; exhaustion was rolling across him in waves. When he brought his hands down, the dark landscape rippled as if reflected in a pool of water. "After that . . . after we look here, Canon, I need sleep. I appreciate what you're doing. But, if I'm going to deal with this . . . with what's happening to me, I've got to sleep."

The older man put the car in gear and crunched over icy ruts. A couple of hundred yards in, something shimmered in the headlights, and they rolled to a stop before a thicket of ice-covered limbs.

A pine had split from stump to crown under the weight of clinging ice. Half the tree stood upright. Limbs and needles lined one side as if unaware that they now grew from a dead thing; on the other side, an open gash of yellow wood ran from jagged treetop to frozen ground. The butchered tree's spindlier half was down across the roadway.

Canon put the transmission in park. "You feel like walkin' in this mess?"

Scott shook his head as he popped open the door. "I didn't even feel like riding." But he stepped out into the slush and slammed the door shut. He heard Canon do the same, but he never looked back. Something was pushing him now. Too many events had conspired to keep him away from this place—first his own illogical fears bolstered by Canon Walker's warnings, then the weather, the lack of sleep, even the downed tree blocking the roadway. He could either give up or push ahead. Without thought, he had chosen the latter.

Outside the reach of the headlights, the frozen roadway cut through crystallized tangles of trees and brush that showed in silver and black. As Scott cleared the stand of pines, a weathered vacation home emerged from the smudged line of dark woods behind it—its white-trimmed doors and windows floating against gray-weathered siding, like stage props in a production of *Our Town*.

Scott could hear the older man's footsteps. "Canon?"

"Yeah?" The answer was whispered.

"This seems like a pretty good way to get shot. Walking up on a country house in the middle of the night like this."

"I was thinkin' the same thing." Scott turned back to speak, but Canon added, "We here now. Might as well bow up and do it."

Scott tried to read the old man's face, but his dark skin showed nothing in the night.

The gated yard held an old oak with splattered, ice-coated limbs, and each footstep sent splinters of ice cascading down in tinkling bursts. Long needles of ice hung from a satellite dish at the corner of the roof.

Scott stopped in the yard and called out. "Hello?" He glanced at Canon, who said nothing, then turned back to the house and called out louder this time. "Hello!"

Canon spoke. "No cars."

"Yeah, I know." Scott walked up wide steps to the front porch. He rapped at the door frame, and each knock sent a jolt of pain running through the bones in his hand and forearm. The cold made him feel breakable.

Again, he knocked on the door frame and called out. "No one's here. What now?"

The old man shrugged.

Scott reached up and ran numb fingers along the top of the door frame.

Walker said, "Check under the mat there."

Scott did as instructed, but found nothing. "See any flower pots or anything?"

"Here." Canon leaned over and picked up a red clay pot that made a popping noise as it came loose from the edge of the porch. Dirt now formed a neat circle around a brass key that had been secreted beneath the pot.

The key was covered in grit, and Scott wiped it on the leg of his jeans before fitting it into the dead bolt. Behind him, he heard Canon whisper. "Call out again when you get it open."

The dead bolt turned, the door swung open without a hint of sound, and Scott called out to the darkness. It did not answer. Swiping the wall next to the door, he managed to find a light switch and flip it. The house seemed to burst alive, but it was only by way of contrast with the dark. The switch worked only a small overhead fixture in the foyer.

"Step in."

Scott's mind was still swimming in exhaustion. "What?"

Canon placed a hand on Scott's back and pushed gently. "We here now. Can't look around standin' out on the porch." He shoved harder at the small of the young man's back. "Go, boy."

Both men stepped inside. Canon called out now—not just hello, but that his name was Walker, that his car broke down, that he needed help, that he needed to use a phone, that he was just an old man. Pretty much anything and everything he could think of not to get shot.

Finally, he seemed satisfied. "Okay. You want upstairs or down here?"

Scott ran his hand through his hair. "Neither."

"Too late." Canon pointed to a dark room on the left. "You go that way. Meet you at the back of the house, then we can head upstairs." The older man moved quietly away, leaving Scott standing alone beneath the foyer light.

The room Scott entered was some kind of office or study. He located a small desk lamp and clicked it on; a forty-watt bulb bathed the room in stained yellow light. The furnishings were bare but serviceable. Nothing but a particle-board door on sawhorses for a desk, but the computer was a new desktop with high-speed Internet access that—this far out in the country—was probably hooked up to the icicle-covered satellite dish outside. The desktop also held typing paper and a dark red Harvard mug full of ballpoint pens. A cheap task chair sat neatly beneath the desk; a printer squatted on the floor.

Nothing else. Nothing personal. Nothing to reflect the life or personality of the owner.

This, it seemed, was a house with no history—a place where someone was only preparing to live. Scott was thinking that he had committed breaking and entering for no more viable reason than lack of sleep when he heard movement in the foyer behind him. Turning, Scott came face to face with the man who had driven him to this place.

"What is it?"

Walker's voice came dry and hoarse. "I need you to come this way."

"What? It looks in here like somebody's just moving in. What'd you find?"

The old man's eyes narrowed. All he said was "Now," but he gestured awkwardly with his hand and arm when he said it. Scott glanced down. Cannonball Walker gripped a small black revolver in his bony fist, and the muzzle was pointed at Scott's chest.

CHAPTER 12

"What the hell?" Scott couldn't move his eyes from the gun.

"Now." Canon motioned again. "You don't wanna be fuckin' with me right now."

"You're going to just shoot me?" Scott's mind felt weighed down with the sludge of exhaustion. He felt the room tipping. "Is that why you brought me out here, Canon? Get me out in the country away from everybody and put a bullet in me?"

"Startin' to think maybe you brought *me*."

"How . . ."

"Sent the girl, Kate, to my hotel. And then you all hang-dog when I found you with the po-lice. I'm thinkin' you worked me, Doc." Canon blinked hard as if he didn't believe it himself. "Don't matter. Get in here now, or I'm gonna pull this trigger." He shrugged. "Nothin' else I can do."

Scott moved unsteadily across the room. The old bluesman backed through the foyer into a large, brightly lit living room. The whole time he kept the barrel pointed at Scott's abdomen, as if pulling him along by an invisible line.

A thrift-store easy chair was visible through the doorway. Canon backed to it and sat down. His eyes drooped. His blue-black skin looked ashen. For the first time since Scott had met the man, Canon Walker looked old and tired and ready to quit life.

"Keep comin', Doc."

Scott stepped into the living room and froze.

All four walls were plastered with pornographic images of women being mounted by tall, short, skinny, fat men—pale-skinned women on all fours mounted from behind, spread-eagle women mounted from above, contorted women mounted from the side and from below in ugly tangles of legs and arms. Scattered among the copulating nudes were black-and-white photos of naked women roped to chairs and handcuffed to bedposts, pictures of women chained wrists-to-ankles with long black nightsticks shoved into them. At the far end of the room, a horrible life-size nude poster of a bruised and lacerated female homicide victim stretched from ceiling to floor.

And on each of these pictures, over every female head, someone had glued a photograph of Patricia Hunter's smiling face. And worse. Over the faces of every hairy, slack-butted, dog-collared man, someone had pasted a blow-up of Scott's own picture from the Harvard yearbook.

It was too much. The room spun and slipped. Scott looked at Canon, the old man swung from side-to-side as if in a sideways rocking chair, and Scott Thomas's body hit the hardwood floor in a slack and unconscious heap.

Canon Walker didn't move. The fainting had looked real, but he was too old to tangle with some young stud playing possum. So he sat and watched. Minutes passed. If the boy was dead, well, he was dead. But if he had just passed out, he'd come around. Folks always rush around grabbing smelling salts and slapping faces whenever somebody faints, but he'd never heard of anyone he knew dying from it.

Canon leaned forward to get a better look. "Wake up or don't." But he felt bad as soon as he'd said it. He did wish for the first time in his life, though, that he had a cell phone. He let his eyes move over the images taped to the white Sheetrock walls. "Sick bastard."

The old man stood to stretch his legs, and Scott moaned. Canon waited. The younger man reached up to rub at his face, then pushed up on one hand and got his butt under him. "What happened?"

"Passed out."

"Fainted?"

"Women faint. Men pass out." The old man shook his head. "From the look of this, though"—he waved an open hand at the walls—"callin' you a man is an insult to every other human being with a set of balls."

"I didn't do this."

"Uh-huh."

Scott got slowly to his feet. "Why would I do something like this?" He walked toward Canon.

Canon brought the gun up. "Stop your ass right there." He glanced at the wall. "I don't know why anybody'd do somethin' like this. Sick sonofabitch, I guess. Ain't no explaining it. Some people are just . . ."

"Evil?"

Canon nodded.

"What can I do to convince you?"

"Nothin'."

"What about that gun? That's evil, isn't it? I didn't come out here packing a gun."

"Shit." The old man chuckled, but there was no mirth in it. "A gun is a tool. It can do evil, and it can stop evil. An old bluesman like me, hell, I wouldn't be alive after some of the juke joints I played if it wasn't for this little thirty-eight."

Scott tried to think. "What now?"

"Back to town." He motioned with the gun. "You gonna get a ride in the trunk. Sorry. Don't see no other way."

"Can I at least get some water before we go? My head's swimming."

Canon shrugged. "Where's the kitchen?"

"I don't fucking know!" Scott felt his face flush and realized he'd been screaming. "I've never been here before."

"You want water. Calm the hell down." Canon pointed at a door at the back of the inside wall. "Try through there. Slow. I don't want to, but I will shoot your ass if I have to."

Scott started to walk past the old man, but then hesitated. Canon reacted by impatiently jerking the muzzle of his revolver at the door. That was all the opening Scott needed. He grabbed the older man's wrist, shoved it hard away from him, and at the same time clamped down on the small bones in Canon's wrist.

A sound like a cherry bomb exploded from the older man's hand. Before Canon could pull the trigger a second time, Scott had grabbed the cylinder with his left hand and twisted the gun loose. The young ex-wrestler swept the gun away from Canon's reach while quickly stepping back and ducking under a surprisingly swift elbow the older man had aimed at his ear.

When Scott had retreated three paces, he stopped and waited.

Canon was breathing hard and rubbing his wrist. "I'm too old to run. So"—he pulled in a deep breath—"do what you're gonna do."

Scott looked down at the gun. "How do you take the bullets out of this thing?"

"Huh?"

"How do you . . ."

"Little button there on the left side. Push it up, and the cylinder swings out."

Holding the grip in his palm, Scott discovered that his thumb came to rest naturally on an indented lever. He pushed and the cylinder moved slightly to the left. Walker said, "Flop it to the left," and he did. The cylinder swung full out. Scott pointed the muzzle at the ceiling and four bullets hit the floor. Canon was ready to be helpful now. "See that steel rod sticking up on the front end? Push down on it. It'll pop out the other two bullets."

The last two cartridges hit the floor. One of them was spent. He looked up into Walker's eyes. "You're a crazy old bastard. You know that?" His eyes dropped. "Did I hurt your wrist?"

"Shit, yeah, you hurt it. What'd you think?"

Scott grinned. "I thought a crazy old man was getting ready to kill me. Here"—he held out the gun—"take this before I hurt myself."

Canon glanced at the pistol but didn't reach for it. He said, "You move pretty good for somebody with a messed-up, no-sleep frontal lobe." The old bluesman massaged his wrist. "Where'd you learn to do that? What was that, some kind of special forces move or somethin'?"

Scott grinned more broadly. "I don't think a special forces move would've had bullets bouncing around the room. I just grabbed your wrist with one hand and twisted the gun loose with the other."

"Fastest thing I've ever seen."

Scott walked over and dropped into the easy chair vacated by Canon. "I was a wrestler in college."

Canon still didn't move. "That wasn't no wrastlin' move I ever saw."

Scott could see the old man was scared. He tried to explain. "Everybody . . . almost everybody has some kind of gift." He looked around the room and sighed. "Look, I'm not quick *because* I was a wrestler. I started wrestling because I could just naturally move a little faster than most people. The coach . . . the wrestling coach at my prep school . . . saw a bunch of us boxing on the green one Sunday afternoon. He talked me into trying out for the wrestling team, and I was a state champion the first year." Scott stopped and screwed his eyes shut. "I'm kind of rambling here. Bottom line is, I never did anything like that before in my life. I'm just quick, that's all. Always have been. Nothing sinister, okay? The hell with it. You going to sit down or what?"

Next to the easy chair, someone had placed a sofa that looked like something you'd find next to a dumpster in a trailer park. Scott tossed the empty pistol onto the sofa. Canon sat down and picked up the gun. "I don't like being in this sick place." He dropped the pistol into the side pocket of his overcoat.

Scott looked around the room. "How do you think I feel?"

"That's the problem, ain't it? I don't know how you feel about it. Don't know if it turns your stomach. Don't know if you think this sick-ass room is the happiest place on earth."

"So." Scott leaned back against stained polyester cushions. "Now what?"

Darryl Simmons had been online now for seventeen hours. The apartment lights were off. Outside, the ice storm had stopped and the sounds of city traffic grew steadily as more cars ventured back out onto frozen streets.

Here, alone in his small apartment, Simmons wore black-rimmed glasses as he peered into the glow of a huge flat-panel computer screen. He had been hacking credit card numbers. It was his bread and butter.

A phone rang. Simmons muted the classical music

blasting from his computer speakers and picked up the receiver. "Yeah?"

"Is this Click?"

"Never can tell. Who wants to know?"

A few seconds passed, then the voice said, "Jimmy Lee down to the 7-Eleven. Jimmy Lee said call this number and ask for Click."

"Guess you can follow instructions."

"Uh, yeah. Well, look, Jimmy Lee says you hookin' folks up with online pussy. Uh, cut-rate porn site access numbers. You know?"

"Say the magic words."

"Oh." The caller hesitated. "Oh, yeah. Jimmy Lee said to say 'Gandalf lives.' "

Simmons, a.k.a. Click, leaned back and pulled off his glasses. "How many?"

"How many what?"

"How many IDs you need? I don't be selling retail, jack. Ten's the minimum. You need ten ID numbers, it'll be ten bucks each. A hundred flat. You need fifty numbers, I can go five bucks a pop. The access numbers are guaranteed good for two months."

"How many for a thousand?"

Click grinned. "I'll shoot you, say, two hundred-forty private memberships in the nookie site of your choice for a grand. That's"—Click barely missed a beat—"four bucks sixty-six cents a pop. And this is the good stuff. I can do Playboy Members Only, Penthouse Players Club, or we can get nasty with some online sex-show stuff. So, what you waitin' on? We got a deal or what?"

"Let's do it."

Click stood and walked to the window. "Go back to Jimmy. Show him the money, then have him call me with an e-mail address where you want the stuff delivered. When Jimmy puts the cash in my palm, the access numbers hit your computer."

"And I'm just supposed to trust Jimmy and you with a thousand bucks? Just say okay and walk out and hope you'll send the numbers?"

"Only way it's gonna happen, jack. You don't see me. I don't see you. You get the porno access numbers by e-mail routed through a dummy address." Click scanned the street beneath his window. "You found Jimmy and me, so you know who you're dealing with. And you and me both know you can hit any high school in the city and turn your one grand into three or four in a day or two. You don't wanna do it . . . fuck it. Up to you."

Seconds passed. Click had already walked to the desk to hang up when the caller said, "I'm taking the money now. Send me the sex-show access numbers. Like you said, the nasty stuff."

"You got it. I'm waitin' on Jimmy's call."

The caller said, "Like you said, I guess I know who I'm dealing with. I know Jimmy Lee, anyhow." He paused. "Don't you wanna know who you're talking to?"

"No," Click said, "that's kind of the friggin' point."

"Listen up, smartass. You may not wanna know who I am, but I promise you I'm not somebody you wanna screw over. You hear me? You don't do what you say you're gonna do, I'll be coming to see you with a nine."

"Right." Click hung up the phone.

He glanced out at the street again before settling back in front of the keyboard. He never printed anything. He never made notes, never kept passwords or addresses. It was all in his head. He'd learned that much, and not much else, from his old man. Leroy Simmons had been a numbers runner for the Irish mafia from way back. Old-timers in the neighborhood swore that Click's old man, Leroy, could keep a week's worth of football, baseball, and horse-racing odds *and* wagers between his ears. Smart as hell, they said, until the whisky finally ate his brain.

Click heard the sound of his own voice now in the dark apartment. It sounded eerily like his father's. "Can't go to jail for what's in your head." It was the Simmons family motto.

The computer screen held a day's worth of coded credit card orders to an online electronics retailer. He would unscramble the numbers later. For now, he uploaded everything he had to an online server and deleted all local files. Then, using administrative access and a sweeper program, he erased all evidence of his footprints across the Internet by expunging all incriminating entries in the server logs of the computers he had just accessed. Years ago he would have simply deleted the logs themselves, but that could raise alerts. Leaving the logs intact while erasing only his own entries was much more sophisticated. It was, he thought, more elegant.

When he was done, Click pushed away from the keyboard and stumbled into the next room where he collapsed onto a king-size bed. It was time to sleep. He'd gotten a request for something new on the shrink over at the hospital. Nothing complicated. Just keyboard time. But now he needed to sleep. Scott Thomas would have to wait.

CHAPTER 13

When Canon said he was going to the car for a bottle, Scott was sure the old man was cranking his Caddy, retreating down those ruts of heavy slush, and leaving him alone in that horrible house. So he was surprised when Canon stepped back into the foyer holding a fifth of Jack Daniel's.

He motioned to Scott. "Other room. That's turning my stomach in there."

Scott stood and followed Canon into the little makeshift study. The older man plopped down in the only chair, unscrewed the cap on his bottle, and took a swallow. Then he extended the bottle to Scott.

Scott shook his head. "I'm having enough trouble without that. Probably put me in a coma."

Canon asked, "What's upstairs?"

"I told you. I've never been inside this house in my life."

The old man bobbed his head and took another swallow.

Scott pushed his rump up onto the particle-board desk and let his feet dangle. "You reload your gun?"

Canon snorted a kind of brief chuckle. "Bet your ass."

"Try not to shoot me."

"Can't promise anything." The old man took another

pull from the bottle, then looked around the room. All he said was "Convince me."

"That I've never been here before?"

Canon Walker nodded his head, reared back in the chair, and propped a pointy-toed shoe on the edge of the desk.

"Okay." Scott rubbed his eyes and reached out. "Give me a sip of that." The bottle was cold. The whisky felt cool on his tongue, warm inside his throat and stomach. "I guess . . . I guess you've got two choices. One, I'm innocent of any of this—the murder or putting up that filth in there. Or two, I'm not only crazy as hell, but I'm going to extraordinary measures to announce that fact to the world." He paused. "That sound about right?"

"Uh-huh."

"So let's take the last one. Why would I bring you out here to see this? Why would I make up a burglary, smash up all my own stuff, and tell a lie about some unseen burglar admitting to murdering one of my patients?"

"Like you said. Crazy."

"Okay, why would I faint . . . sorry, pass out when I saw that awful room?"

"Actin'."

"You really think I was acting, Canon?"

The old man screwed the top on his bottle and set it on the desk. "No. Not makin' much of an argument for your innocence, either, though." He stood. "Fire up that computer. I wanna see what's on it."

"Good idea."

"Yeah. I'm goin' upstairs and look around. See what I can find. And, Doc?"

"Yeah?"

"If you're tellin' the truth, I'd keep a eye and ear peeled for anybody comin' around. We don't wanna get caught flatfooted by whoever put together that picture show in the next room."

Scott hopped off the desk and walked to the window. Nothing out there but moonlit pastures and charcoal clumps of trees. When he turned back, Canon had disappeared.

He turned his attention to the computer. The front panel showed a DVD player, a CD writer, a floppy drive, two USB ports, and a firewire. He punched the ON button and watched the nineteen-inch screen come to life. *Windows XP*. Scott zoned out as the operating system loaded. When the hourglass disappeared from beside the cursor, he clicked on START, opened the Control Panel, and clicked SYSTEM.

"Oh, shit."

The screen read:

```
Registered to: Scott Thomas
Gateway, Inc.
          Intel (R)
Pentium (R) 4 CPU 1.90 Ghz
1.90 GHz
256 MB of RAM
```

"Shit, shit, shit!"

"What is it?" Canon had quietly returned downstairs and was standing behind him.

"Guess I'm not only a pervert, I'm a stupid pervert to boot." Scott pointed to his name on the screen.

Walker straightened up. "Already got your picture all over that mess in the living room. Don't see where your name on the computer makes much difference."

"Depends on what kind of cookies they've been accepting. What kind of security. If they downloaded those pictures off the Internet . . ." His eyes scanned the desktop. Nothing there but Office Suite programs and Internet access. He clicked on START again and opened the Programs menu. "Look."

Canon leaned over the screen. "What the hell am I looking at?"

"A cheap version of Adobe Photoshop, Paint Shop Pro. Three or four other graphics programs."

"What's that . . ."

"Hang on." Scott opened Photoshop and hit OPEN. The My Pictures window opened. "Oh, shit."

"What!"

"There are a couple of hundred files here." He chose one at random and double clicked. The screen filled with a closeup of a gynecologist's work area.

Canon said, "That what I think it is?"

"Can't you tell?"

"Kinda hard to place things with no point of reference like that."

Scott chose another numbered file at random from the menu. The next screen had a barnyard theme.

"Burn it," the old man said abruptly. "Burn the whole house down."

"We can't do that."

Canon took his hand off the loaded pistol in his pocket and motioned at the house with an empty palm. "What if somebody finds this? You can't explain this shit. You haven't even been able to explain it to me. What you gonna tell the po-lice? Damn. I'm tellin' you, Doc, you gonna give that de-tective in your apartment this afternoon, you gonna give the man a month of wet dreams handin' over sick-ass evidence like this. This ain't no fuckin' movie. You give the cops this kinda evidence, hell, they gonna lock your ass up and throw away the key. Nobody . . . no-damn-body on earth gonna look any farther for who snuffed that poor woman in the hospital if they see this."

"What about you?"

"What about me?"

"You've seen all this. And I guess you believe me. Otherwise, I don't think you'd be telling me to set fire to some stranger's house."

"Two things." Canon walked to the window and scanned the pasture outside. "First"—he turned back and tried to smile—"you're forgettin' I can see evil on people."

"Yeah, right."

"And, boy—you got about as much evil on you as a new puppy stumblin' around trying to find its momma's tit."

Scott turned off the computer. "What's second?"

"Second is that it don't benefit me to think you killed that woman. The cops wanna solve this crime. You said . . . What's the woman's name?"

"Patricia Hunter."

"You said this Hunter woman is rich. Got a big-dog husband. Well, big dog don't matter to me, but you can bet your ass it matters to the po-lice. They'll slap a set of cuffs on you and parade your ass in front of every reporter in town." He looked out again at the frozen fields. "It ain't my job to talk you into savin' yourself. You wanna call the cops and get 'em out here to look at this, knock yourself out. I'm just sayin', if it was me, I'd set a match to the place."

"I have a history with fire."

"Oh." Canon didn't know what else to say.

"The pictures are here." Scott waved his hand at the desk. "Inside this computer. Now my fingerprints are all over the place, too." He paused. "What'd you find upstairs?"

"Nothin'."

"Nothing important or . . ."

"I mean nothin'. Not a bed. Not a chair or a table." Canon moved away from the window to stand over Scott. "I'm tellin' you, this whole place doesn't feel right.

It's more like a stage that's half ready for a show than a place where somebody lives or works. And I'll tell you somethin' else. I don't think you'd be burnin' down somebody else's house, the way you said."

"What do you mean? It has to belong to somebody."

"Got your name on the computer. All those nasty pictures in the other room. We might as well assume there's a lease or a bill of sale somewhere has your name on it. All the rest don't make sense otherwise. The cops discover this place, they got to check on who pays the rent. All the rest don't work if that person ain't you."

"So you say put a match to the whole house."

"Nothin' else you can do. You strip out those pictures, bust up this computer, they're just gonna fill it up again. Or set you up somewhere else."

"But either way—burn it or empty it—and they can still set me up again in another house or apartment." Canon started to speak, but Scott held up a palm to stop him. "Just a minute. You think it looks like whoever did this isn't through."

"No way to know for sure. But, yeah, looks that way to me."

"So that means they're coming back."

The old man grinned. "Yeah. It does. Doesn't it?"

Scott could feel the haze clearing inside his head. "If you'll take that pistol and stand watch out by the road, I'm going to build a hell of a fire in the fireplace." He leaned down to pick the CPU up off the floor. Placing it on the desktop, he asked, "You got a knife on you?"

Canon reached into his hip pocket. "Yeah, sure. What you gonna do?"

"Well, after I put a match to those pictures in the living room"—he rested his hand on the computer—"I'm going to come back in here and cut this thing's heart out."

CHAPTER 14

Kate Billings had turned on the answering machine in case Charles Hunter returned her call. She waited for his voice after the sixth ring, but heard Scott Thomas instead.

"Kate? If you're there, please pick up. I really need to talk to you. Please, pick—"

She grabbed the receiver. "What's wrong?"

"Oh, hi. Sorry to call so late."

"Don't worry about it. I was just working out." Lying naked on the bed, Kate allowed her fingers to pause just below the dimple of her navel. She drew soft circles in the beads of perspiration on her stomach.

A soft hum filled her earpiece. Seconds passed before Scott asked, "Is there any way I could come by there tonight and talk with you? I wouldn't ask but . . ."

"Come on."

"Now?"

"Now." The timbre of her voice changed. "Where are you calling from?"

Scott looked out at the dark oily pavement separating him from a brightly lit Citgo station. "I'm on a pay phone at a service station. I guess about forty minutes away from the hospital, if that's close to your place."

"You've never been to my apartment, have you?"

"No. You had me drop you at that coffee shop when we left the blues club on Bleeker. Remember?"

"Right. Well, I'm not far from where you dropped me." Kate laid out simple, straightforward directions, said, "See you soon," and hung up.

She strolled across the rug to her mirror, where she paused to study sweat-glistened skin and blood-gorged muscles before continuing on to the bathroom. She had just enough time to shower and pick something interesting to wear before Scott showed up.

Scott dropped the heavy phone into its cradle and popped open the folding glass door. The old Caddy sat between Scott and the light, so that Canon looked flat and black like a carnival silhouette.

Back inside the car, Scott relayed the conversation.

"Just said to come on over?"

Scott studied Canon Walker's impassive features. "Yeah."

"Thought you were tired."

Scott bent forward and propped an elbow on each knee. "I'm tired as hell, but I've gotten past the place where I was sleepy. Anyway, I don't see me getting a lot of sleep until I ask Kate why she came to see you today."

Walker looked straight ahead and dropped the transmission into drive. "Gotta get to bed myself. Got a couple days off before headin' out to Baltimore. Old men can only take so much."

"Young ones, too."

"Yeah." Walker nodded his head. "I guess that's right."

Kate lived in one of those steep-roofed, white-and-brown apartment complexes that are supposed to look like an alpine village. It seemed like a hip theme in the seventies, and most major cities had half a dozen of the places. The faux-carved sign at the turn-in read *Apres Ski Villas.*

Cruising between rows of identical buildings, Scott maneuvered his Land Cruiser through jagged lines of back bumpers. The instructions had been "Two rights, and I'm the third building on the left. Building G. Number 1103." Scott repeated Kate's apartment number out loud.

He was lost. Every building looked the same. At a dead end, he turned around and started back out. Three minutes later, he was at the entrance again. *Apres Ski Villas.* "Yeah," he said, "I know."

The second run-through, Scott found a turn he'd missed before. He parked against a yellow curb next to a building with a giant old-English-looking G glued to its side.

Apartment 1103 turned out to be on the second floor. Scott ascended through a center orifice of the building, passed into a long inside hallway, and found the right number on a metal security door.

He knocked. Nothing happened. Scott knocked again. Nothing. It was late. He was tired. He was miserable. He pounded too loudly. A door three apartments down opened about a foot, and a bespectacled male face popped out.

"Can I help you?"

Scott shook his head. "I doubt it."

"People are trying to sleep."

"Yeah. Sorry about the noise. I guess she fell asleep."

The man just kept looking.

It had been a long, hard day. Scott said, "Go away."

The man snorted, getting ready to say something or other, just as Kate's door opened. He started again. "Everything all right down there?"

Kate ignored her neighbor. Her eyes scanned Scott's face. "I think you better come in before you fall down."

Her apartment was painted white. The carpeting was pale, the furniture generic. Scott walked to a sofa and plopped down without being asked.

"What happened?" Kate stood before him wrapped in an oversized, terry-cloth bathrobe. Her hair was still moist from the shower. "You look awful." As she spoke, she dropped to one knee in front of Scott and her robe separated to her hip.

Scott was too tired to notice. "I'm sorry to come by this late."

"You said that on the phone. It's okay. I like to work out at night. I'd just finished when you called."

"Good." He rubbed his eyes and thought about how to start. "Canon Walker told me you came to his hotel today."

Kate studied Scott's face. "Do you want some coffee or something?"

"I was wondering why you'd do that."

"Talk to Mr. Walker about your problems?"

"Right."

She rose to her feet, then sat sideways on the sofa next to Scott and tucked her feet underneath her. "I didn't mean to upset you."

"I'm not upset. At least, I'm not upset about anything you've done. I just don't understand why you did it. I mean, going to an old man I barely know—somebody who isn't a lawyer, who's basically just passing through—and asking him to help me with a legal problem . . . It doesn't make sense."

"I don't know."

"Well, you must have had some reason . . ."

Kate gently laid her hand on Scott's arm. "I was going to say that, although I'm not completely sure why I chose Mr. Walker, I guess I just thought you needed some help." She paused. "Help, I guess, from someone who has nothing to do with the hospital."

Scott turned to look at the blank screen of Kate's television. "Dr. Reynolds was helpful. There wasn't that much he could do. He's as disturbed by Patricia Hunter's murder as the rest of us. But he stepped in and tried to run interference for me."

"Maybe." Kate slid her hand up Scott's arm and began to massage his shoulder. A sprinkling of chills scattered across his neck as pockets of tension dissolved. "And just maybe the hospital's going to look after *itself*. When you spoke with Dr. Reynolds, the hospital lawyers hadn't gotten involved. Patricia Hunter was a rich woman, and her husband, from what I hear, has a lot of pull." Her fingers moved up to massage Scott's neck at the base of his skull. "Anyway, like I said, I'm not sure why I went to Canon Walker. I guess I thought he was a better friend of yours than he is."

Scott leaned forward. Kate's answers weren't helping much, but her fingers were. He almost asked about the watcher—the young man with the plastic face—but changed his mind.

Scott tried to smile. "I guess I'm also asking why you're trying to help me. We had one date. You hated the music, and I took you home early."

"I didn't hate you. I wanted you to ask me out again."

"Well"—Scott slid forward on the sofa, preparing to stand—"that's really all I wanted to know. You were nice to let me come over. I guess I better—"

She smiled and shook her head. "You're not going anywhere. You're about to pass out sitting there talking to me. I'm not about to let you get in a car and drive home like this. How long has it been since you slept?"

Scott tried to smile. "I had . . ." He struggled to

process the numbers. "I, uh, slept two or three hours last night. That's . . ." His mind fuzzed.

"It's two in the morning now." She did the math. "*If you got a good night's sleep two nights ago, then you've still only had three hours sleep in the past forty-three hours. For God's sake, you're slurring your words, Scott. Like I said, you have no business trying to drive. You can stay here tonight, and we'll talk more in the morning.*"

"Are you sure?"

"Positive. I think I've got a new toothbrush you can use. I don't know what we're going to do about pajamas." She grabbed Scott's hand and pulled him to his feet. "Are you a boxers or briefs man? There's not much difference in boxers and short pajamas when you get right down to it, so that'd be fine. Don't think I could handle the tighty-whiteys thing, though." She smiled. "I'd never be able to look at you the same way again." As Kate talked, she led Scott through her bedroom and into the bath, where she retrieved a new toothbrush from the cabinet and placed it in his hand. "I've only got one bed. But it's a queen size, so we can remain chaste."

Scott looked in the mirror at a slack, puffy face. "I can sleep on the sofa. Right now, I'm so tired I could probably sleep on your coffee table."

"That's ridiculous. We're both grown-ups, and you're too exhausted to be dangerous. I'm being nice here. Shut up and let me do it."

Scott pressed his lips together and smiled.

"Good." She pointed at the sink. "When you're done here, you can get undressed in the bedroom. Just put your clothes on the yellow chair in there. And don't worry. I've actually seen a man in his boxers before." As she turned to leave, she added, "I've gotta go double lock the door and shut off lights. I like the side of the bed next to the alarm clock." And she was gone.

Scott turned on the hot water and held his fingers under the stream until steam billowed up out of the basin. He twisted the cold water handle to bring the water from steaming to warm. Cupping his hands under the running water, he washed and rubbed at his face with handful after handful of warm water. It was something his father had taught him as a little kid. The warmth always seemed to calm and center his thoughts without jolting him awake.

Back out in the bedroom, he was alone as he stripped down to boxers and tossed his clothes over a yellow, overstuffed chair. Scott was at ease with his body the way men are who've spent half their lives in locker rooms.

He had just flipped back the covers on the right side of the bed when he heard Kate talking. At first, he thought someone else had come to the apartment. For some reason he didn't fully understand, Scott tiptoed across the room and pressed his ear to the closed door. Kate's was the only voice. It had the volume and cadence of someone speaking on the phone.

As Scott turned to walk away, he heard his name. He leaned back against the door to hear more, but the conversation was over. He walked to the bed and slipped inside cool crisp sheets.

His own place was usually clean, but it was guy clean. He picked up newspapers, threw out pizza boxes, and visited the Laundromat every couple of weeks. He had a bottle of spray cleaner and a broom. Anything else he considered evidence of OCD. But *this* was nice. The sheets and pillowcases were pressed. They had sharp creases ironed into them, for God's sake. The place even smelled clean. No sickening floral scent, no baskets of potpourri everywhere you looked; the whole apartment was just unbelievably, preternaturally *clean*.

He heard Kate step into the bedroom and close the door behind her. "Find everything you need?"

"A sink and a toothbrush was pretty much it."

"Good. Flip on the bedside lamp."

Scott rolled across Kate's side of the bed and stretched to click the light on. When he did, Kate killed the overhead light and walked to her dresser. He watched as she opened the top drawer and pulled out a large red T-shirt. Keeping her back to the bed, Kate pulled off her bathrobe, carefully folded it in half, and placed it on the seat of a small stool. She wore blue panties and no bra, and she had a beautiful back.

Kate put her hands inside the shirt and raised her arms to pull it over her head. Scott could see the perfect roundness of her left breast—that teasing view from behind a woman that she never sees and that every man knows. He closed his eyes and turned away. He needed sleep, and staring at Kate Billings's curves was no way to get it.

He felt the bed move as Kate slid under the covers and turned off the lamp.

Sleep was already pouring over him like a warm bath, but, as he drifted off, a question prickled the back of his mind and tugged him back. He turned and looked up at the dark ceiling. "Kate?"

"Yes?"

"There's a, uh, patient I promised to keep tabs on for the family. A Mrs. Winton."

"Paranoid schizophrenic. Cooked her kid's cat for lunch."

"God." He paused to order thoughts that seemed to flit in every direction, like a flock of canaries tossed in the air. "Do me a favor. Tell Dr. Reynolds that I promised to keep the family informed, but with everything that's going on . . . Anyway, tell him there's a little girl who's going to need to talk with someone . . ."

"I thought you were tired."

"Can you take care of that for me? Tell him I'll speak with him about it as soon as I can."

"Not a problem."

Scott lay still, listening to the soft rush of Kate's breathing. "Can I ask you something?"

"Nope. You can sleep in my bed with me, but asking a question is way over the line."

Scott smiled in the darkness. "I was just wondering about something. The other nurses at the hospital wear blue and green uniforms. Some have designs on them. This is weird, but I was wondering . . ."

She quietly interrupted. "Why I always wear white?"

"Right." Seconds floated by. He felt the nearby warmth of her back beneath the covers. He felt the rhythm of her breathing. "I guess you just like white."

Silence settled over the darkened room. Kate fluffed her pillow. "Good night, Scott."

He pulled the blanket under his chin and felt his aching body begin its plunge into unconsciousness. Scott said, "Good night, Kate"—and he was gone.

Sharp-edged flames roared against the night, stabbing at the house, carving it into irregular blackened chunks. Scott saw fleeting human shadows at the windows. He tried to call out from the yard; he tried to stand, to run for help. Words choked to nothing deep inside his throat; his legs turned dead beneath him. The ground began to sway and swirl, and suddenly he was inside a long hospital corridor. Summoning all his strength, Scott called out for his father.

"Scott? Scott?"

The room was pitch black.

"Are you okay?"

He cleared his throat. "Sorry."

"Nightmare?"

"Yeah." He could feel his face color in the dark, even as he struggled to control his breathing. "Sorry I woke you."

The mattress rocked gently as Kate got out of bed. Seconds later, the bathroom door opened and closed. A bright L of light showed underneath and along one side of the door, and Scott heard water running. He closed his eyes.

The door clicked open, and bathroom light cut a yellow gash across the bedspread. Scott watched as Kate sat down on his side of the bed. She held a glass of water in one hand.

"I have some sleeping pills, if you think that would help."

"No, thanks. I'm fine."

"It's just Benadryl."

"Really, I'm okay."

Kate put two white and red capsules on the bedside table. "They're there if you want them. Here." She held out the glass.

Scott took the glass and sat up. The woman had gotten out of bed to help. The least he could do was drink some water. "Thank you." He put the glass on the bedside table. Kate picked it up and slid a magazine under it in place of a coaster.

She walked over to turn off the bathroom light.

Lying in the dark, Scott heard the soft brush of Kate's feet against the carpet. The whispered sound of cloth against skin came just before Kate slipped back into bed. The mattress swayed as she slid over to press against his back. Her right hand passed beneath his arm and circled his ribs. The warmth of her breasts and stomach pressed into Scott's back, and he realized that she had stripped off her shirt.

Scott lay still. Waiting. Nothing happened. Kate's breathing slowed. Her arm grew limp. Exhaustion overpowered any arousal or discomfort Scott felt, and he was asleep.

Some time later—he didn't know how long—he stirred as her hand moved over his stomach in gentle circles. He didn't move. For all he knew, she was still trying to comfort him. Either pushing her away or rolling over to pull her closer could offend in a dozen different ways; so he simply lay there in that warm sensual place between sleep and wakefulness and let her stroke his stomach like a favorite dog.

The fog of sleep was just returning when she slipped her fingers beneath the waistband of his boxers. He reached back to put his hand on her thigh. "Kate? Are you awake?"

She didn't answer, but her hand pushed deeper inside. Her fingers moved gently at first, then she took him into her hand and used his erection as a gentle lever to roll him onto his back. Kate's skin felt unnaturally hot as she found his mouth with hers. There were no cloying kisses, no gentle moist touches. She pushed her tongue deep into his mouth as her hand worked beneath the covers. Sliding up toward the headboard, she pulled her hand away and straddled his stomach. Scott reached for her breasts and found her hands already there. She moved her full hands and then just her fingertips over her breasts, allowing his fingers to linger on the backs of her hands as she touched herself. Finally, she grasped his left hand and pressed it against the round heat of her right breast. His other hand she guided down over her stomach and inside her panties, where she pressed both his finger and hers deep inside.

Scott said Kate's name once more before she leaned forward and crushed her mouth against his.

CHAPTER 15

Winter light had begun to angle high through the bed-room windows when Scott stirred. He turned onto his back, blinked at the ceiling, and felt at peace for the half minute it took for reality to settle into his thoughts.

His jeans and shirt were on the yellow chair, not in a haphazard pile the way he'd left them but perfectly folded into squares. His belt lay on top of the jeans, neatly coiled like a sleeping serpent.

"Kate?"

He listened and heard the shower running. Crossing the room, he tapped on the door and heard Kate tell him to come in.

He spoke to a fogged figure on the other side of frosted glass. "I'd like to get a shower, if you don't mind."

Kate popped open the door and poked her head out. "Sure. I was just getting ready to step out." She closed the door. Scott watched her blurry form through the glass. She turned away from the spray, tilted her chin, and arched her back to rinse her hair. "Just a sec."

"Thanks." Scott turned to the sink to brush his teeth.

Kate turned off the water just as he dropped his toothbrush into a plastic cup on the basin. "Toss me a towel, please. One of the big ones on the chrome shelf, there."

Scott pulled down a towel off a head-high shelf and placed it into a slippery wet hand that reached through the space over the shower door. He watched through frosted glass as Kate patted herself dry and carefully wrapped the towel low around her waist like a sarong. She pushed back wet hair with her fingertips before opening the door and stepping out.

Scott's eyes fixed on Kate's breasts, which was what she had intended. The towel-sarong was designed to hide the imaginary extra pound or two that Kate carried on her hips. A dim bedroom lamp had been one thing, but this was harsh bathroom lighting. Scott understood without giving it a second thought. For years, he'd seen throngs of slim, beautiful girls at the beach hurrying to tug on shorts or wrap towels around their hips the second they emerged from the water. He was sorry, though, that the towel was there. Men are visual.

"You're really beautiful."

Kate smiled. "You're not looking at my eyes."

"I've seen your eyes." He kissed her lightly on the lips. "Thanks for letting me stay. I feel a hundred percent better."

"Glad you enjoyed your stay. We're a full-service inn, here." Kate reached up to scratch against Scott's whiskers with the backs of her fingers. "Get in the shower. I've got some disposable razors around here somewhere. I'll put one on the sink for you." She lingered, unabashedly watching him turn on the shower and step out of his boxers. "I see you're wide awake."

"Naked women have that effect on me."

"Good for you."

"Yeah," he said, "I'm pretty happy about it. Look, why don't you step back into the shower with me for a few minutes and help me find the shampoo and conditioner?" He leaned into the shower and glanced around. "Looks complicated in there. I could use some help."

Kate stepped forward and softly kissed Scott's mouth. As their lips parted, she reached down to take him into her hand. "I'm going to make a nice brunch for us." She gave his erection a playful squeeze. "You can help yourself."

And she walked out.

When Scott mounted the wooden steps to his apartment a few minutes past noon, he found an envelope taped to the front door. His name was written across the front in blue ballpoint. The embossed return address was that of the Ashtons—the address of his landlords who lived forty feet away in the big house facing Welder Avenue. Obviously, they were back from skiing in Colorado.

He worked the key in the lock, stepped inside, and quickly shut the door against the cold. Then he examined the envelope and his stomach tightened. He ripped it open and unfolded one sheet of paper. The lady of the house had written a short note with the same cheap ballpoint.

> Scott—
> We were so very sorry to hear about your
> problems at the hospital. Steven ran into Dr.
> Reynolds last night and heard about the whole mess.
> I know you must be devastated.
> Unfortunately, this situation places us in a delicate
> position. While both Steven and I are certain you will
> emerge from this problem vindicated and stronger for
> the experience, we cannot come to terms with the idea
> of someone involved in a murder investigation living
> so close to our home and our children.
> Please vacate the apartment no later than one
> week from today.
>   God Bless,
>   Michelle Ashton

Scott spoke one word out loud. "Perfect." Then he walked into the bedroom and found the red message light blinking on the answering machine next to his unmade bed.

The first message was from Dr. Reynolds. "I'm calling to inform you, Scott, that you've been placed on administrative leave. And let me tell you up front that this is no reflection on you *or* your value to the hospital. This is standard operating procedure in matters of this kind." The good doctor went on from there, attempting to salve Scott's feelings. It was all prattle. Scott wondered how stupid someone would have to be to believe that the hospital had a "standard operating procedure" for handling staff members accused of murdering patients. Alternatively, if the hospital really did have such a policy, how scary was that?

He punched the SKIP button in the middle of Reynolds's soliloquy. The next message was from Cannonball Walker. All he said was "You need help on this. Think about it. Don't do it alone. Cops gonna eat you up."

Finally, Kate's voice came teasing and breathless from the tiny speaker. "Late for work. Just wanted to say 'Great night.' Call me and we'll—" The phone rang, shutting off the message in midsentence.

Scott picked up the receiver. "Hello?"

"How'd you like your house?"

"What?"

"How'd you like the way we decorated your country house?" The voice had a mechanical, singsong quality— as if it were being spoken through some kind of electronic filter—yet the tone sounded vaguely familiar. "I thought it came off pretty good. Not the picture of you from the Harvard yearbook. The pixels couldn't handle that kind of enlargement. But the other pictures? How'd you like the pictures we picked out for you, Scotty?"

It's amazing how frightening an unknown voice can

be. An old saying ran through Scott's mind: *Nothing's more frightening than an unseen knock on the other side of a lonely door*. He tried to sound assured. "Who the hell is this?"

"We've got better pictures of you now, Scotty. Shots of you on the porch and standing in the front hallway. Even got a couple through the window. I like the one of you working at your computer."

"Are you the same asshole who broke into my apartment?"

"What'd you do with your hard drive, Scotty? That was irritating. We spent a lot of time building it, making it reflect your personality. It wasn't nice to tear it out that way."

Scott scrambled to identify the memory triggered by the synthesized voice, and it came to him. The guy sounded like the caller who terrorized Doris Day in *Midnight Lace*. Still, something in the voice was more familiar than a half-remembered late-night movie. "I've heard your voice before."

For the first time, there was hesitation. Finally, the caller simply said, "No."

For the first time, Scott felt some control flowing his way. "I know you, don't I?"

Again, seconds passed before the caller spoke. "No. But you will, Scotty. You will." The line went dead.

Scott's breathing had grown quick and shallow; he struggled to control it, as he realized the phone was trembling. It was trembling because he was.

Seconds passed. He pressed the OFF button, punched in *69, and pressed the PHONE button again. Three beeps, and a different mechanical voice informed him that the number he was seeking was unavailable. He dropped the receiver into its cradle and sat on the bed. He'd had a full night's sleep; he'd eaten a great breakfast; hell, he'd even gotten laid. It was time to focus. Time to think.

Scott walked to his desk, sat down in the straight-back chair, and pulled a yellow pad from the top drawer. He grabbed a pen from the Harvard mug on the desktop and started to write.

1. *2 gangbangers break into apartment, take nothing.*
2. *Early next moring, unidentified caller tells me to come to hospital.*
3. *Patricia Hunter murdered.*
4. *Same 2 gangbangers (I think) break into apartment again. Trash living room. Still take nothing. Cops flood place with investigators.*
5. *Country house found full of pornography— pictures from the Internet. My face. Patricia Hunter's face.*
6. *Caller with mechanical voice knows I took hard drive. (Maybe) has pictures of me at the house. Knows how to electronically disguise voice. Knows how to block *69.*

Out loud, to the empty room, he said, "Too complicated." Even if someone wanted to frame me for murder, he thought, this is too complicated. There's too much that could go wrong.

He pushed back and propped his feet on the corner of the oak desk. His eyes raked the brief list.

In undergraduate school, his advisor had told him early on that life is like anything else—a math problem, a poem, whatever; things that appear complicated only look that way when you don't understand them. It had seemed obvious advice to a freshman psych student. But the idea had stuck, especially as Scott began to work with patients in therapy. After all, the whole basis of his profession was that complicated emotional problems cease to be complicated, and in fact become solvable, once you understand the root causes.

He looked back down at his list.

He had it. Not much. Just something. Something that was worth pursuing. He grabbed his coat, rushed through the outside door, and ran down icy steps to his Land Cruiser.

CHAPTER 16

A morning thunderstorm had washed the city clean, leaving a silvery sheen in its wake. Scott maneuvered through a series of narrow, rain-slicked urban canyons to Harvard Square. Turning onto Massachusetts Avenue, he headed east through Central Square to the fire station where he forked left onto Main. Four blocks later, he bumped across railroad tracks and started looking for somewhere to park. He found the Charles River Basin; he found lots of ugly buildings; he did not find a parking space.

Scott made a quick U-turn, rumbled back across the tracks, and finally found a road that cut between a new glass-and-steel building on one side and an older academic building on the other. There is no parking in Cambridge. He invented a place next to a construction dumpster and walked through a glass door into the older building. A receptionist manned a built-in desk in the foyer. On the wall over her head hung the letters *LCS*. Beneath that, in smaller print, a stainless steel sign read: MIT LABORATORY FOR COMPUTER SCIENCE. The sign had a high-tech–looking abstract design in one corner.

"Good afternoon."

The twenty-something receptionist wore a pair of severe, Teutonic glasses and a wrinkled sweatshirt. Frizzy brown hair, parted in a wandering, topographic path, started low on her forehead and ended just past a blue scrunchy at the base of her neck. She didn't speak. She glanced up. She looked tired.

"Can you help me?"

She closed a thick book on the desk and sighed. "How much help do you need?"

Scott smiled. "Not much." He produced his wallet and fished out a Harvard student ID. "I'm a doctoral student at Harvard."

"Higher education for the mathematically challenged."

He smiled again. "I'm working on a doctorate in psychology."

"Like I said."

"You see, my dissertation is about the psychological effects of technology on modern society."

She opened her book. "Sounds unoriginal."

"Yes, well, my advisor spoke to someone at the lab here and said there was a guy I could talk to about all this. I don't have a name."

"Then how do you expect . . ."

"He's supposed to be in some bar around here. Someplace where all the computer geeks—sorry, that's the way it was described—somewhere all the MIT computer geeks hang out at night."

She didn't look up. "Geeks are running the world. I don't guess they've heard about that in the psychology department at *Harvard*." The name of the school seemed to leave a bad taste in her mouth.

"Like I said, no offense. If you could just . . ."

"It's closed."

"What is?"

"The restaurant. You know, Colleen's Chinese Cuisine?" She waited for the *ah-hah* and didn't get it. "Grokking Chinese. Surely they've heard of *that* even at Harvard."

"Sorry, I really don't know . . ."

"Bill Gosper, Richard Stallman?" She waited again. "It's famous, okay. Back in the seventies, a group of MIT grad students used to meet a Colleen's Chinese Cuisine. Over time, they noticed that they never got the same dishes as the Chinese customers, even when they ordered the same thing. So, they started Grokking Chinese."

"Grokking? I'm sorry but—"

"What do they teach you people? *Grok* refers to Martian understanding. It's from *Stranger in a Strange Land.*" She huffed. "By Robert Anson Heinlein?" She shook her head in disgust. After all, making a Harvard student feel stupid was the only reason she was telling any of it. Scott knew that if he *had* known what she was talking about, she would have been sorely disappointed. "Forget it. Suffice it to say that these MIT guys started mixing up Chinese characters from the menu and insisting on whatever combination they came up with. Sometimes they'd get sweet and sour bamboo shoots. Other times stuff like fried rice with peaches. But, little by little, they figured out the characters for all the ingredients on the menu. You know, so they could get the same dishes the Chinese customers were getting."

Scott smiled. "But it's closed."

The girl sighed. "Yeah. Now it's called the Royal East Restaurant, over on Main Street."

"So that's where I need to go."

"No." She looked back down at her book. "Try P.J.'s"

"What?"

"It's a bar. You can find it in the phone book."

"Then why did you tell me—"

She tilted the book up. "Look, I've got to study. Are we done here?"

"Sure. Thank you."

She didn't respond. Apparently, he wasn't all that welcome.

*   *   *

P.J.'s served a decent clam chowder. But then, every bar in Boston with a menu served a decent clam chowder. Scott had located the place off Vassar Street, near the MIT campus, just after three o'clock that afternoon. Now he occupied a back corner booth.

Hexagonal oyster crackers floated in half a bowl of white chowder. He'd gone through three packages. Every few bites, he'd tear open a new wrapper and dump in more crackers. It was good chowder; he just liked crackers.

A blond waitress dropped another handful of the little packages on his table. "Want some soup with your crackers?"

"Maybe another Guinness."

She said, "Sure," and walked to the bar. When she returned, Scott invited her to sit down. "Can't. I'm working."

Scott looked around. "I'm the only one here."

She glanced back at the old-fashioned oak bar. "I live with the bartender, honey." The blonde lowered her voice. "Maybe I could just give you my cell number. We could get together somewhere else."

"Your boyfriend mind if we just talk? I'm here to meet someone, and I really don't know who."

She set her round drink tray on the table and slid into the other side of the booth. "How do you meet somebody . . . Oh. You mean like a blind date? You answering a personal or something?"

"No, no. I'm a graduate student. My advisor told me about some computer whiz who hangs out here. He didn't have a name. Just said to stop by tonight, and the guy would be here."

"Oh, sure. This place is geek central." She swept a highly manicured hand in a circle to indicate she was talking about the bar. "Don't ask me why. You're the first guy in here in a month looks like he might have enough dick to get my number."

"Thanks."

"Look. I don't want Freddie to see me give you anything. You got a pretty good memory?"

Scott nodded.

"Good." She recited her number. "Wait till I leave to write it down, okay? And use some judgment. Freddie's here till two in the morning. I get off after dinner. So use it sometime between, say, seven and midnight and I'm all yours." She picked up a package of crackers, tore it open with tiny white teeth, and dumped the contents into Scott's chowder. "My name's Ginger." Scott felt a strange pressure and looked down to see five stockinged toes massaging his crotch. He moved back, and the tickling toes followed. Scott swallowed. Ginger met his eyes when he looked up. She bit down suggestively on the tip of her tongue, then said, "How's the service?"

"Who"—Scott struggled to concentrate—"ah, who should I talk to about my project? I need the head geek, if you know what I mean. Somebody who knows about hackers and computer theft, that kind of thing."

"Oh, sure." She shot a furtive glance at the bar. "There's this guy comes in here for dinner every night. Eats the same damn thing every night, too. And we're talking the king-fucking-geek of all time, here. His name's . . ." She looked into the distance and tapped a long glossy nail against her lips. "His name's, uh . . . it's Victor Ellroy."

Ginger talked about Ellroy and his alleged geekiness for another couple of minutes. To Scott, it seemed much longer. By the time Ginger left the booth, she had recited every piece of information she knew about Victor Ellroy. And Scott had gotten his first and last toe job.

Two beers and a sandwich later, Ginger caught Scott's eye and nodded at a bulbous man sporting an oily pageboy and black-rimmed glasses. Scott mouthed the name "Ellroy," and the waitress nodded. Scott immediately stood and waved to the man as if greeting an old friend.

"Victor?"

The master geek waddled in Scott's direction, his eyes narrowing to slits as he tried to place the smiling face. "Uh, yes, yes, yes. Great to see you again."

Some clichés have no basis in fact. That computer geeks have poor social skills is not one of them. Ellroy refused to believe that he did not know Scott from somewhere, and he was thrilled to have been recommended as the preeminent computer geek at MIT.

It took an hour.

Scott left P.J.'s with two names, not including Ginger's. Ellroy had first selected a guy in South Boston named Darryl Simmons—a hacker who was reputedly some kind of master computer criminal. Class brain turned gangbanger, Simmons was fast becoming a legend among self-taught "street geeks."

When Ellroy had finished describing Darryl Simmons, Scott grimaced. "Sounds like the kind of guy who might decide to kill me during the interview."

Ellroy's round features had slackened in thought. Finally, he'd said, "I was just trying to get you the best person for your interview. Uh, don't guess it'd do much good if . . . Yes, yes, yes, you're right. Guy's supposed to be a little psycho."

Next, Ellroy had named Peter Budzik, saying, "This is the guy for you. Georgia Tech undergraduate. MIT graduate school till he got the boot. Budzik's on the shady side, but he's not physically dangerous. Piss him off, he'll ruin your life. But he'll do it with his mind and a computer. Yes, yes, yes. More I think, yes, yes, yes, you need Budzik."

"Ruin my life?"

"Well, yes. Legend is, probably true . . . yes, yes, yes, probably true . . . legend is Budzik got pissed at some girl in a freshman class he was teaching. Seems Pete had the hots for the girl and she wasn't interested. Told him to fuck off, called him some names in front of other students. Anyway, word is Budzik canceled the kid's credit cards, changed her grades on the mainframe, emptied some bank accounts. You know, stuff like that. Even put her name and phone number on an Internet dating service, with her interests listed as something like, uh, 'blowjobs and threesomes.' "

"No wonder they booted him."

Ellroy swallowed half a glass of Coors Light in one gulp and shook his head. "Well, yeah. Maybe. Wasn't all that so much as, well, this girl goes nuts and kills herself." He'd then taken a second to drain the rest of his beer. "Lucky old Pete didn't go to prison. Ruined his life, though." The master geek had then belched loudly. "Crazy as hell. Budzik I mean, not the girl. Crazy as hell, but he's the man you need. Old Pete's the best I know."

Scott had smiled. "Good as you?"

The big man had grinned broadly. "Nope. But I'm an academic. Budzik is pure hacker." Ginger had walked over to bring more Coors Light. When she'd left, Ellroy added, "I'll tell you how good he is. Pete's close to what I'd be on the dark side of the force. And"—he'd paused to roll out another aromatic beer belch—"I know how to find him."

CHAPTER 17

Spinnaker Island, a thick green worm of land in the upper third of the Outer Banks, had been abandoned by everyone but environmentalists for half a century. Charles Hunter had lobbied for most of a decade to build his town of the future there—arguing that he would protect and enhance the beaches and wildlife, that the state of North Carolina would never find another developer who was more interested in perfection than money. He had contributed to political campaigns; he'd hired the state's top lawyers and flown down from Boston at every opportunity to smooch the backsides of every city, county, and state official he could find. The whole process had been expensive and exasperating and often demeaning.

But it had worked.

On this bright afternoon—only one day after Scott Thomas had gotten his balls stroked by Ginger's toes in a Boston bar and three short weeks before the vernal equinox—Charles Hunter was standing on a undulating beach outside his North Carolina home. All around him black-headed laughing gulls cawed and dove in jumbled clusters; pelicans soared the coastline, fishing in groups of three and four; and tender new growth pebbled the limbs of wind-tortured oaks and dark-fingered brush.

Inland—worked carefully into natural spaces beside dense patches of trees, shrubs, and sea grass—lay a scattering of *perfect* buildings. At least, they seemed that way to the man who had designed them. Cedar siding to withstand decades of Atlantic storms and blend with the island's vegetation; copper roofs that would age gracefully to reflect the green of the sea; walkways, natural spaces, and manicured squares—all forming the framework for the perfect town that would follow.

Charles stood on the beach in worn khakis and a nylon windbreaker. He breathed in ocean air and shuddered just a little. He was too content even to smile.

A cell phone jingled in his pocket. "Charles Hunter." He listened, said, "On the way," and clicked the flip phone shut. He lingered for three long minutes before walking up the beach to his home, where he climbed into a convertible Jeep and headed down a sandy roadway.

His office had been the first building erected on Spinnaker Island in a hundred years. That had been a year ago. Now he drove past five new houses in the space of the mile that separated his home and office. In the town proper, at the island's highest elevation, the Jeep's tires slid to a dusty stop on an oyster-shell parking lot. He stepped out of the Jeep, leaving his keys in the ignition. It was a purposeful act.

Like every structure on Spinnaker Island, the offices of Hunter & Petring were at once modern and traditional. Charles pushed through tall doors into a central open space, reminiscent of the dog runs found in old Southern homes. The room rose two stories high and ran straight through to a bank of windows at the rear overlooking the North Carolina coastline.

Turning right, he walked into the drafting room.

Three young professionals—two builders and a freshly minted architect—were huddled around his junior partner, Carol Petring.

The group stopped in midconversation as the great man approached. Carol asked, "Nice late lunch?"

Charles, who hadn't stopped to eat until past three, said, "Drove home, grilled a shark steak and vegetables out on the deck, ate, and took a walk on the beach." He paused. "And left here less than an hour ago."

Everyone but the new architect laughed. One of the builders, a beefy guy with blond hair and permanently sunburned jowls, said, "We get it, Charles. It's a nice place."

Charles grinned. "Bullshit. It's *perfect*. Anyway, Sarah's coming out tonight. Let's do whatever we need to do. I've gotta cross over to the mainland and get to the airport by seven."

The young architect, a guy named Olivetti, asked, "I thought Sarah was like ten years old."

Charles's smile faded. "She is. Obviously she's not flying alone." An uncomfortable silence settled over the group, and Charles behaved uncharacteristically by filling it. "My wife Patricia's former nurse, a young woman named Kate Billings, is bringing her down." He turned to Carol. "Ms. Billings will be staying on as Sarah's nanny, at least for the time being."

Carol nodded. "I understand, Charles. That's very kind of you." The group grew quiet again, and Carol realized that the North Carolina builders had no idea what she was talking about. Quickly, she reached under a stack of drawings on a nearby work table and extracted a topographic map. "Charles. If you'll look here. Killian, the commercial artist who bought lot fifty-seven, is being a pain in the ass about the orientation of his house. Insists he needs northern light at the rear elevation . . ."

* * *

Cold air had rolled in behind yesterday's rain, and Scott Thomas could see his breath inside the car. He leaned down to push against a heater control that was already at its highest level. Outside of Cambridge now, he drove through Boston proper as dusk enveloped the streets like a black mist.

Following directions happily supplied by a drunken academic, Scott passed along monotonous queues of ancient brick warehouses, searching for a numbered intersection and a faded electrical parts sign. He missed the intersection, but spotted the vertical sign suspended from the corner of a pollution-stained brick cube.

Here he found parking. No one wanted to come to this neighborhood, not even the residents. As Scott popped open the driver's door and stepped out onto wet pavement, the oily, briny scent of commercial docks filled his sinuses. Here, in these brick caverns with asphalt floors, the cold seemed sharper, the dark more profound.

He turned, reached under the driver's seat, and pulled out a messy bundle that looked something like a paperback novel wrapped in newspaper and rubber bands. Unzipping his Marmot shell, he slid the package into a webbed inner pocket.

At the front of the brick warehouse, an eight-foot cube had been left out of the larger cube formed by the building. A heavy metal door, replete with four or five oddly artistic spray-paint tags, was set into the back of the entrance cube. On the left, the brick wall held three brass buzzers, plus one raw wire where a former buzzer had died. Scott looked for a name, but saw only the numbers 3, 4, and 5. The second floor had to make do with the bare wire.

Scott glanced at his watch. It was a few minutes past six. Dinnertime. A normal time for lost keys, for visitors, and for armloads of groceries and takeout that would make it more convenient to push a buzzer than to fish in pockets for a key. It was a good time to push buzzers; so he pushed all three. The security door hummed at him. Scott shoved through the door and heard it slam shut as he stepped inside.

The lobby, if it could be called that, seemed to have been some kind of light manufacturing plant at one time. Bare lightbulbs centered on each of the four walls cast a yellow glow across rows of metal workstands. Some still supported the heavy bases of drill presses; others held the dark shapes of gears and wires, beer cans and waste paper. Intersecting layers of pipes—some no thicker than a thumb, others a foot in diameter—squirmed across the ceiling like steel serpents.

In the center of this harsh dreamscape, open metal stairs pushed upward through the tangled ceiling. Scott started up the steps and banged his forehead on the dark boards that closed it off.

He stepped back down to the floor. In a dark back corner, he could just make out the metal cage of a commercial elevator. He crossed through dead workstations, shoved open an accordion gate, and stepped into the elevator.

And jumped inside his skin.

"Who are you?"

The disembodied voice sounded calm. Scott looked around for a camera, and the voice came again. *"Over your head."*

He looked up into the lens of a Radio Shack security camera. "Oh."

"Do you have a name?"

"I'm Scott Thomas. Victor Ellroy, over at MIT, told me to come by."

"Vic called. Hold up your driver's license."

Scott fished out his wallet and did as instructed.

"*Okay. Close the gate.*"

Scott shoved the metal accordion gate shut. "What now? Do I . . ."

The elevator shuddered and started and began to creep upward. He counted two floors, and the lift stopped on the third. Scott pulled open the gate and stepped out into a square foyer. The floor was coated in black peel-and-stick tiles. Scarred walls and a patterned tin ceiling had been painted flat white. It was not a professional job. Smears of other, earlier colors showed in places where the paint roller had begun to run dry.

Straight ahead, beneath a wash of blue light from a wall fixture, an industrial steel door opened, and a little bald man stepped into the doorway. "Dr. Thomas?"

"I'm not a doctor." Scott walked forward. The little man stepped back to let him pass through into a cavern of exposed brick and open space divided by white canvas walls on little rollers. "Nice of you to see me."

Peter Budzik shut his front door. "Vic said you needed the best." He grinned, and his left eyelid made a spastic, fluttering movement. "I crave recognition."

Scott smiled back, not because he wanted to but because it was expected. He studied the little hacker and something tugged at his memory. His eyes moved over the man's egg-shape head and thin-lipped smile; he looked hard into pale blue eyes that peeked out from oversized, horn-rimmed glasses. "Do we know each other?"

"No."

"Are you sure we've never met? There's something about . . ."

"Moby."

"What?"

"The musician Moby. I look like him. I've had to sign autographs in town to get kids to leave me alone."

Scott nodded, and the little man motioned at a black leather chair.

Scott sat down. Budzik perched like a nervous parakeet on the edge of a yellow and red sofa that had suspended round cushions for a back. Scott couldn't place the designer, but he knew the thing was expensive. He started, "Victor Ellroy spoke highly of you."

Budzik's smile faded, and his spastic twitch went into overdrive. "Vic is a useless blob of beer-soaked lard. His opinions are of no value to me." He leaned back against the suspended disks, feigning a relaxed attitude despite the jittery eye. "You told Vic some story about a doctoral thesis on the psychological effects of technology on society."

Scott tried to focus on Budzik's one still eye. It was easier to ignore the blinking. He didn't want to start twitching himself out of some kind of strained empathy—the way a cough or an itch can be contagious. He grinned. "I guess that's been done."

The little hacker may have been a walking dictionary of neuroses, but he wasn't buying any of Scott's bullshit about a thesis. "No more than a few thousand times, not to mention a dozen articles a year in *Time* and *Newsweek*." Budzik shrugged and pointed to a barely noticeable lump under Scott's coat. "What'd you bring me?"

The little geek didn't miss much. Scott unzipped his coat and pulled out the bundle. "It's a hard drive."

Budzik reached out. "Let's have a look at it."

"I need to explain . . . to get you to understand what's happening to me." Scott looked down at the package. Inside was the hard disk he'd removed from the computer at the porno country house. "There's some disturbing stuff on here."

The little Moby look-alike reached back to lace delicate fingers behind a smooth egg of a head and crossed an ankle over a knee. His toes began to bounce with nervous energy, echoing the spasms in his eyelid. "I'm sure poor sloppy Victor told you about my suicidal student." He smiled—not a calculated smile. It was a real smile. Thinking of the tragedy made the man happy. "I've learned that it is that very point where most allegedly *normal* people become disturbed that I just start to get interested." He pointed at the wrapped hard disk. "You have me intrigued. This sounds like something I'm going to enjoy."

Scott held the package out, and Budzik accepted it. Scott started to stand. "Should I check back tomorrow or what?"

Budzik's smile disappeared. "This is fifteen minutes' work. You should sit and wait." The little hacker smiled again. "I'll bet Victor told you that I'm on the 'dark side of the force,' didn't he?" He waved his hand in dismissal. "No need to answer. The man's a Star Wars loser from way back. Finds all his analogies for life in Obi Wan and Yoda, mostly because he's never read anything but computer code in his life. Anyway"—he stood— "right now, you need help from someone on the dark side. Otherwise, you wouldn't be here. So sit there and read one of my magazines. Turn on the television if you want. But you aren't going anywhere. Not until I take a look at this hard drive and figure out exactly what it is you're up to." He pointed at the door. "Try to leave before I say it's okay, and you'll find out just how dark life can be."

Time slowed as Scott studied the mini-asylum he'd wandered into. Budzik stood very still now, watching— waiting to see what effect his words were having. Scott understood that the little man wanted to see how much shit he would eat. Unlike the little hacker, Scott didn't have anything to prove, but he did need the man's help.

What he didn't need was to look vulnerable to a neurotic, possibly psychotic criminal.

Scott stood. "You've got two choices. You can look over the hard drive, analyze what's there, and I'll pay you very well for your time. *Or* you can give me that package back right now, and I'll walk out of here and leave you alone. But telling me what to do and when to sit are not things you're going to get to do." He stopped to watch the little man's face grow red. "This is a business deal. Nothing else." Scott paused. "What's it going to be?"

Budzik spoke through tight lips. "I don't think I'm in the mood to do this tonight. Come back tomorrow."

Scott nodded and walked out.

When he was back on the street, Scott paused in the dark to catch his breath. The cold felt good in his chest. The sidewalk felt substantial, as if he'd just stepped off a carnival ride and back onto solid ground.

There had been something uniquely disturbing about Peter Budzik, something that continued to both pull at Scott's thoughts and stir an uneasy feeling in his gut. Some people shake your hand and you can't wait to wash off the imagined residue of their contact. After sitting in that strange man's chair—after talking with him and breathing his air—Scott needed cool wind in his face. He needed clean thoughts. Maybe a shower. He needed to wash away the residual filth of Peter Budzik.

As Scott turned the corner, he found two teenagers in baggy clothes and knit caps leaning against his Land Cruiser. He stopped. One, a wiry black kid in unlaced hightops, flipped a lit cigarette at Scott's chest. Without thinking, Scott reached out and caught the cigarette between his thumb and forefinger. The kid's smile faded.

Scott rolled the still-burning cigarette between his thumb and middle finger and flipped it hard between the two boys. It hit his car door in a spray of embers. He reached into his hip pocket, pulled out a twenty, and held it up. "Twenty do it?"

The wiry kid nodded.

Scott stepped over to the side of Budzik's building, where he folded the bill twice and pushed it into a crack in the bricks. "Step away from the car."

The second one, a fat kid who hadn't spoken before, said, "Fuck you. You give up a Jackson that easy, you gonna give up more if we beat on yo' white ass."

The wiry kid pushed off the car. "Twenty's enough."

The fat one's head snapped around. "I'm tellin' you—"

"Shut up, Beebo. I said twenty's enough." He motioned at Scott with his chin. "Man's down here to do business. And . . ." He shrugged. "Looks and moves like a fighter. Two of us, though." He walked over to lean against the building. "Jus' business. Twenty a businesslike number." He raised his chin again in Scott's direction. "Move away."

Scott crossed the sidewalk and stepped into the street. He kept both kids in view as the skinny one retrieved the twenty and walked away. The fat boy glared at Scott, mumbled something or other, then followed.

When they were half a block distant, Scott unlocked the Land Cruiser, stepped inside, and immediately relocked the door. He didn't realize he'd been holding his breath until the engine turned over and he let out a chestful of air. As he pulled out and passed the two teens, the fat one flashed a hand signal that looked like a gang sign. Probably bullshit to scare the white guy, but you never know.

Scott glanced in the rearview mirror and saw a third guy step out of a sheltered doorway. The dark figure hunched his shoulders against the cold and hurried down the sidewalk, his gaze seemingly fixed on the two teenage extortionists.

Scott wondered briefly whether the two teens would get to keep his twenty.

He reached over to make sure the passenger door was locked, checked his gas gauge, and pointed the headlights toward Cambridge.

CHAPTER 18

Charles Hunter's ten-year-old daughter, Sarah, dangled her feet from a plastic chair in one of the hundreds of identical, impersonal waiting areas at Logan International Airport. She wore jeans and an Old Navy sweatshirt. On the empty chair to her left lay a folded, light blue topcoat with a faux fur collar. The coat was her favorite.

Sarah watched everything. CNN rattled out of a television monitor over her head. Outside, on the other side of huge sheets of plate glass, men in ear protectors and dirty coats waved at jumbo jets with orange-capped flashlights; tiny wagon trains of luggage wound through a crisscross maze of yellow lights that cut the tarmac into vague geometric shapes. Across from her, a fat man with a beard drooled in his sleep, which struck Sarah as kind of funny and disgusting at the same time.

Sarah loved "people watching"—that's what her mother, her *real* mother, Jennie, had called it. She loved it, but now her stomach hurt from missing lunch. Sarah couldn't move, though. It was her job to guard the bags. Kate had made that clear. It was Sarah's job to make sure nothing happened to their bags. *I can eat when Kate gets back.* It was becoming a silent mantra. *I can eat when Kate gets back.*

Kate Billings had picked up Sarah from school at noon. Kate never ate lunch, and it had never occurred to her to ask whether Sarah was hungry; Kate had too much to do to think of such things. The call from Charles—the one she'd been waiting for, the one telling her to come to the island and be a small part of the architect's new life—had come just the night before.

At the hospital that morning, Kate had turned in her resignation and taken accumulated leave to cover the required two weeks' notice. Now she stood at an open phone booth, trying to reach Scott Thomas for the fourth time that afternoon. Kate needed to say good-bye so things wouldn't get strange. She had left a message on his machine, telling him that she was leaving, that Mrs. Hunter's death was just too upsetting. But that wasn't enough. Their good-byes should have been in person. That was impossible now.

Kate dropped the receiver into its chrome cradle and counted to ten. As she started punching in numbers again, somewhere in the back of her mind, she wondered if Sarah was old enough to be left alone in an airport like that. A busy signal beeped through the earpiece, interrupting her thoughts. Kate slammed down the receiver, hard. A triangle of plastic flew off the front of the pay phone, and people began to stare at the beautiful woman having a mini-tantrum.

As Kate navigated the jumbled mass of hurried travelers on her way to find Sarah, it occurred to her that she needed to eat something. Kate hesitated outside a Wall Street Deli and almost went in, then the thought entered her mind that maybe Sarah was hungry, too.

Kate sighed and walked to the gate to collect Charles's little girl for dinner. Thinking of Sarah's needs was something she was going to have to get used to.

* * *

Cambridge looked like a place imagined after the trip through south Boston. Smooth streets, clipped hedges, and rows of well-kept houses. Scott turned into the drive on Welder Avenue, parked in back, and stepped out onto herringbone-pattern brick that shone wet in the moonlight.

The fog of his breath preceded him up the wooden steps to his front door. Inside, he flipped on the overhead light. His apartment was trashed. He knew it had been trashed. He knew he hadn't made much of an effort to set it straight; yet still he was shocked, the way you can be shocked by a dying friend's appearance even if you think you're prepared.

He glanced at his watch. Just past eight. Too early for bed. He tugged off his coat, tossed it onto the shredded sofa, and bent down to pick up a mangled copy of *Civilization and Its Discontents*—one of the last books Freud wrote before his death, it was an exploration of the conflict between the egotistical individual and society's pressure to inhibit instinctual drives. Nothing but a cheap paperback—its spine torn—now permanently opened to page eleven. Scott let his finger trace an underlined quotation Freud had lifted from *Hannibal*: "We cannot fall out of this world."

The door creaked open behind him. "Scott?"

Scott spun to face the door.

"Whoa." His landlord, Steve Ashton, held up both palms. "It's just me." A physically distinguished man, Ashton always looked like he'd just stepped out of the clubhouse at Augusta National. Now worry creased his deep snow tan. He surveyed the room with a landlord's eye. "What's happened here?"

"Couple of guys broke in the other night."

The older man nodded. He knew about the break-in. "They do all this?"

Scott nodded.

Ashton stepped farther into the room. "We can't have this, Scott."

It had been a long day. Scott said, "You think I'm happy about it?"

The older man's eyes flashed. "I think you should begin looking for another apartment." Scott started to speak, and Ashton held up a palm. He said one more word before leaving. "Tomorrow."

It was just past noon when Scott parked against the curb outside Budzik's warehouse. In daylight, the neighborhood was a different place. Transfer trucks rumbled up and down pockmarked pavement, occasionally pausing to back into a loading dock or stop at curbside to be loaded by workers in knit caps and down coats.

Scott stepped out and circled around to the warehouse entrance, where he picked a buzzer and pressed. The door buzzed open, and he pushed through.

When the elevator door opened onto Budzik's white foyer, the metal door was already open. An attractive twenty-something woman stood in the doorway.

"Is Budzik in?"

She smiled a welcoming, Junior League smile. "Of course. Are you Mr. Thomas?"

He nodded. "Scott."

"Wonderful." She beamed. "Please come in."

Scott walked through the door and stopped.

His hostess carefully closed the heavy door and then walked over to offer her hand. "I'm Cindy Travers. I live here with Peter."

Scott shook the tiny hand. "Nice to meet you."

Cindy stood looking at her guest, as if she expected something from him. Scott looked back. Finally she said, "Peter is busy in his lab. You can go up if you'd like."

"Okay."

She led the way to a set of stairs. "One flight up." She paused. "Oh. I'm sorry. Can I offer you anything? I've just put on a pot of tea."

"No. Thank you. I really just need to talk to Peter."

"Of course. Well, just call out if you need anything."

Budzik's lab occupied the entire fourth floor of the warehouse. Here, there were no movable panels. Just bare brick walls, a dozen stainless steel tables with black rubber mats, and, everywhere, computers and computer screens, printers and keyboards. Scattered among the recognizable components were various metal boxes with gauges and knobs.

Budzik sat in a designer chair, his narrow shoulders hunched over a keyboard, his huge glasses reflecting lines of code from the computer screen before him.

Scott cleared his throat. "Find anything useful?"

Budzik glanced back. "Interesting stuff."

Scott shrugged. "The porn on that disk isn't mine. I tried to tell you—"

"Screw the porn. I don't care about that. I'm talking about you murdering your whole family when you were ten. I mean, I may be a bad guy, but you were a frigging *prodigy*."

"My family died in a house fire. It wasn't anybody's fault." It was a practiced line that rang false even to his ears.

Budzik spun in his chair to face the screen. He closed the coding program and opened a web page. "This is your very own page on a site called 'The Ones Who Got Away dot com.'" He pointed to a school photo of a young boy. "You were a nice-looking kid. No wonder they let you go."

Scott tried again. "It was a fire . . ."

Budzik's voice turned shrill. "I know it was a fire, you moron! Everybody knows it was a fire. What we're discussing is who *set* the frigging fire." Budzik was breathing hard; Scott was hardly breathing at all. Without looking up, the hacker said, "Better sit down. You look like shit."

The world floated by as Scott moved across the room. His hand found the back of a gray chair on casters. He pulled it near Budzik and sat. His eyes moved to the computer screen. "Who would do something like this?"

Budzik shrugged. "That would be somebody who, *one*, needed a hobby and, *two*, decided to ruin your life."

"But it's not true."

The hacker pushed away from the computer. He laced his fingers behind his head and crossed his legs. He smiled. "I know."

Scott was in sensory overload. It took a few seconds to process the words. "What? You said you *know* it's not true?"

Nervous, happy energy wiggled the hacker's foot. "I should clarify. For all I know, you fried your parents and younger brother . . . What was his name, by the way?"

Scott glared at the hacker. "Bobby." He spoke the name like a challenge. "My brother was named Bobby."

"Well, for all I know you burned Mom, Dad, and little Bobby alive and enjoyed every second of it. I don't know about that. What I do know"—he pointed to the screen—"is that this site is bullshit. Most of it cobbled together from other web sites about killers and capital punishment, stuff like that. Only your page is original to the web-site designer."

"How can you . . . ?"

"Shut your hole and listen."

Scott leaned back and tried to control growing irritation. "I'm listening."

"How kind of you. Try not to interrupt again." The geek was bullying the jock, and enjoying every second of it. He continued. "Reconstituting your hard drive took ten minutes. This"—he motioned at the web page—"turned up a few seconds later. What took a little time was downloading the page and checking the code. I also had to run some searches to find where most of this came from. But the bottom line, as far as you're concerned, is that someone is defecating heavily onto your life." He motioned at the screen again with his free hand. "This is all brand new, by the way. Put together in just the last few days. Also, in case you didn't know it, you are a dues-paying member of some of the nastiest porno sites on the Web."

Scott stood. Budzik glared at him. "Sit back down."

He'd had enough. "No." Scott motioned at the screen. "If I pay you, can you wipe all this out and keep it from coming back?"

The little man shook his head. "Wipe it out? Yes. Keep it from coming back? Nobody can do that. Well, if you can get to the web designer who did it—and to whoever hired the designer—then, yeah, you could stop it."

Scott reread the account of how he allegedly torched his family. "So, can you tell me who put the site together? Can you run some kind of trace or something?"

Budzik smiled. "Cost you five grand."

Scott hesitated to do some mental math. "I could give you two."

Now Budzik laughed. "I can give you the man or woman who's ruining your life, and you're trying to get a bargain? Fuck off. I don't need the aggravation."

Scott forced his eyes away from the screen. "Okay. Five thousand dollars."

"Uh-uh. Too late. You irritated me. Now it's fifty-five hundred."

He studied the little bald hacker—a pencil-necked geek who liked to talk tough, who needed desperately to feel like more of a man than he believed himself to be. The price would rise until Budzik convinced himself that he'd completely dominated the Harvard jock.

Scott nodded. "Done. When will you have the name?"

"It won't take long, not for me. Tell you what. Give me

twenty-four hours. Put the money in my hand tomorrow night, and you'll get the name of the web designer. Probably can get the street address, too. Whatever you need."

Scott started for the door. "I'll bring the money tomorrow."

"Hold on a minute." Budzik stood. "How'd you like my girlfriend?"

"She seemed very nice."

"Too nice for me, huh?"

Scott could tell he was expected to agree. "Yes. She is."

"Looks can be deceiving, Scott. That little girl is the sister of my student who killed herself."

Scott glared at the hacker. "You mean the one you drove to suicide?"

Budzik smiled. "That's the one. And that little lady downstairs—who knows all about what I did to her sister—will happily do anything I tell her to. *Anything*."

"What's your point?"

"There are no good people, Scott." He motioned at a window, as if to indicate everyone except the two of them. "They're all just walking meat sticks with competing neuroses."

Scott studied Budzik's smiling face. He said, "Bullshit," then descended the steps and left the building.

Lieutenant Cedris, along with two uniformed officers, secured the country house while three other policemen hooked a chain to the downed pine blocking the driveway. A motor roared. Minutes later, the sound of chains being stowed rattled in the afternoon air, and two patrol cars crunched onto frozen ground at the front of the house. Swirling red and blue lights washed the winter landscape.

Cedris mounted the front porch. "Thomas! Scott Thomas! This is the police. We have a warrant to search this residence." The lieutenant stood to one side and nodded at a policeman who held a thick, four-foot length of cast iron by rubber handles. The officer approached the door, took a practice swing for momentum, then smashed the door open.

Cedris and another officer rushed into the dark house.

The gray afternoon exploded with yellow light. Flames erupted out of the roof and flowed down the sides of the house like syrup over pancakes. Men screamed and rushed inside to save others, only to be pushed back out by the flames. A window shattered. Cedris and the other policemen dove out onto frozen ground, where they rolled and scrambled clear of the heat and flames.

All the while—standing inside the cover of thick timber a hundred yards away—a man in a stocking cap stood and watched. Even at that distance, yellow flames highlighted shiny skin drawn tight across misshapen features.

The young man stood silently for several minutes; then he picked up an empty gas can, turned his back on the screaming police officers, and walked into the woods.

CHAPTER 19

Lights burned inside the Ashton home when Scott turned into the driveway. As he rounded the main house, a jumbled stack of pasteboard boxes blocked his path. He cut the engine and stepped out, leaving the headlights on to illuminate the makeshift blockade.

The boxes were labeled in black marker. SCOTT THOMAS—BOOKS. All bore his name. One read LINENS, others COMPUTER, STEREO, and CLOTHES. He stopped to look at the Ashtons' big house, then mounted the wooden steps to what had been his garage apartment. An envelope was taped to the door; a new brass dead bolt shone in the moonlight. Scott pulled the envelope free and angled the folded paper to read by the moon's reflection.

Mrs. Ashton had used the security deposit to rent a storage unit in his name. A van would pick up the boxes the next morning.

Nice people. Thoughtful.

Scott descended the steps—his legs aching, his thoughts quietened by a soft buzz that filled his head. He walked down the driveway, cut across the front lawn, and stepped onto the Ashtons' portico. A television deep inside the house scattered muffled voices into the early evening.

He rang the bell. No one answered. Scott wanted to apologize for upsetting his landlords' lives, but no one wanted to hear it.

He walked back to the boxes, tossed the ones marked CLOTHES and COMPUTER into his Land Cruiser, and then rummaged until he found his answering machine, which he dropped into a box with his computer.

The four-by-four cranked. He backed out onto Welder Avenue, yanked the gearshift into first, and pulled away.

With a stomach full of free "continental breakfast"— grapes, stale cinnamon rolls, and coffee—Scott returned to the bleak motel room where he had tossed all night. He spent the better part of an hour unpacking and then hooked up his computer. He opened Microsoft Outlook, found the number of his trust officer in Birmingham, and grabbed a grimy pastel phone. Seconds later, a secretary passed him through to John Pastings.

"Scott?"

"Mr. Pastings? Yes. Good morning."

"Good morning, Scott. Haven't heard from you in months. How are things up there at Harvard? Uh, doing well, I'm sure."

"Not that well, to tell you the truth. That's why I'm calling. I need to know how much I have in my trust account."

The banker let the earpiece fill with static before answering. "Of course. You're over twenty-one now, Scott. The money's all yours to do with as you please. But if I could . . ."

"I need a total, Mr. Pastings."

"Right. I'm pulling that up now." The patter of computer keys sounded in the background. "Market's not the best it's ever been, Scott. Would have been more a few years ago."

"Mr. Pastings . . ."

"Right. Okay. Here it is. As of close of business yesterday, your balance stood at twenty-nine thousand, three hundred eleven dollars, and eighty-two cents."

"It should be twice that."

"Like I said, the market . . ." The old banker stumbled. "Well, look here. We're showing thirty thousand withdrawn last week. Like I said, you're over twenty-one and the money's yours, but—"

"I'm twenty-five, Mr. Pastings, and I haven't withdrawn any money."

"I'm sorry. What?"

"I didn't withdraw any money last week."

"Well, ah, ah, ah. Here it is. A computer withdrawal of thirty thousand dollars a week ago today. Hold on." The tapping of computer keys sounded in Scott's earpiece. "I have a bank routing code and an account number here." The old man rattled off the numbers as Scott jotted them on motel stationery.

"How could this happen?"

"We've heard some disturbing rumors, Scott. Are you sure you didn't . . ."

A tiny alarm at the back of Scott's mind broke through the day's panic. "What have you heard? Has someone contacted the bank?"

Static again. Seconds passed before the banker said, "Well, yes. The police asked us not to say anything, but the way I see it our allegiance is to you . . . and your father's memory. I still think of your dad, Scott."

Scott tried to think. "What police? Who contacted you?"

"The police up there. Boston or Cambridge. I'm not sure which. Guy with a funny name. Greek or something."

"Cedris?"

"That's it. He called late yesterday. Said you were mixed up in a homicide, Scott. Of course, I didn't believe him. But . . ."

"But what?"

Pastings cleared his throat. "This Cedris was asking about how your father died."

"And Bobby."

The old man hesitated. "Of course. Bobby, too. We'll never forget any of it. Such a waste."

"So." Scott looked out the motel window at a jumbled parking lot. "What did you tell him?"

Pastings didn't answer.

Scott drew a deep breath. "Yesterday—for the first time in my life—somebody . . . not even somebody. It was a frigging web site. This web site said I had gotten away with torching my whole family when I was ten years old." The banker remained silent. "Is that what Cedris wanted to know about?"

"Yes."

"Mr. Pastings? Was that the first time you'd heard me called a murderer?"

"Look, Scott . . ."

Scott's voice came more loudly than he'd expected. "Was it?"

"No."

"Is that what everyone down there thinks?"

"Of course not, Scott. I set up this trust for you after your father died. Divided the money. Got you out of town. I did the best I could for you."

Scott screwed his eyes shut. He rubbed hard at his temples with thumb and forefinger. "So you *got me out of town*, huh?"

"People gossip. That's all. People gossip, and a kid who'd lost his family didn't need that. I did what I thought best, Scott. I hope you believe that. You had no competent relatives. No one, really. So I managed to get appointed your guardian. Your dad's life insurance didn't pay out, so I sold off everything your parents had and put it all into a trust fund. Scott, you've been to two of the best boarding schools in the country on that money. Vanderbilt, too. And now Harvard. I think you should appreciate what I—what the bank has done for you all these years."

"Back up a minute. What do you mean you 'divided the money'? Divided it with whom?"

"Are you questioning my honesty, Scott?"

"This isn't about you, Mr. Pastings. And changing the subject won't work."

The banker remained silent.

"Are you going to answer me?"

"No, Scott. I don't think I am."

Acid churned Scott's stomach. "I need whatever money is left. I need it now."

"Nothing we can do about the thirty thousand. I mean, we can investigate if you ask us to, but right now that money's gone. . . . Of course, the twenty-nine thousand and change is available to you." The old man stopped to think. "May I make a suggestion? Find two banks there in Boston, both a good distance from your home. Let me send you two separate wires, one at each bank, for nine thousand dollars."

The old man understood more than he was letting on. Scott stood and walked to the bed. "Something about ten thousand triggering a report to the feds?"

"I don't know how much that matters to you. But if you're concerned about keeping your assets, well, keeping them private . . ."

Scott sat on the bedspread and lay back against stacked pillows. "Two wires totaling eighteen thousand? What about the other eleven thousand?"

"I'll stand ready to wire it anywhere you ask. Do you have a cell phone?"

"Why? No. I don't like the things."

"Get one. Then give me the number. If anything comes up, I'll call you immediately."

Scott closed his eyes. "Why would you do that?"

The older man sighed deeply. "Good-bye, Scott. Call me with those banks so I can wire the funds. Do it today." He hesitated. "And I'll close out your Internet banking account, if you want me to."

"Yes. Please do. Can you restrict any future withdrawals to require your signature?"

"Sure. I'll take care of it the minute I get off the phone."

"Thank you. Mr. Pastings?"

"Yes?"

"You're hiding something from me, aren't you?"

The old man hung up without responding.

Scott lay on the motel bedspread, looking up at a framed picture of the Wright Brothers at Kitty Hawk, North Carolina. The cardboard print had fake brush-strokes pressed into its surface. Sleep caressed his thoughts. His arms and legs went limp just before he jerked awake and sat up.

Scott's brain was trying to shut down, trying to protect emotional circuits from overload. His unconscious wanted to give up.

Scott sat up and swung his feet onto cheap carpet.

By noon, Scott Thomas had cashed out wired funds at two branches of two different national banks. At the second bank—a NationsBank branch—he leased a safe deposit box and left eight thousand in cash locked inside. The rest of the afternoon he spent driving south from Boston.

Forty miles down the coast, in the tiny town of Marion on Buzzard's Bay, he found what he wanted.

Nestled in among the cedar-shaked bookstores and quaint eateries, he found an old-brick cube with FIRST FARMERS stenciled across the front window. Inside, two tellers manned the counter. A loan officer sat in one corner behind a tiny desk still trimmed with plastic pine needles and Styrofoam berries from the Christmas season months before. Scott approached the birdlike woman at the desk.

He pointed at the decorations. "Festive."

She glanced up over half reading glasses. "What?"

Scott smiled. "I'd like to speak to someone about opening a checking account."

She returned his smile as if it hurt. "Yes. Sit down."

"I need the ability to wire funds here as they're needed. Is that going—"

She rifled through a file drawer. "Not a problem." She dropped the form in front of him. "You can fill that out at the counter. One of the tellers will process it."

First Farmers was not part of a huge conglomerate that could search every branch transaction in seconds, and the personnel were accustomed to dealing with well-heeled vacationers who regularly transferred large sums for the yachting season. It was, in short, the best place he could find to cash out a quick eleven thousand from Mr. Pastings if the need arose.

After filling out the paperwork with an invented address, he deposited two thousand dollars, took his imprinted counter checks, and left.

Five miles outside town, Scott swerved onto a grassy shoulder and stepped out into winter air. Leaning over, he vomited into snow-frosted grass.

*   *   *

Lingering sunlight still tinged the Boston skyline as Scott rolled to a stop outside Peter Budzik's warehouse loft. Half a block down, a grizzled old man in a black topcoat carried on a casual conversation with a hooker. As they spoke, the old man unzipped his pants and turned to urinate against Budzik's building. The hooker walked away laughing as the man stumbled and then slumped on the sidewalk next to his steaming puddle.

Scott stepped out into bitter air, steadied himself against a cold fender, and breathed deeply. When he looked up, the hooker was walking in his direction. Scott shook his head at her, but she kept coming. He turned and walked into the alcove to Budzik's building, where he was immediately buzzed inside.

He was, after all, expected.

The service elevator opened as he approached. Upstairs, the stainless steel door to Budzik's apartment was already open when the elevator doors parted. But this time little Cindy was nowhere to be seen.

Scott paused outside the door and tried to shake the growing sense that something had changed. He jumped when Cindy appeared. The chipper Junior Leaguer he'd met the day before was gone. The tiny woman before him looked physically and emotionally bruised. Makeup covered an oblong lump over her right eye.

Scott spoke first. "Hello."

"Please come in." She stepped aside.

Scott first pretended not to notice her condition. "Peter is expecting me."

"Go on up." She hesitated as if gathering her thoughts, but all she added was "Please."

He started for the stairs, then turned back. "Are you all right?"

She shrugged.

Scott looked around the room. "Get your things

together. When I come back down, you're leaving here with me."

"I can't." Tears began to roll down swollen cheeks, cutting crooked paths through heavy makeup. "You don't understand. He needs me."

The phrase "born victim" floated through his mind. But Scott knew better. *Not* born. *No.* Someone had made her this way, someone long before Peter Budzik. The hacker had only spotted a wounded bird and then taken the opportunity to stab, pull, and pick at the existing wound.

Some people you can't help. Some you have to help in spite of themselves. "Be ready when I come down."

She visibly trembled. "You don't know what he'll do to me—"

"Cindy!" Scott snapped her name. "You'd do better to worry about what I'll do to both of you if you don't leave here with me. Now get your butt to wherever your stuff is and get packed. I'll be down shortly."

Her face softened. "You won't hurt me, will you?"

Nausea began to gnaw at his gut. "Get ready." He turned to leave. By the time he'd reached the stairs, Cindy had disappeared.

On the fourth floor, he found Budzik bent over the same computer screen.

Scott said, "I have your money."

The little man turned. His shoulders relaxed. "Show me."

Scott reached inside his coat and fished out a plain envelope. He thumbed it open with one hand to show the bills.

"Okay."

Scott tossed the envelope onto the computer table.

"Scott Thomas. I got your man, but"—Budzik smiled—"*you* are in a world of shit."

CHAPTER 20

Cannonball Walker's stomach growled. The bellman should have come up by now. The old man had held the hotel room late—paying for a night he wouldn't sleep in Boston—waiting by the phone, needing to hear from Scott Thomas and dreading it at the same time. Now there was just enough time for dinner if he was going to make it to New York and a soft bed by midnight.

The old man walked into the bathroom. He filled a squat glass with tap water and drank. A knock sounded on the outside door, and he walked out to answer.

"Yes?"

"Mr. Walker?"

The old bluesman opened the door and studied the visitor in the hallway. "You a cop?"

The detective nodded. He let his eyes wander over the old man's dark clothes. "Can I come in?"

"Got a name?"

"Cedris. Detective. I met you at Scott Thomas's apartment."

Walker nodded and stepped aside. "Waitin' on some-body to carry down my bags." He turned and walked into the room, leaving the door open behind him. "Gettin' ready to leave." The old man sat down in the only chair. "Hope you ain't gonna mess that up."

"Have you heard from Scott Thomas?"

"You saw me with him."

"Today. Have you heard from him today?"

"Nope."

"Do you know where he is?"

"Nope."

"You're not being very helpful, Mr. Walker."

"Like it better if I lied to you?"

"Well, if you do see him, tell him he needs to turn himself in to the police. Can you do that?"

Walker smiled. "I can tell him that's what *you* say."

Cedris grunted and walked out. The door was still open when a uniformed bellman appeared. The young man put on his tip face and stepped into the room.

Peter Budzik's fingers played over the keyboard like ants swarming an anthill.

Scott's eyes searched the screen. "What's his name?"

"It's not that simple."

"That doesn't sound like a five-thousand-dollar answer."

Budzik shook his head and pushed back from the screen. "We're just getting started. I said I could get you what you need for five grand, five hundred, and that's what I'm going to do." He crossed one leg over the other and began to wiggle his foot. "I want you along for the ride, Scott. I want you to know when you get a name that it's the right name."

Scott studied the little man's face. "Okay" was all he said.

"Let's start with the web site, The Ones Who Got Away dot com. Yesterday when we talked, I'd already downloaded the code from the site. What I did earlier today was print everything out and take a more thorough look at it." He pushed nervously at the nosepiece of horn-rimmed glasses, and Scott saw that the little man's delicate knuckles were red from hitting something or someone. "You see, whenever anyone creates a web site, that site has to be registered with a service that is approved by the federal government. Understand?"

"So far."

"Nobody can create a site without registering it. And you can't register a web site without a valid e-mail address. Of course, the registration group requires a hell of a lot more than that. Names, addresses, lots of stuff. But the only thing they ever check is the e-mail address. The registering company *always* contacts the listed e-mail address to verify that the web-site administrator is, in fact, at that address."

The guy turned Scott's stomach. He tried to cut the lecture short. "So we've got the creator's e-mail address, right?"

Budzik shook his egg of a head. "Would that it were that simple. What I have is *one* of the creator's e-mail addresses. I mean, if it were a legitimate site, like a business or a school or something, we'd have a valid address."

"I thought you said it had to be valid to register the site."

Budzik shook his head some more. "That's why I'm explaining all this to you. You've got to listen. The registered e-mail address has to be *a* valid address. It doesn't have to be the creator's only address. Neither does it have to be registered in the creator's real name."

"So," Scott said, "all we've got is an e-mail address that can't be tied to anyone."

Budzik sighed. "Not exactly. We've got an e-mail address that can be Googled. And we can search news groups—which, by the way, are the nastiest places on the Internet. We can do a lot.

"Also—and this is our second clue—you need to understand that every time *anyone* visits a web site, they leave a fingerprint." The little man picked up a sheaf of papers from the desktop and leafed through the pages. "Here, look at this."

Scott took the sheet and studied a page-long list of abbreviations and strings of numbers separated and punctuated by slashes and brackets. "Okay. Now, what the hell am I looking at?"

"That"—he grinned—"is what you leave behind every time you visit a web site."

"You're kidding."

"Nope. All that. And right there at the beginning is the IP, or Internet Protocol, address of the computer that logged onto the site. Every computer on the Internet is assigned an IP number whenever it logs on. That means that if you're using a dial-up connection—you know, a regular phone line—then you've got a different IP number every time you log on. But—and this is the good part—if you have cable access or a DSL connection, then you're *always* connected."

"And you've always got the same IP number."

"Right. And no self-respecting hacker uses a dial-up connection. So, in that one way, hackers can be easier to trace than a casual user. And here's something that could come in useful in the future if you want to check who this guy is working with. Every e-mail ever sent contains the sending computer's IP address."

"I've never seen anything like that on my e-mail."

Budzik rolled his eyes. "That's because almost every ISP—America Online, Earthlink, Yahoo, the Bell companies, pretty much everybody—hides the IP number as a default setting. It's there, you just don't see it."

"And how's that . . ."

"You've got the IP address, right? Well, if you think the guy is communicating with someone at your hospital, for example, you can go to the system administrator and ask him to run a search for the number. The printout should show which e-mail addresses at the hospital

the guy's been contacting." He shook his head as if trying to rattle something inside. "But we're getting off the
point. You want to know how I found your guy this time."

"Actually, I just need a name."

Budzik seemed not to hear. "Okay, now we can narrow the search by going to the American Registry of
Internet Numbers at arin dot net. See here." He typed
the IP address into a box at the upper right of the screen.
"Look." He pointed to a reply line reading: `OrgName:`
`BellAtlantic.net Inc.` "So it's looking more like
the hacker's in Boston, since he's on Bell Atlantic. But
we can check this further by doing a nslookup from a
Windows 2000 DOS prompt." He changed screens and
typed in the IP address again.

This time, along with the usual geek-speak, the reply
read: `Server: ns.bos.bellatlantic.net.`

"You see the b-o-s?" Budzik tapped the screen excit-
edly. "That verifies that your guy is right here in Boston."

"And his name is?"

"Okay, okay. We're getting there. Here's the deal.
Nobody—and I mean nobody—ever created a web site
without logging on to check out his or her handiwork.
You know, to make sure the thing looks good and works
the way it's supposed to. And"—he changed web sites
and tapped the screen where Scott's own disturbing little page was displayed—"this site just ain't been up that
long. So"—he beamed—"I managed to find a frequent
visitor that I could trace to the registered e-mail address." Budzik reached back and laced his fingers behind
his head. Clearly, the little man felt some sense of ac-
complishment that Scott did not share.

"And?"

"And"—Budzik's wiggling foot went into overdrive—
"I *got* the motherfucker. Traced his ass to a phreak bulletin board."

"You think you could spare me the brilliance and just . . ."

Budzik waved him off. "You see, a phreak is a phone hacker. They have bulletin boards set up on the Internet where they share information on stealing cell phone access. Stuff like chip hacking, phone company employees who'll take a bribe, model weaknesses, stuff like that."

"Budzik . . ."

"Dumbass used his standard hacker name." He paused to build the drama, then said: "Click."

"And—please tell me—you came up with some brilliant way of tracing this guy's hacker name to a real person."

"Nothing particularly brilliant about it." Budzik smiled. "I know the guy." He unlaced his fingers and made a so-so motion in the air with one hand. "Self-taught. Pure hacker outlaw. Smart, but no match for me." The little man paused, milking the situation for drama. "Your five-thousand-dollar name is Darryl Simmons."

Something tickled at the back of Scott's memory. "Your MIT buddy Ellroy mentioned Simmons. Made the guy sound . . . well, violent."

"Yep. That's young Simmons in a nutshell. Does that scare you?"

Scott rose to his feet as he thought about the question. He was surprised at his conclusion. "No."

Budzik's expression changed. Some of the cockiness faded. "Maybe you don't know what you're dealing with."

"Maybe. In any event, you earned your money."

"Bet your ass." Budzik picked up a printout and read Click's address out loud.

Scott nodded and walked to the top of the stairs. "One more thing . . . I saw Cindy's eye. I don't like that kind of thing."

"Tough shit. She does."

Scott looked into the man's eyes and saw something very much like pure evil. *Evil*. You get scared enough, you can believe in anything. "I asked her to take a ride."

Budzik strode forward. "She's not going any—" Scott stepped up to meet him, and Budzik's voice broke.

"I'm giving her a chance," Scott said. "She may come back to you. Nothing I can do about that. But for now, Cindy's leaving here with me. You're not going to do anything or say anything to stop her, and you're not going to follow us."

"We had a deal."

"We still do. I bought your time, and I paid in full. But right now, I'm going to give a new friend a ride."

As Scott turned to leave, Budzik blurted out, "I'll tell Click. I'll tell Simmons and he'll kill your ass."

"What are you going to tell him? That you hacked his identity and sold it to me for five grand? He's not going to believe I did it on my own. And, even if I had, how would you know about it? You tell Click about our deal and you've got two problems. One, he'll probably kill you himself. And, two, I'll definitely be back to pay you a visit. Or, you can just let it go. I'll go away. Click will never know you messed around in his life. And you'll still be fifty-five hundred dollars richer."

Scott turned and descended the stairs. He half expected Budzik to come running after him, but heard nothing. Cindy waited by the door. She had put on an expensive suede coat. A weekend bag sat by her feet. She smiled tremulously as Scott approached. "Are we ready?"

Scott nodded, then reached down to pick up her bag.

Her eyebrows arched, and he could see blue skin beneath the makeup. "What'd Peter say?" There was pleasure in her tone.

Scott opened the door and stepped aside. "Not much he could say."

She looked around the loft one last time and then stepped out into the foyer.

Forty minutes later, Scott dropped Cindy off at a home for battered women. He flashed his hospital ID and dropped his mentor's name to get her admitted.

She was not happy.

Maybe she'd go back to Budzik. Maybe to someone else. Someone even worse. But there was nothing he could do about that. Tears & Roses was a good place; some of the best physicians and shrinks in Boston volunteered time and resources there.

Most people in trouble want help. He hoped Cindy Travers was ready to take it.

CHAPTER 21

Scott Thomas's digital watch read 12:00. Straight up midnight.

Four hours' drive south of Boston, Cannonball Walker's mind raced and occasionally jabbed at his conscience as he checked into the Madison Hotel on Central Park West. He checked a gold pocket watch and decided to call Scott when he got to the room, regardless of the time.

Ten hours' drive farther down the Atlantic coast, inside a glass-and-cedar beach house on Spinnaker Island, Charles Hunter stood in the door of his daughter's bedroom watching the child sleep. Twenty feet away, Kate Billings paused while unpacking her bags. She walked to the window, where she gazed at moonlit ocean and felt the same calm and fulfillment that Charles felt watching Sarah sleep safe in her bed.

Scott was alone now. He stood deep inside the shadow of an inset doorway, watching the second-floor apartment of Darryl Simmons. This part of Boston was old. It was a place where decades of stale odors mixed with the clean metallic scent of New England winter. He shifted his weight, tapping one foot against the other for warmth.

Occasionally, Click's dark silhouette would float across drawn curtains, and Scott would move farther back into the shadows to wait, to force himself to stay quiet. A couple of times, a group of teenage boys had wandered by, catching Scott's eye, puffing out their chests and talking trash—their slurred words hanging in the winter air inside visible puffs of fog. But anger and desperation so filled the young graduate student that the teenagers had sensed enough to leave him alone.

This was a bad neighborhood, bad as they get in modern America. Any man who stood alone in a darkened doorway had to be more predator than victim. And Scott felt predatory. He watched Click's form move across cheap, drawn curtains and visualized kicking the hacker's door down. He could almost feel the man's weight in his hands as he imagined slamming Simmons into the wall until he lost consciousness.

Scott shook his head. He tried not to think about hurting the man. He tried not to think about hurting anyone. But he felt empty without the fantasy. He felt warm in its presence.

The sound of a door opening cut into his thoughts, and he hastily stepped deeper into the inset doorway. Click, dressed in heavy topcoat and stocking cap, trotted across the asphalt and turned right in Scott's direction. Scott thought of stepping out. He thought of taking the guy down as he passed, of twisting arms until they snapped, of forcing Darryl Simmons to tell everything he knew.

But they were stupid thoughts.

What Scott needed was to get inside Darryl Simmons's life the way Simmons had gotten inside his. He needed to know motivations and means. He needed to know *why*. So he leaned his back against the door, propped one foot against the kickplate, and bowed his head to look at the ground. Simmons passed by without so much as a sidelong glance.

As the hacker's footfalls faded, Scott stepped into the street and followed.

Three blocks over, Simmons disappeared into an ancient parking garage and emerged minutes later driving the blue Lexus with chrome wheels—the same car the two burglars had driven a week earlier after breaking in to Scott's apartment on Welder Avenue.

Now Scott intended to return the favor.

He retraced his steps to the doorway across from Click's apartment window, where he waited ten more minutes. Watching. Listening for some sound that would warn him not to enter the dark apartment. At exactly 12:20 A.M., he stepped out of the recessed doorway.

The apartment building was a dump. Gaps showed in the steps where bricks had been pried up and used as doorstops or makeshift weapons; spray-tagged plywood covered what had been a glass rectangle in the front door; the twin scents of smoke and grease reeked from a metal grate on the sidewalk.

Scott paused to glance up and down the deserted street. He reached inside his coat and rummaged inside a nylon bag hung from his shoulder, coming out with a thin-bladed chisel. Scott had never jimmied a door before. But, as it turned out, it was a surprisingly easy thing to do. Most crime is relatively unskilled—that's why people who fail at everything else are drawn to it. At least, most crimes are easy right up until the time you get caught; so he'd thought quite a bit about the best way to commit burglary. Lingering would look suspicious. Scott planned to move with purpose, to get in and out as quickly as possible.

He pushed into the foyer, where radiator heat burned and stung his cheeks. He smelled more grease, more smoke. A tangled hum of domestic noises—televisions and radios, clinking dishes and muffled voices—echoed in the dark stairwell.

One flight up, Scott paused outside a painted wooden door that bore the apartment number he'd gotten from Budzik. He stopped to listen. The background noises remained steady. The loudest sounds were Scott's own breathing, the beat of his own heart. He tapped lightly on the ancient door. No answer. The thin chisel slid easily between door frame and cheap molding. Scott felt for the dead bolt, got a corner of the chisel wedged into its side, and levered the bolt back into the lock. He held his breath and swung the door open.

The lights were off, but ambient light from the street showed a room about twice the size of his former living room on Welder Avenue. He could make out a couch, two chairs, a worktable, and four computers. This was Click's office, not his apartment.

Scott closed the door and pressed his back against paint-caked panels.

The street had been relatively bright. Inside now, he needed to adjust quickly to the dark. He stood very still and closed his eyes. *One step at a time*. It was his mantra for the evening. He'd planned out everything. *One step at a time*. A full minute passed, and he opened his eyes. Moving easily around and through tables and chairs, pasteboard boxes and thick cables, Scott made his way to the room's only window and parted cheap curtains. The street was empty.

He unbuttoned his coat and pulled out the nylon bag, swapping the chisel for a metal penlight. Sweeping the disk of light across the walls, he located two doors. One turned out to be a closet filled with electronic equipment; the other was a bathroom. Neither held any danger. Scott turned to grab a wooden chair and wedge it under the front door knob. He'd once seen a reformed professional burglar on *Oprah*. The trick, the guy had said, was to lock or barricade the bedroom or apartment door and have an alternate escape route available. Scott went in search of alternate escape routes.

The bathroom window would have let out onto an ancient, rusted fire escape if only it hadn't been painted shut. Scott clamped the penlight in his teeth and went to work with the chisel. Rivulets of sweat ran down the small of his back. His heartbeat sounded like boots marching through muck. It took four and half minutes, but the sash popped loose and moved up. Scott cussed into the rush of winter air that flooded the bathroom.

One more thing before he could work. He turned and ripped down a dark blue, mildewed shower curtain. Back out in the main room, he pulled duct tape from the nylon bag and sealed the shower curtain over the window that faced the street. Finally, he walked over and flipped on a desk lamp.

The front door was barricaded, an escape route was ready, and he could work in decent light without anyone seeing from the street. It had all taken just under ten minutes.

Oprah's professional burglar had sworn it had never taken him more than eight minutes from the time he entered a home until the time he walked out with every valuable in the place. But Scott wasn't here to steal cash or jewels. He wanted information, and that was going to take time.

The desk drawers held almost nothing—just pens, highlighters, and printer cartridges. A pyramid of pasteboard boxes occupied a back corner. The top box held two or three dozen PDAs—Palms, Visors, Blackberries, Pocket PCs, and Sony Clies. All used. Scott remembered reading that the information on stolen PDAs was generally more valuable to the crook than the device itself.

A thought glowed at the back of his mind.

A beat-up Palm Vx stood in a charger next to one of Click's computers. It was a slightly newer version of his own Palm V. He picked up Click's PDA and dropped it into the nylon bag. Then he went back to the pasteboard box and picked out a similar device. After unscrewing the top off of the stylus, he used the pin to press the reset button on the back of the Palm, dropped the device into Click's charger, and pressed the hotsync button to copy the backup files of the Palm's contents from the computer's hard drive to the virgin Palm.

The closet held stacks of equipment and brown boxes. In one, Scott found a treasure trove of cell phones. Budzik had called Click a phreak—a phone hacker. Scott chose a new Motorola flip phone in a case with its own charger. It worked. He dropped it into his bag.

Finally, Scott tried the computers. Here Click's professionalism showed. Scott couldn't get past a welcome screen without multiple passwords. He'd just powered on the last of four computers, vainly hoping that one was accessible, when a light knock came at the door.

"Click? Open the door, boy. I got somethin' for you."

Seven hundred miles south along the Atlantic coastline, Kate Billings lay in bed staring at the ceiling of her new room. Unseasonably warm breezes wafted through open windows, ruffling linen curtains and caressing her arms and face. The soft rhythmic rush of the surf filled the room.

Kate had never lived in a place without traffic noises. She'd never even lived in a place where she could open ground-level windows at night without worrying. The young nurse sighed deeply and pushed back the covers so she could feel the breeze on her bare legs. She wondered if Charles Hunter was sleeping; she wondered if having a beautiful young woman in the house was keeping him awake at night.

She glanced at the bedside clock: 1:33 A.M. Kate smiled as she rolled out of bed.

It was time to go exploring.

CHAPTER 22

Kate Billings pulled on jeans, leaving her tee-shirt night-gown untucked and hanging to mid-thigh. Trotting across to her closet, she slipped her feet into untied cross-trainers, then thought better of it and tossed the shoes into the closet using her toes.

Out in the hallway, she brushed fingertips down the wall to guide her steps. Houses, she thought, have a different feel at night. Colors disappear into grays and blacks; windows throw pale planes of dissected moonlight onto floors and furniture; the black silhouettes of plants contrast sharply with the straight lines of walls and tables, seeming even more alive, more organic, than in full light.

She paused outside Sarah's bedroom, then pushed the door open. The little girl lay in a fetal position, her covers kicked to the foot of the bed. Kate moved silently across the floor, stopping next to the bed. Sarah's long hair had fallen across her face, and it occurred to Kate that the girl looked somehow generic—more an impersonal representation of childhood than an actual child. The thought sent a chill along Kate's spine, and she reached out with painted fingernails to brush the hair back.

Sarah stirred as her new nanny pulled the sheet and comforter up to her chin. Kate watched as the girl instinctually grasped the comforter in her fingers and straightened her legs to paw at the covers with curled toes. Kate paused a few seconds more, thinking about the events that had led her here.

Back in the hallway, Kate found her way to the great room and snuggled into an oversized leather chair. Charles Hunter's reading glasses were on the side table, perched atop a well-worn copy of a book titled *Rebecca* by a woman named Daphne something-or-other. She picked up her employer's glasses and tried them on. As she did, a soft breeze tickled her bare toes.

Kate moved carefully through the unfamiliar house, all the while following the feel and scent of fresh air. One of the beach-side french doors was ajar. She had already placed her hand on the knob to pull it shut when the sound of glass on glass drifted in from the patio.

Nerves tingled in the pit of Kate's stomach as she stepped through the door. The stone steps were cold against the soles of her feet.

"Kate?"

She jumped and spun to her left, where her eyes found a man's shape in one of the big wicker chairs facing the Atlantic. "Mr. Hunter?"

"Trouble sleeping?"

Kate walked toward the masculine silhouette. "New place, I guess."

"Have a seat." He motioned at a second chair. "Wish I had that excuse."

She lowered herself into the chair as Hunter picked up a glass that smelled of whisky. He drank deeply. When he put the glass back down on the tabletop, Kate heard the same clinking that had drawn her out onto the patio. "It's nice here."

He nodded, his eyes fixed on the ocean.

"I know this is a hard time for you and Sarah. Mrs. Hunter's death, especially the way it happened . . ."

Now Charles Hunter turned to face the new nanny. "I'd prefer not to discuss Patricia's death." His voice was sharp.

Kate began, "I understand you'd—"

"No," he interrupted. "You don't."

Some time passed. Hunter drank more whisky, and Kate watched waves tug at the pebbled beach. Finally he said, "Sorry. Didn't mean to snap." He paused. "The Boston police called tonight. There's been, ah . . . there's been an arrest warrant issued for that grad student who was taking care of Patricia. What was his name? Scott . . ."

"Thomas."

"Right." Charles Hunter picked up his glass, killed the contents, and repeated the word. "Right."

Kate got up and left the famous architect alone. Back in her room, she placed a call to a Boston hotel where she was given a forwarding number in New York.

The phone rang a dozen times before a hoarse "hello" came over the line.

"Is this Canon Walker?"

"Who wants to know?"

"This is Kate Billings, Scott's friend." There was no response. "Do you know how to get a message to Scott? It's important." She told Canon about the arrest warrant. She begged him to get Scott out of Boston, to help him stay away from the police until he could prove his innocence.

Canon hardly spoke. When Kate said good-bye, the line simply went dead.

Kate punched the END button on her cell phone and walked to the open window. She breathed deeply of the scents of early spring, carried on heavy salt air. She had almost hoped it wouldn't come to this. Almost. She sighed and punched in the number of a cell phone in Boston.

When a man's voice answered, she could hear music in the background. She didn't know it was Wagner. Click knew. He said, "Yeah?"

"It's Kate."

Silence.

She went on. "There's a warrant out for Scott Thomas."

"Good."

Kate watched whitecaps roll across the black Atlantic. "I don't think so. He found the house, the porno . . ."

Click interrupted. "Took the hard disk from the computer, too. And somebody's been trackin' me through bulletin boards, trying to find me on the Net."

She spun away from the window. "Shit!"

"Tell me about it." His voice was calm. "Want me to kill him?"

Kate answered quickly, her voice clear. "Yes."

"Sure?"

"Yes."

"Cost you another five grand. Would be more, but I need the guy to go away, too. Figure killing him benefits you and benefits me. I could've emptied his bank account early on, and you insisted . . ."

"If we'd taken everything, his checks would've started bouncing. He'd have known in no time that someone had access to his funds. And he may have called in the cops before we had time to convince him to try to handle things on his own." She stopped to think. "You'll also remember that you wanted me to bang Scott and plant his semen at the scene."

Click cussed. "Well, what's the hell's wrong with that? It's a lot less complicated than renting that house out in the country and filling it up with porno."

"God." Kate looked out at the waves. "The semen would've been dead by the time it got placed on the body. Remember, Patricia Hunter was in a hospital. We didn't have hours and hours before she was found. And, more important than that, every other cop show on television has someone getting framed with sperm." She sighed. "No, Click. You're the computer jock. You know about computers. I'm a nurse. I know about biological evidence. That's why I'm doing the thinking. This is not a slash-and-burn operation."

"Still," he insisted, "I did what you wanted. Passed up thirty grand in Thomas's bank account. Could've emptied the whole thing. And now you gotta find more money to get the man dead. Shit. Like I said, killing Thomas benefits us both. But if I do all the work, I get paid for your benefit." He paused. "Five grand."

"You hear anybody arguing with you?" Her voice was hard. Sharp. "Just kill the bastard. And don't get cute and try to empty his accounts after he's dead. We've done pretty well. No need to give the cops something suspicious now."

"Not a problem. Do whatever you gotta do to get the five grand together. I'll let you know where to send it."

Kate walked across the room in bare feet and plopped onto the bed. Her eyes scanned the ceiling. She was thinking. "Let me know now. I'll wire the money tomorrow. This can't wait."

"Always in a hurry. Always have been. Don't worry. I don't need the money in hand to do the job." Click chuckled softly. "How long we known each other, Kate?"

"Since I was ten."

"Think you know me pretty well?"

"I think so."

He chuckled again. "What'll you think I'll do if I snuff this guy and you *don't* pay me?"

Kate's eyes stopped roaming. Her gaze came to rest on a water stain—an ugly discoloration in one corner of the otherwise perfect white ceiling. Something quivered in the pit of her stomach. "I'll pay you."

"Yeah, Kate." He paused. "I know you will."

She let the threat pass. "One other thing. I just called that old guitar player Scott likes. He's in New York now at the Madison Hotel. I told him to tell Scott about the arrest warrant. Told him to get him out of Boston."

"Why the hell—"

She cut him off impatiently. "*Again,* we don't need Scott talking to the cops. He's got more of this figured out than he knows." Kate paused to take a deep breath. "Listen. This Cannonball Walker's a mean-ass old black guy who's got bad news written all over him. Probably been dodging cops since he was born. I used him for this once before. Don't worry. People like Walker don't go to the cops for help. They duck and dodge and slip out of town in the middle of the night. I'm telling you, the old man's going to keep Scott away from the cops, and that's going to give you the chance you need to finish him."

Click laughed. "Katie? You are one devious fuckin' bitch."

She ignored him. "Just make sure you get him. Everything else is working. All you have to do is make sure you stop Scott before he talks to anyone else."

"He's good as gone. I guess that's it for business. Now, speaking of sperm. How 'bout telling me some of the kinky shit you're doing to help Charles Hunter through his grief? I bet you're wearing his old ass out."

Kate punched the END button.

Squeezing through the bathroom window like toothpaste from a tube, Scott hit the rusted fire escape on the point of his left shoulder, rolled forward to get onto his feet, and almost pitched feet-first over the railing.

Inside, the quiet knocking had amplified into a banging fist. The last words Scott heard before scrambling down the rickety escape ladder were "Click! Where you at, boy?"

A filth-filled alley fed onto the street that fronted the building—the empty pavement wet and black. Scott waited, flattened against old brick that infused the thick muscles along his spine with aching cold.

No friend of Click's was likely to call the cops. More likely that some dumbass with a Glock would come charging out of the building, firing rounds intended to put the idiot in solid with Click.

Scott needed to move. He'd parked in the right place—a space chosen so he wouldn't have to cross in front of the building if he had to leave from the rear.

The muddy boots of a racing pulse stomped louder in his ears. His breath came fast, as if he'd been running. But still he pushed slowly off the brick wall, and he walked. Hands in pockets. Shoulders hunched against the wind. He walked through the night to his car, climbed inside, and drove away.

Back in his motel room, Scott pulled off layers of clothes and stepped into a steaming shower. He faced the hot spray and let the warmth flow over a sea of knotted muscles that seemed to start in his temples and end in the balls of his feet. He didn't wash. He just stood there. When the hot water was gone, he stepped out.

Stretched out on clean sheets, he tried to get his mind around what was happening. Scott had spent most of his life orphaned, moving from one boarding school to the next with no sense of home or continuity. Yet, at that moment, he felt a crushing, almost physical weight of loneliness settle over him. He turned on his side and faced the bedside table. A soiled motel phone offered escape. But he had no one to call. It was past two in the morning. Even if Kate Billings or Canon Walker had been in town . . .

And he was asleep.

* * *

Charles Hunter sat immobile on the patio for an hour after Kate went inside. The last slivers of ice had melted inside his glass. He tossed whisky-flavored water out onto the stone patio and reached down to pick up a bottle of Macallan from beside his chair. After tugging at the cork, he poured half a tumbler of scotch and took in a mouthful of warm bliss.

Charles tried to set the crystal tumbler on the stones and misjudged the distance. He felt it shatter and raised his fingers in the moonlight. Black blood rolled down from his ring finger into his palm. Charles chuckled. He got up, staggered a bit as he wound through wicker patio furniture, and picked up a ceramic jar from the breakfast table.

He examined the jar containing Patricia Hunter's ashes as if he'd never seen it. "You get the bloody hand, Lady Macbeth." He stood there and chuckled again at his joke. "It's time."

The architect stumbled as he crossed the patio and stepped onto the beach. Hard, cold pebbles punched at bare feet as he hobbled to the surf. He paused at the high-tide mark. Cold waves lapped his toes, and Charles struggled to stop his upper body from swaying. A purple mist hovered over the dark Atlantic. Pink and orange halos surrounded the moon. He was an architect, an artist, and he believed that such things uniquely resonated within his mind or soul or, he thought, wherever it was that his talent, his view of the world, resided.

He turned to look off down the crooked line of beach—to examine how the purple mist turned the blue-black of India ink in the distance.

And he saw him.

As real as the funeral urn in his hands—as real as the sand and surf and fog—Charles Hunter saw his son, Trey, running along the shoreline. It was something his track-star son had done a thousand times, training for the four-forty, running in deep sand to build his calves and hone his balance. Then, just as suddenly as he'd appeared, Trey's beautiful form dissolved into the fog.

It wasn't real. Charles knew that. And it was because it wasn't real that the tears came.

With the jar held between forearm and ribs, he tugged hard at the lid of Patricia's funeral jar, twisting and yanking and cursing. It was dark; he was drunk; it wouldn't budge. He mumbled something that sounded like "Stubborn bitch."

Standing alone on the dark shoreline, Charles Hunter smiled. He held the jar in both hands now, extending it out in front of his body. With a bounce, he stepped forward, tossed the heavy jar into the air, and punted it hard with his bare right foot. The jar exploded; a cloud of billowing gray ash floated out over the churning waters.

Inside her bedroom, Kate heard an anguished scream pierce the warm sounds of wind and surf. She sprinted down the hallway, though the great room, and out onto the patio. Her hands trembled.

Mumbling.

Kate forced her breathing to slow. She listened and followed the sound. Her employer was lying on his back in the cold surf.

"Mr. Hunter?"

More mumbling.

"Mr. Hunter? Are you all right?"

His eyes rolled up at the night sky. "Fucking bitch."

"What?"

"Ruined my life. Fucking bitch."

"Mr. Hunter!"

His head shuddered, and he met her eyes. "Hello, Kate."

"Are you okay?"

He laughed. "Think I broke my foot."

Kate leaned down and pulled his right arm around her shoulders. When he was up, she said, "Who were you cussing?"

"Huh?"

Kate repeated the question as she struggled to help a hundred-eighty-pound drunk with a broken foot navigate the uneven beach.

"Oh. Sorry. It sure wasn't you. Sorry. It was a ghost, Kate. Just a ghost. She's gone now."

Kate glanced back at the broken shards of pottery on the sand, then got her patient moving again. "Good thing I'm a nurse."

"Yeah." Charles Hunter flashed a drunken smile. "I'm a lucky bastard."

CHAPTER 23

Strange noises. Popping. Tools rattling. Lights somewhere flickered like flames, and Scott tried to open his eyes. His mother stood at the foot of his bed, a heavy metal bucket of some kind in her hand. Scott tried to speak, but the words choked to nothing as she held a finger to her lips. Something—gasoline? or maybe lighter fluid?—filled his sinuses. Scott screwed his eyes shut, and the gas smell turned to smoke. He tried to sit up, to reach out for his mother, but he couldn't move. He opened his eyes, and he was alone. Flames curled through the cracks around the door, and finally he screamed.

Scott rolled over and tried to fit the surroundings into his memory.

A fist banged the door.

He cleared his throat. "What?"

"Housekeeping." Hesitation, then:"Are you okay, sir?"

Scott glanced at his watch. It read 10:33 A.M. "I'm fine. Come back later."

He heard a muffled, heavily accented "Yes, sir" as the maid turned away.

Scott stumbled into the bathroom, where another hot shower—this one complete with soap and shampoo—washed away most of the befuddlement. He started to shave and thought better of it. Maybe, he thought, I'll need a beard to hide out. It was a ridiculous idea, but his life had taken a ridiculous turn.

Scott rummaged in a moving box for clothes. His landlord had done a neat job. He took out underwear and socks, pulled them on, and went back for jeans, a shirt, and an oversized sweater from L.L. Bean.

Dressed now, he reached for the nylon bag of burglar's tools. On top was Click's Palm Pilot. Scott smiled. He dropped onto the bed and punched the green power button at the top right of the Palm. The category was set to *Date Book*.

Scott froze.

Using the toggle button under the screen, he began to flip through the calendar.

"That sonofabitch." He ran to the moving box marked COMPUTER, rummaged around for his Palm V, and clicked it on. Everything was just as he'd left it. Same dates, same contacts, same bubblet and chess games.

He reached for the phone and punched in seven numbers. Budzik's answering machine picked up. "Budzik. This is Scott Thomas. I paid you more than five grand, and I need something. Pick up the phone."

Seconds passed before he heard the click of Budzik lifting his receiver. The hacker began, "You've got some nerve calling here after what you did."

"The woman is mixed up. You were taking advantage. And you know damn well you told me about it to see what I'd do."

Budzik sounded pouty when he answered. "Maybe I wanted to see what you'd say . . . Anyway, don't you shrinks believe love is bullshit to begin with? Nothing but—what's the term?—'a compendium of needs.' That's it, isn't it? People don't fall in love. They simply recognize the right stew of insecurities and neuroses in their soul mates. One set of neuroses balances another." His voice trailed off. "I'm done with you, man. I already earned my money. Five grand doesn't make me your daddy."

"I went to Click's apartment."

Long seconds passed before Budzik spoke. "You didn't tell him about me?"

"No. I didn't tell him about me, either. I broke in when he wasn't there. By today, he'll know somebody was in his place, but that's it."

"So why am I supposed to care?"

Budzik was being pissy, but Scott could hear in the hacker's voice that he cared very much. "I lifted his Palm Pilot."

"You're kidding." Budzik was laughing. "That's got to have all kinds of great stuff in it. But why call me? Does he have it password-protected?"

"I wish. When I turned the thing on it was mine."

"What?"

"It's not physically mine. I've got my Palm here in my hand. But the data on the Palm Pilot I lifted from a charger in Click's apartment is a carbon copy of what's on my PDA."

"Click copied your . . ."

"I know."

"You think he got into your place? Or, I don't know, have you noticed anything recently that'd make you think someone had been in—"

Scott interrupted. "Two guys dressed like gang-bangers broke into my apartment a week ago. I saw them leaving. I thought it was weird because they didn't take anything."

"They took *everything*." The little man was thinking. "What'd they get? Computer passwords? Credit card numbers? What?"

"Somebody withdrew thirty thousand dollars from my investment account last week."

"Internet banking."

Scott nodded at the empty motel room.

"They broke in and beamed your bank account number, your ID, and your passwords all into a second PDA. Have you at least changed your bank passwords?"

"I closed out my Internet banking account."

"I guess now we know where Click got the money to rent that country house with all the porno on the walls."

Scott shook his head. "I don't know. They would've had to do it all in a day. The two kids broke into my apartment just one day before we found the house. It doesn't seem possible . . ."

Budzik made a derisive snort. "How long do think it takes to hang some porno and put in a makeshift office? The whole house was probably rigged four hours after they got your banking information. Hell, if Click was planning this all along, he could've rented the place a week or two ago using a stolen credit card to hold the place just until he got his hands on your money."

Scott stared at the motel print of the Wright Brothers. "Is there anything I can do?"

"About the stolen information? Not much. You can go through Click's Palm page by page and make sure there's nothing else in there he can use to hurt you." He chuckled. "That's about it."

Scott looked at the bedspread.

When Budzik spoke again, his tone was less hostile. "Truth is, you didn't do anything half the country doesn't do. Almost everybody has information on their PDAs, their computers, or both that could be used to ruin them. You," he said, "just got caught bending over for the soap."

Two beats passed before Scott spoke. "Budzik?"

"Yeah?"

"I want to ruin this guy."

"Uh-huh. But in a battle between you and Click . . ."

Budzik seemed to stumble for a facile putdown. Instead he simply said, "You're screwed"—and hung up.

Scott spoke to the dead receiver. "Sure looks like it."

It took most of an hour to scroll through every screen in the stolen PDA. When Scott was satisfied that nothing else could be used to hurt him, he grabbed the motel phone and punched in a number in Birmingham.

The banker answered his own phone.

"Mr. Pastings? This is Scott . . ."

"We have a problem, Scott."

"If it's the thirty thousand, we need to trace the withdrawal, but I've figured out how it happened."

The older man cleared his throat. "That's fine, but . . . Scott, something bad has happened. That detective in Boston, he called last night. Claims a house you rented outside Boston there was . . . It was, ah . . . The place burned night before last, Scott. The detective says it was arson."

"I know about the house. I've been there, but I never rented it. I swear. Somebody's setting me up for the murder of one of my patients."

"Save that for later, Scott. Just listen. Lieutenant Cedris has contacted the Birmingham police, and he's got someone down here listening. They're talking about reopening the investigation into the fire that left you alone in the world." He paused. "You understand what I'm saying here?"

"You think I killed my family." It was a statement.

"Do you have any memory of that night? Has it ever come back?"

"Just nightmares." Scott reached under his glasses and massaged his eyes.

"You don't want this investigation opened back up, Scott," the old man said. "Take my word for that. If you

can make this mess in Boston go away, then do it. Turn
yourself in there, and the cops here are going to let a
fifteen-year-old fire go into history."

Turn yourself in. Scott turned the phrase over in his
head. "Who are you protecting?" The banker tried to
speak, and Scott spoke over him. " 'Turn yourself in?' I
mean, advising me to work with the police to clear myself is one thing. But you're worried about the fire. More
worried about that than a murder charge in Boston."

"I'm trying to do what's best, Scott. That's all. That's
all I've ever done."

Scott glanced at a sheet of paper. "I need the rest of
my funds. Wire everything to First Farmers in Marion,
Massachusetts." Scott relayed the account and routing
numbers. "Can you do that today?"

"As soon as I hang up."

"I'm going to come down and see you. I don't know
when. As soon as I can make some headway in clearing
up this mess up here."

The old banker didn't respond.

"You know something about my family that I don't,
Mr. Pastings. I'm going to come down. And we're going
to have a talk."

"I can't tell you . . ."

"Oh, you're going to tell me. I've lived with nightmares and questions for fifteen years. Whatever it
takes, believe me, you're going to tell me. And the
money better be in Marion today. Are we clear on that,
Mr. Pastings?"

"We're clear, Scott. We're clear."

When he hung up, Scott crossed the room to rummage again in his nylon bag of burglar's tools. This time
he came out with the Motorola phone he'd stolen from
Click.

On the chance that his voice mail at the hospital
hadn't been disconnected, Scott punched in the number.

He entered the code and got the usual recording. *"Press one for current messages."*

The first few messages were "involuntary leave of absence" notices from the hospital and from the graduate program. Finally, a friendly voice sounded through the little cell phone.

"Scott. This is Canon. Cannonball Walker. Your lady friend, Kate, she called from down in North Carolina. Said the po-lice got an arrest warrant out for you." The old man sighed. *"I don't know why I'm fuckin' with you, boy. Guess you're my stray puppy or somethin'. Look, call me. I'm stayin' at the Madison Hotel in New York."* He gave the number. *"You're in a world of hurt, boy. Call me. Let me see if I can help you out."*

Scott shut the little phone as a light knock sounded against the motel door. "Housekeeping."

He walked to the door and used the peephole. A round-faced Hispanic woman stood placidly waiting. He opened the door.

"Come back later, sir?" Her accent was heavy. Spanish was her native tongue, but the accent didn't sound Mexican.

He smiled. "No. Please. Come on in."

The woman pushed a stainless steel cart into the room. Towels covered the top shelf, sheets were on the bottom. Cleaning supplies stood in a well in front of the handle.

Scott dropped into the foam rubber guest chair. He tried to think. "What's your name?"

The maid froze. Her head turned so that she could examine Scott out of the corner of one dark eye. Seconds passed before she said, "Rosalita."

"Well, Rosalita. Mind if I ask you something?"

"Sir?"

"Can I ask you a question?"

"*Sí.* Yes, sir. If you need something, I can get it for you."

"No. I just need an answer. What, dear Rosalita, is the only thing that can defeat evil?"

"¿Que?"

"Yeah." Scott nodded. "That's the same answer I got."

She frowned and emptied his wastebasket. He picked up the stolen Motorola and punched in the number of the Madison Hotel in New York City. The hotel operator connected him.

"Canon? Yeah, it's me. Thanks for the message. Listen, I've got a proposition for you. How long has it been since you were in Birmingham?"

The day passed slowly. For hours Scott hunched over the tiny motel desk, making lists, drawing diagrams on lined notebook paper, and then wadding up most of it for the trash can. At six he turned on the TV.

The nightly news in Boston looked pretty much like a broadcast from Phoenix or Nashville or Dallas, with a few local names inserted and a different guy with too much hairspray mouthing bad segues. Tonight, though, the news felt different. Tonight, Scott heard his own name announced as the primary suspect in the "murder of socialite Patricia Hunter, wife of internationally acclaimed Boston architect Charles Hunter."

CHAPTER 24

Morning came and went. The flight from New York descended into a mist that seemed to swallow the plane whole. The *clunk* of the landing gear lowering resonated inside the cabin, and the lights of Birmingham emerged from pale gray nothing.

Minutes later, Cannonball Walker eased his battered Gibson out of the seat next to his. The flight crew smiled their generic smiles, and the old musician stepped into the suspended orifice leading into the terminal. It was the first week of March, and Canon remembered the South being warmer.

Inside the terminal, he pulled out a brand-new cell phone and punched in a Boston number. Scott Thomas answered on the second ring.

"That you?"

Scott smiled. "It's me, Canon. You get the phone I FedEx'd?"

"Talkin' on it. Just landed in Birmingham. Standin' in line at the Hertz counter right now."

"Get out of line."

The old man stepped to one side and lowered his backside onto a plastic-coated metal bench.

Scott went on. "Grab a cab. There's a room waiting for you at the Tutwiler Hotel; it's downtown across from the gas company building. That'll put you within walking distance of Mr. Pastings's office at the bank."

"I thought you hadn't been here in fifteen years."

"I haven't. But I've got my computer up and running, and I just pulled up a map of the Birmingham business district on the Internet." He paused to think. "You got the phone; so I guess you got the power of attorney, too."

Canon's fingers traced the outline of a thick envelope inside his overcoat. "I got it. Gonna be shocked out of my mind if anybody lets me use it. Old black blues player walkin' in a bank, sayin' I'm the personal rep-re-sent-a-tive of some white kid at Harvard. Be lucky if I'm not arrested."

Scott laughed. "Too late now. You're there."

"I don't know. Lookin' like this little trip might be the hardest five grand I ever earned."

"Not bad for a week's work, though."

"No." Canon stood and walked toward the cab stand. "Not bad. Hell, stealin' is more like it, considering how much good I'm likely to do."

"Canon? Having someone I can trust checking things out down there would be worth twice that."

"Fine. Then pay me twice."

Scott Thomas closed the map of Birmingham and gathered up his notes from the day before. Nothing made much sense. Not yet. But he was getting organized. He was thinking.

Scott spread out his notes on the bed and started work again. Hours passed. He ran across the street for a take-out sandwich, hurried back to the room, and kept working. Something was just out of sight. Something vital was there in the blanks, between the lines of his notes.

He jumped when the phone rang. He grabbed the receiver. "Canon?"

Lots of static, then, "No. It's Budzik. I need to see you."

Scott hesitated. "You sound strange."

"Cell phone. Breaking . . ."

"What?" Scott raised his voice.

"Come . . . warehouse. My place. Come to my place."

"Why? What's happened?"

Scott thought he may have heard the word "hurry" before the line went dead. He punched a button on the cradle to end the call, then immediately entered Budzik's home number. The answering machine picked up. Scott left a message for the little hacker to call the motel, then hung up.

He spoke to the room. "Probably finally getting what you deserve." But two minutes later he grabbed his coat and ran out the door.

Cannonball Walker arrived early for his afternoon appointment with John Pastings. A young black woman brought him coffee. She had rhinestones set into fake fingernails and a beautiful smile. He smiled back.

"Mr. Pastings will be just a few more minutes." She straightened up after setting his coffee on an end table. "Did you have any trouble finding us?"

He shook his head. "Not really. Just had to figure out which one y'all were. Never seen so many banks all set together like this."

"More banks headquartered here than anywhere outside New York City."

Canon didn't care, but he smiled. "How 'bout that."

Time passed, and no one came to fetch the old man. Bad coffee turned cold. Eleven o'clock came and went. Canon went looking for the girl with the rhinestone fingernails. He found a plump little peach of a woman sitting behind a large desk. Behind her, next to an oak door, a brass sign read EXECUTIVE OFFICES.

The old man nodded. "I'm Canon Walker. I was supposed to have an eleven o'clock appointment with John Pastings."

She raised her eyebrows. "Regarding?"

"Regarding"—he raised his voice a bit—"thirty thousand dollars missin' from the account of my client, Scott Thomas."

"What do you mean missing—"

"This bank lost *thirty thousand dollars* of his money. That's what I mean. And this John Pastings agreed to talk to me about it. Here it is"—he glanced at his watch—"eleven-forty-eight, and I'm gonna be sittin' out here coolin' my heels while he leaves and takes a banker's lunch. I flew down from New York for this meeting."

The woman's round face flushed. "I'm sure Mr. Pastings has every intention of seeing you. If you could just be patient . . ."

"I guess maybe when I called from New York Mr. Pastings didn't know I was black. Tell me. How long you think I'd be waitin' if I had white skin and a thousand-dollar suit?"

Beads of perspiration had begun to form above the woman's thick lipstick. "I can assure you that has nothing to do with it. Mr. Pastings is a busy man. If you'll just wait here for one more minute, I'll step back and see what I can do."

Three minutes later, Cannonball Walker was ushered into John Pastings's office.

Now Cannonball was all smiles. "Good mornin', Mr. Pastings. Thank you for seein' me."

The banker sported three chins and rosy drinker's cheeks. He reached out to shake Canon's hand. "Scott told me you'd be coming. We'll get to business in a minute, but first I want to know what kind of crap you thought you were pulling with the receptionist."

Canon just smiled.

"Don't play the race card with me, Mr. Walker. It's counterproductive."

Canon studied the banker's rosy jowls. "Got me in here."

Pastings's eyes narrowed. "So would have stamping your feet and crying. What you've got to ask yourself is how much good that sort of tactic is going to do you once you get through the door."

Canon's smile broadened. If the man wanted to lecture, that was fine. So long as he got what he wanted in the end. "About Scott Thomas's account and the missin' funds. Scott wanted me to get copies of all transactions—"

"Sorry. We can't do that."

"Oh." Canon reached inside his coat and pulled out the folded power of attorney. "Scott made this up. Said it'll give me authority to look into his business here."

Pastings reached out for the document. His eyes scanned down to Scott's signature. "I'm afraid this won't be sufficient."

"And why is that?"

"Well"—he dropped the document on his desk—"first of all, our legal department would have to take a look at it. Then, of course, we'd have to verify Scott's signature."

"You tellin' me you don't have a copy of Scott's signature here at the bank?"

"No, no. It's just that this could take a few days—maybe even a few weeks—to process your request."

"It's Scott's request, not mine."

"Right." Pastings leaned back in his leather chair and laced his fingers over a painfully round gut. "In any event . . ."

Canon waited for Pastings to finish his thought. He never did. "Is this 'cause we got started on the wrong foot?"

The banker shook his head. "No, no. I understand Scott's concerns, and I understand that you're apparently here as his representative. The whole thing will just take a while to work through."

Canon leaned back in the guest chair and sighed. "So long that I might as well go back where I came from. Is that what you're sayin'?"

"That's completely up to you."

"What if I get a lawyer?"

"That's certainly your prerogative. Although, if you don't mind my saying so, it's not really the way to go if you want this information as soon as possible. Our litigation attorneys would have to become involved. Scott would no doubt have to put in an appearance. No, no. Now you're talking about turning weeks into months."

Canon rose to his feet. "I'm not leavin' town."

"That's totally up to you." With some difficulty, Pastings managed to push his poundage into a standing position. "If you do stay, be sure to check out our Botanical Gardens. Not much longer till azalea season, you know."

"Yeah." Canon turned to leave. "One more thing."

Pastings flashed his banker's smile.

"Scott told me to tell you that his brother, Bobby, is in Boston." He tried hard to make the statement sound more certain than it was. It was Scott's *guess*, maybe just his hope. But no more.

The man's features went slack. He took a step backward and steadied himself against the chair. As he regained composure, Pastings's eyes fell to the desktop. Still, he didn't speak.

Canon studied the banker. "Scott wanted to know what you think about that."

Slowly, Pastings's eyes rose to meet Canon's stare. All he said was "Good-bye, Mr. Walker."

Scott arrived at Budzik's warehouse a little after six. He was hungry, and apprehension stabbed at his empty stomach. He parked and sat still to watch.

Transfer trucks rumbled over broken pavement. Three shabbily dressed men wandered from alley to dumpster to steaming grate. The same hooker he'd seen before worked a corner two blocks up.

Scott popped open the door and stepped out into cold evening air.

At the entrance to the hacker's building, everything looked the same. He punched the second-floor buzzer and the front door clicked open.

He whispered, "Shit," then stepped inside and paused for his eyes to adjust to the dim, yellow lighting. Everything looked fine. He had just rounded the boarded stairs, when he heard her voice.

CHAPTER 25

The shadows changed, almost imperceptibly at first. Then a dark leg appeared behind the stairs. Scott moved around the stairwell for a better look.

"Cindy?"

Cindy Travers nodded. Scott stepped forward and gasped in a short, quick breath.

Budzik's girlfriend had come back for more, and she'd gotten it. Both eyes were swelled into purple globes. Blood trickled from the slit of one eye, and a thick red mass bathed her chin beneath mashed and swollen lips. Her clothes were torn. Her arms and legs, her shirt and pants, all looked as though someone had used her to mop the floor.

"Oh, my God. Cindy. What did he do to you?"

Tears rolled out of slits that had been eyes, mixing with a rouge of smeared blood on her cheeks. She shook her head hard and reached out with a hand where two manicured nails had been ripped from the flesh.

"Come on, Cindy. It's all right. My car's outside."

He stopped as she began to tremble with exertion. She was trying to speak.

"Don't. We'll talk later. Just come—"

"*Rurh!*" It was a guttural sound, one that seemed to physically shoot her pain into Scott's chest. He shook his head, and she tried again. The swollen slits of her eyes gaped open. Her head tilted back, and Cindy Travers screeched out one horrible word.

"*Run!*"

Scott could feel the danger, even before his mind translated impressions into thought. He kept his voice even. "Where?"

"Here," a man's voice said, behind him.

Click stood twelve feet away. The outlaw hacker held a stainless steel automatic pistol in his right fist. "You know who I am?"

Scott nodded.

"Say it."

"I know you're Darryl Simmons." Scott motioned over his shoulder at Cindy. "I don't know if you're the piece of shit who did this."

"Keep talkin'. Gonna shoot your ass, anyhow. Might as well say what you want."

"I want to know *why*."

Click shrugged. "Why what? Why'd we decide you looked good for the murder of the Hunter woman? Or"—he pointed at Cindy Travers with his gun—"why'd I fuck up Budzik's girlfriend?"

"Her, I understand. You're a sadistic asshole."

"That a professional analysis?" The hacker grinned.

"Yeah, it is." Something moved in the shadows behind Click's left shoulder, and Scott felt his eyes flicker. Maybe it was Click's backup. Maybe it was Budzik. Whoever it was, Click seemed unaware of the movement. Scott tried to control his line of sight. "What I want to know is why set me up. Why so complicated?"

"You?" He chuckled. "Beats me. That was somebody else's idea. But complicated? Nothin' complicated about it. She-it. All we did was junk up some computers with porno, break into your cheap-ass crib a couple times, and rent that house out in the boondocks. Nothin' to it."

More movement. A dark form, a man, moved silently toward Click's back. Sweat trickled along Scott's spine. He needed to talk—to calm his nerves, to buy time, to make some noise to cover the approach of the dark man pausing now in the shadow of an old workstation.

"One more thing."

Click shook his head. His eyes narrowed. "Fuck you. You're standin' there dead. It's over."

"If I'm dead, what difference does it make? I just want to know who hired you. Who set me up?"

The hacker shook his head and raised the gun.

"Had to be someone at the hospital. Had to be. Didn't it? You can tell me that much."

"For a Harvard boy, you ain't all that smart, are you?" Click sighed. "Yeah. It was somebody at the hospital. I won't give a name. Not even to a dead man. I don't do that." He raised the barrel. "Good-bye, asshole."

A black shape sprang from the floor behind Click. Scott dove hard to his right just as the blast from the automatic shattered the cool air inside the old factory. Scott rolled and sprang back onto his feet, sprinting to a metal workstation where he hunkered down.

Someone cussed.

Scott peeked out to see the wax-faced stranger standing over Click. The watcher held the gun. Click was doing the cussing.

Scott rose to his feet. The watcher, without taking his eyes from Click, extended a hand in Scott's direction and crooked his fingers. As Scott approached the pair, the young man's coal-black eyes burned only in Click's direction.

"Who the hell are you?" Click was speaking to the watcher. "Burglar? Rapist?" He pointed over at Cindy Travers, who had collapsed onto the floor. "You want the girl?"

Fearing Cindy had been hit by the wild gunshot,

Scott knelt down beside her. The round had missed. She was crying—her thin shoulders trembling, then heaving with sobs. Scott stroked her hair, then stood.

Click got to one knee. He was studying the watcher. "You're one ugly bastard, aren't you? Look like you had a job as a taste tester in an acid factory." He laughed. "Don't imagine you got women lined up around the block. I think you better get you some of that before she kicks. She's messed up, but you don't fuck the face. Right?"

The watcher's scarred features showed no expression. Not anger or fear, not even interest. His eyes locked into Click's. "I don't want her." His voice came out like a rusty whisper—as hard and sparse and damaged as his face.

Click hesitated, taken aback by the voice. "What do you want?" He motioned at Scott. "You with him?"

The watcher shrugged, then turned to Scott. "That girl your friend?"

Scott glanced back at the broken soul on the floor. He thought about Budzik's smug abuse, about taking Cindy to the shelter, and about what Click had done to her now. He nodded. "Yeah."

The halting whisper came again. "You want this one?" He motioned at Click with the barrel of the handgun.

Scott needed Click. He needed him for information. He needed him to clear his name. Right now, he needed to kick his ass. "I want him."

The watcher stepped backward. He held Click's handgun up in front of his face as if he'd never seen it before, his black eyes glimmering beside the stainless steel barrel.

Scott feared what the watcher might do. "I don't want him dead."

The watcher shrugged. He made a quick step toward Scott, then tossed the automatic through the air. As Scott reached out to catch the gun, he caught a blur of movement. Click was moving. Scott caught the pistol by its black rubber grip and dropped to the floor as a gunshot from a second gun exploded in his ears. Two more blasts sounded.

Click had a short black revolver, and he was unloading in the direction where the watcher had been standing. Scott's eyes went to the target, but the wax-faced stranger had disappeared. His eyes moved back to Click. Scott's hands fumbled with the stainless automatic. There was no time to aim. He pointed and fired. And fired again and again. Click was running.

Scott heard himself scream "Stop!" It was a stupid thing to say. No one stops to be shot.

Click was gone. So was the watcher.

Cindy had crawled under the boarded stairs and curled into a tight fetal position. As Scott leaned down to check her breathing, Click's voice echoed throughout the factory.

"You're dead! You hear me, you prick. On the street, in jail—it don't matter. You're fucking *dead*."

Scott stood and aimed the automatic at the voice, but the only other sound was the front door slamming. The young shrink moved carefully through the ground floor of the warehouse, checking behind old workstations, listening hard for the soft sounds of movement and breathing. When he was satisfied that he and Cindy were alone, he placed Click's handgun on a nearby workbench and went to help Cindy to her feet.

She cringed.

He knew not to rush her. She needed time. Scott kneeled on the cold concrete floor and talked softly to her. He told her that no one would hurt her; he talked about getting her to a hospital. Mostly he kept his voice soothing, and he waited.

Minutes passed. The soft brush of a shoe on the

gritty floor sent a jolt through him. He reached for the handgun, but it was gone. He cussed under his breath.

"Who is she?" The voice was a raspy whisper.

The watcher stood there again. He held Click's gun in his right fist.

The air felt thick. Seconds passed. Scott shook his head. "You don't want to kill me."

The watcher glanced at the gun, took a few steps, and tossed it onto a metal worktable. All he said was "No."

"You've been following me."

No response.

"I need to know who you are."

Again, the whispered "No."

Scott moved forward. "I don't want to hurt you, either."

The cold, expressionless eyes watched every move.

"But you're going to talk to me." Scott reached out, and the younger man stepped backward. "Okay." Scott shot forward and executed a perfect takedown, hooking the man's heels with his ankle and driving his shoulder into the guy's midsection. The watcher was taken unaware, but, as soon as Scott had him on the floor, the man simply disappeared out of his grasp.

Scott spun up onto one knee and caught the blur of a foot aimed at his temple. He rolled and came up on both feet. The watcher came in fast, his head tucked low, his fists raised like a boxer's. Scott dodged a quick jab, then stepped inside a right cross that hooked behind his head. Grabbing the man's right elbow and jamming an arm between his thighs, Scott used the momentum of the punch to roll backward into a fireman's carry. Again, the watcher hit the concrete floor. This time, Scott moved up fast to clamp an arm around his waist before he could move away.

Scott pushed up, shooting a hand forward to grab a wrist and break him down. But the stranger twisted left and planted a hard elbow in the center of Scott's forehead. And he was up.

Now Scott got to his feet and staggered as the swirling room coalesced into a steady focus. Their undignified scuffle had taken less than five seconds. Scott gingerly touched his forehead. "Why won't you talk to me? Who are you working for?" He bent forward and gripped his knees to keep from falling. The world swirled again and then settled back into place. "You've been following me and my friends. I need to know why."

The man dropped his fists to his sides. "No."

Scott breathed deeply. Nothing to do but ask. "Are you Bobby?" His voice cracked when he spoke the name. "Are you my brother?"

The watcher stared into Scott's eyes, managing to somehow convey confusion and amusement without moving a muscle in that melted face. His eyes drifted around the room once more, and he was gone. Just like that.

As the heavy front door bumped closed, Scott looked down again at Cindy Travers. The girl met his eyes.

"Can you stand?"

She nodded.

Scott walked to the workstation where the watcher had been standing and retrieved the stainless automatic. He pushed the cold metal under the waistband of his jeans. "I need to secure the doors. Okay? I'll just be a few seconds."

She nodded again.

The first floor had filled with freezing air. Scott locked the front door, then trotted through the maze of workstations to find the back door propped wide open. He stepped through into the alley.

A breeze ruffled cardboard beer cartons, torn newspapers, and scattered bits of plastic trash bags. The ancient alley was paved with bricks that gleamed with spilled oil and frozen mist. Scott looked up at smudged stars glowing pale in the muddy sky above the alley and between square rooftops. He breathed deeply and thought of running. He wanted to run. He wanted it more than anything he could imagine.

The mix of thoughts and fractured pictures filling his mind coalesced into one sentence: *My nightmares have faces.*

It was a new thought, and he was surprised that getting a good hard look at Click and the wax-faced watcher had helped. The nightmares had now become real, and that was progress. Demons can eat you alive. Bad guys are just bad guys.

Scott stepped inside out of the alley, locked the door, and walked forward to find Cindy Travers on her feet.

"You need an ambulance." He paused. "Sorry. I need to check out Budzik's apartment. He called. That's why I showed up here tonight. He may be hurt, too." He glanced around the ugly warehouse. "He's nothing, but . . . there's a phone up there. So we can call for help. Do you want to wait here?"

She shook her swollen face.

Scott's eyes scanned the ugly factory floor. "You're right." He tried to sound reassuring. "Don't worry. The man who hurt you is gone. And I can handle Budzik." Scott glanced back at the old elevator. "Come on." He put an arm around her waist. "Let's go."

CHAPTER 26

Sarah Hunter loved the stars. "See, those are the Pleiades. You find 'em by finding the Big Dipper first and then following its handle."

Kate studied the child's face.

"No." The little girl giggled. "It would help if you looked at the sky, Kate."

Kate Billings looked upward. "How is it possible to have more stars here than in Boston? God," she said with a sigh, "it *is* beautiful here."

Sarah looked over at her new nanny. "You know there aren't really more stars here, don't you?" She was teasing—trying hard to do as her father had asked and "build a relationship" with Kate.

A car horn sounded on the other side of the house.

The little girl cried out, "Daddy's home," and took off running.

Kate followed at a slower pace, then veered toward the kitchen door. She was taking dinner out of the oven as Charles came in holding a cane in one hand and Sarah's hand in the other.

Kate smiled. "How's the foot?"

Charles chuckled. "Broken. What's for dinner? Sarah *claims* she made it all by herself."

"She did." Kate put a round platter on the center island. "Homemade pizza."

Sarah laughed. "Bisquick and Ragu with mozzarella cheese on top. The recipe was on the box."

"Sounds wonderful." Charles ran his hand over Sarah's long brown hair. "Why don't you go get washed up. I'll be right behind you."

Sarah skipped out of the room, and Charles lowered his voice. "Kate? I've got to run up to Boston for a few days. There's a, uh . . . there's a problem I have to take care of personally. So I was wondering." He sat on a stool to take the weight off his cast. "I was wondering if you think Sarah would be comfortable staying alone here with you. I know you two are just starting to get to know each other . . ."

Kate showed her teeth. "Absolutely."

"Really? Because I could make other arrangements."

"No way. I guess Sarah's the person you really need to ask, but I think we're good to go. She was just out on the beach trying to show me how to find the Pleiades."

Charles smiled. "Well, okay then. Of course, I'll talk to Sarah. But"—he stepped gingerly down off the stool—"I don't foresee any problems. The place will be all yours for a few days. I just hope you won't get bored during the day when Sarah's in school on the mainland." He paused. "But I guess you're pretty much alone here even when I'm at the office a mile away."

"I like it." Kate showed her teeth again. "Enjoy your trip. I've got things here under control."

Charles hobbled out to wash up for dinner, and Kate pulled a chef's knife from a maple block on the counter. As she pressed the heavy blade through hot cheese and tomato sauce to cut through the crust, she began to sing quietly to herself.

And, for the first time that evening, a genuine smile crept across Kate Billings's face.

*   *   *

The elevator clanged noisily on the way up to Budzik's apartment. For the first time in Scott's experience, the panel buttons inside the thing worked. Apparently Budzik had engaged a manual override.

When the lift door slid open, the apartment door was ajar. Scott pulled the red STOP knob and reached a protective arm across Cindy's midsection. "Wait here."

"No."

He looked into her swollen eyes. "I have a gun. Nobody's getting past me."

She looked trapped. "No." It was all she could comfortably say through broken lips.

"Stay behind me."

Cindy nodded, and he stepped quickly out of the elevator. Scott didn't know how to enter a room with a gun. His reference points were scenes from James Bond movies. He pointed to the side of the door, and Cindy flattened herself against the wall. Scott braced, then kicked the door wide and went in fast.

The room was empty.

Motioning Cindy inside, he said, "Watch the stairs." He moved around the perimeter of the living room and through the open kitchen to the hallway. "Anything?" His voice a loud whisper.

Cindy Travers mouthed, "No."

"Come on."

When Cindy was beside him, Scott explained, "If Budzik's here, he's probably in his lab upstairs. I'm going to check out the bedrooms, make sure they're clear. Then I want you to stay put while I go upstairs." His eyes roamed her face. "Can you do that?"

A long breath trembled inside Cindy's chest, and she nodded.

"Okay, here we go." He glanced down the dark hallway. "Which room is Budzik's?"

She pointed at the far door.

Scott motioned at the other door. "And this one?"

"Like a guest room." It was the most she'd said since he found her downstairs.

He moved to the first door and quietly eased it open. Scott glanced back at Cindy and shook his head. Next he tried the master bedroom.

Scott half expected the door to be locked. It wasn't. The cool metal turned easily in his hand. The door swung open. A human shape lay perfectly still in the bed, swaddled in tangled sheets and blankets.

"Budzik? Budzik? You okay? Is anyone else . . ." Scott's voice choked to nothing. And, without taking another step, he understood instinctively that he was talking to a corpse.

Scott quickly inspected the room, the closets, and the adjoining bathroom before making his way to the bedside. Protruding from the covers, up near the pillows, he saw the pink, fleshy globe of the little man's shaved head. Scott took a deep breath and pulled back the covers. Budzik was on his back. Nude. Milky eyes stared at nothing; blood spread out like cardinal's wings on either side of his shoulders; and a fleshy red gash spread from one earlobe to the other.

Scott's breathing came quick, and he heard Cindy gasp behind him. Fighting the taste of bile at the back of his throat, he spun around and spoke sharply to the girl. "Get out." She hesitated, and his voice grew harsher. "Go!"

He pushed the girl out ahead of him and closed the door.

In the hallway, he flattened against the wall and breathed in clean air. Images blew through his mind's eye like autumn leaves in the wind—coagulating blood and torn tissue, milky eyes and bloodstained sheets. Nausea licked at his throat.

Someone else could still be in the apartment. Scott

needed to focus; he needed to call an ambulance for Cindy, to call the cops and then get out ahead of them. Cindy had dropped out of reality again—her eyes focused on a point in midair, her mind gone to an empty place to protect itself from further horror.

Scott led Cindy into the next bedroom and helped her lie down on the bed. She didn't object to being left behind this time. This time, she couldn't.

The loft was quiet. Only the soft hush of central heat blowing through floor vents—a white noise even quieter than nothing. He moved out at a run. Scott had had enough of slow. Through the living room and up the stairs to the lab, he sprinted quietly on the balls of his feet. Always holding the gun in front. Always ready to pull the trigger.

But there was nothing. Nothing at all. No one in the lab. No one waiting on the top floors. He dropped into a chair and picked up Budzik's phone.

The 911 operator didn't like no street address. Scott gave the intersection. He explained about the elevator and told exactly where Cindy Travers could be found. When he was done, Scott walked downstairs to wait with Cindy.

She was sitting up on the edge of the bed when he came in. Glancing up, she tried a small smile. "This is awful." It sounded like *Dis ee awfoo.*

Scott sat beside her. "An ambulance is on the way. You'll be okay."

"Nothing broken, I think."

He nodded. "Look, when the paramedics get here, I need to get out fast. Don't worry, I'll wait till I know you're okay. But I can't stay around."

She raised a thumb in the direction of Budzik's bedroom. "Because of that?"

"No. Well, not *just* that."

"You'll be in trouble." Cindy reached out with an unnaturally cold hand and squeezed his wrist. "Go. I'll be fine. They're on the way."

"No." Scott lay back. "You've got enough to deal with without trying to explain what happened in the next room."

The young woman's irises, just visible through swollen slits, bounced from side to side. "I can handle it. That man downstairs—the pale one with the guns. He beat me up and killed Peter. You came by, ran him off, and called for help." She squeezed his wrist again. "Really, I'll be fine." She paused. "Downstairs, I told you to run and you didn't do it. Now I'm telling you—*run*. I don't want to cause you pain. I couldn't stand that. Please, run."

Scott pushed up off the bed and walked to the door. "You need anything before I go? Water? Or . . ."

She pointed at the door. "Run." *Rurh*.

As he stepped off the elevator, Scott could hear commotion in the street outside. He walked forward to unlock the front door. But as he pushed it open, he saw the mix of swirling emergency lights on the street. Some red, some white, and some blue. Blue meant the police. He stepped back inside, flattened his back against the wall, and tried to think. His brain wouldn't work. The pieces wouldn't fit. No way had the cops gotten there so quickly after his emergency call.

Maybe Click had called the cops to set him up for Budzik's murder. Maybe someone in the neighborhood had heard the gunshots. Maybe . . . he didn't know. But he couldn't give up. There was too much left to do.

Sprinting through a graveyard of abandoned work-stations, he hit the elevator just as the warehouse door slammed open. Scott punched the top button. The elevator creaked and shimmied and seemed to take minutes to rise four floors. Finally, he stepped out into a brick cube on the roof, turned, and punched the 1 button so the cops and paramedics could get to Cindy.

Now what?

Panic began to overtake him. Scott's heart felt as though someone had reached into his chest and gripped the muscle. He fought to slow his breathing, to control the flow of adrenaline flooding his bloodstream. His eyes came to rest on the rusty metal door leading out onto the roof.

CHAPTER 27

Scott ran to the edge of the warehouse roof and peered down through the night into the alley below. Uniformed cops flanked the back door. He crouched down. He needed to think. If only for a few seconds, he needed to concentrate.

Across the alley and at the back left corner of the roof—a short ten feet away—sat another warehouse that was shorter by one floor than the one where he stood. Scott got to his feet and glanced down into the alley once more. A policeman looked up. Scott ducked down and waited. He needed only one unobserved second.

Scott glanced down to see one of the patrolmen disappear into the building. He had no more time. He checked the lone cop in the alley once more, backed up twenty feet, and ran hard for the edge of the roof.

Sunrise. Purples, yellows, and blood reds streaked the distant horizon of lead-gray waters. A light breeze rolled off the Atlantic, bringing the scents of the sea and—it seemed to Kate Billings—of life. She sighed.

"Feeds your soul, doesn't it?"

The voice startled Kate. She turned to see Charles Hunter standing behind her. She nodded. "It's so peaceful here. I grew up in Boston, but, even if you ever see a sunrise away from buildings and cars, it's still sort of busy with ships and planes and . . ." Her voice grew softer. "Always something. Not like this."

"I've decided to say good-bye to Sarah here on the island. There's no school today, so there's no need for the two of you getting a chill on the boat."

Kate thought the temperature was perfect, but she nodded again. "Okay. We'll go over to the bay side with you. Sarah can watch your boat cross over."

Charles turned and walked inside. Kate paused to drink in the sunrise for a few more minutes before going in to rouse Sarah from sleep.

Forty minutes later, Kate stood on the bay-side dock with Charles and Sarah. The father had dropped to one knee to gather his little girl up in his arms. When their good-byes were done, Charles turned to Kate. "Here." He handed her an envelope and smiled. "There's three hundred in there. Should be enough to last the few days I'll be gone. If something comes up, and you need more, just drop by the office and see Carol Petring. She'll advance you whatever you need. I'll call around dinner every night. Please have Sarah available so I can speak with her."

Kate smiled. "No problem. Have a nice trip."

Charles nodded. He picked up Sarah for one more hug, then stepped into an idling Boston Whaler.

As the boat cut a white curve through dark water, Kate put her arm around Sarah and squeezed her shoulder.

"Ow!"

Kate looked down. "What's wrong?"

"You're squeezing too hard."

"Oh." Kate looked back at the receding boat. "I'm sorry, sweetheart. I was thinking about something else." She kneeled down to look into Sarah's eyes. "We've got a whole day ahead of us. No school. Nothing. I was wondering . . . Is there anything here on the island that you've always wanted to do? Something"—Kate winked—"that maybe your dad wouldn't let you do. Some kind of adventure maybe?"

The little girl's eyes shimmered. "Uh, Dad told me to quit asking until I'm older, but . . ."

Kate nodded encouragingly. "It's okay. What is it?"

"I've always wanted to take the Sunfish out by myself. I need somebody to show me what to do first. You know, I can sail a little. I go with my dad all the time. But you know . . ." Quiet pleading filled the child's eyes.

Kate reached over to gently massage the shoulder she had hurt. "If you don't tell your dad . . ."

Sarah squealed. "Oh, I won't, Kate! I promise, I won't."

Kate smiled. "Then I think we can definitely get you in a boat. Don't worry, Sarah. We're going to make that wish come true."

Kate stood and walked down the dock toward Charles's Jeep. Sarah looked out once more at her father's boat chugging toward the mainland, then the ten-year-old turned and ran after her nanny.

Time passed slowly inside the abandoned warehouse. For endless hours, Scott's heart jumped every time a rat scuffled through the storage closet where he hid from the police. A dozen times, some muffled street noise or a distant creak convinced him that Lieutenant Cedris had entered his hideout.

At sunup, he crept out of the closet, crossed a tangle of flophouse mattresses, plastic syringes, and broken crack vials. He peered through pollution-caked windows to see the cop cars still parked outside Budzik's loft. An hour later, he ventured out again to find the streets empty.

Scott rolled his shoulders to squeeze out some of the

tension. He started carefully down rusted metal steps. On the first floor, metal doors with busted locks had been chained shut. But someone had been using the mattresses upstairs during warmer weather. They'd had to get in somehow.

Methodically working the perimeter of the building, he finally found a wide, loading dock door that was loose enough on one side for a man to squeeze through. He glanced through the crack and pushed out.

The jump down from the loading dock sent shocks of pain through cold ankles and knees. Scott moved out though the dock to the street, where he paused. The same hooker he'd seen before leaned against a soiled brick wall across the street.

She caught his eye. Scott shook his head. The woman stared back hard. He was about to step into the street when she shook her head.

He pointed to his chest.

She nodded again and, keeping her hand down next to her hip, angled up a palm as if to say *stop*.

Scott eased back a few feet. The woman turned her head from side to side and then pushed off the wall. She crossed over a few paces north of the loading dock, turned, and casually strolled to the edge of the dock. The streetwalker stood only a few feet from Scott now, and he could see that the woman he'd seen from a distance was, at most, sixteen.

Keeping her back to Scott, she fished a cigarette pack out of her purse and placed a white filter between deep red lips. As she did, the girl said, "The cops are still here." She pushed the pack of cigarettes back into her purse and long-nailed fingers came out with a lighter. She cupped her hands around the flame. "Gimme a second. Just makin' sure they ain't lookin'." The girl took a deep drag, blew a stream of smoke into the air, and turned to walk into the loading dock.

Scott's eyes moved over the heavy makeup and dirty hair, over a faux-fur coat to black hose in high-heeled pumps.

She grinned and opened her coat to reveal a black bustier and red leather miniskirt. "Gettin' a good look?"

Scott shook his head. "How old are you?"

Her grin faded. "Older than you'll ever be."

"Did the police see you come in here?"

"I know what I'm doin'." She gathered her coat around her. "Never been arrested. Not once in three years turnin' tricks." She glanced back out at the street. "But they're out there. Inside the building where that bald geek lived. One's watchin' that old Jeep of yours."

"Damn."

"Ain't that the truth." She sucked in a lungful of carcinogens. "I oughta be mad at you." Smoke puffed out of her nose and mouth when she spoke. "Fucked up my whole night. Not that there's much business this early. But you had them fuckin' cops here all night. And, you know, even this late I can usually pick up a trick or two— old guys gettin' off the night shift down at the lightbulb factory on Twenty-eighth. But you got the cops swarmin' the place. So, what? You kill somebody or somethin'?"

Scott shook his head.

Her eyes narrowed. "Right." She stepped toward Scott. "Whatever you did, you look like shit. You okay?"

"No, I'm not. I need to get across town. To Boston Hospital."

She sniffed a runny nose. "You sick or hurt?"

"Both," he said, "but not the way you mean."

"Oh." She shrugged. "You got money for a cab?"

"Sure."

"Got some extra for me?"

"Yeah." Scott tried to focus on the task at hand. "Get me to a cab and I'll give you a hundred dollars."

Her eyes moved over Scott's face. "I must be fuckin'

stupid. First of all, I ought not to be screwin' around with some guy probably a murderer. Second, I guess I could hold you up for two or three hundred, kind of shape you're in." She paused, then turned toward the street. "What the hell. Wait here. I'll tell you when to come out."

CHAPTER 28

Cannonball Walker sat in the restaurant of the Tutwiler Hotel. Outside, the oaks in Linn Park were starting to bud. He watched a group of first graders heading for the downtown library, each child holding tightly to a bright yellow rope that stretched from one teacher in front to another in the back, the children decorating the middle like carved beads. The old man tried to feel good about what he was seeing, but a bitter taste twisted his throat. Scott wasn't answering. Canon had tried the number six times after his meeting with Pastings.

The waiter brought iced tea. Canon took a sip and thought of his mother's perfume; the tea was mostly something like Luzianne, but with just a hint of Earl Grey. He punched in Scott's number for the seventh time and got nothing. But, as he hit the END button on the cell phone, it rang in his hand.

"Scott?"

"Yeah."

"Doc? Where the hell are you? Been tryin' to get you all day."

"Sorry. I'm . . . Well, I'm in the apartment of a sixteen-year-old hooker at the moment, but . . ."

The old bluesman snorted. "We ain't got time for that now."

"I'm not up here getting laid, Canon. She's calling a cab for me. I can't go into everything here, but we found the computer hacker who set me up at the country house."

"Good."

"Wait. We found him, but he found us, too. The other hacker. The one who was helping me. Budzik. He's dead."

Canon sighed. "And the cops think you did it."

"Probably. I'm going to the hospital as soon as the cab gets here. There's someone there who I think might help me with this."

Canon glanced up as the waiter put a club sandwich in front of him. "Sounds to me like you fixin' to screw up."

"Maybe. Tell me about your meeting with Mr. Pastings."

"Man don't care about you, Doc. That's the way it looks. Kept me waitin', wouldn't show me your bank records, nothin'."

"What about the power of attorney I sent you? He doesn't have any choice but to—"

"He got a choice. And he took it. Said he'd get back with me in a few weeks after his legal folks looked over the paper."

"What'd he say about Bobby? Did you tell him I think Bobby's alive and here in Boston?"

"Man said good-bye."

"What?"

"That's what he said. I asked him about Bobby, the way you told me to. And that old fat banker just looked at me and said, 'Good-bye, Mr. Walker.'" Canon took a sip of tea and thought again of his mother. "Looks like you're payin' me for nothin', Doc. Figured I'd load up and head out this afternoon."

"No. Please don't do that. We've just got to come at this from a different angle. I know about the thirty thousand, and Pastings is pretty much out of my business now. My problem is what they're saying about the fire that killed my parents."

Canon heard the hooker's voice in the background, saying, "Cab's here. You need to go."

"Canon? There's a street there called Roseland Drive. It's in Homewood. A suburb. I don't know addresses, but our neighbors there were named Pongeraytor. That's a pretty unusual name. Yugoslavian or something. Anyway, if you could run them down, maybe they know what happened. I mean, your next-door neighbor's house burning down has to be a big event in anybody's life."

Canon looked out the window at passing traffic.

"Canon?"

"Yeah," he said, "I'm here. I'll see what I can do."

The teenage girl spoke again. "Come on! Cabbies don't even like comin' to this neighborhood. You make him sit, he's gonna take off."

Scott said something unintelligible to the girl, then said, "Thank you, Canon. I know this is more than you bargained for."

"Don't worry about it." Canon looked down at his lunch. "Take more than a fat banker to knock me out of this."

Scott stepped out of the backseat into a wet gray afternoon, then leaned back inside to pay the cab driver. He hurried to get under a canvas awning, out of the March mist. Three doors down, a hanging sign read JOEY'S ITALIAN-IRISH EATERY. He trotted through hard mist and pushed through heavy double doors.

A college-age girl with masses of curly black hair showed him to a back booth. Scott hadn't eaten since the night before. He ordered lamb stew and Guinness.

When the same girl brought his check, Scott asked about a barber shop in the area.

"No. But Judy cuts men's hair. Just two blocks down. Tell her Casey sent you."

Five minutes later, he stepped into Judy's Style Shop—a one-woman beauty parlor slash barber shop slash tanning salon. Judy—a petite woman with overprocessed hair and a silicone chest—was experiencing a midafternoon lull.

He sat down, and she spun the chair so that Scott faced the mirror. In traditional male shops, they usually have the decency to face you the other way. Scott examined his sorry reflection.

Judy make a *tsk-tsk* noise. "First thing we have to do is wash this out." She tugged gently at a wayward curl. "Who's been cutting your hair?"

"Different people. But it's going to curl like that no matter what you do." Scott looked at the reflection of Judy's eyes. "So I was thinking I want it cut off."

"I could fix it."

Scott smiled. "No. I'm tired of fooling with it. I want it short."

"Okay." She sounded doubtful. "But listen to me on this one. You're too cute to have that scraggly beard all over your face."

Scott looked at his week's growth. "I kind of want to keep it. Think you could shape it up for me?"

She brightened. "Absolutely. I'm good with a razor. Just this past Valentine's Day, I shaved eight regulars . . . you know, down there"—she pointed—"in the shape of a heart." Judy blushed a bit. "Only women, of course."

Judy sprayed Scott's hair with warm water and started to work in handfuls of lather. Scott leaned back and tried to relax. "You think you could point me at a decent men's store around here? Somebody who has a tailor on the premises. I need a suit for a meeting this afternoon. And"—he glanced at a desk near the front—"could I use your phone for a local call? A friend of mine is in the hospital. I want to make sure she's okay."

Judy cocked her head to one side. "Sure." She winked. "But you've gotta let me shave your beard in the shape of a heart."

Standing on the sidewalk outside the hospital, Scott removed his gold-rimmed glasses and tucked them inside the breast pocket of the white dress shirt he'd purchased to go with his new suit and tie. Uncreased oxfords pinched his feet.

Without his glasses, the world had turned a little squiggly around the edges, but he only had to make it in and out—just this one trip—without being recognized. He found the main entrance—the one with the most visitors and the fewest doctors and nurses—and stepped in out of the mist.

Moving quickly past the information desk, he made his way to the fire door leading to the main stairs. He reached for the handle, and the heavy door swung open untouched. Two doctors in white coats charged through, nearly running him down as they stepped into the hallway. One he knew, a surgeon named Smithers, glanced at Scott and mumbled, "Sorry."

Scott couldn't move. He tried to get past them, to look purposeful but unhurried, but he geeked out—frozen in place like a frightened child. Dr. Smithers had already turned away to continue a conversation with his friend. Now, as Scott stood frozen in place, the doctor turned back. "I *said* I was sorry."

Finally, Scott's brain kicked into gear, and he brushed past the doctors without answering. Before the door closed, he heard the doctor say one more word. "Jerk."

Scott trotted down one flight of stairs and pushed the

release bar on a door leading into the hospital's IT section. He'd been only part time—nothing but a student counselor, or "baby doc" as they were known around the hospital—and he'd had almost no interaction with the hordes of worker bees in Information Technology.

Almost.

There was one person. Natalie Friedman had been fresh out of Boston College and chained to the PC help desk when Scott first arrived at the hospital. Natalie had set up Scott's access to the hospital's IT system, and she'd solved a printer spooling problem for him a month later. She'd even had dinner with him in the hospital cafeteria on two or three occasions. The two young professionals had connected. Scott now hoped that would be enough.

A face approached in the hallway without triggering any sense of familiarity. Scott waited for the stranger to get inside the limited range of his vision and glanced at the security name tag dangling from his belt. CLEMENT PEOPLES. The man's name was no more familiar than his face. This was as good as it was going to get.

"Excuse me."

Clement Peoples turned to meet Scott's eyes. "Yes."

"I'm looking for the help desk. Natalie Friedman."

Peoples pointed past Scott's shoulder. "Go to the end of the hall and hang a left. You'll go down a short set of steps and dead end at some double doors. Turn right, and you'll run into the help desk offices. Natalie's stuck at one of the cubes in there." He snorted out a little chuckle. "Unless she's out showing some dork where the delete key is on his computer."

Scott said, "Thanks," and turned away.

The time was creeping toward five now, and Scott hurried. If she had gone home, he'd have to take the same chances all over again the next day.

When he turned at the double doors, Scott came

face to face with four young men. They were leaving the help desk office, carrying coats and briefcases. Scott lowered his head and brushed past. Through a tiny window in the office door, he saw three women preparing to leave for the day. One of them was Natalie Friedman.

The women pushed through the door and brushed past. No one asked why he was there. No one offered to help. It was quitting time. If he wasn't going to speak up, they weren't going to volunteer.

Scott turned to see his hope leaving in the person of Natalie Friedman.

Shit. "Natalie!"

One of her friends giggled. "You got caught. See you tomorrow."

Natalie sighed and turned. As she did, Scott was already stepping through the door to her office.

The young programmer wrinkled her brow, then marched down the hallway and pushed open the door. "You really shouldn't be in here. If you need help, the second shift will be on at eight."

Scott turned to face her. "I need *your* help, Natalie." For a moment, he thought she might scream. White showed around her dark irises. "Someone's trying to frame me for murder. A man named Darryl Simmons. His hacker name is Click."

Her expression changed, and Scott could tell that Natalie had heard Click's name before.

"I have Click's IP address. He was working with someone here at the hospital." His eyes dropped. "At least, I think he was. It's the only thing that makes sense." Scott looked back up into her eyes. "I need your help, Natalie. I don't know where else to turn."

Natalie stepped backward and put her hand on the door. She pointed to a plastic chair ten feet distant. "Sit there."

"What?"

"Sit down or I'm leaving right now. Sit!"

Scott obeyed. "Okay, what now?"

"Tell me about this alleged frame. Tell me about Click and how you got the IP address of one of the most notorious hackers in New England. Explain it. I'll listen as long as it makes sense. But"—she pointed at Scott like a teacher warning an unruly student—"move an inch, try to stand up, even raise your voice, and I'll scream bloody murder. You got that?"

"I've got it. Is it okay if I put my glasses on?"

"You can put your glasses on." Her voice turned softer. "Now start talking."

CHAPTER 29

Dusk had settled outside the windowless basement offices. The streets were a different place now from when Scott stepped through the hospital's glass doors only minutes before. People hurried more and spoke less. Drivers swerved, slammed brakes, and blared horns, trying too hard to maintain a reputation as the most aggressive commuters in the world.

Inside the IT dungeon, fluorescent light was constant. Day and night, winter, spring, summer, and fall, computer jockeys moved through halls and offices as unchanging as a photograph.

"Can we go somewhere else to talk?"

Natalie Friedman shook her head. "No. We can't."

"Somebody could come in—"

"So I'm supposed to go off with an accused murderer to God knows where? I don't think so." Natalie pressed her bottom against the door to make sure it was ajar. "Talk now, talk here, and talk fast, or I'm gone."

Scott looped his glasses over his ears and tried to slow his breathing. He studied Natalie's face. She was definitely nice to look at, but not magazine-cover beautiful. Not really. But she had something more than that. Intelligence and empathy combined with . . . something. She was just astoundingly *attractive*. That was the word.

He decided to dive in. "Patricia Hunter was murdered while I was at home, asleep in bed. Somebody—I don't know who—called me at three A.M. and told me about it. I came down to the hospital, and the cops started treating me like a suspect." Scott examined Natalie's face. Her eyes watched his. She knew something. The biggest mistake he could make would be to tell her a lie or to gloss over incriminating facts she already knew. He decided to tell her everything. Almost everything. "My apartment was burglarized the day before this happened. At the time, I thought nothing was taken. Later I found out that the two burglars brought an empty Palm Pilot. They beamed everything in my Palm into the one they had, put mine back in the charger, and left without taking anything. Without taking anything I'd notice missing."

Natalie nodded. This was something she knew about.

Scott needed to keep her nodding. "My Palm had everything in it. They got my online banking passwords and used it to steal thirty thousand dollars from my trust account in Birmingham."

"Was that all the money in the account?"

"No. The account had everything left from my father's estate. Just enough to finish my doctorate. They took about half of what was there."

"Why would they only take half if . . ." Her voice trailed off.

"I don't know. Maybe taking everything would have triggered too much interest at the bank. Maybe . . . I don't know. I *do* know they used the funds to try to frame me for Patricia Hunter's murder."

Natalie's eyes darted around the help desk room. "Who are 'they'?"

"Darryl Simmons. Click. I know that for sure. I found a Palm with my data in it on a desk in his office."

"How'd you . . . ?"

"I broke in. The man's a criminal. He invaded my life. And I broke in to what I thought was his apartment to find out why. He has a kind of office—with four computers and boxes of stolen cell phones and PDAs—set up in an old tenement apartment."

Her eyes narrowed. "And I guess you've got a good excuse for torching your house."

She must have seen the web site. Scott objected. "I didn't torch anything. I was ten years old."

"No, Scott. The house out in the country south of here. It was in the papers. The police arrived to serve a warrant, and the place burst into flames with two or maybe three officers inside."

Scott shook his head. His eyes dropped and moved over the floor. "I know the place." He stopped talking as a horrible thought worked through. "Are the cops . . . did they get caught in the fire?"

"They're fine."

"Good." Scott shook off the image of burned bodies. "Someone rented the house in my name and put a computer and a bunch of porno in there."

"On your computer here at the hospital, too."

He looked up. "Huh?"

"Porno. We found some nasty stuff on your hard drive."

"I didn't have a computer. I was a part-time student analyst. I was lucky they gave me a cubicle and a phone."

"Oh. Well, it was *one* of the psych ward computers. There were all these S and M pictures—dirty, nasty, black-and-white photos of . . ."

Scott could tell he was losing her. He looped back to something she could understand. "It had to be Click. Somebody hired him. He told me. Somebody hired him to ruin my life. To frame me for Patricia Hunter's murder."

Natalie began to edge backward. The door pushed open another inch.

Now or never. "He was working with someone here at the hospital. I paid a computer hacker to help me work through this. He said the hospital's system administrator could pull up a list of all the e-mails that have come through here. I've got Click's IP address. All I need is to check it against—"

"No way." Natalie's voice was harsh. But she was no longer inching backward.

"You know you can do it."

"I *can* do a lot of things. I'm not even supposed to know how to do what you're asking."

Scott tried a smile. "But you *do* know how, don't you?"

"I know how to do a lot of things that could get me fired."

Scott started to stand. She tensed, and he eased back into the formed plastic seat. Seconds passed. Both of them were thinking. Finally, he said, "This is the only thing I could come up with. I don't know what else to do."

More time passed. Natalie exhaled as if she'd been holding her breath. "You've exhausted everything else? Every other way to check into this?"

He almost admitted that there were other loose ends out there, but thought better of it. He needed to know who Click was working with at the hospital. So, in the end, he lied. "Yes. I don't know what else I could do."

Lines formed between her eyebrows. "If you find something—if you find someone here at the hospital who was communicating with this Click person—will you turn yourself in and give that information to the police?"

"They won't listen."

She was shaking her head before he got out the third word. "It's the only way I'm going to help you."

Scott tried to read her face. All he said was "Okay."

Natalie glanced at her watch. "The next shift comes

in at eight. That means you've got about two and half hours to find what you need and get out of here." She swept her hand around the room. "Pick a computer. I'll walk you through the logon and password procedures."

Scott smiled. "Are you going to stay there in the doorway, like you've got a wild animal in the room?"

"Yes." She didn't smile. "That's exactly what I'm going to do. I'll get you into the system. Then I'm out of here. You can sit here and scroll through the e-mails by yourself. Now"—she made an impatient gesture with her hand—"pick a computer. You've got a few thousand e-mails to scroll through, and not much time to do it."

Two uniformed cops loitered at the first-floor information desk. One—a skinny kid with acne scars—stood with his back to the receptionist. His arms were folded. He rocked on his feet from heel to toe. The second cop was all beef and attitude. He leaned forward, ropy forearms resting on the tall Formica counter, his mouth working overtime. "We need to see this Clement Peoples, uh, in your IT department. He called in a—" The receptionist's phone rang. She reached for the receiver, and the cop barked, "Stop!"

The woman jumped in her seat. "There's no need . . ."

The beefy cop took a deep breath. "I been standin' here for five minutes not able to get a sentence out 'cause you been pickin' up that phone every time I get started." She tried to speak, but he kept talking. "I know it's your job to answer that thing, but it's my job to find a murderer." Now he had her attention. "We got a 911 call about an hour ago from some guy named Clement Peoples. Said he'd wait here for us. Said he spotted a fugitive here at the hospital."

The receptionist nodded. "I'll ring his extension."

Seconds passed. "I'm sorry, he's not in. Maybe he got tired of waiting . . ."

"You got an emergency contact number for him?"

"No. I don't, but they'll have one in IT."

"Call 'em."

The woman's fingers shook as she punched in the number.

Leaving Scott alone in the help desk room, Natalie had walked immediately down the hallway to the night manager's cubicle. Like Scott, she had a little over two hours before the night shift came on at eight. She would be fired, or worse, if anyone caught her. But she needed the monitoring software on the manager's hard drive.

Natalie began to review every keystroke Scott had made since he logged in to the system. She wanted to help. But she wasn't crazy. One wrong move by Scott, one improper inquiry, one attempt to sabotage anything, and she would call security.

For almost an hour, she watched the young shrink stumble through thousands of e-mails—finding reams of nothing—until she had begun to simultaneously feel both deep sympathy and growing distrust for him. She'd been almost ready to give up on him when he got his first hit.

Click—if that was really who belonged to the IP address—had sent an e-mail to someone at the hospital with the in-house address bill13k@boshosp.com. Natalie halved the size of her monitoring window and opened the manager's e-mail program. Three or four seconds, and the program popped on screen. She clicked **address book** and scrolled through for bill13k. There was no such address.

She glanced over. Scott had two more hits. Now he was opening the e-mails, printing each in turn. Natalie couldn't see the texts, and she couldn't open the notes on the manager's computer while Scott had them open at the help desk. She waited, her fingers poised over the keys, her breathing slow and shallow.

The phone rang, and Natalie jumped inside her skin. She glanced around. She was where she was. No pretending otherwise. If someone knew she was in the manager's cubicle and she didn't answer the phone, well, how bad would that look?

Natalie grabbed the receiver. "Manager's desk."

"Yes. Is this Susan?"

"No. This is Natalie." No need for last names. "I was working in this area and heard the phone ring."

"Oh. Uh, this is Ms. Selma at the information desk on one. I've got two police officers here who need an emergency contact number for Clement Peoples. Do you have access to that information?"

"Is something wrong?"

"I think it's about that woman getting murdered here in the hospital." A grumbling male voice sounded in the background, and the receptionist said "Sorry" with her mouth away from the receiver, as if speaking to someone else. "Look, hon." She was back. "They don't want me talking about it. Just give me that number, okay?"

Thought scattered and then seemed to coalese in Natalie's mind. "Sure. I can get that for you. Just give me about five minutes to pull it up, and I'll ring you right back."

"Okay, hon. Thanks a lot. I'm at extension ten-eleven. Talk to you in a few minutes."

After hanging up, Natalie glanced at the program monitoring Scott's keystrokes. An involuntary shudder ran up her spine. She closed all programs, logged off the computer, and turned off the power. She was outside the cubicle and walking too fast when she spun and went back.

Natalie fished a packet of Handi-wipes from her purse, pulled out a white sheet, and went to work. She wiped down the keyboard and mouse, the desk and chair. A separate wipe took care of the telephone.

She stepped back to inspect the area. The chair was right, the desk neat. Everything was exactly as she'd found it, except . . . Natalie bent down to wipe the power button on the minitower, then dropped both towelettes into her purse. She was moving fast as she left the room of cubicles and turned down a fluorescent-lighted hallway.

The receptionist would expect Natalie to call back in two minutes. A minute after that, the receptionist would try to call her. Then it would be a matter of seconds before the police decided to check out just what the hell was going on in the IT department. All in all, she figured Scott had about four minutes before the cops started looking for someone, anyone, working in the department.

Unfortunately, at 7:08 P.M.—fifty-two minutes before the start of the night shift—Scott would be the only one there.

CHAPTER 30

She almost left him there. For all Natalie knew, she'd provided hospital-wide system access to a murderer. But Click's alleged IP address had turned up a number of hits, all to the same e-mail address inside the hospital. That's what stopped her.

Natalie glanced at her watch and broke into a run. As she rounded the corner outside the help desk office and burst through double doors, she called his name. "Scott!"

He swiveled in the task chair and shot to his feet. When his eyes met hers, he said, "Don't do that. You scared me to death."

"Log off the computer."

"Why? I'm finding—" Her panic broke through his, and he began to think. "Who's coming?"

"The police are at the information desk out front. The receptionist called back. Someone spotted you coming in."

Scott turned and started punching keys. Natalie pushed him aside. "Move." As her fingers began to fly over the keyboard, she called back, "Check the door."

Before she finished her sentence he was through the door, glancing down the long hallway outside. He leaned back into the room. "Nothing." Then he seemed to freeze. "Wait."

He stepped back into the hallway. Seconds passed. Natalie felt the tingle of adrenaline flowing into her blood. "What?" Her voice was sharp. "Wait on what?" She logged off the computer.

Scott stepped back into the room. "The cops—two in uniforms—they've got a woman with them. They're checking the offices." He stopped to examine the horrified face of the woman who'd let him sneak into the hospital's brain. He felt sick. "I'm sorry. I'm so sorry, Natalie." His eyes bounced around the room, looking for a way out that wasn't there. He walked toward her. "Start screaming."

"What?"

"Start screaming. Run out into the hallway. I'll give you a couple of seconds head start and run out behind you."

"They'll shoot you."

"No, they won't. Just say you were working late and I came in. I'll give myself up. It'll be fine. Don't worry. Soon as I lay eyes on the cops, my hands are going in the air." Natalie shook her head as Scott spoke. Then they both froze as a loud knock echoed in the hallway. He whispered, "Go! They're here."

"It was next door."

"But they'll be here . . ."

"Drop your pants." Natalie began to unbutton her blouse. Scott watched without understanding. "Now!" Her blouse was open. She yanked it off one shoulder.

Now he understood. "You sure?"

"Get over here." She reached out to pull Scott close as he undid his belt then worked the clasp and zipper on his new suit pants. She tugged at a loose bra strap—just enough to reveal the rounded top of her breast—and reached up to put her arms around his neck. "Your boxers, too. If you have to turn around, you don't want them looking at your face." Scott hesitated. She let out a huff of air, then reached down with both hands and yanked his boxers to his knees.

"What—"

"Hush!" Her voice a whisper. "Somebody's moving outside the door. Damn it, kiss me."

Scott pressed his closed mouth against hers. There was no passion, only fear. If anything, he could feel his manhood retreating—an ancient involuntary muscle contraction made in anticipation of attack.

Natalie grabbed a handful of fabric at his lower back and lifted the coat and shirt to expose his bare bottom, and the door squeaked open. Scott squeezed Natalie tight around the middle and continued their chaste kiss.

"Break it up."

Scott jerked his head to the side and looked back at two grinning cops. "Get out of here!" Natalie continued to hold tight to his coat and shirt, making sure Scott's full moon eclipsed any interest the two might have in his face.

A female voice came from the doorway. "She works here, Officer."

"What about him?"

The same woman simply said, "Please."

One of the cops unfolded a fuzzy photocopy of Scott's Harvard yearbook picture. Still maintaining a semirespectful distance, he held it up, comparing the wild-haired, bespectacled academic in the photo to the pantless yuppie before him.

"This your boyfriend, ma'am?"

"What's it look like?"

"Okay, okay." The cop turned to the door. "You two, go get a room. And, for God's sake, buddy, pull your pants up."

Scott reached down to tug at his boxers, and both

cops took the opportunity to check out Natalie's bra. She spat words at them. "Get a good look?"

There was no apology, just laughter, and they were gone.

Scott had his pants up. Natalie looped the loose bra strap over her shoulder and pulled on her blouse. "Follow me." She walked quickly past Scott and out the door, buttoning her blouse as she went. He grabbed half a dozen e-mail printouts off a nearby desk and ran to catch up.

Nighttime traffic flowed along both sides of Natalie's old ragtop Saab, the headlights of every oncoming car momentarily dividing her face into bright planes and hard shadows. Scott tried to look elsewhere, mostly watching ugly queues of fast food joints, service stations, and strip malls roll by.

They both were silent. Scott was buried in his thoughts, Natalie in hers. Occasionally, Scott glanced over to catch her watching him out of the corner of her eye. She was, he thought, carrying on an internal debate over what, exactly, to do with her fugitive cargo.

She clicked on her turn signal, and a sickly green pulse highlighted her face. Sliding expertly through traffic into a slot in the rightmost lane, Natalie braked and cut into the parking lot of a twenty-four-hour Kinko's. She pushed the transmission into park and cut the headlights.

Seconds passed. Scott asked, "Is this where I get out?"

Natalie nodded absently, as if agreeing with some internal thought rather than Scott's question. "I need copies of those e-mails."

"Can I ask why? The text of all these is nothing but a list of numbers separated by commas."

"No, you can't. I think you owe me at least that much."

"You're right." He stepped out into cold night air and swung the door shut. No sooner had the latch clicked into place than he heard Natalie lock the doors. He walked around to the front bumper and tried to see her face through the windshield, but the interior was hidden by ugly reflections of red and blue neon. Scott turned and walked into the building, fully expecting that he would be left alone the second the door shut behind him.

He used a self-service machine to make three copies of each e-mail. After paying a sleepy college student behind the counter, he stepped back out into the parking lot. Natalie's Saab was still there, and he was surprised by how extraordinarily relieved and grateful he felt.

Scott tapped on the passenger door, and the electric window lowered two inches. He leaned down to peer inside.

"Hand me the copies." Her voice sounded muffled through the tiny opening. He hesitated, and she added, "Do you want my help or not?"

Scott separated out one full copy of the e-mails and fished the stack of pages through the window. "What now?"

"You got a pen?"

"Yeah." He reached into the suit jacket's inside pocket.

Natalie told him her phone number. As he jotted numbers, she said, "See that Omelette Shoppe, like three or four blocks down?"

He turned to look and nodded.

"Go get some dinner. In thirty minutes, call my number. You do have a cell phone, don't you?"

"No, but I can find a pay phone."

She sighed. "Here." A stainless flip phone jutted through the window. Scott took it. She pointed a finger at him. "Remember. Half an hour. Maybe I'll know something by then. Maybe not. But call, okay?"

"Okay."

The window went up, and she drove away without saying good-bye. Scott stood in the freezing parking lot, watching her taillights recede and realizing that any feelings of calm or relief he'd had were disappearing down that ugly street along with the person of Natalie Friedman.

Kate Billings watched waves lap the pebbled beach. She reached for a glass on the patio next to her chair, picked up the cold tumbler, and tilted Charles Hunter's good scotch onto her tongue. Through a huge window that let in to the living room, she could see Sarah stretched out on the floor working on a project for school. The kid had called it a diorama of the Lost Colony. It looked like nonsense to Kate—nothing but a shoe box with colored paper and plastic figures glued inside. But the ten-year-old was quiet. That was good. Sarah's father would call soon, and Kate would quickly remind Sarah to keep their secret.

Sarah had turned out to be a natural sailor, piloting her little Sunfish halfway across the bay and back without incident as Kate watched from the dock.

Kate had fantasized about a more interesting day— one with distraught and hurried calls to the Coast Guard and, later, to Sarah's father. It hadn't happened that way, of course, but she had plenty of time. It was too early anyway. Another lost child might have pushed Charles over the edge. Kate glanced in again at Sarah, and the aftertaste of Charles's Longmorn scotch turned bitter on her tongue. She made a face, swirled ice and whisky in her glass, and killed her drink.

"Are you at the Omelette Shoppe?"

Scott looked around the dark urban park. "No."

Natalie Friedman asked, "Why not?" When he didn't answer, she sighed. "You think I was sending the cops to get you? I mean, after I got you out of the hospital?"

Every syllable he uttered sounded too loud in the deserted park. Each word struck Scott as an invitation to unseen dangers. "People have second thoughts. I couldn't blame you."

"And I *did* lock you out of my car."

"Well . . . yeah."

"I needed to check some things. I called somebody I work with, somebody who I thought might have an old e-mail roster." She hesitated. "Those e-mails you printed off, they went to a valid address. One in the psych department."

"Who?"

"Do you have money for a cab?"

"Who was it?"

"Do you have money?" Her voice grew insistent.

"Yes."

"Come to 1238 Bittermeyer. It's an old quadraplex. I live in the back right corner. Apartment C."

"I'll get a cab." Scott coughed. "But please give me the name now."

Natalie let some time pass. She said, "I'll see you in a few minutes," and hung up.

Scott sat on the bench and breathed in cold air. His forehead ached where the watcher had planted an elbow. Somewhere across town, Cindy Travers lay in a hospital bed, working through her own set of problems; Peter Budzik's corpse awaited the coroner's knife and— Scott imagined—Click was working harder than ever to ruin his life.

This was a lonely place. Scott let his eyes scan the park and then move to the teeming street to the east. He wondered if the wax-faced watcher was there, wondered who else might be out there watching and following. He got to his feet. The bench had been cold. His legs were stiff and sore. It was around dinnertime. Lots of traffic. He'd get a cab easily enough, and then, if Natalie was telling the truth, he'd finally get a name. Hell, he'd get *the* name.

Stamping his feet to get the blood flowing, Scott walked stiffly over frozen ground in the direction of streaming, rush-hour traffic.

CHAPTER 31

The two-story brick building looked to be at least a century old, but it had been a well-tended century. Manicured boxwoods lined the bottom floor. Freshly painted shutters flanked every window. The front entrance was bright and welcoming.

Scott pushed a buzzer labeled C.

"Yes?"

"It's Scott." The door clicked, and he pushed through into the central hallway. Apartments A and B were immediately inside the foyer, on his right and left. Scott continued down the hall, and the back right door swung open. Natalie stood in the doorway, her clothes casual now, her hair soft and loose.

As he approached, she tried a weak smile. "I was worried about you. Did you get something to eat?"

He shook his head as he stepped past her into the apartment. "Not yet. I needed to think about . . . things."

Natalie closed the door and turned to face him. "Like whether I was sending the cops to the Omelette Shop to arrest you?"

"Like whose e-mail address kept popping up at the hospital."

"Have a seat."

Scott could feel anger pushing blood into his face. He pushed back against emotions that had less to do with Natalie than almost anything else. But he wanted a name. "I need to know who Click was contacting in the psych ward at the hospital."

Natalie circled around to an overstuffed chair and waved her hand at the sofa. Scott walked over and dropped onto soft cushions. Natalie sat down, crossed her ankles in the chair, and leaned forward. "Just so you'll know I'm right, let me quickly explain something." Her eyes examined Scott's face, and the irritation registered. "I said *quickly.* It'll help. Okay?" She took a breath. "Like pretty much every company on earth, the hospital has a procedure for assigning e-mail addresses. You can't just let people choose whatever they want, like at home. It'd be chaos. So the hospital uses a combination of letters from the employee's name and a department code number. Specifically, we use the first four letters of the last name, followed by the department code, followed by the first letter of the employee's first name. Sounds complicated, but—"

Scott cut her off in midsentence. "It was . . . bill-thirteen-k at boston hospital dot com. If thirteen is the psychiatry department"—he stumbled as his mind tripped over the idea—"Click was writing to Kate Billings." His eyes bounced around the room, then locked into Natalie's. "That's it, isn't it?"

Natalie nodded. "That's it, but what does it mean? Who is Kate Billings? She wasn't on my e-mail list because her name was automatically expunged when she terminated her employment at the hospital."

"She was Patricia Hunter's private nurse." Scott rose to his feet and walked around the room, stopping at a window overlooking a small courtyard. "I went to her for help. We slept together the night before she left

Boston." He turned to face Natalie. "After Mrs. Hunter's murder, Kate said she was too upset to continue at the hospital."

"But apparently not too upset to boink you a couple of days later."

"I thought it was about shared trauma."

"For God's sake. What the hell are they teaching you guys over there at Harvard? Snap out of it. Most of the time, sex is just sex. Two people decide they want some and then come up with justifications for banging around like billy goats. With Kate, you just went to a bad person for help. She strung you along, then decided to take advantage of the situation and ride the baloney pony." She shook her head. "Damn, Scott. How far are you into this woman? Does she know enough to have set you up for the Hunter woman's murder? Are you still in contact with her?" He didn't answer. "Well?"

A low chuckle started at the back of Scott's throat.

Natalie leaned forward again. "Are you all right? You're not flipping out on me, are you?"

A tired grin spread across his face. All he said was "Baloney pony?"

"Cute." Natalie wasn't smiling. "There was one other e-mail to a separate address. r-e-y-n-thirteen-o-at-boshosp."

"Right. I'd just found a second e-mail from Click to that address when you shoved me out of the way and logged off."

"I could have left you there."

"I'm not complaining. Just . . ." He picked up the e-mails and thumbed through the pages. "Here it is. Reyn13o. So it's another address in the psych department, and . . ." Scott's thoughts stumbled. "It's . . ." He stopped again to think. "If it were r-e-y-n-thirteen-p, that would be Phil Reynolds, the department head." He looked at the e-mail again. Natalie let him look. This was going to be hard for him. Finally, he looked up at her. "It's Dr. Reynolds, isn't it?"

She nodded. "I already checked. The O is for Oscar." She looked frightened. Her face had gone pale. "Oscar Phillip Reynolds."

Scott looked back down at the e-mail. All he said was "Shit."

Weak morning light floated through gauze curtains. Scott's whole body felt cramped. He tried to turn over, rolled off Natalie's sofa, and hit the carpet with a thud. A gravelly moan followed the fall. He gripped the edge of the coffee table and got to a sitting position.

He was rubbing his eyes, and considering the probability of achieving a full upright position, when Natalie's bedroom door opened. "You okay?"

"I'm alive."

"Good to know." Natalie walked into the living room and leaned down to click on a lamp. Her eyes moved over her rumpled guest, and she looked amused. "You've looked better. That I-didn't-shave-this-week beard went out with Wham!, by the way."

Scott tried to smile. "It's part of my crafty disguise."

"Umm." She moved around the room, opening curtains and clicking on more lights. "Worked like a charm. Some guy you didn't even know recognized you from a picture on the nightly news. I'm going to make some breakfast. Go get a shower." She opened the refrigerator and pulled out butter and a cardboard carton of eggs. "Go! And do yourself a favor: Shave the beard. By now the cops have a report you're wearing one, and"—she gave a theatrical shudder—"it makes you look like an extra on *Miami Vice*."

Scott had been watching her move around the

apartment. It had been a nice view. Now he pointed to her bedroom door. "Through there?"

Natalie smiled, and there was something in it to let Scott know that she approved of being watched. "Yes," she said. "Through there. Hurry. Eggs'll be ready in ten minutes."

Natalie's bed had the look of being made up by someone in a hurry. Scott walked through into the bathroom, where he found a marble-topped vanity overflowing with tubes of mascara, blue jars of Noxzema, and pastel disks of powder and blush and tinted, scented creams.

The place fairly reeked of girl. And Scott smiled at the calming normalcy of it.

Inside the shower, the full weight of Kate Billings's involvement began to settle over him. The thought of sleeping in her bed, of being inside her, turned Scott's stomach. He found himself literally shaking his head to clear the mental pictures of Kate smiling down at him, her round breasts bouncing wildly as she rode the baloney pony. He almost smiled at the perfection of Natalie's expression. It captured his and Kate's sexual encounter—at once ridiculous and crass.

Kate's involvement in setting him up explained a lot, but it raised a hell of a lot of questions at the same time. It explained how Click gained access to the hospital computer system, how the porno ended up on the psych department hard drive, and, most tellingly, how Click knew enough to frame him. Scott had no doubt that—somewhere between Kate's smile and her bare bouncing breasts—some poor slob in IT or human resources would have told her everything in Scott's personnel file. "No parents, no family. Gee, I don't know why you'd want his social security number, but here it is."

Maybe it had been more complicated than that. Probably not. What had Click said in Budzik's warehouse? "Nothin' complicated about it." Scott turned to let steaming water wash over his skull and face, and Click's words came back. "All we did was junk up some computers with porno, break into your cheap-ass crib a couple times, and rent that house out in the boondocks. Nothin' to it."

Is it really that easy, he wondered, to ruin a person's life?

Reynolds fit in there somewhere. Could it be that someone of his stature would get involved in murder just for sex with a younger woman?

A draft of cool air cut through the steam. "Natalie?"

Scott's heart pumped harder. Someone moved in the bathroom. He pushed at his hair, yanked open the door, and stepped out with his fist raised.

Natalie screamed.

Scott reached for a towel. "What the hell are you doing?"

She held her hand over her heart. "Jeez. You've been in here forever, so I looked in to check on you. I was just gathering up your clothes. This"—she held up a wadded pile of clothing—"is no way to treat a suit."

Scott wrapped the towel around his waist. "Why didn't you answer me?"

"Didn't hear you. Shower running, I guess." Natalie nodded at the sink. "There's a fresh disposable razor there for you." She smiled. "I see you've warmed up. I never really believed men when they said temperature made that much difference."

"What are you talking about?"

Natalie turned to leave.

As she stepped through the door, Scott's face colored. All he said was "Oh."

After shaving and brushing his hair, Scott stepped out into the bedroom. She'd taken his clothes. A set of blue doctor's scrubs was laid out on the bed. He dropped the towel and pulled them on.

Natalie was curled up on the living room sofa. She glanced up as he came in. "They fit okay?"

"Yeah. Perfect." He examined her smiling face. "Old boyfriend?"

"Dated a doc last year." She shrugged. "Too little time, too much ego."

He nodded. "My clothes . . ."

"Your suit is hanging in my closet. You should steam it later in the bathroom. I threw your shirt and underwear in the wash with some things of mine."

Scott walked over to sit on the sofa beside her. "Thank you." He could see a plate of eggs and toast growing cold on the kitchen counter.

"No problem. You're a guest, and . . . well, you've been through hell. The least I could do was toss your clothes in the wash."

"You've done a hell of a lot more than that."

She turned to face him on the sofa, crossing her legs Indian style. Leaning forward, she said, "I've been thinking about that. Some guy recognized you at the hospital, right?" She didn't wait for an answer. "Saw you with the beard and shorter hair. Saw your new suit."

"So much for the disguise."

"Right, but . . . I think I'm gonna have a problem. The cops are eventually going to talk to the guy who said he saw you. When they do, somebody's very likely to realize that the guy's description of you in your disguise is identical to the description the cops have of the man I was"—she cleared her throat—"*caught with* in the help desk room."

"But there's no way for them to prove anything. You can't be arrested for making out with a guy who resembles someone who may look like me. Problem is—"

"The problem is," she interrupted, "I might not get

arrested, but I can get fired. Forget for a minute that I have no name to go with my bare-assed beau—which will not make the cops happy—the hospital's not going to put up with an employee having sex in her office. Particularly one she shares with seven other people."

"What about Jim Mardy? He nailed some nurse in front of a security camera. A guard finally turned on the intercom to tell Mardy he was on camera. Hell, everyone in the hospital knows that story, and Mardy's still on the fast track to chief resident."

"Mardy's a physician. I'm a lowly computer jock." She shook her head. "Different rules. And it's not worth debating. Look, I made a couple of calls while you were in the shower. Everything you say about this Kate Billings checks out. There's even been some gossip around the hospital." She hesitated. "Some of it—to be honest—about you and her. But more than a few people thought her leaving was . . ." She struggled for the word.

"Opportune?"

"No." She shook her head. "I guess the word is *uncharacteristic*. Apparently, Nurse Billings was not really known for her tender heart. People liked her—that's what my friend says—but the word is that she wasn't particularly emotional, and she didn't scare.

"I'm getting off point here. The bottom line is that I'm going to have a problem as soon as the cops get hold of whoever ID'd you. I won't get arrested. At least, I don't think they can do that. But I'm going to have a very uncomfortable meeting with my supervisor. And the cops are going to come see me. No way around that."

Scott got to his feet. "I can't believe I didn't think of that."

"We were both exhausted when we got here last night."

"I need to get out of here, fast."

"*We*."

"Huh?" His mind was elsewhere, already planning a return to Click's neighborhood.

"I said 'we.' *We* need to get out of here fast."

Now she had his attention. "No way."

"Scott . . ."

"No way in hell." His voice rose. "This could screw up your whole life. Mine is probably already screwed. I'm just trying to stay out of jail. My future is already shit. Just forget—" A bell *ding-dong*ed somewhere in the apartment, and Scott stopped short.

"Someone's at the door out front. Hang on. It's probably nothing." Natalie walked to the apartment door and pressed an intercom. "Yes?"

The voice came, full of static. "Police, Ms. Friedman. We have a warrant. The backyard is covered. We don't want to damage the door or upset your neighbors. Please open up."

She glanced back at Scott, who sighed audibly then nodded. She pressed the entry buzzer.

Scott walked quickly across the room and took Natalie's shoulders in his hands. He locked his eyes into hers. "Listen. I only have time to say this once. You knew I was a suspect in Patricia Hunter's murder. You did not know I was wanted by the police. Got that? *You didn't know.*"

She nodded.

"Good. I came to you in the hospital asking for help. You refused."

"They're going to find the printouts. They'll know—"

"No they won't. You just printed off some e-mail lists, checking for dummy addresses or something."

A loud knock startled them.

"Listen!" Scott whispered, but his tone was sharp. "The sex was real. We've been to lunch together a couple of times, always liked each other. Okay? And—with everyone gone for the day—we just got carried away when we were alone together in the office."

A fist sounded as though it would shatter the door. "Ms. Friedman! Open the door. This is your last chance. Open up now!"

Natalie unlocked the dead bolt. As she twisted the knob to let the police inside, she simply nodded at Scott.

CHAPTER 32

The interrogation room at Boston PD looked like the ones on TV—gray walls, metal chairs, and a folding table with a top that was supposed to look like walnut. Across the tabletop, wisps of particleboard showed through plastic woodgrain in the forms of obscenities and initials. A few of the previous accused had gouged out creative anatomical sketches. Some of the more offensive pictures and phrases had been blacked in with Magic-Marker by someone trying to maintain some minimal level of decency, but not trying very hard.

Scott sat and looked at the two-way mirror built into the wall—again, just like on television. He stood and walked around the room, stopping in front of the mirror.

Gazing hard at his reflection, Scott said, "I'd like to make a statement. I'd like to make it now. Otherwise, you can get me a lawyer. Your choice. But I don't plan to sit here any longer."

Three minutes later, the door opened. Detectives Cedris and Tandy—the same cops who had questioned him the night of Patricia Hunter's murder—stepped into the room. Cedris had led the arrest team at Natalie Friedman's apartment. This was the first time Scott had seen Tandy since the night of the murder.

Tandy began the conversation. "Hello, you sick fuck. Kill any helpless women lately?"

Scott trained his eyes on Cedris. "I'd like to make a statement."

Tandy kept it up. "We don't give a shit what you want. We're here to ask you some questions."

Lieutenant Cedris sat in a chair opposite the one occupied by Scott.

Tandy walked around the table and perched a fat butt cheek on the table six inches from Scott's elbow. He leaned over Scott, saturating the younger man with sour breath. "So, we hear you got caught at the hospital last night fuckin' the Friedman woman." A nasty wet grin spread across his face. "Course, I always figured you was nailin' the Hunter woman before you snuffed her out. Most of this kind of shit is sex related." He turned his head. "Ain't that right, Lieutenant?"

Cedris shrugged.

Scott leaned back, crossed his arms, and studied the two officers.

"So that's my first question," Tandy persisted. "Were you fuckin' the Hunter woman?" He winked. "You know, havin' sexual relations with the victim while she was under your care?"

Scott looked across at Cedris. "You two need a new act."

Cedris didn't answer. He just studied Scott's face.

Scott pointed a thumb at Tandy. "He's got to go."

"You ain't in charge here, Harvard boy." Tandy was going at it full bore, playing the crazy mean cop to perfection.

Scott kept his eyes on the lieutenant. "It's up to you. But if you want a statement, the bad cop in your little scenario has to leave. I want to make a statement, but not like this. If Detective Tandy stays, I'm done. *And* I'm formally requesting legal representation. On the other hand, if he leaves we can talk, and I'll forget about the lawyer. For now, at least."

Tandy jumped down off the table and slammed an open hand against the tabletop. "Fuckin' little brainiac, ain't you? If it wasn't for my partner, I'd be bouncin' that brain of yours around inside your skull."

Cedris simply said his partner's name.

"I'm leaving." Tandy kept his eyes on Scott. "I'm leaving, but I'll be back for my turn. Guess I got some time to kill. Let me see if I can't line you up a big black buck with a hard-on for a cell mate."

"Tandy!"

"I'm gone. I'm gone." Tandy's eyes went to Scott, and he winked. "See you later, smart boy."

The door slammed. Cedris still didn't speak.

"Someone should explain to your partner that graduate students don't really consider 'smart boy' to be a putdown," Scott said.

Cedris took in a deep breath. "I'm pretty smart myself, Scott."

"Congratulations."

"Detective Tandy has a temper, especially when a woman's been hurt. Sometimes it's a useful trait."

"Maybe."

"You calling me a liar?"

The young shrink shrugged.

"Maybe what? Maybe he doesn't like women being hurt? Or maybe it's a useful trait?"

"I've been sitting in here for two hours. Could I get something to drink? A Coke or something?"

Cedris shook his head. "You give me something first. Answer my question about Detective Tandy."

"Okay. You're not exactly playing good cop. You're the . . . let's call you the 'smart cop.' Maybe 'reasonable cop' is more accurate. You make it clear that you are the path of reason. I'm supposed to believe that if I can only explain my problem to you logically, then you'll understand—maybe even come over to my side."

"I didn't ask about me."

"But your partner, Detective Tandy, he's not nearly so sly. Tandy is playing the bad cop to perfection, probably exactly the way some old cop taught him when he joined the force ten years ago. It's ridiculous. Yelling, threatening. Hovering over me and invading my personal space. His job is to shoo me to you—like a faithful spaniel flushing a covey of quail for his master to blow out of the sky."

Cedris leaned back again and smiled. "My, my. You really do think you're smart, don't you?"

"Not really. But smart enough to know that Tandy wanted me to ask him to leave. That's why he was pushing so hard. And—give him credit—he *is* irritating. So, when I said I wouldn't talk until he left, that gave you the opening to be Reasonable Cop and take over the interview alone."

Cedris allowed himself a small laugh. Scott couldn't tell whether it was appreciative or derisive. "Anything else, Dr. Thomas?"

The lieutenant was smart. He had remembered that Scott had asked at the hospital *not* to be addressed as doctor. Tandy had used the unearned title to needle Scott the night of the murder, and Cedris was using it now for the same reason.

"Just one more thing." Scott breathed deeply to control the fear expanding inside his chest. "You don't care what I think—except as it applies to Patricia Hunter's murder. You asked me to explain my comment regarding Detective Tandy to get me talking. You wanted to open a dialogue—to pry open my mind and get me comfortable sharing my thoughts with you."

Cedris smiled again. "Seems to have worked."

Scott tried to smile back. "Could be. Could also be

that I wanted you to know that the statement I'm about to make is being made because I want to make it. Because it's true, and because I have nothing to hide. Not because you and your hypertensive partner ran some B-movie scam on me."

Cedris didn't smile now. He got stiffly to his feet. "You said you wanted a Coke?"

"Please."

"But when I get back, I want that statement."

"You'll get it." Scott held his gaze. "You could have had it ten minutes ago if you'd just asked for it instead of trying the Abbott and Costello routine."

The lieutenant nodded once and exited the interrogation room.

Scott sat very still. He was pretty sure he'd throw up if he moved.

Scott told his story to Lieutenant Cedris. He rattled off the litany of anonymous phone calls, break-ins, and threats. He told all about Click, about Kate Billings and her connection with Patricia Hunter, about Peter Budzik and his abuse of Cindy Travers. Scott even talked about the wax-faced watcher, without speculating to the detective about the man's real identity. The only things he left out were the e-mails from Click to Kate and Dr. Reynolds. Discussing those would have implicated Natalie.

Cedris listened and took notes. When Scott was through, the detective asked him to repeat everything. Finally, Cedris disappeared and Scott thought he was through talking until the lieutenant came back with a court reporter. Scott drank a second Coke as he relayed everything again.

Cedris left. The court reporter followed. Scott was alone.

The nausea faded.

Talking to the detective had made him feel better. But talking could be a dangerous antidote to nerves. He rolled his shoulders to release tension and glanced at his watch. He and Natalie had been picked up four hours earlier—just after 9:00 A.M. He felt jittery and weak from having nothing in his stomach all day except two Cokes. But a case of the jitters was better than puking, which was where he had been headed earlier in the day.

Scott stood and walked to the mirror again. "Don't you guys have to feed me?"

Nothing.

At four that afternoon—seven hours after being nabbed at Natalie's place—Scott saw the knob turn. A skinny woman with dishwater blond hair stepped into the room. Her blue lawyer suit was worn at the hem and shiny across her butt. She looked tired and official.

Cedris stepped in behind her and closed the door. "Scott, this is Assistant District Attorney Anne Foucher. She wants to speak with you."

The woman sat on the edge of the table, not in an intimidating or energetic way but as if she didn't have the energy to lower herself into a chair. "You tell a good story, Mr. Thomas." She leafed through a stack of papers—some looked like the detective's notes, others were typed. "Very consistent from one version to another. Just enough changes in wording, just enough little errors, to make it look believable."

"The truth's funny that way." Scott studied her face.

Some small energy flashed in the ADA's irises. This one had a short fuse. "Don't get smart with me, Scott. I may even be smarter than you are."

"I doubt it." It had been seven hours of this crap. Scott had had enough. "Lieutenant Cedris tells me he's smarter than me, too. Looks like I should get to be smarter than someone around here."

"Listen to the mouth on this one." She glanced back

at Cedris, then turned her eyes on Scott. "I'm smart enough to know that several of your hairs were found in Patricia Hunter's hand."

Scott bounced forward in his chair. The reaction was involuntary, and he hated that he'd let them see it.

"Uh-huh. Ready to quit being cute now?"

"Mrs. Hunter was my patient. I imagine you can find trace evidence all over the room showing I was there. Look—I volunteered a statement and gave it three times. You're the ones trying to get cute. Someone—Kate Billings or this Click guy or both—is trying to ruin my life. I don't think there's anything cute about this. Everything I've worked for is falling apart, and all I get from you people is some bullshit act you've seen on *Law & Order*."

Anne Foucher's face colored. "Oh, we're just getting started here, Scott." She tossed his typed and handwritten statements onto the tabletop a little harder than she intended, and two sheets floated onto the floor. She ignored them. "Tell me about your bare-assed adventure with Natalie Friedman." She motioned at the spilled papers. "You managed to leave that out of your statements."

"Nothing to tell. Natalie and I have always been attracted to each other. I was hoping she could explain—"

The ADA interrupted. "I heard she was blowing you when the officers interrupted. Tell me, you manage to get your rocks off?" The ADA knew her facts were bull. She was angry and pushing to get Scott to say something he'd rather not say.

"This is getting tiresome. The detective's partner already tried that route. At least he was trying to get thrown out so his partner could get me talking. I'm not sure what you think you're trying to do."

The ADA jerked her thumb at the door. "Friedman is in the holding room next door. She claims you two were just getting started—kissing and petting—when the officers caught you. Now, I can understand why that's the version she wants to put out there. I mean, hell, she's probably gonna lose her job over this as it is. Throw in that she was gulping tube steak, and—"

That was enough. "You aren't a very attractive person, are you, Ms. Foucher?"

"I'm not here for you to like me, Scott."

"No, no. That's not what I mean. Obviously, you're a waste of oxygen as a human being. But I was talking about your physical appearance. I'm not talking about the shape of your nose or the width of your butt. I'm talking about someone who looks like she didn't bathe this morning. Someone whose hate and bitterness flows out of every pore."

Cedris stepped up. "Shut up, Thomas."

"She started it. I thought Anne here wanted to get personal." He turned his eyes back to the ADA. "No ring on your finger. What are you, thirty-six, maybe thirty-eight? Spend all your time at work. No social life to speak of. *Talking* about sex is about all you've got, isn't it? I mean, when life's been as disappointing for someone as it's been for you . . . who can blame you for wanting other people to be as miserable as you are? Sure, you could get out there and meet someone, but then you'd have to quit hating everyone you meet. You might have to admit that life hasn't turned out the way you expected.

"What happened to you, Anne? When did you go from being a woman to slumping around—pissed off at the world—in a frayed, ten-year-old suit? I'm sorry. I'm getting off the subject. You wanted to talk about sex. Preferably something degrading? Something that makes you feel better about your own miserable little life? Is that it, Anne? You want to degrade Natalie and me because we were doing something that you've either forgotten about or never could handle to begin with?"

ADA Foucher was on her feet now. She opened her mouth, closed it, and opened it again. Finally, she blurted out one word—"Asshole"—and stormed out of the room, slamming the door behind her.

"That was shitty." Lieutenant Cedris leaned against the far wall, studying Scott's face. "You happy with yourself?"

"No."

"Then what was that performance supposed to prove?"

"You people come in here and insult me and everything I stand for. You play with my mind. Try to degrade me. Try everything nasty you can think of to make me angry enough to say something incriminating, when I haven't done a damn thing wrong." Scott fought the queasy knot working around in the pit of his stomach. "I thought Assistant District Attorney Anne Foucher needed to see what it feels like."

"And," Cedris said, "she insulted your friend."

"Yeah"—he leaned forward—"she did."

The lieutenant pushed off the wall. "Okay, come with me. We're cutting you loose . . . for now. The ADA you just attacked says we don't have enough to hold you."

"Then what was all her trash talk about?" Scott stood. "If anything, that makes her comments about Natalie that much worse."

"Oh, she thinks you did it. No question about that. We just don't have enough to indict you on either the Hunter or the Budzik murder. Not *yet*, anyhow."

As Scott followed the lieutenant through the door, he asked about Natalie.

"You trust this Friedman woman?"

"Why wouldn't I?"

Cedris didn't answer. He just started walking again. "She's waiting for you out front." He spoke without looking back. "Both of you will be expected to stay in the Boston area, by the way."

The young shrink mumbled, "Expect away."

"What?"

Scott didn't answer.

CHAPTER 33

Outside the taxi, the hint of spring gently pushed against winter air. The wind was up, the afternoon sun shining brightly. Inside, Scott and Natalie rode in silence, the scents of mold and perspiration wafting up from nylon seats and carpeting. Natalie looked pale. Her fingers trembled when they weren't clenched.

Scott spoke first. "I didn't tell them anything about your helping me."

She glanced over without speaking.

"I think all you're going to have to deal with is the sex thing. Improper behavior. Whatever."

"The police station." Natalie swallowed. "It was horrible, Scott. Horrible," she repeated in a husky whisper.

Scott thought back to his plan to use Natalie's friendship to break into the hospital's computer system. Not a lot of thought there for anyone else. He looked out the window and silently agreed with the district attorney. *Asshole.*

Without looking back, he said, "We need to eat."

Nothing.

"I'd like to take you to dinner. If you can stand it." The passing buildings had turned residential. He watched concrete stoops flash by.

Natalie reached over and patted his knee, but the

contact felt stiff and mechanical. "Sure." She quickly withdrew her hand. "There's a place up here on the right. See. There."

Scott leaned forward. "Pull over."

The cabdriver swerved to the curve. Natalie got out. Scott paid and stepped out. Natalie was looking up at the sky, breathing deeply. "I'm feeling a little sorry for myself. Just gotta get my mind around this. Bottom line is I helped a friend in trouble. I mean, a reputation for getting laid at the office is a minor thing. Even if it costs my job, it's a minor thing." She nodded at Scott. "You're free. You've got the names of two people at the hospital who were in cahoots with this Click guy. And," she said, "the cops had to let you go." She looked off down the street. "I think you're ahead of the game. At least, you don't have to look over your shoulder anymore. The cops have had their shot. They can't do anything else to you without more evidence. So"—she turned to face Scott— "if nothing else, you're free now to find out what happened without having to look behind you every other second."

Scott tried to smile. All he said was "Yeah," but even that didn't sound convincing.

Warm sunlight cut through the window over the sink, throwing bright shapes on kitchen tile. The tiny TV on the counter was tuned to the NBC affiliate out of Raleigh—some story about a terrorist bomber who'd been hiding out in the North Carolina mountains.

Kate Billings was aware of voices floating through the television speaker, but not much else. She chopped lettuce for a salad. The kid was having hot dogs for dinner. Not something Kate planned to put into her body. Not after all the work she'd done to make it perfect. Now more than ever, she needed to look perfect.

Charles is coming home tomorrow, she thought. I'll make steaks. Maybe asparagus . . .

The phone rang, snapping her thoughts in half. She reached for the receiver. "Hello?"

A man said, "We have a problem."

As he finished the sentence, a child's voice came from another extension in the house. "Hello?"

Kate said, "Hang up, Sarah. It's for me."

"Is that you, Dad?"

"Hang up, Sarah."

"I want to talk to him. I'm not going to hang up."

Kate's face flushed. "Sarah! It's not your father. It's a *private* call for me, and you're being rude. Now hang up the damn phone!"

A sharp *click* sounded over the line, and a faint hum went away.

Kate fought to calm her temper. "What is it?"

Click said, "We've got a problem."

"You said that."

Click let some silence settle into the line. Seconds passed before he said, "Your boyfriend—the Harvard shrink—got arrested."

"Which—"

"Which one? Is that the question?" Click chuckled. "You're somethin' else, Katie. I'm talking about Thomas. He was picked up by the cops early this morning."

Kate cut her eyes around the kitchen to make sure no little ears were listening, then spoke into the receiver in a harsh whisper. "You were supposed to get rid of him. This is *exactly* what you were supposed to prevent."

Click ignored her. He'd called to convey information, not to listen to Kate Billings bitch. "He's out. They didn't hold him."

"You dumb fuck!" Kate spat the words into the phone. "That means they believed him, at least enough to put off any indictment." She stopped to breathe—to try to regain control—but a new wave of fury washed over her. "Shit! Shit! Shit!" She was screaming now.

"Kate?" Sarah Hunter stood in the doorway. "I'm sorry."

Kate spoke into the phone. "Hang on." she smiled. "I'm not mad at you, sweetheart. That was a bad word. I shouldn't have said it, but I'm not mad at you." She leaned down to look into the child's eyes and found tears forming. "A friend of mine in Boston is in trouble. I'm just upset. That's all. It's not you, Sarah." Kate smiled again. "Now go back in the other room. Please. I need to talk to my friend."

Sarah swiped at a tear, turned, and left the kitchen.

"Goddammit, Click!" Her tone was venomous but muffled. "Now Scott's got his side of the story on the record. Goddammit! This is exactly, *exactly* what we didn't need. I cannot believe you fucked this up."

"Careful, Kate." Click's voice was quiet, but his tone scattered chills across Kate's spine. "We've known each other a long time. Been through a lot. Don't fuck it up now." He paused. "Kate?" She didn't answer. "Kate? You had best answer me."

"What?" The volume of her speech was lower still, but contempt was piled heavy.

"You speak to me like that again, and you can quit worryin' about Scott Thomas. I'll take a trip. A vacation. Come see you." He let the idea sink in. "You understand, Kate? You remember who you're dealin' with? I will fuckin' end you you lip off at me like that again."

Kate's anger turned cold inside her gut. Some day she would kill Click. But not now. He was bought and paid for, and she needed him. "I'm sorry, honey. You know me. Emotional, right? I just thought Scott was dead meat the minute you said you'd take him out. You're usually so . . . so efficient. I was surprised, that's all. Okay?"

He didn't answer.

She tried to put a friendly lilt into her voice. "Anything else?"

"It gets worse." Click almost sounded bored. He wasn't. "Thomas was picked up at the apartment of a chick named Natalie Friedman."

"So?"

"She works in the IT department at the hospital."

Irritation began to creep back into Kate's voice. "I still don't see what the problem is. I guess she could've been helping Scott erase some of the porno you put on the hospital computers, but other than that . . ."

"No, Kate." Click was continually amazed at how dumb people could be. "That's not all she can do. If the Friedman woman's any good, she's probably already found something to connect us. Phone calls, e-mails. Something."

Kate fought hard to hold her temper. "You told me that couldn't be done, Click."

"I was using a safe IP address. Safe as you can get, anyway. But Thomas got help. A hacker here in Boston named Budzik. Little squirrely asshole used to teach over at MIT. Guy spent days tracking down my IP address, and—"

"What the hell is an IP address?"

"It's a number that identifies your computer every time you log on the Internet." She tried to ask something else, and he cut her off. "Don't worry about it. You understanding what I'm talking about ain't gonna change anything. All you need to know is that I hid my e-mails to you behind a dummy address that no one should've been able to trace to either one of us."

"Then how . . . ?"

"I told you. The boy shrink tracked down Budzik. Weak, but—tell you the truth—man would've been the best hacker up here if it wasn't for me."

Kate stepped around the counter to make sure Sarah wasn't eavesdropping. "Would have been?"

"I cut his throat."

"Good." She didn't miss a beat. "What about Scott?"

"We had a run-in." Seconds ticked by while Click thought back on his fight with Scott and the wax-faced man. "Truth is, I'd kill him now even if you begged me not to."

"You hear any begging?" Kate stopped to think. "What about the girl?"

"Friedman?"

"Uh-huh. Could be a loose end."

"It ain't gonna be gratis."

"I don't have much more cash, Click."

"Shit." He paused to think. "But you will soon."

The thought triggered a pleasant tingling sensation in Kate's stomach. She said, "You're right. I will." And hung up.

The café was dark. A recording of an old Rat Pack stage show played over the sound system. No one interrupted Frank, but he and Dean interrupted every line Sammy sang with a joke. The waitress smiled, but the food had no taste. Natalie ate little. Scott devoured a twelve-ounce ribeye.

They lingered at the table after the dishes were cleared. Natalie was lost in thought. Scott watched the woman who had ruined her life for him. He examined the shape of Natalie's face and the curve of chestnut hair where it touched her shoulder. He allowed his gaze to linger on her eyes—eyes so pale green that the irises looked almost transparent in profile. And, despite the frown of concentration and the shadow of sadness, this woman still pulled at something deep inside him. He reached out to touch her hand. "I'd feel better if you'd let me sleep on your sofa again tonight."

She'd been studying the tabletop. "I'm sorry. What?"

"I'm sure you're fine. As fine as you can be after what happened. But still, I'd feel better if you'd let me stay over tonight on your sofa."

"You planning to protect me?" Her voice was tired.

"I'm sure it won't be necessary." His eyes roamed over her face. "Forget it. I've imposed . . ." He almost ended the sentence with "enough," but what he'd done to her was a hell of a lot more than an imposition.

"Why would anyone want to hurt me? I'm just your dumb squeeze." She tried a smile. "Natalie Friedman, sex machine."

Scott smiled back. "Another good reason to stay over."

"In your dreams." She drank some coffee. "I've got things to do. Some other time."

He nodded and motioned at the waitress for the check. Scott needed to find Click, but tonight would be spent lurking outside Natalie's apartment building—watching.

CHAPTER 34

The afternoon breeze had turned hard at sunset, gaining speed as the night wore on and sweeping the street outside Natalie Friedman's apartment with bone-chilling gusts. Scott huddled inside the wet mouth of an alley, his suit coat pulled up around his neck like a *GQ* model, his shoes awash in scattered trash. He glanced at his watch: 11:03.

Earlier he'd ventured over to find a way into Natalie's back courtyard. It would be tricky . . .

A Mercedes SUV—one of the boxy, ninety-thousand-dollar jobs—rolled to a stop outside Natalie's building, and Scott stepped farther back into the shadows. Dr. Oscar Phillip Reynolds—e-mail address reyn13o—stepped out onto the street. The old man's dark topcoat flapped in the wind; leaves and candy wrappers tumbled past his shoes.

Reynolds slammed the door and took two steps. Then the famous shrink just stood there frozen in place, his hands pushed deep into overcoat pockets, his cotton-ball eyebrows squeezed down low over his eyes.

Scott could have sworn that the old man fairly radiated fear. And fear makes people do things they'd never do otherwise. Fear causes accidents and death. Fear can push a gentle man to violence.

Just as Scott decided to step out and confront the
older man, Reynolds trotted around the front bumper
of his vehicle and mounted the steps to Natalie's building. It seemed that someone inside had been waiting for
him. He'd barely touched the doorbell when the door
clicked open.

Scott looked both ways down the empty street and
then sprinted to a brick wall that connected to the apartment building. He checked the street again, pausing this
time to scan lighted windows for curious faces. Turning,
he hooked his hands over the top of the seven-foot wall
and bounced high onto his palms. After quickly looking
over into the inside courtyard, he worked his left knee
onto the wall and got to his feet. The wall was a foot
thick, capped with slabs of limestone, and it was easy
enough to walk along the top.

The first courtyard belonged to apartment A on the
building's front right corner. Scott made his way around
the edge to the second square of bricks—the one outlin-
ing the small, formal courtyard outside Natalie's apartment. From atop the wall, he could see into her living
room, where the back of Dr. Reynolds's head was visible.
Natalie was nowhere to be seen, but then most of the
room wasn't visible, either. Scott took a breath and
dropped the seven feet into the yard.

Boxwoods and dormant grass are the same color at
night—especially if you've just been staring into a
lighted apartment. His left foot hit grass. His right
caught on a waist-high boxwood, flipping him sideways
into a concrete urn filled with leftover potting soil from
last summer. A gust of air and a guttural "*ugh*" escaped
from Scott's throat as the urn's lip caught him in the ribs.

He felt the urn hit and flipped hard in midair, managing to trade broken ribs for what was going to be a hell
of a bruise. The ground came up fast, and Scott rolled to
break his fall. Less than a second after carefully jumping

down off the wall, he stopped rolling and sat up in a bed of dormant tulip bulbs. Severed boxwood limbs protruded from one leg of his pants. He spat, and potting soil came out mixed with saliva. He touched his ribs. It hurt to breathe.

Scott got to his feet. Natalie was alone inside with Dr. Reynolds.

Pressing a hand against his ribs, trying to hold in the hurt, he trotted across the small yard and mounted the back steps. The screen door creaked. Deciding that a short squeak was better than a long one, he yanked the door open and reached for the inside knob. It turned in his hand, and he was inside Natalie's kitchen.

Tiptoeing across the tiled floor, Scott got a glimpse of both Natalie and Reynolds. The doctor was facing away from Scott at a forty-five-degree angle. Natalie was facing the kitchen at the same angle. Neither of them seemed to have heard his Jerry Lewis approach through the courtyard, which, as pitiful as it was, had taken less than a minute.

Reynolds's deep baritone floated into the kitchen. ". . . called me. Asked me to come out here."

Natalie said, "You came."

"You've been through a traumatic day, Natalie." The old man was using his analyst's voice. Smooth. Understanding. Gently dominating. "I felt you needed to talk to someone. To vent some of your feelings in private."

"You mean, instead of accusing you in public of involvement in Mrs. Hunter's death."

"Come now, Natalie." He was using her first name to establish an intimacy that didn't exist. "We both know you don't want to become involved in making slanderous accusations." He paused. "You said something about an e-mail . . ." His voice trailed off.

"Good. I'm glad we're through with the I'm-here-because-I'm-so-good-and-caring crap. You want to know what I have on you."

"Natalie . . ."

"Save it, Dr. Reynolds. What I have is an e-mail to you at the hospital from a man named Darryl Simmons."

"Natalie, I get hundreds of e-mails a day . . ."

"You may know him better as Click." She paused. But he either didn't or couldn't respond. "Yeah, I thought that might get your attention."

Seconds passed. Finally the old man said, "Natalie, you may not know this, but I'm an on-air analyst for CNN. Psychological profiles of terrorists, kidnappers, that sort of thing. In any event, since I took on that job, I've been getting tons of e-mail from . . . let's say, disturbed individuals all over the country. Now, if you could tell me what this e-mail said, maybe I could try to remember if it was one of the ones I answered."

Natalie stood and walked to the fireplace. Gas logs burned too perfectly, throwing dancing flames across the rug. "As I'm sure you know, the content of the e-mails was nothing but a series of numbers."

"Well, you can't expect—"

"I expect you to remember communicating with Kate Billings's insane friend." Natalie's eyes searched the old man's face. She was gambling.

Some time passed before Reynolds asked, "How much do you know?"

"I know she used you."

"Some might say I used her. A man in my position with the hospital, ah, dating a young nurse under my supervision. It's . . ." He breathed deeply. "It's an embarrassing situation. Nothing else." Now he was gambling.

"I don't think so." Natalie propped her elbow on the mantel. Yellow light from the fire silhouetted her tight upper body through a cotton blouse, and Scott wondered whether she knew what she was doing—whether the revealing view was planned to manipulate an old man who like younger women. "Did you know, Dr. Reynolds, that Mr. Simmons—you know him better as Click—did you know that Click is famous? Really. He is. If you were a computer jock like me, instead of a head shrinker like you, you'd know that Click may be about the most famous outlaw computer hacker in Boston." She paused for emphasis. "And he's violent, Dr. Reynolds. Did you know that? Click isn't a backroom hacker. He's what we call a street hacker. Self-taught. Brilliant. And the word is that the man will kill you in a heartbeat."

The old man cleared his throat. "What has this got to do with me? I admit to having an affair with Kate Billings. If this Click person was a friend of hers, well, that's regrettable, but it has nothing to do with me." His voice wavered a little at the end. The man was starting to fold.

"I think you let him into the hospital's computer system."

"You can't prove . . ."

"Oh, yes I can. I can backtrack e-mails from Click to you. I can trace passwords used to plant pornographic material on Scott Thomas's computer. Believe me, if you had anything to do with Click—if you supplied passwords, dial-up access numbers, anything—I can trace every bit of it back to you."

Seconds passed without anyone speaking. Scott saw Dr. Reynolds turn his face to the side so he wouldn't have to meet Natalie's eyes. Finally, the old man said, "What do you want?"

"I want to keep my job."

Reynolds didn't hesitate. "That's not a problem."

"And I want to know what you gave him."

"Click?"

"Right."

"Nothing."

"Dr. Reynolds!" Her voice rose with implied threat. "I thought we were going to help each other."

"We are. I mean, I'm going to help you. And I'm not lying. I . . ." His voice faded.

Natalie pushed away from the mantel and walked across the room to stand over Reynolds, changing her position from teasing to dominating. "You gave the information to Kate Billings, didn't you?"

Reynolds head drooped, and he nodded at the floor.

"But you knew Click."

"After Kate quit her job and left the hospital . . ." He looked up into Natalie's eyes. "This Click character called me and said he knew all about the passwords and computer access information I'd been supplying to Kate. He wanted money."

Natalie frowned. "He blackmailed you?"

The old man nodded again. "The stuff I'd given Kate was only good for accessing employee records." In the kitchen, Scott felt a little jolt. Reynolds went on. "Nothing financial. Nothing so they could get to private patient records. But this Click wanted money and access to the hospital's banking and accounting records. I told him I couldn't . . ."

Natalie sat in an overstuffed chair next to the hearth. "Did you give him any money?"

He nodded. "Five thousand dollars. But I said no to letting him into the hospital's finances. I figured, you know, it's my mess and the money is mine. But I draw the line at corrupting the hospital for my sins."

"What do you call giving Kate Billings access to employee records? I guess corrupting the hospital is okay if you're getting some nookie for your trouble."

"That's not what happened." The old man snapped his words at her. "I thought Kate wanted the information to help her career. To find out who was going places and who wasn't."

"Is that what she told you?"

"Well . . . yes."

"What about Scott Thomas?"

"I told you. I'll cover for you at the hospital. You two are old friends, lovers, whatever. I'll make it look like a momentary lapse in judgment. Several young doctors have been caught in similar circumstances. I'll play the gender card if I have to."

"No." She shook her head. "That's not what I mean. I'm asking what you're going to do about the murder charges against Scott."

"Why should I do anything?"

"Because"—she leaned forward—"Kate Billings and Click killed Patricia Hunter, and you helped them do it."

He sprang to his feet. "Now see here!"

"They used the personnel information—his social security number, his birth information, probably his driver's license number and his direct deposit banking information—to frame Scott for the murder."

The old man shook his head violently from side to side. "You can't know that. You—" He stopped speaking abruptly and dropped back into the chair, running his fingers through thick white hair. "Oh, God."

Natalie let some time pass before asking again, "What about Scott?"

Reynolds pushed his fingers up under his glasses and massaged his eyes. "You say that Kate and Click framed Scott, but . . . but that's just your opinion. You can't prove it, and neither can anyone else. So, for all I know, Scott murdered that poor woman in her sleep." Natalie started to speak, and he held up a palm to stop her. "Just hear me out.

"Now, all you know for sure is that *you* didn't kill her. You're guessing that Scott didn't, but you're only guessing. And, if you think about it, you know two more things. One, Scott came to you for help and almost ruined your life. Remember, if I weren't going to help you, your career would be over. Natalie, you'd be out the hospital door and flipping burgers at McDonald's before you knew what hit you. Anyway, that's one. And, two, you should know that I didn't kill Mrs. Hunter. At least, I don't think you've gone far enough off the deep end to accuse me of that.

"So, that leaves us with Kate, Click, or Scott. Do the police have any evidence of any kind pointing to anyone but Scott? I don't know for certain, but, from everything I've heard, the answer is no."

Natalie finally spoke. "So we should just throw Scott to the wolves?"

"We're not throwing him to the wolves. The evidence is. And I can't see coming forward and confessing to an affair with Kate, admitting that I supplied her with computer access and so on, if there's no evidence that any of that had any bearing on Patricia Hunter's murder. A story like that would only serve to ruin my reputation, destroy my marriage, and blacken the hospital's name.

"Natalie, it's just like the situation you find yourself in: You gave in to lust. You got caught playing slap-and-tickle in your office. Should that ruin your life and your career?" He paused. "Should my lapse of judgment with Kate ruin mine? Let's face it, Scott's the best candidate here to take the fall. The truth is, he probably *did* commit the murder. And if he didn't, the police will find that out in good time."

Dr. Reynolds let his argument sink in. Natalie seemed to be running it over in her head. Finally, she said, "Just tell me one thing. Do you honestly believe that Scott Thomas murdered Patricia Hunter in her bed while she slept?"

The old man rose to his feet and picked up his overcoat from the sofa. "No, I don't. But if you ever tell anyone I said that, I'll call you a liar. Look, we can help each other here. I can not only save your career, I can make it take off like a rocket. I see you moving up very quickly in the future, Natalie."

Seconds passed before she nodded. "Okay. I think we have a deal. I keep quiet, you save my job, and Scott Thomas is on his own. But what if Kate comes back?"

The back of the old man's neck colored. "I think she will, Natalie. And that should change nothing."

"You think Kate's coming back to you, don't you?"

"We'll talk again tomorrow, Natalie. Come by my office after lunch. We'll start putting your career back together."

As the apartment door closed, Scott stepped into the living room and Natalie let out a little shriek. Scott held his index finger to his lips. He crossed the room and pressed his ear to the door. Seconds passed. He stepped out and trotted down the hallway.

CHAPTER 35

Two full minutes ticked by before Scott returned from tailing Dr. Reynolds down the hall. When Scott reentered the apartment, Natalie looked horrified. "What happened? You look like somebody threw you through a tree."

"I fell." He walked over and sat in a black Windsor chair beside the fire. It was painted wood, and Scott figured the leaves and potting soil he was wearing wouldn't ruin it. He nodded at the door. "Looks like you almost killed the guy. He was out there bent over the hood of his Mercedes. At first, I thought he was throwing up. But the old man was just getting his head down—probably trying not to faint."

Natalie walked over to stand beside Scott. She brushed dirt out of his hair. "I told you to stay away tonight."

"So you could meet with Reynolds?"

She nodded. "I was trying to get information."

Scott's eyes searched her face. "Sounded like you were making a deal to bury me."

Something changed in Natalie's eyes, and she smiled. "Yeah. I'm a real bitch." Her expression changed again. "Could you believe how easy it was for the world-famous doctor to bury you to save his career? The Mr.

Sensitivity act goes out the window pretty fast when it's his ass on the line."

This still didn't feel right. "And you were just playing along?"

Her jaw flexed. "I recorded him."

"What?"

"I recorded every word the bastard said. You can have the recording if you want it." She shook her head and changed the subject. "The guy's a real scumball."

"It's . . ." Scott stopped and began again. "Everyone worships success. But the personality profile of extraordinarily successful people—like Dr. Reynolds—isn't as flattering as you'd think. You've got to be pretty egocentric to get that far in life. It also helps to have something to prove. Obviously it varies, but an only child with an overbearing mother is usually a pretty good bet."

"Sounds like psychobabble made up by someone who needed to explain her own mediocrity."

"Jeez." Scott leaned back against wooden spindles. "Why don't you say what you really think?"

Natalie shrugged and crossed to the sofa.

"I get your point. But, no, that's not it. Highly successful people tend to be self-promoting and self-centered. *But*—and it's a big but—the world would be a pretty sad place without them. Self-promoting, self-centered, egomaniacal people build skyscrapers and airplanes. In the past, they discovered continents and flew to the moon. But Frank Lloyd Wright, Thomas Edison, and most of the world's great leaders were not really people you'd want to go fishing with."

"I didn't mean to set you off." She nodded. "I guess I know what you mean, though. I dated a lawyer a couple of years back. Guy specialized in corporate litigation—you know, like one big company suing another over a contract or something. Anyway, he always harped on what terrible witnesses corporate presidents were. These rich guys get on the witness stand and think they know everything, or they think they're *supposed* to know everything and they fake it. Ted—that was his name, by the way—Ted said the worst witness on earth is one who doesn't know when to say 'I don't know' or 'I can't recall.'"

"But," Scott interrupted, "these rich guys didn't get where they are by admitting ignorance or fallibility. The truth is, most of them won't admit imperfection because they think it doesn't apply to them."

Natalie snuggled back against the sofa cushions. "By the way, why are we having this moderately boring, philosophical discussion ten minutes after I—your only friend, by the way—and your mentor—Dr. Reynolds—made a pact to sell you down the river?"

"Three reasons." He clicked them off on his fingers. "One, I needed to think a little about what motivates rich old men like Phil Reynolds. Two, you—I hope—didn't mean what you said to him. And, three, Reynolds meant what he said, but you got him on tape saying it."

Natalie stood and walked across to a pine cabinet shaped like an antique wardrobe. She pulled open a door. "No one tapes anything anymore, Scott. It's not 1980." Natalie pushed a button, a small panel slid out of a black box, and she fished out a silver disk. "We've got Dr. Oscar Phillip Reynolds right here in all his digital glory. I voice-dated it and identified the parties while you were down the hallway watching the good doctor faint. Fortunately, you didn't say anything when you came into the room. So we've got a nice, pristine recording here."

Scott's eyes wandered to the ceiling.

Natalie twisted the shiny disk in midair. "Hello?"

"Are you going by to see him tomorrow?"

"Who? Oh. Dr. Reynolds?" She stopped and shook

her head as if rattling ideas into place inside her skull. "I'm not sure. I guess I need to think about that, don't I?"

Scott finally turned over at midmorning, this time managing to grab a handful of cushion to keep from flipping off Natalie's couch onto the carpet. He found his feet, stumbled to her bedroom door, and knocked. No answer. He peeked inside. No one in bed. No one in the bath. Natalie was long gone. After washing his face and running a brush over his teeth, he found a note on the fridge.

> *Eat whatever you want. Be home after*
> *my meet w/Dr. Reynolds.*
>
> > Nat

He opened the refrigerator and smiled. "Whatever you want" consisted of one egg, four cartons of yogurt, and a scattering of stained pagoda boxes from a Chinese takeout place. Sweet and sour pork is not a breakfast food, but the peach yogurt smelled okay. He found a spoon.

A half hour later, Scott stepped out of a steam-filled bathroom to answer the phone. It was on its second run of insistent ringing, and he thought Natalie might be trying to reach him. He tucked a towel around his waist and flopped into a small chair next to the bed.

Unsure of whether he should answer her phone, he picked up the receiver but didn't speak.

A woman's voice said, "Natalie?"

There was something familiar about the caller's voice. He said, "Hello?"

The woman's voice asked his name.

Scott hesitated. "May I ask who's calling?"

"Is this Scott?"

He stood and walked out into the living room, still holding the handset. The front door was locked. Everything looked fine. "Who is this?"

"I'm a friend of Kate's." She let a few seconds tick by. "Does that mean anything to you?"

"Yeah. It means something."

"So, this is Scott Thomas."

"Yes." Now he let some time pass, but she didn't say anything else. His mind raced, trying to place the voice. "I know you, don't I?"

"Kate's worried about you."

"Have you seen Kate?"

"Sure. She wants to see you."

Scott wandered to the window, but the apartment was on the back corner of the quadraplex. All he could see was the empty courtyard. "When did she tell you this?"

"Last night. Kate heard about your arrest, and she wants to talk."

"Why?"

She hesitated before answering. "She's just worried about you. That's all." The familiar voice paused. "She said you two were, you know, intimate or dating or whatever, but . . . If you don't wanna see her, I can tell her that."

"No, no. I'll see her. But not here. I'm staying with a friend. How did you find me? How do you know Natalie?"

"Kate said you were arrested with a woman from the hospital named Natalie Friedman. I guess it was in the phone book. Kate gave me the name and number." She paused, and Scott could hear her breathing—the breath coming in short huffs now. The woman with the familiar voice was nervous. "Look, it's no sweat off my . . . What I mean is, it's up to you. Kate wants to see you. She's worried. If you got better things to do, just say so. I'll pass along the message."

The call waiting signal beeped in his earpiece. "Hold on a minute. I've got another call coming in."

Now she spoke quickly. "No need. Just keep tonight open. I'll call back with a time and place." And the phone went dead.

A frightening daisy chain of thoughts had already begun to spin through Scott's mind when call waiting beeped again in his ear. He hit the flash button on the receiver. "Hello?"

"You still asleep?"

"Natalie?"

"Who'd you think it was? You must've been dead to the world."

"What do you mean?"

She laughed. "The phone rang about fifteen times before you picked it up." She stopped, then her voice changed. "Are you all right, Scott? Has something happened?"

Scott thought of the caller asking for Natalie—asking for her with something like familiarity in her voice. His eyes searched the carpet at his feet. "I need to know where Kate went when she left the hospital."

"We talked about that, Scott. No one seems to know."

He tried to slow his thoughts. "What about her last paycheck? Maybe reports on her 401-k? Continuation of insurance coverage? Somebody's gotta be sending her something. You don't just walk away from a professional job at the beginning of the twenty-first century and not have paperwork following you around."

"You're right. Let me think." Most of minute passed, and he heard Natalie speaking with someone away from the phone. Finally, she came back on the line. "I'm going to have to use a favor."

Scott began, "Who are you talking to? I—"

She cut him off. "Can't say right now."

"Oh. Okay. If the favor isn't too much to ask . . ."

"No, no. I don't mind a bit. It's just . . . Well, I don't know how many favors I've got left around here."

Scott cussed. "I'm sorry. I got a phone call that freaked me out a little. How did your meeting with Reynolds go?"

"Nice of you to ask." She laughed. "A reprimand is going in my file, and I've got a two-week suspension with pay. But that's it."

"With pay, huh?"

"Yeah. How about that? If I'd known it'd get me a paid vacation, I'd have yanked down some guy's pants at the office a year ago."

Scott smiled.

"Now," Natalie said, "about Kate Billings . . ."

"Some woman called, allegedly with a message from Kate. Said Kate wants to meet me tonight."

"Holy shit. Do you think the call was for real?"

"I don't know. But you need to know that the caller asked for *you*. She knows your name." Natalie didn't respond, and he went on. "But if Kate is looking for me—if she knows about you, too—I'd rather find her before she finds us."

"Right. Look, I'm waiting around here for Reynolds's secretary to finish typing my reprimand so I can have indignity of reading and signing it." She paused. "Don't worry. I'll get what you want. Will you be there when I get home?"

"With dinner on the table."

She laughed again. "Aren't you sweet."

"Hell," Scott said, "I can order takeout with the best of them." He tried hard to sound less anxious than he felt.

* * *

The call came just after three that afternoon. Kate Billings would meet Scott on the street, just outside the entrance to the hospital parking lot, at ten P.M. Again, Scott thought he recognized the woman's voice on the phone. And again, she denied ever meeting him. But as she denied it, Scott placed the voice: the girl hitchhiker who had helped carjack his Land Cruiser.

Natalie breezed into her apartment less than an hour later. "Where's dinner?"

Scott smiled. "Cute. It's not even four o'clock yet."

"You said dinner on the table. I'm looking at the table and . . ." She shrugged.

"That woman called again. I think it was the girl who stole my car the night all this started. Anyway"—he shook his head—"she said Kate wants to meet me tonight at ten, outside the hospital parking lot."

Natalie's smile faded. "So, basically you're supposed to hang around the street at night waiting for someone to drive by and shoot at you."

Scott nodded. "Basically."

"Or this Kate Billings is actually going to show up and explain everything."

Scott just looked at her.

"I found out that Kate's final paycheck was mailed to a Boston address."

Scott glanced up. "At least she's in the city."

"Well, maybe. It went to the architectural firm of Hunter & Petring. Patricia Hunter's husband is the Hunter." Her eyes searched Scott's face. "Do you want to know what I think?"

"Of course."

"I think Kate Billings is long gone from Boston. Think about it. If she had an address here, she wouldn't need her checks to go through Hunter's office. I think she's out of town but still tied into this Hunter guy somehow, and she's having her mail routed through his business address so no one will know where she is."

"You think Charles Hunter had something to do with his wife's death? Is that what you're getting at?"

"Not necessarily. Could just be that Kate has insinuated herself into his life somehow, which would mean . . ."

"That he's in trouble, too."

Natalie walked to the refrigerator and opened the door. "What did you eat today?"

"Yogurt."

"Sorry. Not much of a cook." She shut the door and turned back to Scott. "All I know is that Kate Billings is tied to Charles Hunter, and—more important at the moment—she is *not* currently living in Boston. What you have to decide is whether she's planning a return trip to meet you so she can straighten out your life. Considering that she didn't place the call herself, that she hasn't bothered to write or call before now, and that she allegedly wants to rekindle your relationship on a dark street in the middle of the night . . ."

"Ten o'clock is not the middle of the night."

"You get my point, though."

Scott ran his hand through his hair and pushed at his glasses. "Got a phone book?"

"Sure." Natalie opened a drawer and pulled out a Bell Atlantic book for Greater Boston. She tossed the monster directory onto Scott's lap.

He flipped pages, then reached for the phone next to the sofa.

Natalie asked, "What are you doing?"

He held up a palm. "Yes. Could I speak to Mr. Hunter's assistant, please?" He paused. "Sure. I'd be glad to hold." He put a palm over the mouthpiece. "Who's the benefits manager at the hospital?"

"Bridget Palmer."

Scott stared at her. "I think my voice is too low."

"Oh." She blushed. "Say you're Tim O'Rourke. He's a flunky in personnel. Does a little bit of everything."

Seconds passed. "Yes. This is Tim O'Rourke in employee benefits at Boston Hospital. Our records show that a former employee, Kate Billings, had her last paycheck sent to your address. Uh-huh, uh-huh. Right. Listen, I need to speak with Ms. Billings regarding a 401-k election. I could write, but if she wants the full tax benefit, I really need to speak with her in the next day or two. So, I was wondering . . . Uh-huh, uh-huh." Scott wiggled his fingers at Natalie, and she handed him a pen from her purse. "Okay, go ahead. Got it. Thank you very much. Good-bye."

Natalie grinned at him. "Sneaky, aren't we?"

Scott didn't repond.

"What's the matter?"

"The number has a two-five-two area code." He flipped to the front of the Bell Atlantic phone book and ran his finger over a map of the country. "That's North Carolina."

"So?"

"Nothing." He punched in the number. On the fifth ring, a child answered the phone. "Hello?"

"Yes. May I speak to Kate please?"

"Okay." The sound of the receiver being dropped rang in his ears, then he heard the child's voice again— this time distant and muffled. "Kate? Kate! Telephone. It's for you."

Seconds passed before he heard the next voice. "Hello?"

Scott pressed the OFF button on the phone and tossed the receiver onto the sofa. "She's in North Carolina."

Natalie shook her head. "Don't guess she's gonna be waiting outside the parking deck tonight."

"No."

Her eyes roamed over his face. "You're not still going, are you?"

"Yeah," he almost whispered. "I think I have to."

CHAPTER 36

Roseland Drive was short. Maybe a couple of miles was all. On the phone that morning, Cannonball had asked when Mr. Pongeraytor would be home, not wanting to show up in the middle of the day when just the wife would be there. The old man wasn't assuming prejudice—not just because of his color. But Cannonball Walker knew what he looked like. Living fifty years every night in a bar—every night breathing smoke and washing down bar food with bourbon, eating whatever the kitchen served up—the life took its toll. Walker was a hard man. He looked it. And it scared people sometimes.

The Pongeraytor place was a white clapboard house sandwiched between two small brick Tudors. The front grass looked like a putting green, the shrubs like they had been grown inside perfect, rectangular forms. He mounted the steps and rang the doorbell.

Some time passed before the door swung open and a white-haired man stepped out. "Yes?"

"I'm Canon Walker. I spoke to your wife earlier today on the telephone."

"Right, right." He stepped aside. "She told me about it. Come on in." They walked past a Victorian living room and through a long kitchen with pine cabinets and vinyl flooring. "Such a nice day. Thought we could talk out here on the patio." Mr. Pongeraytor opened a rear door and led Cannonball down three steps onto a brick patio. "Please." He motioned at a white wrought-iron chair. "Have a seat."

Cannonball nodded and sat. "Appreciate you seeing me. A stranger calling like that."

"Right." He hesitated as if not sure what to say next. "I don't think I told you my name. I'm John Pongeraytor." He hesitated again. "You said something about representing the Thomas boy?"

"That's right. I flew in a couple of days ago. Scott Thomas asked me . . ."

The back door squeaked on its hinges, and a sixtyish woman with light red hair brought a tray of iced tea out onto the patio. John smiled. "Thank you, honey. This is the man who called today." He glanced at Cannonball. "Canon Walker, right?"

He nodded.

"This is my wife, Alice."

She held out her hand. "Reverend."

Cannonball smiled. He knew Southerners were friendly, but the quick invitation and the tray of tea had seemed suspect. These nice people thought that Scott Thomas's minister had come to call on family business. The old bluesman had his mouth open to correct their mistake when he thought better of it. Instead, he simply said, "Nice to meet you, Alice. I hope you're going to join us."

Deep crow's feet formed at the corners of blue eyes when she smiled. "Of course. Truth be known, I'm curious about what the older Thomas boy is up to after all these years."

Cannonball smiled back. "He's done well for himself. In school at Harvard, working on his doctorate."

Alice lowered her tiny backside into a metal chair. A hand went to her chest. "My goodness. That is nice."

"But something has come up that . . . Well, something very disturbing for Scott has happened recently. Two things, really." Cannonball took a glass of tea from Alice's outstretched hand, took a sip, and smiled appreciatively before going on. "First of all, someone at the Birmingham Police Department has reopened the investigation into the fire that killed his family."

The Pongeraytors shared a look, then John asked, "What's the second problem?"

"Strange as it may sound, a young man—uh, someone whose face looks shiny like it was burned—has shown up in Boston. He's following Scott. Showing up in the strangest situations." He stopped to think, to decide how much to tell, and John interrupted.

"Bobby" was all he said. His wife nodded her tinted hair.

Cannonball was genuinely shocked. "That's what Scott thought. You do mean Scott's brother? You think this young man is Bobby Thomas. Is that what you're saying?"

"Makes sense. Had to happen sooner or later. Bobby got out of the hospital about a year ago."

Cannonball tried to think. "A year ago?"

"Well." Alice spoke up. "John's putting a nice face on it. It's true that Bobby was hospitalized for months and months following the fire, but . . ." She looked off into the distance and straightened her dress. "This is so . . . unpleasant."

"I need to know, if you can tell me."

She sighed. "I guess it's common knowledge. You see, Bobby was burned so badly in the fire that he just never looked like a normal boy. And, well, you know how cruel children can be."

"Oh, good Lord," John Pongeraytor interrupted. "The kid's a thug. He started out beating up other kids and moved on to teachers and coaches. They kicked him out over there at the high school, and the next thing we heard he'd killed a guy over a six-pack of beer."

"When did this happen?"

"Oh"—John looked at his wife—"about seven, eight years ago. I guess he was about fourteen at the time."

"Young enough to get youthful offender status," Alice said.

"And he just got out?"

Alice sipped her tea. "Like we said, about a year ago."

Cannonball started to ask something, and John held up his hand to stop him. "Let's back up a minute. There's something wrong about the first problem you mentioned, too. You know, what you said about the Birmingham police reopening the fire investigation." Cannonball could see a fine intelligence working in the man's eyes. John said, "Let me explain something about Birmingham. It's gotten to be a pretty big place. Lots of people in what they call the Metro Area. But what we all call Birmingham is really a collection of mostly small towns. Course, Birmingham itself is big, but the suburbs—Homewood, Vestavia, Mountain Brook, Hoover—they're all independent, incorporated cities."

"I don't understand what that has to do—"

"The fire was here in Homewood." He pointed to a brick Tudor next door. "That house right there. Birmingham police got nothing to say about what happens in Homewood."

"Oh."

"Now, like I said, most people just say Birmingham to talk about the whole area, and maybe that's what somebody meant when they said the Birmingham police were reopening the investigation, but . . ." He paused. "It seems fishy, anyhow."

Cannonball noticed the glass in his hand and placed it on a glass table. "What do you mean, fishy?"

Alice spoke up. "What did you say your relationship with Scott was?"

Cannonball could actually feel his face blush. They couldn't see it, but he could feel it just the same. These were not people he wanted to mislead. "I'm his friend."

"His minister?"

"No. I'm his friend. I guess I'm more of an advisor than anything else."

John said, "Canon Walker? I hope you won't be insulted if I ask for proof that you're here to represent the Thomas boy's interests."

"No, sir. Not insulted at all." Cannonball reached into his inside coat pocket and pulled out a copy of the power of attorney executed by Scott. He unfolded the document and handed it to John.

John smiled and handed the document in turn to his wife. "Alice was a legal assistant at the biggest firm in the state for thirty years."

Now Alice blushed. She said, "Just a secretary, really." But she consumed the document with extraordinary speed and focus before looking up to nod at her husband. "I think we can quit worrying about Canon Walker's intentions." She turned to smile at Cannonball. "He's here for Scott." Her voice sounded soft now, almost appreciative.

The old bluesman's eyes moved from Alice's face to John's. Both looked hard into his eyes. Both looked a little bruised by what had to be said. John broke the silence, first by speaking to his wife. "The boy doesn't know."

She shook her head.

John turned to Cannonball. "Nobody's going to

reopen that investigation. Heck, it wasn't much of an investigation to begin with. Everybody knew what happened." He took a deep breath. "Scott's father, Robert, got in some trouble at the bank. Nobody knew it until after the fire, but apparently he'd been embezzling funds. He worked in the trust department, you know."

Cannonball just shook his head.

"Well, anyway, poor Robert burned down his house for the insurance money." He paused, searching for something to add. "It's just that simple. There was never . . . never any question about what happened." John picked up his tea and killed a third of it. "And something else. Scott's *family* didn't die in that fire."

The bluesman sat bolt upright in his chair. "You talkin' about Bobby?"

"I mean Robert Thomas managed to mess up the fire just like he'd messed up his job at the bank. We were living next door even back then."

Cannonball nodded. "Scott told me. That's why he asked me to look you up."

"Right. I knew Scott. Not as anything but a little tow-headed boy on a bike, but I knew him. His parents, Robert and Nancy, had us over for cookouts a few times. We returned the favor."

"I understand what you're tellin' me ain't gossip, Mr. Pongeraytor. You knew these folks."

"Right." He drank more tea. "Anyway, Robert was an A-1 fuck-up."

Alice shamed John by the way she said his name.

"I'm sorry, Reverend. But it's true. Man just couldn't get his act together. I never understood how he got Nancy. Woman was sharp as a tack. Good-looking, too. In any event, the investigator from the fire department stopped by about a week after the fire and came over here to use our phone. This guy tells me that Robert used an accelerant to start the fire—probably gasoline he kept around for his lawnmower. Said it wasn't a secret. That it'd be in the papers. And it was. But he also told me that Robert's body was burned—"

Alice rose out of her seat, said "Excuse me, please," and hurried into the house.

Cannonball grimaced. "Sorry to make y'all talk about this."

John nodded. "It's all right. Alice was close to Nancy."

His words began to fall into place inside Cannonball's head. "Are you tellin' me that Robert Thomas was the only one killed in the fire?"

John let out a breath and his shoulders visibly relaxed. "That's what I'm telling you. Robert died. Bobby and his mother were badly burned. Neither of 'em ever been the same. Scott got out."

Cannonball decided to trust this man. "Robert Thomas's old boss at the bank told Scott that people around here blamed him. Blamed Scott, I mean."

"That, Canon Walker, is bullshit. I don't know what this guy's trying to pull, but nobody—and I mean nobody—ever blamed that boy for getting out alive."

A heavy silence settled between the two men. Somewhere on the street a dog barked. Alice's azaleas blew in the breeze—small, pink buds bouncing with each gust. Minutes passed before Cannonball asked, "What about the mother?"

"Nancy? She's not dead, but she's not much alive either. Pretty woman like that all burned up." John shook his head. "Bad scars, you know? Don't know whether it was the physical part or something else—her husband ruined, her family . . . God, it kills me just to think about it. Scott was well out of here, I can tell you that. His father dead and a crook. His mother burned and

half crazy. His brother . . . his little brother scarred and
all-the-way crazy from what they tell me." He shook his
head. "No. Sounds like Scott's done okay for himself. He
was well out of here."

"What I meant was, where is Scott's mother? Is she
in a nursin' home? Is she somewhere where I could visit
with her?"

John raised his hand and pointed at the house
next door. "Still lives right there. Got a nurse lives in
full time."

"I thought it burned."

"Gutted. And I mean big time. But they say the bank
paid to have it cleaned up and rebuilt for the widow."

"Nice of 'em."

"I always thought it was kinda curious myself."

Cannonball stood to get a better look at the brick
Tudor where Scott Thomas's mother lived. "Think she'll
talk to me?"

"I doubt it."

Acid had chewed at Kate Billings's stomach for hours.
The kid, Sarah, was more than she could take. So Kate
had made a show of feeling the little girl's forehead at
dinner and proclaiming that the child had a slight fever.

"I feel fine, Kate."

"I'm a nurse, Sarah." She produced three pink pills.
"Take these and you'll keep feeling fine."

"But . . ."

"If you're not going to mind, I'll have to speak with
your father about keeping you in bed all weekend until
you're better." Kate smiled. "Come on, Sarah. It's not
like I'm poisoning you or anything."

Sarah gritted her teeth and clenched her fists beneath the table, but she took the three tablets and
washed them down with milk. A half hour later, she was

sound asleep on top of the covers in her bedroom. The tablets were just antihistamines, but so are almost all over-the-counter sleeping pills. The kid would be out for hours.

Now, finally, Kate Billings could think.

CHAPTER 37

Winter was slowly wasting away—the salty scents of the Atlantic growing stronger at night, pushing aside auto exhaust and industrial stink. Natalie Friedman drove without speaking. Standing water hissed beneath the Saab's tires. A dense spray—more thick fog than raindrops—washed the windshield between sweeps of wiper blades. The passenger-side window whistled next to Scott's ear where the convertible top didn't seal.

"So we're just gonna hide and watch?" Natalie gripped the steering wheel, her knuckles glowing white through the car's dim interior.

"Right."

"And you don't think that's exactly what the caller expects you to do?"

Scott looked out at rows of buildings gone dark for the night. A stuttering stream of windows returning blank stares. "Probably."

"Then why are you doing it?"

"I don't know what else to do." He shrugged in the dark. "No reason for you to hang around, though."

"Don't worry."

Scott turned to face Natalie's profile. Her sharp nose and full lips glowed with soft green hues from the wash of dashboard lights. Her pale eyes had gone wide and seemed too green in the reflected the glow of the instrument panel. "Leave, but don't go home. Whoever set this up may go to your place when I don't show up."

"I won't." She glanced over and caught Scott's eyes lingering on her face. Her cheeks colored a bit in the dark car. "How about this? What if we give it a quick drive-by first? I'd like to get a look at things."

Scott weighted the idea. "Natalie? That's just exactly what I'd *like* to do."

She nodded her head. "Good."

Scott shook his. "It's what I'd like because I'm scared. The truth is, I don't want to get out of this car and I don't want to be left alone. Every chickenshit impulse I have is screaming for you to stay with me as long as possible—which is exactly why you shouldn't do it. I'm scared because I'd have be a moron not to be scared. Somebody—probably Click—is waiting on a dark street for me. We don't know why . . ."

"We know why."

He shrugged again in the dark.

Natalie said, "He doesn't know my car."

"I wouldn't bet my life on it."

"I'm driving by." She used that tone. The discussion was over.

Scott smiled. "Chickenshit and his trusty sidekick Dumbass."

Natalie Friedman didn't smile. "Lean your seat back. The control's on the side of the seat. It'll make you harder to see."

"And harder to shoot."

"Right."

The two were silent again as she steered the car along familiar streets to the hospital. She'd driven the same route every weekday for two years on her way to work. It was as familiar to her as the layout of her living room, as familiar as her parents' backyard in Pennsylvania.

A block south of the parking garage, she slowed to a crawl.

"Don't." Scott's voice was a whisper. "Go the speed limit. You're not driving like someone passing through."

She nodded and sped up to twenty-five. Seconds passed. "Look." Natalie pointed through the windshield at the tall craggy form of Dr. Phil Reynolds. "What the hell's he doing here?"

Scott's mind raced with disjointed thoughts. "Speed up."

"What? You said—"

"They're going to kill him. We linked Click to Dr. Reynolds through those e-mails. He and I were both invited here tonight. Click is going—"

"What do you want me to do?" Natalie was almost screaming now.

He changed his mind. "Pull over here. I'm getting out. When I'm out, you haul ass. I'll get Reynolds inside the hospital."

"I can't just—"

"Do it!"

Natalie slammed the brake pedal and swerved to the curb. Scott swung open the door and hit the sidewalk before the car quit rolling. Natalie heard the door slam and punched the gas.

Dr. Reynolds's head had snapped around when the car door banged shut. Now he watched the Saab tear by before glancing back to see Scott charging toward him. The old man's eyes went round. His lips gaped open. He managed to mouth the word "no" a millisecond before a loud shot shattered the night air. The old man teetered in place, staring blankly down at his chest.

Scott went down hard, rolling once before springing back onto his feet. He sprinted right, cutting through a

bed of dormant shrubs, ran to the concrete wall of the
parking deck, and dropped onto his stomach behind a
line of ornamental hollies. His heart pounded in his
ears. His breath shot out in hard bursts, blowing up
puffs of dust and dry leaves.

Holly leaves scratched his neck and hands. Grit
caked his teeth. He lay still and listened. But there was
nothing. He needed to move. The shooter would have
seen where he went down, and he needed to move before a bullet whizzed through the flimsy curtain of holly
surrounding him. Scott pushed along the edge of the
parking deck, dragging his belly in the dirt, moving
toward the exit ramp that lay behind Dr. Reynolds.

He could see the lighted parking exit only yards
away now. He pushed up and got his legs under him.
Moving fast, Scott tore through waist-high bushes to the
ramp, grabbed the concrete corner of the opening, and
swung inside.

Bam!

Scott sprang back onto his stomach behind the
thick wall.

A car alarm sounded, then someone screamed and
screamed again. A woman out on the street, a block
down, kept screaming—human wailing adding urgency
to urban background noise. Scott got back onto his feet,
crouched behind a Ford SUV, and waited.

Police sirens sounded in the distance, and still he
waited. Minutes later, when the blue swirl of police
lights began to bathe the parking deck, Scott at last got
to his feet. He stepped outside the garage to see Dr.
Reynolds's corpse surrounded by five uniformed patrolmen. One of the cops saw Scott and placed a cautionary
hand on the butt of his revolver.

Scott spoke up. "It's okay. I was walking down the
sidewalk when he got shot." He looked down at his torn

and soiled clothes. "I dove into the shrubs there and then ran into the deck."

The officer seemed to relax. "Just keep your hands where I can see them. I need to pat you down." He walked toward Scott. "Just procedure. Nothing to worry about. We can walk you right into the hospital here when we're done."

"I don't need a hospital." He stood perfectly still as the officer's hands moved expertly over his waist and pockets. "Is he dead?"

"Yeah. You know him?"

Scott caught sight of Natalie hurrying across the street in his direction. His eyes searched her face.

"I asked if you knew the guy."

Scott turned his attention back to the cop, and he almost said yes. Instead, he tried to hoarsen his voice. "I think I'm going to be sick."

"Yeah, well, puke in the bushes if you have to. I need to see some ID." Scott fished out his wallet and handed over his driver's license. The officer pulled a flashlight from his belt and bounced its beam across the license. "What are you doing out here this time of night?"

"My girlfriend works in the computer department." He pointed at Natalie, who was hanging back from the gathering crowd. "That's her."

The cop motioned for Natalie to come over, then pointed at Scott. "This your boyfriend?"

She nodded at the officer and then reached out to squeeze Scott's arm. "You okay?"

He nodded.

Her eyes scanned his face, searching for a hint of what to say. "What happened?"

"He's fine, ma'am. Do you have any ID that says you work here at the hospital?

"Sure. It's in my car, though."

"That's fine, ma'am." He turned to Scott. "Let's walk

over to the car and clear this up so you folks can get on out of here."

Five minutes later, Natalie was driving quickly away from the scene. "I can't believe they didn't check us out. You know, run our names or whatever."

The streets the two had driven earlier now spun by in reverse order. Scott said, "Good job back there." He paused, and Natalie's question began to work through the confusion. "They'll get around to checking us out." He stopped to look out at vacant storefronts. "You know what? Fumbling around Boston, waiting to get shot . . ." His voice trailed off.

"Sucks, doesn't it?"

Scott turned to look at Natalie's profile. He almost laughed. "Well, yes, it does. I've been thinking, and it looks like I've got three options. We could take your recording of Dr. Reynolds to the cops and hope for the best. Or I could try to kill Click before he kills me."

"That's just stupid. If you're going to talk about killing people, you can get the hell out of my car right now." Her words came fast as she braked the car to the curb. "I mean it. Get the hell out. I'm not going to put up—"

Scott held up his hands in surrender. "Whoa, whoa, whoa. I was just listing the options. Believe me, I'm not planning to kill anyone. I was just saying . . ."

"Okay. I get it." She pulled back out into light traffic. She repeated, "I get it. So, what's the third option?"

Scott looked out at the dark city streets. "Ever been to North Carolina in the spring?"

CHAPTER 38

The house smelled of age, old fabrics and pine disinfectant. Cannonball Walker sat on the edge of a hard, squared-off sofa from the sixties—so old it had come back into style. He held a beaver-felt hat on his lap. Female voices, clear but intertwined and indistinguishable, floated in from the back room. He glanced at his watch and looked up to find the nurse standing in an arched doorway.

"She *say* she see you now."

Cannonball rose. "Thank you."

The old nurse turned. "Mmm-mm. Lucky you know Miz Pongeraytor. Miz Nancy don't meet with anybody. Not usually. Last one came by here got Miz Nancy all beside herself. Askin' questions about her boys."

Cannonball stopped in his tracks. "You said 'the last one.' Who was the last one to bother Mrs. Thomas?"

The nurse looked him up and down. "I don't know who he was. Showed up here a few weeks ago askin' about Scott and Bobby. All I knows is Miz Nancy got into a state, and, right after that, Bobby he disappeared and ain't been seen since." She turned and clunked away ahead of the bluesman, leading him through a hallway to a back den, then turned to glare. "Don't you be long, you hear?"

"I hear."

"Good." The nurse shoved his shoulder a little with her own as she exited the room.

Cannonball glanced back, then turned to face Nancy Thomas and caught his breath up short—not because she was scarred and burned, he'd been ready for that, but because she wasn't. The still-beautiful woman stared at the old man through perfect blue irises. She sat in a wicker rocker. A small white turban covered her hair. A blue-flowered, zippered gown enveloped her from neck to ankles.

Scott Thomas's mother reached out a hand to point at an old recliner—and that's when he saw. Her hand shone in the dim light like a wax claw. As Cannonball made his way across the room and eased down into the chair, his eyes took in more detail. Both of the woman's hands, both dainty feet in white sandals, and what he could see of her ankles and wrists were all discolored, all as hard and shiny as pine resin. Her gown had a Nehru collar, but, as she turned slightly to face him, an irregular swath of scarring showed along the back of her neck and disappeared into the turban.

As far as he could tell, an unscarred face was all Nancy Thomas had left. Everything else, from horribly disfigured hands and feet to her aristocratic neck—maybe even her scalp—seemed to have been engulfed in the fire that took her husband and destroyed her family.

She didn't speak. Her blue eyes roamed the old man's face.

He cleared his throat. "Thank you for seeing me."

"You Alice's new husband?" Her voice sounded smooth and Southern, but still managed a flat mechanical tone.

"Alice . . . ?"

Now she snapped. "Alice Pongeraytor. Next door, dumbass. Next door. You her new husband? Is that it?

That it? You her new husband? John's dead, they tell me. John's dead, and now she's got herself something new. That it?"

Cannonball fingered his hat. "John's fine. I just talked with him. Alice is fine. My name is Canon Walker. I wanted to talk to you."

Nancy leaned back in her chair, closed those blue eyes, and said, "Talk."

Cannonball wished he'd given this more consideration. His only thought now being that this was the hardest money he'd ever earned.

Can't just bust out telling her I'm here for her boy, he thought. Can't ask about her crooked husband.

He let some quiet settle into the room, and she started to hum. He almost interrupted, then something caught his ear and instead he began to sing—low and quiet so only she could hear.

"May the circle be unbroken, by and by, Lord, by and by. There's a better home a waitin' in the sky, Lord, in the sky. In the sky, Lord, in the sky."

The woman smiled. "You can sing."

Cannonball nodded.

"Keep going. Sing something else." She motioned impatiently with her shiny claw. "Go on. Sing something."

Cannonball looked out a window at the eaves of the house next door, and he began to sing "Amazing Grace" in a soft, rusted baritone. Nancy Thomas sat perfectly still—nothing moving but those cold blue irises, ticking from side to side as if jerked by each beat of her heart.

Just as he finished, she interrupted. "They played that at my funeral."

He smiled, trying to convey comfort. "You mean your husband's funeral."

"Same thing." Nancy tossed her sandals with her toes and began to bounce the balls of her feet against the rug, like a child with a full bladder. "Thought you understood. Husband's funeral. My funeral. All the same. Robert's dead, shrinking away in a casket, in a vault, in the ground, under the grass, beneath the sky, by and by, Lord, by and by. He's gone. I'm here. It was our funeral. But, me, I can't die. Won't ever die. Lazarus, that's me. I'm Lady Lazarus. The Highlander. Swoop!" She cut her scarred claw through the air. "There went your head. I'm Duncan McLeod of the Clan of McLeod, and I cannot die." She paused. "Sing something else." Leaning forward in her rocker now: "You're a negro fellow, aren't you? Tell me what you are."

Cannonball cleared his throat and told the truth. "I'm a friend of your son's. I'm a friend of Scott's."

She let out a cackling laugh—high-pitched and disconcerting in the quiet room. "Lord Lazarus himself. My son. My son. My son. My son. Got away. Nothing to bear, nothing to hide. Got clean away. Outliving us all. Swoosh!" Nancy swung her claw through the air again. "Out of here. Off to there. Never seen again. Over the rainbow and down the drain."

This was getting him nowhere. Cannonball studied her face and asked the question. "Who set the fire that killed your husband?"

Nancy grew still again, her gaze drifting to her bare feet.

"Mrs. Thomas?"

"My shoes are gone."

Cannonball stood, picked up her white, strapped sandals off the rug, and knelt in front of her. Nancy Thomas held out one small, scarred foot and then the other for the old bluesman, and he gently placed the sandals on her feet. She smiled down at him.

Still on one knee, Cannonball spoke softly. "Bobby is in Boston with Scott. He won't talk. He just—"

"Bobby doesn't talk. He can. Does when he wants

to. He can. But he doesn't. Ooh, though. Tell Scott to be careful. Bobby's a strange one. Always the smartest. Don't be fooled about that. Even as babies, always the smart one. Just different now. Seared by the flame of redemption. Licked by the fires of hell. Licked hot and crazy. Be careful, they said. Be careful."

"Scott's smart, too, Mrs. Thomas. You'd be very proud of him."

"There's smart and smart. Smartest rabbit on earth nothing but dinner to a fox. Nothing but blood on the ground and meat in the belly."

Cannonball kept his voice low. "Why is Bobby in Boston, Nancy? Your nurse said he left a few weeks ago after another man came by to see you."

Nancy had worked forward in her chair so that her pretty face floated only inches from Cannonball's hard features, but now she leaned back and sighed. "I need to sleep now. Come back tomorrow and sing me a song."

By the time Cannonball got to his feet, Nancy Thomas had closed her eyes. By the time he left the small room, she had begun a soft and steady snore.

The nurse never showed again.

He let himself out, walked between neat rows of dark monkey grass, and turned down the sidewalk on Roseland Drive. Poking around in his pocket, he came out with the cell phone Scott had sent to him. The old man punched in Scott's number at the motel in Boston and, for a long time, stood and looked at the numbers. But he never pushed the SEND button. Instead, Cannonball Walker punched END, then entered the number of the cab company. He glanced up at the street sign, gave the address, and asked them to please come get him.

Scott packed up his motel room while Natalie hunkered in the car out front, watching for cops, for Click, for whatever. Her nerves hummed. Her eyes jumped at every passing car. Her breath caught up short every time someone turned into the parking lot. Scott was gone five minutes—one minute up, three minutes to throw everything in boxes, and a minute down. The time stretched Natalie's nerves to exhaustion.

Scott tossed two boxes in back and climbed in. Natalie put the car in drive. "I can't wait to get into my own bed. God."

"Natalie?" He paused. "I don't think your bed is a good place to be tonight if you want a full night's sleep. Maybe it'll be tomorrow before the cops put Dr. Reynolds together with a former protégé accused of murder and a disgruntled employee who he disciplined earlier today for having sex in her office." Scott looked over to examine her face. "Maybe they'll never put it together."

Natalie smiled, but there was no pleasure in it. "That's bullshit, and you know it. It may not be tonight, but they'll link us to Reynolds soon enough."

"But if they do put it together tonight, you're probably going to get a visit."

"So what? We're covered. We've got Reynolds on CD saying he had an affair with Kate Billings. He admitted he gave her access to the hospital's computer system. We can tie Reynolds to Kate and both of them to Click. And—"

Scott shrugged. "And what? What does that prove about who killed Patricia Hunter? And more important, what does it say about who had a motive to shoot Reynolds tonight?"

"Click and Kate, that's who."

"And us."

"Huh?" She spoke more slowly now. "How do you figure that?"

"On the recording, he says he's willing to let me go

down the river for the murder, and he enters into a criminal conspiracy with you to hide his dealings with Click. Think about it. You secretly record him one night, and he gets killed the next. I mean, I'm just spitballing here, but it's not out of the question for the cops to figure it was a criminal conspiracy gone bad."

"That's kind of a leap, Scott."

"I feel like I'm trying too hard to convince you that we're in this together. But I want you to know what's coming. Or, at least, what I think is coming." He hesitated. "You were there at Reynolds's murder. So was I. The cops checked our driver's licenses and made notes. We were there at his murder, Natalie. And if somebody saw me jump out of your car and rush Dr. Reynolds just before he was shot—"

She interrupted. "Or saw me drop you off and then drive by Reynolds just as the shot was fired." Natalie gulped for air. "I need to pull over." Scott reached across to steady the wheel. When they had rolled to a stop, she popped the transmission into park and leaned forward to rest her forehead on the cool top of the steering wheel.

"I'm sorry." Scott stroked her back. "I know that's not much from someone who's ruined you life. But I *am* sorry."

Natalie leaned back in her seat. As she did, Scott began to pull his hand away, and she reached out for it. She wrapped both of her hands around his and held it against her breasts. It was a gesture more intimate than sexual. Holding tight to his hand, she said, "You asked for help. I could have said no. When the police came to the hospital that first night, you tried to get me to run out screaming so you could let them arrest you." She squeezed his hand. "I not only said no, I yanked down your pants and told you to kiss me when the cops came in."

"Natalie . . ."

"Hush. Just be quiet and listen. It was my idea to

record Dr. Reynolds. And, last but not least, I'm the one who insisted on going along when you went to the parking garage tonight. *And* I insisted on . . . what did I say? Giving it a 'quick drive-by' to see who was waiting for you.

"So." She paused to take a deep breath, and Scott saw that she was crying. "What we have here is a woman who has *chosen*—every step of the way—to become more and more involved in your life and your problems. I guess the bottom line is that you're a friend, you're in trouble, and I've got something of a crush on you. And that's about how mature it seems, too. I've got a *crush*." She tried to smile. "Pitiful, isn't it?"

Scott's eyes moved over her face in the darkened car. "I just hope it hasn't ruined your life."

She let go of his hand and wiped at her eyes with the backs of her hands. "No, no. I'm not that stupid. I helped you, Scott Thomas, because it was the right thing to do. The rest is just . . ."

"Nice."

Natalie shot an anxious glance. "Is it?"

"Yes. It is." Scott smiled. "But it raises a question."

Now she smiled. "Why banish the subject of my girlish crush to the sofa?"

"Well . . . yeah."

"Because, Scott, I *said* I have a crush on you. I did *not* say that I'm a ho." The tears had stopped. She looked tired but smiled a little. "It takes a certain number of dates—you know, invested time, shared interests, your basic outlay of cold hard cash—to move into the bedroom."

"So," he said, "we there yet?"

"We're close." Natalie dropped the transmission into drive and pulled back out onto the street. "Yep." She smiled softly again. "I have to say that we're damn close."

Scott leaned back against the seat to think. He knew

that the flirtation was a defense mechanism, that Natalie had endured all she could, and that her brain had protected itself by replacing thoughts of desperation with something simpler—by substituting pleasant emotions for unpleasant. He also knew that people in shared danger develop unnaturally strong feelings for each other that would never exist under normal circumstances.

He knew all this. But, still, the conversation had made him feel better. You can understand, intellectually, that love is nothing but a compendium of needs and still fall head over heels—not that he had, but there was definitely *something*.

The neighborhood looked familiar. Scott sat forward. "Are you going to your apartment?"

Natalie nodded. "If we're going to North Carolina, I need some things."

"Are you sure you want more of this?"

"No." She smiled again. "But I've gotta do something for the next two weeks. Remember? I got suspended from work for being a ho."

Scott laughed. "I thought you said you weren't a ho."

"Complicated, isn't it?"

CHAPTER 39

The remains of a room service omelette cooled on the small table where Cannonball Walker sat with legs crossed and fingers drumming. He'd placed a call to John Pastings, and the old banker was keeping him holding.

Canon would not hang up. He turned in his chair and looked out at the bright start of an unseasonably warm day. Soft green buds peppered the dark limbs of a willow oak on the street corner outside his window. Men in khakis and golf shirts, women in khakis and blazers, trotted up and down the steps of the gas company building across the street. "Business casual" had outfitted the world in khaki.

"Mr. Walker?"

Canon was caught by surprise after the long hold. "Uh. Yeah."

John Pastings asked, "Have you decided to let our attorneys have a look at that power of attorney?"

"No. I don't expect that'd do much good, except maybe to let you drag things out. I called to ask you a question about Nancy Thomas." He paused, but the old banker didn't speak. Canon wondered if it was his imagination that the fat man's breathing seemed to grow louder and more labored with the mention of Scott's mother. "You see, Mr. Pastings, I stopped by to see Nancy yesterday afternoon. It was a very informative visit."

Pastings coughed. "You have to understand something, Mr. Walker. You—you've got to know after visiting Nancy . . ." Pastings stumbled, seemingly unable to weave words into a complete sentence.

"Are you okay, Mr. Pastings?"

"Scott didn't need to know about his mother." The banker was almost yelling. He paused to get his voice under control. "Not with her in that condition. And I don't mean her scars. No. I'm talking about her mind, Mr. Walker. What would Scott be today if he'd grown up with a crazy mother who preferred . . ." His voice trailed off.

Cannonball finished the sentence for him. "Who preferred Bobby? Who preferred her crazy, burned-up son to her healthy one? Is that what you were gonna say?"

Labored breathing filled the earpiece. "You're down here to stir up trouble, and I'm not going to be a part of it. Tell Scott what you will, Mr. Walker, but I won't be made a part of it. My hands are clean. I've done everything I could to help . . ."

"Tell me about the embezzlement scheme, Mr. Pastings. What happened to make Robert Thomas set fire to his home with his family sleepin' inside?"

The line turned silent—not even Pastings's heavy breathing sounded against the hum of the connection. Either he was gone or he'd moved the mouthpiece away from his face.

"Mr. Pastings? You there?"

Seconds passed before Cannonball heard a soft *click* as Pastings placed his phone into its cradle.

The old bluesman sat and looked at the receiver in

his hand. He dropped it back onto its base, and the phone rang almost immediately.

Cannon picked up the phone. "Mr. Pastings?"

"It's me. Scott. What's going on down there?"

Cannonball looked out again at the budding oak. "Still tryin' to get somethin' worth listenin' to out of John Pastings over at the bank. Findin' out some things. Ain't ready to put it all together yet."

"But you're finding out enough to make it worth staying a few more days. Is that what you're saying?"

The old man ran a thickly veined hand across the tight salt-and-pepper curls on his scalp. "I guess that's about the size of it."

"I'm coming South. Everything's leading us that way."

"You comin' to Alabama?"

"No, no. To North Carolina. Kate Billings is there."

Cannonball snorted. "That one's no good. Wears evil like angel's wings."

Scott paused as Cannonball's picture of Kate formed in his mind. He said, "The cops may be looking for me. Dr. Reynolds—my boss at the hospital—got shot last night. I was there when he died."

"Some folks get the stink of bad luck on 'em and can't get clean." The old man sounded disgusted.

"That supposed to make me feel better?"

"Shit, Doc. Damn wonder I believe a word you're sayin'. Hell, me sayin' you're carryin' around the stink of bad luck may be about the nicest thing anybody could say about you right now. It's either that or you're the most evil sonofabitch I ever run across."

"You don't believe me?"

"If I didn't, I wouldn't be down here puttin' up with all the shit I'm puttin' up with from John Pastings to try to help you out. No, Doc. We're just callin' a spade a spade, here. You're an unlucky sonofabitch."

Seconds passed. Finally, Scott said, "I don't believe in bad luck."

"That's too bad, boy, 'cause it sure as hell believes in you."

"What's got you so riled up, Cannonball? Is there something you're not telling me?"

The old man looked out his window some more. He changed the subject. "How you gettin' to Carolina with the cops after you?"

"I'm not sure. Fly, I guess. We need to get there as fast as possible."

"Doc." The old bluesman dropped his head and rubbed hard at his scalp. "Fast and right ain't the same thing. Fast and good ain't, either."

"Yeah, but somebody needs to tell Charles Hunter that he's employing a maniac. Kate has already—"

The old man interrupted. "She already showed she'll do anything to get next to Hunter. I don't think we gotta worry Charles Hunter until Kate is in his will." Cannonball chuckled. "She might be tryin' to screw him to death. But other than that . . ." His voice trailed off. "Now, listen to me." He paused. "Who's with you? Who is this 'we' you're talkin' about?"

"A woman from the hospital. Her name's Natalie Friedman. She helped me tie Kate Billings to Dr. Reynolds. She's . . . she's helped a lot."

The old man leaned back against the bed pillows. "You thinkin' with your dick again, Doc? Your track record with women ain't exactly awe-inspirin'. If you'll remember, you thought Kate Billings was helpin' you, too."

"I appreciate what you're doing for me down there, Cannonball. But—"

"But mind my own fuckin' business."

"Basically."

"Okay, okay. Didn't mean to offend." Both men let

some time pass. "Get back to how you're plannin' to travel. For what it's worth, I don't believe I'd be buyin' an airline ticket with the cops lookin' for me." He paused to think. "Tell you what. Grab a train to New York. Get a cab to the Madison Hotel on Central Park. There's a garage two blocks behind the hotel. My car is there. I know the owner. He'll know you're comin'."

Scott sighed. "You want me to take your car?"

"What I want . . ." The old man stopped to sigh now himself. "What I want is for you to slow the hell down and *think*. Drive down the coast. Talk things over with your woman friend. Stop along the way and get some rest, get some pussy. But mostly just take the time to fuckin' *think*. Folks might stop droppin' dead all around you if you stopped and used that big brain you're supposed to have before you jumped in every pile of shit you come across." Cannonball paused. "You can consider not gettin' your ass arrested at the Boston airport as an added benefit. And," he said, "my thirty-eight's in the glove compartment of the car."

"I don't want it."

"Yeah." The old man sounded tired. "But you might need it."

Scott pushed the END button on Natalie's cell phone just as she walked out of the motel bathroom. She smiled. "You get him?"

"I got him."

She crossed the brown shag rug and sat on the rumpled bed next to Scott. Her hair was damp and smelled of shampoo. She wore a white towel, tucked in at her cleavage. "You look pitiful. What'd he say?"

Without thought, Scott reached over and rested his hand on the smooth skin of her thigh. "Let's see. I've got the *stink* of bad luck on me, I think with my dick, and I need to stop and think instead of jumping in every pile of shit I see." He nodded at the rug. "I think that's about it."

Natalie laughed; then she leaned over to kiss him lightly on the lips before standing. "Sounds like a good friend." She smiled at Scott's discomfort. "Any advice?"

"He said not to fly. Cannonball's car is in New York. He strongly suggested we drive down if we don't want to get arrested."

"Really?" Natalie picked up an overnight bag and walked back toward the bathroom. "I can't wait to meet this guy."

Sarah Hunter climbed onto the deck of the Boston Whaler and turned to wave to Kate. The boat putted away, hauling five island kids to school on the mainland. As the captain pointed his boat away from the morning sun, the little girl ran to the transom and called out. "Kate? Kate!"

Kate waved again.

"Daddy's coming home." The child's face glowed.

Her nanny smiled and flashed a thumbs-up before turning to walk away. She had work to do. The homecoming had to be perfect. Kate was glad that Sarah had piloted her little sailboat without incident—that she, the loving nanny, hadn't had reason to call Charles in Boston with news of his daughter's accident. It was better this way, really. Too much tragedy too soon could have sent Charles Hunter spiraling down into insanity or drunkenness. Neither of which would do anyone any good. Neither of which, she thought, would do *me* any good.

She climbed into Charles's ragtop Jeep and cranked the engine.

*   *   *

The day moved slowly back inside the spotless house.
Groceries from the mainland were delivered late morning. Kate prepared a marinade for the tenderloin of
lamb, placing the spices in a straight line at the top of
her cutting board before starting, washing each bowl
and utensil as she used it. The tenderloin went into
sealed Tupperware with the marinade, the Tupperware
into the fridge.

Too early to start cutting vegetables, she opted instead to carefully wash the asparagus and broccolini,
the Portobello mushrooms and baby carrots. Each stalk
scrubbed under running water, the underside of each
mushroom cap washed until the water ran clear, and
then each piece set in a stainless colander to drain before joining its brethren in Ziploc bags. At exactly 2:00
P.M., Kate mixed yeast dough for homemade rolls. Pre-
cisely fifteen minutes later, she placed the dough in an
opaque glass bowl, covered the bowl with a damp
cloth, and put the bowl on a cleared shelf in the laundry room where the afternoon sun always warmed
the air.

The dough would have exactly two hours to rise.

Kate went to her room to bathe. She went to
prepare.

Dinner was a celebration. Charles sat at the head of the
table as Kate covered the linen cloth with platters of
grilled tenderloin, vegetables sauteed in olive oil, fresh
carrots and tomatoes. She returned with a large basket
of yeast rolls—Charles's favorite thing in the world, according to his daughter—and set the basket at Charles's
elbow.

As Kate brought out the food, Sarah set the table

with silver and napkins. Charles laughed and drank scotch and asked Sarah about school and friends. He was on his third drink since walking in the door an hour before. Kate noticed and brought out a bottle of Saintsbury Pinot Noir.

Charles smiled and held up his tumbler. "I'll just stick with this, but you go ahead with the wine."

"No way." She wanted him drunk, but not too drunk. Kate leaned down in front of Charles and changed her voice to imitate a carnival hypnotist. "Look deep into my eyes." When she stood back up, Kate whisked away his tumbler of scotch.

Sarah laughed at the trick.

Charles colored a little. "Now hold on here."

"No way. I worked on this homecoming meal all afternoon, and that's a great bottle of wine. We're going to do things right tonight." Kate turned to Sarah. "Right, Sarah?"

Sarah nodded her head. "Right!"

Charles raised his hands in surrender. "Okay, okay."

Kate quickly took the tumbler to the kitchen. When she returned, she made a show of tickling Sarah as she guided the child to her chair. Sarah squealed with happiness. Her father was home, and, finally, she seemed to have won over Kate. Her father had instructed her to "build a relationship" with her new nanny. Now it was happening. All the quiet times when her father was away, all the awkward dinners with just her and Kate, were in the past.

This was their life now. Her father would always be there; Kate would make gourmet meals and tickle her and play jokes; nothing else bad would happen.

As Kate took her seat opposite Charles, Sarah said, "This is just perfect, isn't it, Daddy?"

"You know, Sarah, I believe it is."

Kate smiled as she picked up a platter and speared a helping of grilled lamb.

Dinner lasted over an hour, then Charles and Sarah went for a walk on the beach while Kate cleared the dishes and stored leftovers. She made quick work of it and headed for her room to change into a nightgown and robe. By the time father and daughter returned, Kate had arranged herself on the living room sofa—a glass of wine in one hand and a magazine in the other.

"You two have a nice walk?"

Charles held up his cast. He blushed a little at the thought of breaking his foot while drop-kicking the urn containing his wife's ashes out to sea. Kate was, after all, the only living being who knew what had happened. "I wouldn't exactly call it a walk. More of a *sit* in the sand. But we did have a good time." He looked down at Sarah. "Didn't we, monkey britches?"

Sarah gave him a look. "Stop calling me that."

He winked at Kate. "Wow. I can't believe you've gotten all that cleaned up already."

Sarah examined Kate's robe. "And she's already ready for bed, too. Are you tired from cooking, Kate?"

The nanny smiled. "No, I'm not tired. Just wanted to get comfortable and do some reading. But, speaking of tired"—Kate glanced at her watch—"you've got about thirty more minutes before bedtime. I'm afraid it's time for a bath."

"I'm celebrating with Daddy."

Charles laughed. "Nice try. Hit the showers, monkey britches."

Sarah stomped out, making a show of feigned anger, and he laughed appreciatively. He walked to the bar to pour a drink. "You two seem to be getting along."

"I think we are. It took a while but I think we're going to be friends."

"Good. I'm going out on the patio. Call me when Sarah's ready to be tucked in."

"I will, but . . ."

He stopped. "What is it?"

She held up her glass of wine. "I was hoping you'd join me for a drink. I wouldn't mind hearing what's going on back in Boston."

Charles looked longingly out at the dark patio. Kate watched, thinking how the man had gotten used to being alone, how he'd grown accustomed to wallowing in private thoughts. He seemed to be living in some private world out there—living in the presence of ghosts more real than the breathing bodies inside the walls of his home. But after a brief hesitation, he walked over to sit on the opposite end of the sofa from her. He smiled encouragingly. "Of course. What would you like to talk about? I can tell you one thing, the weather down here is heaven compared to the cold wet mess in Boston when I left."

Kate nodded and prodded, carefully listening for subjects that seemed to spark Charles's interest and then pushing and pulling the conversation in whatever direction seemed most amusing to him. They had been talking for twenty minutes when Sarah came in and said good night. Charles left to tuck her in alone, but Kate knew she was on the right track when he came back, mixed another drink, and, without thinking, sat down and picked up their conversation where he'd left off.

Kate's satin robe was proper—floor length, solid, tied at the waist. Her nightgown beneath the robe considerably less proper. Not slutty. Just low and high and lacy.

She used a trip to the bar for more wine as a pretense to let her gown fall open—not too far, just enough—as she sat back down beside Charles. She was

closer now. Close enough for him to smell her cologne.
After all, the man had already downed half a dozen
drinks. She smiled and looked into his eyes. He smiled
and looked at her cleavage. He was forty-five; she was
twenty-eight. He'd been in a loveless marriage and then
alone. And Kate had always known, almost innately, that
men can only take so much.

"Your robe is open." His words slurred a bit at
the ends.

She looked down. "Do you mind?"

"No." He smiled. "I don't mind, but Sarah . . ."

"Sarah's sound asleep. Here." She untied her sash
and let the robe fall away. "Is that better?"

Charles said, "I don't think this is right," but his eyes
continued to roam from legs to breasts and back again.

"I've been thinking about you while you were gone."

"Really?" He slurred again.

Men are idiots. "Sure." She scooted closer. "Can I
hold your hand?"

Charles held out his hand like an obedient child.
She took it in hers, slid his fingers beneath her top, and
pressed his palm against her breast. All she said was
"There."

He began to massage her breast and leaned in for a
hungry, fumbling, overanxious kiss. When he pulled
back, Charles whispered, "It's been a long time." Kate
reached over to squeeze his obvious erection, and he
smiled. "Like riding a bike, huh?"

She began to unzip his fly. "Tell you what, Charles.
You're the one with the cast on his foot, so why don't you
let *me* do the riding this time?"

He kissed her harder, and all Kate could think was
how easy it had been. It should have taken longer. He
should, at the very least, have insisted on going to a
locked bedroom. He should have done a lot of things.

She was on top of him now, pulling off her lace gown, watching his eyes devour her perfect breasts even before his mouth reached her nipples. Kate smiled down at the happy drunk suckling her breast.

Men, she thought, are such idiots.

CHAPTER 40

Scott told the cabby to drop them at the Plaza. Natalie looked surprised, then gently nodded. They went in through the famous front entrance, cut through the ornate lobby, and exited the side door facing Central Park. Scott pointed left. "It's a few blocks up this way."

"You know New York?"

"Not really. I got a couple of mercy invitations for Christmas in the city when I was in prep school. Usually I had more self-respect, but I figured a free trip to New York during the holidays was worth a little compromise."

The day was bright but cold. Natalie turned up the collar on her coat. "I need to make a phone call. And we both need to eat."

"Sorry. Guess I'm on a mission." Scott stopped and looked around. "What are you in the mood for? We're in the heart of New York City, land of ten thousand mediocre restaurants."

"I thought some of the best restaurants in the world were here."

"They are. A handful. It's just that we probably ain't gonna have lunch in one of the world's greatest, and the average eatery in New York is pretty average compared to what you'd find in New Orleans or San Francisco."

Natalie shuddered against the wind. "Just how many mercy invitations did you accept?"

Scott smiled. "Two. The rest is . . ." He looked uncomfortable. "You do a lot of traveling when there's nowhere else to go. No home and hearth, so I drove and bused and hitchhiked all over the country in the summers. I could never afford Europe, but I made it from one end of America to the other."

"Well, Mr. Restaurant, pick a place. But first I need to make that call."

"Okay." He stopped and looked down at the sidewalk. "Who do you need to call? I'm not sure that's a good idea."

Natalie turned to face him. "I wasn't asking permission. My cell's out of juice, and I need to find a public phone. And *who* I'm going to call is my business."

Scott took her elbow and turned left. "Let's try this way."

Two blocks down, he spotted a rare public phone and pointed it out to Natalie. She had a strange look on her face. "Okay. Wait here. This is private."

Scott nodded.

Natalie walked to the telephone. She had memorized the number for safety. Turning her back to Scott, she used zero-plus dialing to place a collect call to Homicide Lieutenant Victor Cedris at the Boston Police Department.

They reached the parking garage a few minutes past two that afternoon. Natalie carried a small suitcase and a computer case, Scott a bulging backpack. He approached a filthy glass cubicle next to the entrance. A small dark man sat inside smoking a thin cigar.

"Hello."

The little man's eyes moved. Nothing else.

"I'm here to pick up Cannonball Walker's car."

"Caneen boll?"

Scott tried to enunciate. "Can-non-ball Wal-ker."

"Caneen boll?"

Scott sighed. Natalie poked him in the ribs. "Say yes."

"What?"

"Say yes."

Scott put his mouth near a round cutout in the glass. "Yes."

"Caneen boll, yes?"

"Cannonball, yes."

The little man nodded and pointed over his shoulder. "Offeece."

Scott leaned in. "What?"

Natalie rolled her eyes. "Good God. Who looked after you on those trips around the country? He's saying to go to the office inside."

"Oh," Scott said, "thanks," and smiled. The little man read the newspaper.

Natalie took the lead, pulling Scott around the wigwag and into the dark garage. Bare bulbs glowed faintly around corners and behind concrete partitions. Cars were jammed into small spaces, with no more than a hand's width between them, making Scott wonder how the attendant opened the doors to get in and drive them out.

As Scott wondered about such things, Natalie followed some innate sense of direction to a glassed-in office at the back corner of the first floor. Inside, another dark man—this one bald and round—sat at a gray metal desk flipping through stacks of small, white papers.

Natalie knocked.

"See the attendant." His accent hovered somewhere between French and Arabic.

She knocked again.

He didn't look up. "See the attendant."

Now she banged on the glass door.

"Goddammit!" He got uncomfortably to his feet. "I said to—"

Natalie matched his tone. "We're here for Cannonball Walker's car. The attendant sent us to *you*."

"Tell man there to step up where I see him."

Scott joined Natalie in front of the glass door. He tried to look unthreatening.

"Your hair supposed to be long."

"I cut it."

The round man nodded. He waddled over, turned a flip dead bolt, and waddled back to his chair. He did not open the door. Scott turned the knob and gave it a shove, stepping aside to let Natalie enter ahead of him.

The man ogled Natalie, but spoke to Scott. "You Cannonball's friend?"

"That's right. Do you need to see some ID?"

The guy acted as though Scott had asked if he wanted acid in his coffee. "No! No ID. Cannonball say you'll be here today. He say with curly hair and glasses, you be with a woman." He shrugged. "Good enough for me." The office was as cold as the street, but sweat beaded on the man's bald pate as he opened a drawer and fished out car keys. "Here. Give to the attendant. He get car for you."

Scott stepped forward and took the keys. "Thanks."

"Sure, sure. I got something for you."

"From Cannonball?"

He shook his sweaty, round head. "No. Man stop by a while ago. Say you two eating lunch. Asked me to give you this." He held out an woman's oxblood billfold. Natalie made a small yelp as she inhaled and reached for the wallet. She unsnapped it and looked at the license. The garage owner looked frightened. "Everything there. You check. Everything there. He say if I take anything, he be back."

Scott spoke first. "Is it yours?"

Natalie nodded. "I had it on the train."

"Shit!" Scott turned to the garage man. "What did he look like?"

The man ignored him. He was focused on Natalie. "Everything there?"

Natalie flipped through papers and photos, credit cards and cash. "Yes. It's all here."

Scott's voice grew louder. "I asked you what he looked like."

The man shook his head, sending rivulets of sweat trickling down bulging jowls. "No way." Scott took a step forward, and the man shook his head again. "You beat me up, but this man he kill me. Look, look, I'm doing Cannonball a favor. Doing you a favor. Leave me alone. Not my fault man came to see me. Not my fault he steal lady's purse." He swiveled in his chair to fully face Scott, held his open hands in front of his belly palms down, and made a gesture like an umpire signaling a runner safe at home. "We done here. Take Cannonball's car and go."

Scott wasn't going to beat information out of an old fat man who'd done nothing wrong, and everyone in the room knew it. Natalie tugged at Scott's sleeve, and they left.

Two hours later, Scott and Natalie were clear of the city and heading south. Fear gnawed at their stomachs. He felt cold and nauseated; so did she. Neither one mentioned it for the next two hundred miles.

Natalie looked out at the Maryland countryside—pastures and timberland split by pavement and an invisible line of lingering exhaust. She broke the silence. "How'd you get her address?"

Scott's mind had grown dull gazing at miles of interstate. "Huh?"

"Kate's address. How'd you get it?"

"Oh. I called Charles Hunter's office in Boston. The

receptionist told me they've got a branch someplace called Spinnaker Island on the North Carolina coast. I don't have Kate's address. Just the office."

Natalie nodded. "Kate's got to be close." She reached into the backseat of Cannonball's big Caddy and picked up a black nylon case. She worked zippers and Velcro and came out with a silver laptop. As she powered it up, Natalie repeated to herself, "Spinnaker Island." A few minutes later, she asked, "P-E-T-R-I-N-G?"

"Yeah. I think so. What are you doing?"

"Googling Spinnaker Island and Hunter ampersand Petring."

"You can get the Internet on that thing?"

Natalie shook her head in amused disbelief. "And on my Handspring, and on my cell phone. But I get full-screen graphics with this."

"Oh." Scott smiled. "*Ampersand*, huh?"

"I may not have gone to Harvard"—she grinned at his teasing—"but, unlike some people, I do know how to use a mobile modem . . . Got it!" Her voice changed cadence as she began to read out loud. "*Spinnaker Island, a different way of living. A simpler way of life we've all forgotten. A traditional village for the twenty-first century. Developed by Hunter & Petring, American Institute of Architects.*"

"Anything else?"

"Yeah." Her fingers tapped keys. "Everything. Pictures, model floor plans, a map of the island. And"—she smiled—"a toll-free number to lease one of the 'guest cottages.'" She paused to scan the sales literature. "They've got four cottages they reserve for . . ."

"Sales prospects."

"Not the words they use, but yeah. So." She fished a cell phone out of her purse. "You want a view of the Atlantic?"

Scott smiled. "Why not?"

"Why not indeed." Natalie began punching numbers.

The morning after Cannonball Walker called on Nancy Thomas, the phone in his hotel room rang at exactly eight thirty. Nine thirty Boston time. Cannonball was on his way to the door, heading downstairs for breakfast. He turned back to answer the ringing. "Hello?"

"Is this Cannonball Walker?"

The old man sat on his bed and sighed. "What can I do for you, De-tective?"

Lieutenant Cedris paused. "You're good with voices. Or did Mr. Pastings at the bank tell you I'd be calling?"

"*Mister* Pastings won't give me the time of day. I got a good ear."

Cedris paused. "I thought I advised you to steer clear of Scott Thomas."

"You thought wrong. You said he was in trouble. Asked me to give him a message."

"You're pretty sharp for your age, Mr. Walker."

Cannonball shook his head at the empty room. "And you're pretty sharp for yours, De-tective."

A thousand miles away, Lieutenant Cedris cringed a little. "Sorry. Look, I need to know where Scott is. His former boss at the hospital, a shrink named Phil Reynolds, was shot to death two nights ago." He paused, but Cannonball let the silence linger. "Scott was there at the scene when it happened." Again he stopped for Cannonball to say something, and again the old bluesman let him wait. "I'm sure you can see that it looks bad for Scott to take off after something like that."

"Do you think he shot this Reynolds fella?"

"I can't really comment—"

"Goddammit!"

"Mr. Walker, I don't really think cussing me out is going to solve—"

Cannonball was on his feet, but didn't remember standing. "Listen to me, Mr. De-tective. Scott Thomas is a good boy. I'm doin' my best to help him out, and I got assholes from Boston to Birmingham sayin' they can't tell me *this* and can't tell me *that*. But, all the time, every one of 'em tellin' me just exactly what he wants me to hear but not a goddamn word about what *I* need to hear." The old man stopped to catch his breath. "You want me to help you, then you help me. 'Cause as far as I can tell, you're more interested in tryin' to screw over this boy than in findin' who killed that poor lady in the hospital."

A few seconds ticked by. Finally, Cedris asked, "Are you done?"

"Done and 'bout ready to hang up the damn phone."

"Okay. Slow down." His voice was calm. "Tell me what you need."

Cannonball plopped down into an occasional chair beside the window. "I'll tell you what I need. I need to know what you got on Scott. I need to know what you know about this John Pastings at the bank down here claiming the Birmingham cops are after Scott for a fire that happened fifteen years ago. And, mostly, I need to know how much of this mess you got figured out, 'cause I'm findin' out everything that I don't need to know and nothin' that I do." The old man hesitated. "And, finally, I need to know everything you got on a woman named Natalie Friedman."

Long-distance static sizzled in the earpiece. Cannonball was just about to ask if Cedris was still on the line when the lieutenant began to speak. "Okay, here it is. I've come to believe that you're trying to do the right thing, Mr. Walker; so I'm going to tell you some things.

But, if I'm going to do this, I expect you to fill in some holes for me when I'm done. Does that sound fair?"

Cannonball looked out the window at the Southern spring morning. "*Sounds* fair. But I'm still waitin' to hear what you have to say."

Cedris sighed. "You might want to grab a pencil. This gets complicated."

CHAPTER 41

Virginia was a logical stopping place. A little town called Havenswood looked right—one main street of businesses, maybe a couple of thousand residents, and one hotel. Whoever had taken Natalie's billfold could still be following. Or it could be that the nameless thief knew everything and had gone ahead to the Carolina coast. No way to tell. But Scott Thomas had no intention of spending the night in a big city with bars and alleys, flophouses and whorehouses—not in any place with a thousand nooks and crannies where a violent soul could hide and wait.

Click would stand out like a sore thumb in Havenswood, Virginia. Bobby would frighten small children and old people.

Dusk hung heavy in the air as Scott turned Cannonball Walker's black Caddy into the parking lot of the Havenswood Arms. Natalie waited in the car while he went inside to register. The night manager peeked out and grinned. Natalie saw the look and smiled. When Scott came out, she said, "That guy thinks we're here to sweat up the sheets."

Scott looked over. "That's pretty much what I told him."

"I guess that's part of our cover."

"Nope," he said. "Just bragging."

Scott smiled and Natalie laughed—each of them trying to keep up a brave front, each wearing a mask betrayed by the fear in their eyes.

Click waited a half mile outside Havenswood's police jurisdiction, napping in the reclined driver's seat of his blue Lexus. Earlier—driving through unfamiliar territory just after dark—he'd found an old logging road that was grown up underneath with vines and tight from side to side with buggy-whip pines. He'd parked there just a couple of hours after Scott and Natalie had checked into the Havenswood Arms.

The pale hacker unscrewed the cap on a sticky-sweet grape soda and chugged a quarter of it. He wadded up greasy waxed paper that smelled of cheeseburger. He looked and felt contented. Darryl Simmons had a plan.

At exactly 2:00 A.M. he would drive into that pissant town and enter the hotel room where Scott Thomas and Natalie Friedman lay sleeping. That asshole, Scott, would die immediately. Click had decided he would use a knife. Quiet and fast. Messy, but that was fine, too. The woman could take longer—a lot longer if she didn't scream. If, he thought, I can just get a towel in her mouth . . .

He reached down to tug at the crotch of his pants as the thought of what lay ahead started to give him an erection.

"That man. He come back with a *git*-tar. I tole him to leave you be, but . . ."

Cannonball couldn't make out Nancy Thomas's response, but seconds later he was ushered into the same back room on Roseland Drive. Tonight, Scott's mother wore a gold, quilted dashiki with a black turban and soft black house shoes.

Her feet began to bounce against the carpet when he entered the room. "You can sing. 'Amazing Grace,' 'May the Circle Be Unbroken.'" Her eyes lighted up. "Scott and Bobby. Tom and Huck. One calm, one wild, and you in the middle like chocolate filling inside pure white divinity."

"How are you this evening, Nancy?"

She didn't answer.

"Mind if I call you Nancy?"

"That's my name. 'Come here, Nancy.' 'Do this, Nancy.' 'Do that, Nancy.' 'You're gonna die, Nancy. You're gonna die.'"

Cannonball sat in the same chair he'd used before. "We're all gonna die. When and how are all that matter."

She waved her shiny claw in the air dismissively. "You come here to sing or what? You said you would. Didn't believe you." She smiled, and it was awful.

Cannonball set out his guitar case on the floor at his feet and flipped the chromed clasps. Folding back Gibson's trademark dark-pink satin, he picked up the battered Les Paul, balanced the heavy body on one knee, and fingered the opening to "Worried Life Blues." Nancy clapped her misshapen little hands together, and the old bluesman began to sing. "Oh, Lordy Lord, Oh, Lordy Lord. Hurts me so bad." As he sang, Cannonball watched the crazy woman bounce and sway, and he could see something of Scott in her. Her boy was a nice-looking man, but this woman had been a beauty. His eyes stayed on her face as he sang. There were hard questions to be asked, and he was looking for . . . something. "But someday, baby, I ain't gonna worry my life anymore." He picked out the last two bars.

"What's the matter with your guitar? It's quiet. Sounds good, but it's quiet."

"It's electric." He smiled. "Don't sound like much without an amp."

"Get it fixed." She chirped like a bird. "Get the damn thing fixed, I say. Too pretty not to hear."

"Thank you." He cleared his throat. "We were talking about your boy Bobby when I was here last time."

Nancy's head cocked to one side. "Were we? That's funny. Not much to tell. Smart and hard—he's the quick and the dead." She leaned back in her chair. "I'm just dead."

"I've seen Bobby. I saw him in Boston, Nancy. He was standing outside a restaurant where I was eating. He . . . the boy seemed to be watching me."

"Run!" Nancy Thomas cackled with glee. "Run for the hills! I told you, 'the quick and the dead.' Bobby's quick and you're dead." She cackled again. "Don't worry. You can sing. You sing to his momma." She slowed down and spaced out her words as if explaining something. "You sing to his momma."

Cannonball nodded. "What happened to Bobby? Why is he the way he is?"

"Fire."

The old man began to pick out the classic blues structure of "Ten Long Years." He tapped the toes of one pointed black shoe in time to the music. "Tell me about it, Nancy. Tell me what happened to Bobby."

She grew quiet, her eyes ticking from side to side in perfect rhythm with the song as if jerked by a wire tied to the toe of Cannonball's shoe. After a time, her head began to bob and a quiet hum started in her throat that morphed into words. For the better part of an hour, Nancy Thomas spoke quietly, and mostly with chilling clarity, about her sons. Convoluted, out-of-nowhere quotes from the King James Bible occasionally snapped sentences and thoughts in two, but even then she made a kind of sense to an old man raised in the Baptist churches of Mississippi.

Nancy Thomas told what had happened to her young sons and why it had happened. And, all the while, Cannonball Walker never missed a note on that battered old guitar.

His footsteps made no noise in the dew-drenched grass along the back of the Havenswood Arms. The air felt cool. The pine and sycamore woods to the south seemed to sigh every so often, bathing the hotel in the scents of grasses and leaves.

A long hall ran along the front of rooms whose back windows looked out at the woods. He counted squares of silver moonlight reflected on panes of glass. Five matched pairs of shining eyes over, Scott and Natalie dreamed inside. He trotted forward, squatting with his back pressed against the cool concrete blocks beneath their windows. Somewhere in the woods, an owl hooted and was answered by some kind of bird that screeched.

And he waited.

Minutes ticked by, and he held up a pale hand in the moonlight to examine half moons of dried blood beneath three fingernails. Picking absentmindedly at the caked blood, he smiled a little and stood to try the window.

The good ones plan ahead. It had been almost too easy to unhook the screen, slip the lock on the window, and squirt a little oil on all the contact points when Scott and Natalie were out having dinner. There's always a way if you plan ahead. Sometimes it's as simple as stealing a key card and going in to replace the safety chain with one six inches longer—one just long enough to be lifted off from the outside. Sometimes it's even easier, like hiding under a bed and waiting. And sometimes, like tonight, the people leave and there's a window facing nothing but grass and trees.

The screen slipped out on oiled runners. The window slid open without effort or noise. He planted his palms wide on the windowsill and jumped up. The curtains were pulled, and he got inside with barely a ruffle or lump in the material.

Stand very still. It was a matter of discipline. Nothing moves. Long seconds ticked by, and the deep steady breathing of REM sleep filled the room in stereo. Both of them were in dreamland.

This was the part he liked best.

"Scott?" A whisper from the bed. "Scott? There's someone in the room."

The soft, swishing sounds of sheets and comforters moving preceded the *click* of the bedside lamp.

For a split second, bright light blinded everyone in the room. But it was only a second, and Scott was able to train Cannonball Walker's gun on the dark form of his brother even before his eyes had adjusted enough to know who was there. "Bobby?"

This time there was no refusal or denial. Bobby Thomas nodded his head.

"What are you doing here?"

The scarred face tilted down as those empty eyes examined his fingernails. "Click followed you."

Natalie spoke for the first time. "And you did, too?"

Bobby looked up. "Cover yourself." He pointed to where the sheet had fallen away to reveal the soft round top of Natalie's left breast. She tugged the sheet up, and he nodded. "I killed him."

Natalie could feel the blood drain from her face. Her arms and legs suddenly felt weak and cold. "You killed Click?"

Bobby switched his gaze to Scott. "He followed you. Here." He tossed a Nike sports bag onto the bedcovers.

Scott didn't move. Neither did the gun. "What's in there?"

"Look" was all he said.

Scott nodded at the bag and said Natalie's name. She leaned forward, taking care not to get between the muzzle and Bobby, and retrieved the bag. Holding the covers against her breasts with one hand, she worked the zipper with the other.

Bobby motioned with his hand. "Careful."

She nodded and turned the contents out onto the bedspread. A serrated, six-inch hunting knife, a roll of duct tape, and a huge, black dildo a foot long spilled out. She looked up and squinted at Bobby. Natalie didn't get it.

Bobby did not like talking. His words sounded sparse and wounded. "That stuff." He pointed again. "That Click was coming here tonight with that. The knife was for you." He motioned at Scott. "The rest—the tape and that rubber dick thing—he brought for her." He nodded at Natalie, who sprang naked from under the covers, ran into the bathroom, and slammed the door. Bobby watched her go with those flat black eyes, then turned back to Scott. "I've got his hand in the trunk outside."

Scott was in emotional overload. "What? You've got what?"

Bobby nodded as if thinking back on the rightness of his actions. "I've got Click's hand in the trunk. So you'd know it was him. You can check the fingerprints so you won't have to worry any more."

The handgun turned slippery with sweat in Scott's hand. "I don't want it."

"I understand." His scarred brother nodded. "You're safe now."

"Why did you steal Natalie's billfold on the train?"

"Identification" was all he said.

Scott nodded, but it meant nothing. He did not understand his brother's reasoning.

Bobby looked longingly at the open window. "I'm leaving." He turned away, but then glanced back. "Don't worry. They won't find him. Probably not ever. But not for a long time and not anywhere near here." Those blank eyes lingered on Scott's face for two more beats before Bobby placed a foot on the windowsill, pivoted, and dropped to the ground as if his body had no weight.

Scott made sure he'd gone, then walked to the bathroom door and knocked. "Are you all right, Natalie?"

She opened the door. Her face was ghostly pale except for deep red circles around the eyes. Standing there naked, she looked impossibly small and vulnerable. "I threw up."

Scott reached out and gathered her up in his arms. "Pretty reasonable thing to do." He glanced back at the window. "We need to get out of here."

"And go to the police." Her words were muffled against his chest. She leaned back to look into his eyes. "Promise me, right now. We're going to the cops with this. I thought I could . . ." Her voice trailed off, and she started again. "I thought I could . . . *manage* this, but it's out of control." Her eyes searched his face, and she repeated, "Promise me."

Scott stroked her bare back, but said nothing.

CHAPTER 42

"This is getting to be a habit for us." John Pastings sounded jovial. He thought he'd won the tug of war with Canon Walker, and the fat banker was enjoying his victory.

Cannonball leaned against a wall in the bank's first-floor lobby. "I'm downstairs." He spoke into a stainless steel cell phone.

"I'm sorry, Mr. Walker, but I have a full morning ahead of—"

"I met again with Nancy Thomas last night." He paused to see if Pastings would try to bullshit him, but the banker remained silent. "It's somethin' the way music can loosen up memory. What shrinks call a 'memory trigger,' I think. Anyway, Nancy—we're on a first-name basis now, by the way—Nancy's got herself a pretty good memory once she gets started."

"I really don't see where—"

"Her nurse was the tough part. But—what with Nancy raisin' hell and me hoverin' over the woman like the angel of death—even that old bat got on board and let me look at her paychecks." Cannonball paused as a group of cloned bankers passed. "The money comes from you, Mr. Pastings."

"Of course it does." The old banker's voice labored

between heavy breaths. "I set up a trust. Scott knows all about it."

"The checks I saw ain't from any trust. They're from your personal account, which means that either you're runnin' the Thomas trust funds through your own account—and that makes you a crook—*or* you, Mr. Pastings, are payin' for Nancy's nursing care out of your own funds—and that makes you . . . what?"

Pastings's voice grew shrill. "The last time I looked, there was no law against charity, Mr. Walker. Scott might do better to worry about the trouble he's in up in Boston than about what I'm doing down here out of the goodness of my heart. I told Scott already that if he keeps messing around and not taking responsibility for whatever happened in that hospital . . . Well, believe me, he does *not* want the Birmingham police to get any more interested in his family's house fire than they are right now." The banker's voice smoothed out as he spoke. This was a man used to having his bullshit believed. "Now, for Scott's good and for his mother's, you need to advise Scott—"

That was enough. Cannonball interrupted. "Mr. Pastings? You wouldn't know the truth if it crawled up your pants leg and bit you on your saggy ball sack."

"Now see here!"

"Shut the fuck up and listen." The old bluesman was angry. "The Birmingham cops aren't interested in the house fire. I asked 'em. And not only did I ask 'em, I checked it out with a de-tective up in Boston named Cedris, and he called bullshit on the whole thing. Goddamn! The Thomas house ain't even inside the Birmingham cops' jurisdiction. If you're gonna lie your ass off, at least give the respect of shinin' up your bullshit with a fact or two." Cannonball stopped to catch his breath. Both men were silent for a time. Finally, Cannonball said, "One more thing. Robert Thomas didn't leave a damn thing to his family. The fire investigator called it arson and said Robert did it. Insurance companies don't pay off on property coverage when a man torches his own house. And I don't think they pay out a lot on life insurance when a man burns his dumb ass up while settin' a fire to commit insurance fraud."

"Robert had investments . . ."

"There you go again. You and me both know that Robert Thomas didn't have shit. That's why it was so easy for everybody down here to believe he'd been embezzlin' funds at the bank. I tell you what. Lots of stuff goin' on back then. Lots of stuff. Nancy showed me this pretty little stack of letters all tied up with ribbon. She's real proud of those letters, Mr. Pastings."

It took Pastings a while to speak. "How much of this does Scott know?"

Cannonball ran things over in his head and decided to tell the truth. "None of it."

"What do you want?" The banker's voice was barely above a whisper.

"I wanna do what's best for Scott and his momma. *And* I wanna come upstairs and talk to you about it without you tryin' to sell me any more Alabama swampland."

"I can't talk here in the office, Mr. Walker. I'm sure you understand."

"I'm smellin' the stink of swamp water. I warned you about that. We're talkin' in your office, or we're talkin' at the po-lice station." He paused for emphasis. "You think I'm gettin' in a car and goin' off somewhere with you . . . Shit. I ain't that stupid."

"No, Mr. Walker. You're many things, but you are not stupid." He sighed. "Come on up. I'll tell my secretary to clear my schedule." The man's voice broke, and Cannonball could have sworn he was crying. "You're going to be reasonable, aren't you? I mean, we're going to be able to work this out, right?"

Cannonball shook his head at the bustling foot traffic in the lobby of John Pastings's bank. "I'll be up in two minutes."

Cannonball's old Caddy droned through the North Carolina countryside. All around the speeding car, fresh leaves and the tender shoots of new grass shone beneath blue skies. Inside, Scott and Natalie rode in strained silence.

Back at the Havenswood Arms, Scott had hurriedly tossed her cases and his backpack into the trunk within minutes after Bobby left their room. He had not stopped to report Click's death to the police. Natalie had mentioned it once, just as the old Caddy passed the southernmost city limits. Scott had simply asked, "What do you want me to tell them?"

Natalie had opened her mouth to answer, but there was no answer. At least, there was no answer that wouldn't stop them in their tracks—no answer that wouldn't leave Kate Billings triumphant and also land both Scott and Natalie in a jail cell awaiting extradition to Massachusetts.

So they had ridden in silence.

Almost three hours passed before Scott said, "We're almost there."

Natalie nodded. Minutes passed. "How far?"

"I think about twelve miles to Buckshead."

Natalie picked up her laptop and got it going. "We're supposed to call thirty minutes before we get there. The development company will send a boat."

"Can you . . ." His words trailed off when he heard the soft beeps of Natalie dialing up the North Carolina offices of Hunter & Petring.

She spoke softly and professionally with an overly happy sales rep, and then dropped the phone back into her purse. "Just keep going the way you're heading. I've got directions through the little town to a safe parking area." She powered down her laptop and put it away. "We're lucky. The boat was already on this side. Some guy named Frank will meet us at the parking lot and take us over." She hesitated. "I think I mentioned to you that there's a party tonight at Charles Hunter's office."

Scott looked out at the idyllic landscape spinning past his window. "I don't remember . . ." He glanced over at Natalie. "We've got to get past this."

"Right." Her voice was filled with disgust. "We've got to get *past* running out when Dr. Reynolds was gunned down right in front of us. And we've got to get *past* your brother killing Click. And, let's not forget, we've got to get *past* the murder charges you've got hanging over your head in Boston. We'll just . . ." She struggled for words that didn't come. "We'll just forget about all that."

"*All that* is why we're here, Natalie. I may have been wrong to come to you in the first place, but no one twisted your arm . . ."

"Shit!"

"What now?"

"I don't want to hear that. I'm mad, and I'm sick. And your logic is just making me madder." She leaned forward to peer through the windshield. "Turn right at the service station, there. The parking lot's a mile up on the left."

Scott wheeled the long Caddy around the intersection. "Is there anything I can do?"

She cussed again. "You know, a couple's first big argument isn't supposed to be over whether to report a murder to the police."

Scott looked over and saw a twisted smile on Natalie's face. "Mind if I say something mushy?"

"Shit." She shook her head. "Later, okay?"

Scott pointed to a sign that read PARKING FOR RESI-

DENTS AND GUESTS OF SPINNAKER ISLAND; then in smaller print, ALL OTHERS WILL BE TOWED, MUN. ORD. 11-2-36. "I guess we're here."

Natalie pointed to a giant, bearded man in khakis and a blue windbreaker. "And," she said, "I guess that's Frank."

Scott was surprised that island transportation was an open Boston Whaler and not a ferry. The trip, however, proved the wisdom of that choice. A storm front had approached from the west, moving in a northeasterly direction across the forests and cities of Georgia and South Carolina before hitting the Outer Banks. The front lip of that storm churned the channel and slapped the Whaler's bow as they made for Spinnaker Island.

As the tough little boat dipped its way eastward, Natalie called out to the captain. "Will they have a party in this?"

He yelled out over the wind. "Ma'am?"

Now she raised her voice. "There's a storm coming."

"Yes, ma'am."

"Will they have the party tonight if it storms?"

He shook his furry face. "Not for me to say, ma'am. But I'll get you there safe enough. Don't worry about that."

Natalie nodded and moved to a seat in the stern. Scott joined her. "What's wrong?"

She shook her head. "If it storms and they don't have the party, that's going to be a problem. I was counting on the party to get Charles Hunter alone and talk to him about Kate. We need to warn him as soon as possible. I also thought we'd be able to find out some things without having to do quite so much snooping."

Scott looked out at the dark line of the approaching barrier island. "Sometimes snooping is good."

"I guess." Natalie pulled her coat tight around her neck. "But with Bobby around, I'm starting to worry about what might be happening to people when we don't have our eyes on them."

"Our eyes didn't help Dr. Reynolds." Something caught the corner of Scott's eye, and he walked forward to stand beside Captain Frank. "What's that?" Scott pointed, and the captain looked along his outstretched arm.

The bearded man shook his head. "Small boat. Just somebody getting in a little fishin'."

Scott squinted into the wind. "In this?"

The captain laughed. "Hell, man. This ain't nothin'. Just a little chop. Don't worry, folks around here been fishin' these waters their whole lives. Gets any worse, he'll know to head in."

Scott looked hard at the distant boat. "He's headed toward the island."

"Like I said." The captain's patience began to wear. "He'll turn around sure enough if the weather turns bad."

Scott nodded and walked back to rejoin Natalie in the stern.

CHAPTER 43

Scott Thomas sat on a teal bedspread and stared at his feet. They seemed particularly ugly to him. Not that feet are ever pretty.

Natalie interrupted his aesthetic evaluation. "What's the matter?"

"I don't know." He stood and walked to look out a window awash with silver rivulets. They heard thunder rolling in the distance. "Something."

"I understand about not reporting Bobby to the police in Virginia. It's just not time yet."

"No. It's not."

"Scott? What's bothering you? What specifically?"

His eyes were fixed on the streaming panes, not the windswept Atlantic. "A couple of things. One is . . . This is weird, but I'm not sure I believe Bobby killed Click. That stuff about having his hand in the trunk . . . Jeez, maybe he is that crazy. Maybe . . . Hell, I don't know."

"It could be that you don't want to believe it," Natalie said softly.

He nodded, and a heavy silence settled over them. Finally, Scott said, "I keep thinking about Bobby when we were little. He was a tough little kid. Used to butt me with his head when he got mad." He smiled at the memory. "And smart. Bobby could read when he was three.

He had these huge brown eyes." His voice cracked, and Natalie pretended not to notice. "How do eyes like that turn black? It's like the fire . . ." The words didn't come.

Natalie interrupted to pull him out of it. "What was the second thing?"

"Huh?"

"You said a couple of things are bothering you."

"Oh, yeah." Scott cleared his throat. "Timing."

"Timing?"

"Timing." He turned to find her eyes, and a tired smile crept over his face. "I need to think."

"So, think." Natalie stepped forward, raised up on her toes, and kissed him on the nose. "Heck, tell me what's bothering you and I'll think, too."

"No party tonight, right?" He reached out and circled her waist with his hands.

"That's what the saleslady said. But we're invited to Charles Hunter's home tomorrow night for dinner. Kind of to make up for it, I think."

"Okay." He looked down into her eyes. "I'm going to do some doodling on a piece of paper. It's how I think. Could you have another look at the e-mails I printed off at the hospital? There were a couple from Click to an address outside the psych department."

"Right. I couldn't find anything on those. They didn't follow usual protocol for assigning in-house addresses. And yes, I'd be glad to have another look." She smiled and reached up to brush his cheek with the backs of her fingers. "Cannonball told you to slow down and think. So, we're slowing down and thinking." Natalie pulled away and walked over to rummage through her case. "Do they have room service in this place?"

Charles Hunter hung up the phone in his office just as Carol Petring strode in. With the quiet familiarity of people who work together for hours a day, he went on with his thoughts while she perched a hip on a metal stool and started flipping through drawings on his drafting table.

Seconds ticked by as Carol perused drawings and Charles simply stared into space. Finally, his eyes snapped into focus as if he'd made up his mind about something. "What are you looking for?"

Carol didn't look up. "I'll find it."

"Can it wait?"

"Sure."

As she walked out, he said, "Close the door behind you." It wasn't rude. Just familiar.

Alone again, Charles looked down at the two names he'd just printed in architectural lettering on the pad in front of him. The letters were all caps, the slant and angles of each stroke a mix of flair and precision. Charles drew rectangles in the corners of the pad and connected each by a straight line, then he scratched diagonals across each connecting line. He was trying to make a decision. Finally, he picked up the phone and spoke to his assistant. "Maria, get me Michael Marion at Boston Hospital. He's chairman of their management board."

A few minutes later, his phone beeped and he picked up. Mike Marion's voice came over the line. "Charles?"

"Mike, how are you?"

"Fine, fine." His voice held no affection for anyone. "What can I do for you?"

Charles picked up the note pad from his desk. "I've just this minute learned that two of your employees—Scott Thomas and a woman named Natalie Friedman—are here on the island."

Marion's words came quickly now. "You should call the police immediately. Do you know . . . Well, of course you know who Thomas is. Apparently this Friedman woman was with Thomas the other night when Dr.

Phillip Reynolds was gunned down right outside the hospital. The police actually interviewed them at the scene and let them go."

Charles had turned his chair to face the big bayside window. Charcoal clouds rolled toward him in layered bunches, casting shadows across dark water. "Right, I'll make that call. But tell me first, what's the status of the investigation into my wife's murder?"

"I, uh, really don't know details, Charles. Just—"

"Then give me someone who does." He paused. "I need that information now, Mike. Do you understand?"

The chairman of Boston Hospital could afford to register irritation at being ordered around by Charles Hunter. He could not, however, afford to ignore that order. After all, he was speaking with a man who had donated his services to design an award-winning children's wing. "I'll have someone call you within the hour." Mike Marion's words were distinct and well spaced, conveying irritation combined with power. He might have to comply with Hunter's request, but he wanted it known that he had the power to make people jump in Boston.

"Thank you, Mike." Charles tried to smooth things out a bit. "This is a difficult situation."

"Right" was all the other man said. Then he hung up.

Fifteen minutes later, the hospital's general counsel was on the phone with Hunter. It was not a comforting report. The investigation was wavering. Scott Thomas had given a detailed account of his movements and theories when he'd been arrested in Boston. And, according to the officer in charge of the investigation, Thomas's story was checking out. Worse. Some assistant DA named Anne Foucher had taken a personal interest in the case. Word was, Thomas had so pissed off this Foucher woman that she was on a vendetta. Unfortunately, "The more she digs, the more loose ends and problems she finds. And"—the attorney paused—"I'm hesitant to mention this . . ."

"Mention what?" Hunter's irritation was growing.

"Mike Marion tells me that Scott Thomas is there on the island with a woman named Natalie Friedman. She was arrested with Thomas in Boston."

"I know."

"Well, one of my contacts in the Boston PD says there's a rumor in the department that Friedman struck some kind of deal with them."

"What kind of deal?"

"*Allegedly,* she agreed to keep an eye on Thomas for the police. But I don't even know if the rumor is fact. And, even if it is, Friedman could've simply told the cops whatever they wanted to hear just to get back out on the street. That's why I wasn't sure whether to tell you about it."

Hunter swiveled around to face his view of the Atlantic. His head was swimming; the room seemed to be closing in. He thought of Scott Thomas sitting in a guest cottage just up the road; he thought of what had been brought into his perfect paradise; and his hands began to shake. "What would be the reaction of the cops if Thomas just fell off the face of the earth?"

"I'm sure you don't mean . . ."

"Answer the question."

"Well, this is just my opinion, Mr. Hunter. But if something happened to Scott Thomas right now, I think we'd all—the hospital, Kate Billings, and even you—we'd all find ourselves in the middle of a giant shit storm."

Obviously this man knew that Kate was working for him, and that did not make Charles happy. He'd never even heard this lawyer's name, and the guy knew who Charles had baby-sitting his daughter. He rolled the new information around in his head and said, "Thank you."

"It's just possible that Scott Thomas didn't kill your wife, Mr. Hunter. Misdirected revenge is a waste."

"Why don't you have that printed on your business cards?" He slammed the receiver down.

Thoughts tumbled through his mind—snapshots of Kate nursing him after he kicked Patricia's ashes into the Atlantic, gauzy mental pictures of the nanny tickling Sarah at dinner, slow-motion reels of that beautiful young woman pulling away her nightgown and lowering herself onto him. He thought of Patricia and what she had done to Trey, to *his* son. Everyone had forgotten about that. The bitch had checked into Boston Hospital after *his* only son had drowned. *Goddammit!* The woman had destroyed Trey's life. Ruined his life. She kept ruining his life. *Goddammit!*

He looked up to find his assistant standing in the open door to his office. She looked frightened. "Are you okay?"

Charles froze in place. Somehow he had gotten to his feet and gotten his hands on a brass desk lamp. The big plate-glass window overlooking the Atlantic was spider-webbed with cracks; the lamp lay at the base of the window. He had no memory of throwing the lamp, not even of hearing it crash against the glass.

"Charles? Are you okay? Can I get you something?"

He struggled to control his breathing as the room swirled around him. "It's okay, Maria. It's okay." He decided on a partial truth. "I just got a call about the murder investigation in Boston. It's . . . upsetting."

Maria walked forward. "Of course it is. Sit down, Charles. I'll bring you a cup of coffee."

"Thank you." As she turned to leave, he sank into the chair. "Maria?"

"Sir?"

"Is my guest here?"

"The contractor from Boston?"

"Yeah." He nodded. "That's the one."

"Yes, sir. We put him in the Beckers' place. They're

on the mainland for a few days, and you didn't want him in the guest cottages."

"Right. Could you get me that number? And, uh, you can forget the coffee. Just the number, please."

Maria wrinkled her forehead and said, "Yes, sir. Won't be a minute."

Scott sat at a painted wooden table on the porch of their cottage. Cold mist sprayed over the legal pad in his lap. Wind ruffled the pages, and he absentmindedly smoothed out his notes. He'd been at it for a couple of hours. The sky was dark. A yellow bulb burned on the wall behind him.

"Got anything?"

He looked up bleary eyed. "Something, yeah. Nothing concrete."

Natalie had put on fresh makeup and a heavy sweater. She pulled the sweater tight around her ribs as the crossed the porch to sit opposite Scott at the little table. Leaning forward, she said, "Tell me."

Scott looked up into her bright, intelligent eyes. "You look happy."

"I am. Yours truly has had some success with the e-mails. But I want to hear first what you've come up with."

"Okay." He placed the pad facedown on his lap, not to hide his notes but because he didn't need them. "The timing of everything that's happened has always bothered me. First, two gangbangers broke into my apartment and stole information out of my Palm Pilot. Then there was the phone call from some unidentified person at the hospital the night Patricia Hunter was killed. So, okay, somebody's trying to set me up. That's simple enough. Especially when you put it together with the country house that Cannonball and I found with all the porno on the walls."

She interrupted. "And on your computer at work."

"Right. Make it nasty, and everyone will abandon the little orphan boy."

Natalie pushed her hair back with one hand and laughed. "Little orphan boy with a trust fund and a Harvard education."

Scott smiled. "I wasn't trying to sound pitiful. Just telling why Kate and Click thought it would work. I have no real family. And who else stands by perverts who smother older women in their sleep?"

Natalie leaned back away from him and squirmed in her chair. "God."

"Sorry. But what I'm getting to is this—when I outlined everything that had been done to frame me, which I thought was almost overkill, Click just laughs and says there was nothing to it. Something to the effect of 'all we did was make a few calls, break into your crib a couple of times, and put some porno in a rented house.'"

Natalie was leaning toward him again, focusing—both elbows propped on the table, her cheeks resting on closed fists. "So . . . I'm trying here, Scott. But I don't see . . ."

"I think Click was telling the truth," Scott said. "He was planning to kill me at the time, so why lie?"

She sat back in exasperation. "I still don't get your point."

"I'm not there yet."

"Well, get there."

"Sorry. This is it. Click didn't know about Bobby. But Bobby knew about him and about Cannonball and about me. And look at when my long-lost brother decides to show up. Right at the point in my life when I've been accused of murder. Right when I need help. Think about it. What was it? Destiny? Karma? I don't believe in that stuff."

Natalie shook her head. "Neither do I."

"So what's that leave?"

"Maybe somebody brought Bobby into the picture. Maybe . . . hell, I don't know."

"Well"—Scott stood again—"I still think that someone higher up in the world than Click was pulling strings."

"Kate?"

He shook his head. "Remember Dr. Reynolds? We were supposed to be standing out there with him. No. No way. Both Click and Kate wanted us dead. I mean, we don't know for sure it was Click, but you'll never convince me . . ."

Natalie stood and walked over to stand facing Scott. "Me, either." She slapped her head. "God! The other e-mails to the hospital. Come inside. I need to show you something."

CHAPTER 44

The courtesy golf cart bounced and weaved over the island's sandy roads. Natalie sat in the passenger seat, a nylon windbreaker zipped up tight over a sweater and jeans. Scott manned the tiny steering wheel.

"I feel like a dork."

Natalie looked over in the dark and grinned. His curls were soaked, his glasses misted with rainwater. "You look like a dork."

"Thanks." He came to a jolting stop at a wooden street sign and leaned forward to peer through dripping lenses. "Which way?"

She shone a tiny penlight on a map of the island. "Right . . . I think."

"You sure?"

"Sort of."

Scott turned right. Five minutes later, Charles Hunter's house came into view. Scott slowed, then pulled off the road to guide the cart around a dune to a clump of seagrass and brambles. They both stepped out without speaking. Natalie, whose vision was better even when it wasn't raining, led the way. Staying low, she cut alongside the last fifty yards of roadway before turning off to the right away from Hunter's house.

It was a beautiful place. Copper roof and weathered

cedar. Leaded glass and stonework. The yard was softly
lit by glowing globes of varying sizes—like some alien
life-form had deposited giant, luminescent eggs among
the rock outcroppings and natural flows of vegetation
surrounding the house. It was just enough. Strange and
beautiful.

Natalie hunkered behind a rock. "It's too well
lighted. They're gonna see us if we go up there."

Scott nodded. "If anybody's looking."

"Would 'duh' be an inappropriate—"

"Do you sit in your living room at night watching
outside for peeping Toms or burglars or some other kind
of bad guy?"

"Well"—Natalie sighed—"no."

"Neither does anyone else. They'll watch the sea, if
anything. Maybe glance out at the front drive once in a
while if they're expecting someone."

"So you've done this before?"

"It's just human nature."

She shrugged, and Scott trotted off to approach the
house from the darkest side. It was easy enough. No one
lights the side of a house next to a child's bedroom, not
unless they like torturing a sleepy kid. In minutes, he
was beside the house and looking through an open
window.

A little girl sat cross-legged on the floor of her bedroom. A dozen pages of notebook paper were spread out
around her. She leaned forward and marked in a text-
book with a highlighter.

Easing carefully along the outside wall, Scott
ducked under her window and made it to just outside
the living room. The glass door was open. Music floated
out, mixing with the sounds of rain and surf.

The only thing that saved him was Kate calling out
through the open door. "Charles?"

Less than five paces to Scott's left, a male voice answered. "Is it time?"

"You said eight, right?"

Scott began easing backward. He'd gotten close because the storm covered his footfalls. He hit a shadowed corner where two walls formed an inside angle, and he squatted down to watch.

The dark form of Charles Hunter rose up on the stone patio. He paused and looked out at the ocean, then placed a tumbler on a table before turning to go inside. Just outside the glass door, the famous architect paused and turned back toward the beach. "Is that you?"

Scott could hear his own heartbeat. He tried not even to breathe.

Again, "Is that you? Answer me."

Scott could see Hunter's face now. The man's hair was plastered against his skull. Water ran from the tip of his nose and dripped from thick eyebrows. His pants, beneath the protection of a green slicker, were soaked. Scott wondered why Hunter had been drinking alone on his patio, in the pouring rain, without an umbrella or hat. He studied the man's features. Tension tugged at Hunter's voice when he spoke. Lines cut worried paths in his tanned face.

Seconds passed. Finally, Hunter stepped inside, then closed and locked the glass door.

That was enough. Scott made good time getting back to the dark side of the house, and he was getting ready for a dash across the roadway when the engine of Hunter's ragtop Jeep roared to life.

Headlights swept the house, and Scott dropped onto his stomach in wet sand. In no time, Hunter was past the spot where they had hidden the golf cart, and Scott started to run. He hoped Natalie would understand enough to meet him back at the cart. If she didn't, he wondered if he would still go. Every second counted, since he needed to follow Hunter's Jeep and a golf cart was going to be a pitiful way to do it.

He was in the cart when he saw Natalie running toward him. "Wait!"

Scott spun the cart around and was pointed out toward the road by the time she jumped in beside him. "Hold on."

Scott swerved onto the road and stomped the little electric go-pedal. Natalie reached over to grab his hand. "This is ridiculous. We could run faster than this."

He nodded. "But not as far. Just see if you can tell which way his headlights are going."

"Look!" Natalie pointed off to the right. "He's headed north."

"Good."

"Why good?"

"There's not much on that end of the island yet. We'll be able to find his Jeep."

Scott stopped the tiny cart in the middle of a sandy road. Cool rainwater shot through the cart in gusts, drenching already drenched clothes and sending shivers through both occupants. "See anything?"

Natalie shook her head.

"Know where we are?"

"Nope."

"Mad?"

"I was sitting right here with you. I got us here as much as you did." She got out of the cart and walked around. She cussed and got back in. As she sat down, Natalie pointed down the twin beams of their head-lights. "Look."

A thin man walked slowly toward the cart. He was fifty feet away and strolling through the thunderstorm like it was a sunny afternoon. Scott squinted through misted glasses. "It looks like Bobby."

"Are you sure?"

He shook his head. "No."

"Can we get the hell out of here, then?"

Scott hesitated, and Natalie called out his name. He stepped on the accelerator and turned the cart.

A hoarse voice cut through the wind and rain, the way a rusty hinge creaking open slices into conversation and thought. "I know where he is."

Scott cut the lights back toward the approaching figure. "Did you hear that? I think it's Bobby."

Natalie grew even more frantic as she recognized Scott's scarred and lonely brother. "Scott!"

Bobby was only twenty feet away now. His rusty voice came again. "I'll take you to him."

Natalie grabbed Scott's arm, and he stepped on the go-pedal. The little cart began to move away down the road. Natalie looked back and gasped.

Scott tried a backward glance. "What's he doing? Is he running after us?"

Her nails dug into Scott's arm.

"Dammit, Natalie. Is he coming?"

"No." Her grip relaxed. "He's just standing there alone in the rain. He looks . . ."

Scott leaned into the rain trying to get a better view of the road. "What? He looks what?"

"Sad. I don't know why, but he somehow looks sad standing there in the storm."

As they crested a small hill, Scott saw the lights of the town square in the distance. Twenty minutes later, they were back in the guest cottage and the message light on the phone was blinking. Scott dialed voice mail. It was Cannonball. The message was simple. "Somebody else's been down here lookin' into your family. Some time back, right around when all this mess started. Bobby took off right after that. Probably didn't know you were alive, either. Not till then. Thought you might wanna know. Oh, sorry to tell you like this, but your little brother has killed at least one person in his life. Spent time in some kinda nut house for doin' it. Be careful."

That night, Scott and Natalie showered together to wash away the chill. They cuddled under the homemade quilts that came with the cottage. They listened for Scott's brother and for Kate Billings and for any noise that didn't fit the night. They did not make love. They lay very still and listened.

CHAPTER 45

Spinnaker Island had one hotel—a vaguely Victorian affair with stylized trim and a decent restaurant. At least according to the sales rep, the place was pretty good. So, around eleven, Scott and Natalie eschewed the mud-caked golf cart in favor of a leisurely stroll into town.

It really was a beautiful place.

Planned developments tend to go one of two ways—big chunks of brick and stucco on postage-stamp lots or overly cute gingerbread cottages with happily painted birdhouses and cute cottages with names over the doors. But Charles Hunter had gotten this one just right. The center of this otherwise sparsely developed island looked like an early-American village. There was a town square surrounded by medical offices, two banks, one bookstore, and half a dozen small markets and shops. The town hall—an imposing structure at the head of the square—was balanced by the hotel at the other end. In between, children played on jungle gyms and people of all ages ate lunches on concrete picnic tables—too many people, in fact, for them all to be residents. It seemed that Charles Hunter's island had become something of a day-trip destination for Carolina mainlanders.

The designers had valued the imperfect in pursuing perfection. The playground wasn't hidden behind a building or a clump of trees. And, while the design of the buildings clearly had a central guiding hand, they were different enough in materials and design to make the place look real. No carpets of delicate lawn or mani-cured beds of roses here. The grass was made for run-ning on and the plants looked as though they'd grown undisturbed there for decades.

Spinnaker Island wasn't cute. It just looked the way an American town should, but probably never had.

It took only minutes to get a table. When they were seated and had ordered iced tea, Natalie asked if it was her turn.

Scott scanned the gaggle of happy faces around the other tables. "What do you mean?"

"We've been talking about *timing* all day. I want to tell you about my discoveries."

Scott turned so that he could watch the entrance to the restaurant.

"Hello?"

His eyes moved to Natalie's face. "Sorry."

She smiled. "I want to talk about me now."

His eyes moved over her face, and he smiled back. "You said you broke the code in the e-mails, but the lists of numbers were nothing but addresses."

"That's what I mean." She took a sip of tea, tore open a third pack of sugar, and dumped it in. "You get to go on and on about timing and guiding influences, and I get one sentence to describe brilliance."

"Sorry. Tell me."

It was a lot like listening to Peter Budzik describing how he discovered Click's identity on the Internet. The thought sent chills through Scott's gut. The last time he'd seen Budzik, the little hacker had been lying naked in bed with his throat cut. But Natalie was not Budzik.

She stopped in midsentence. "Are you all right? You look awful."

Scott drank some tea. In his mind's eye, he had been thinking of the night before and picturing Bobby, standing alone in the rain and watching his big brother drive away as if fleeing a monster. He shook his head to clear the picture. "Sorry. A lot of bad things have happened . . ."

She tried to change the subject, but Scott wanted to know what she'd found and how she'd found it. It could be important, he said.

She looked pleased. "Okay, here it is. I cheated. After staring at a list of numbers for an hour, I called a friend at Boston College. I told him what I had—a list of numbers separated by commas and spaces and with every few numbers in bold. Apparently, Click ain't all that original. My friend said it's an old encryption trick. The bold numbers—and the first number in every e-mail was bolded—tell how many keys to count on the keyboard before starting the code. For example, if the first number is, say, seventeen, you'd start at the upper left key on the keyboard—the one with that squiggly thing at the top—and count across and down until you come to the 'e.' I remember that one. Anyway, the 'e' in this case would be the key to the rest of the numbers. If the next number is a six, you don't start back over at the top. You just count over six letters from the 'e,' which"—she looked at the ceiling and squinted—"I believe is an 'o.' Then if the next number is a four, you back up to the 'e' and count over to the 'y.' " The next word starts with the next bold number."

Scott said one word. "Cool." And he meant it.

"Yeah." She grinned. "It kind of is."

"But you said the addresses didn't mean anything to you."

An effeminate man came over and took their orders. When he left, Scott asked, "Do you remember any of the addresses?"

She reached down and grabbed her purse. "They're right here. Have a look."

He scanned down the list and cussed. "Well, the fifth one is mine."

"Oops."

"Yeah. I forgot you've never been to my apartment in Cambridge." He studied the other addresses. Most were near the hospital, but otherwise they meant nothing to him. He handed the list back to Natalie as the waiter placed two salads on the table.

The food was good. Scott tried to make pleasant conversation—to divert Natalie's mind and his own from the task at hand. But when the meal was done and Natalie had ordered coffee, he told her he had to go. "Bobby wanted to talk to me last night. I need to go back and try to find him."

Natalie's expression never changed, but the skin around her mouth turned pale. "He scares me, Scott. Do you really have to . . ." Her voice trailed off, the answer obvious.

"I'll be careful."

Natalie laughed, but there was no humor in it. "Bull. I haven't known you that long, but 'careful' is not how I'd describe you."

Scott got up from the table. "Stay in town, okay?"

She looked puzzled.

"Around lots of people."

"Oh."

He said, "Back soon," and headed off across the town green.

Charles Hunter had not gone to work that morning. Now he sat in his usual chair on the patio and watched Sarah play on the beach. At not quite noon, he was already drinking. His only bow to propriety being in the form of a Bloody Mary rather than his usual single-malt.

Kate sat on the rock-strewn sand near Sarah. Charles called out for her, and both girls came. He smiled at his daughter. "I've got some grown-up talk to do with Kate. Run along and play for a few minutes."

"I want to stay and listen."

He shook his head. "Go on, now. I mean it."

Sarah kicked at the ground and wandered slowly back out on the beach. Charles waited patiently until she was out of earshot.

He motioned at a chair. "Please. Sit down."

Kate managed to walk just a little too close to her boss as she crossed to the chair and draped one suntanned leg carefully over the other. When she was comfortable, the nanny looked into his eyes. "What is it, Charles?"

He took a long pull at his drink and plunked it down on the table. "How long have we known each other, Kate?"

She smiled. "You and I became friends about six . . . no, seven months ago. It was just before the dedication of the new children's wing at the hospital."

"Right."

"Everyone was talking about the famous architect Charles Hunter who had donated his services to help the hospital." She reached over to gently place her fingertips on his forearm. Just a quick touch. "I asked Dr. Reynolds to introduce us."

"Even then," he said, "we talked about your coming here to the island to work for me, either as a nanny or for one of the physicians on the square." He picked up his glass and looked into it, then put it back on the table. "You were very understanding after Trey died. I don't know if I've ever told you, Kate, how much I appreciated your concern. Then you managed to get assigned to Patricia—to keep me up to speed on what was happening." He paused. "You understood what she had done to my family."

Kate reached over and squeezed his arm. "She seduced Trey, her own son. Even if it was by marriage. She was his mother, and she drove the poor kid to—"

"Kate . . ."

"No. I won't stop. Patricia was a horrible person. You made that clear to me, and everything I saw at the hospital only confirmed your worst stories about her." She leaned forward to look into his eyes. "I shouldn't say this, but I'm glad she's dead, Charles. And you shouldn't feel guilty. Not one bit. You checked out Scott Thomas. Found out all about his childhood and his family. You told me about him, about how concerned you were that he might harm Patricia. And you could've had him fired—an important man like you—but . . ." A bright fire burned in her eyes. "Let's just say we're both better off. The woman who dirtied your son is dead. You're free, and I have a whole new life."

"You're going to have to leave here, Kate."

Her face flushed. "What?" She caught her tone and softened it. "Have I done something to upset you? I'm sorry I brought up Patricia's abuse of poor Trey. That I talked about what she . . . what she drove him to do."

Charles concentrated on her face. Kate was a hard woman to read, and he knew he'd only see flashes of any real emotions. "Your friend Click is on the island."

"Who?" She never missed a beat.

"Click. Darryl Simmons. I met with him last night. That's where I had to go at eight. The man you hired to kill my wife. He's here on the island."

Kate began to cry. The tears were real. "Charles, I don't know how you can say—"

"Scott Thomas is here, too."

Now her mouth turned hard. "Goddammit, Charles. How can you allow that murderer to be here in your special place? He's the one who killed poor Patricia. The cops have already—"

He cut her off. "The police are having problems with the case against Thomas." He killed the watery remains of vodka-laced tomato juice and looked hard into Kate's eyes. "He's staying in one of the guest cottages. I talked to people who *know* in Boston. I mean really *know* what's going on. And the cops are coming, Kate. The only reason they're not here already is the time it's taking to get arrest warrants.

"Look." He reached out, put an index finger under her chin, and tilted her face up toward his. "I'm only telling you the facts. What you do with them is your business."

Kate's eyes bounced around the yard and sky, her brain spinning like a rat's exercise wheel. "What if the police clear me?"

His voice was calm. "They won't if they find Scott."

"You mean . . ."

"You can come back if you're cleared, Kate. I'd be wrong to say anything else. But there has to be *nothing* linking you with Patricia's death. Do you understand, Kate? Do you *understand* what I'm saying?"

Kate wiped at tears with her fingertips. Her pupils focused into pinpoints. "Tell me this. Where is this Click person supposed to be? Where is this person who you say killed Patricia?"

Charles Hunter leaned back in his chair and looked out at the Atlantic Ocean. "He's staying in the Beckers' house out on Gull Way."

"What if I—"

He held up a palm to stop her. "I've said too much already. Now, go."

* * *

Scott wandered over the sandy island road in a general northerly direction. The perfume of approaching spring, mixed with the scents of salt and sea, filled his lungs. The sun warmed his shoulders; he pulled off his windbreaker and tied it around his waist like a kid in school.

The island wasn't the flat mix of sand and sea grass, briars and twisted pines he'd seen on Florida's barrier islands. This place seemed older—not because of any structure but because of the stones and trees, the rough beaches and outcroppings of rock. The road rose up before him, and Scott worked up a light sweat getting to the top of the hill overlooking the village.

Up ahead a hundred yards or so was where he'd seen his brother, standing alone in the storm and talking about knowing where *he* was. Who the hell was *he*?

The road here was rough—a smooth finish waiting on more development on this end of the island. Scott's eyes scanned the dusty roadway, searching for an easy path among the washouts and fist-size stones that pocked and pebbled his path.

The spot came and went, and Bobby did not appear. Minutes passed with nothing but the twin ruts of the road to show humans had ever been on this part of the island. Then he saw it. A small stone house squatted in a dip between two dunes. Scraggy rocks, the same color as those naturally poking out into the Atlantic, had been stacked into an old-fashioned, New England–style stone wall surrounding the property.

Scott's heart beat faster. He told himself that it was only a house, and a nice house at that. The kind of place he could be comfortable. The kind of place . . . He rounded a turn, the far side of the house came into view, and Scott felt reality melting away. Parked on the shell drive was his Land Cruiser—the same Land Cruiser he'd left in Boston days before. His knees buckled.

It was a little thing, and it wasn't. The presence of

his old four-by-four was the last punch in a series of blows to his life, to his privacy, maybe even to his view of what the world was supposed to be.

Scott stopped to catch his breath. He put his hands on his knees and looked down at the ground. When he looked back up, all sense of being violated and overwhelmed morphed into pure white anger. Someone was in that house who had messed in his life. Someone who had taken a lot of things that were his—not physical things, but things he had built through hard work, determination, and, too often, endless hours of loneliness.

A figure moved at one of the windows, and Scott began walking toward the front door.

CHAPTER 46

Bobby Thomas stepped out of a heavy front door and said one word. "Stop."

Scott kept walking.

Bobby's scarred features never changed expression. "I said stop."

Scott walked until he was within three feet of his brother. "Whose house is this?"

"Doesn't matter."

"It matters to me. And it matters to you, too, or you'd tell me."

"Some people named Becker. They're gone off somewhere else. Don't even know I'm here."

"Okay." Scott pointed to the driveway. "Then who stole my Land Cruiser?"

"Nobody. I drove it. I'm your brother."

It was almost a touching statement. Almost. Scott's eyes searched the man's melted features. He looked for something familiar in those dark eyes. "I know who you are. How'd you get the car over here on the island?"

Bobby just shrugged. "You should leave." He paused, then added, "I'm trying to do you a favor."

"Would you leave if you were me?" Scott waited for an answer but got none. He glanced over Bobby's shoulder. "Click's not dead, is he?"

The younger Thomas seemed almost ready to smile, the effort made his left eyelid spasm. Again, he shrugged.

"Why the act in Virginia?"

"I wanted you to know that Click wouldn't bother you anymore." Then he added, "You're my brother," as if that explained everything.

Scott shook his head. "If he's not dead . . . He's inside the house, isn't he?" Again there was no response. He pushed ahead. "What about his hand? You said you had Click's hand in the trunk. What would you have done if I'd wanted it for fingerprints, the way you said?"

Bobby sighed. His jaw tightened, his right hand formed a fist, and the thick muscles in both shoulders bunched. Then, just as quickly, he seemed to change his mind about something and relax. Finally, he said, "That's not you. People like you and that Natalie girl don't want to see cut-off hands."

"So you didn't . . ."

He shook his head.

"But Click *was* in your trunk."

Bobby nodded. "He was gonna kill you. And the girl."

"And you thought offering up a chopped-off hand would make me feel better."

Bobby looked again as though he might actually smile. "It's funny when you say it like that."

"Who killed Peter Budzik?"

"Who?"

"Budzik. The bald hacker who lived in the warehouse in Boston. That first time you ran off Click, I went upstairs and found Budzik with his throat cut."

Bobby looked bored. "Wasn't me. That Click was up there before you came. I didn't follow him in."

Scott examined the shiny, scarred face, trying with every skill he'd developed as an analyst to determine if his brother was telling the truth, but all the usual minutia of expression and nonverbal communication had been burned away years ago. "Can you tell me—"

"That girl okay?"

It took Scott a few seconds to figure out that Bobby was asking about Cindy Travers, Budzik's abused girlfriend. "The girl Click beat up?"

Bobby nodded.

"I hope so. I called an ambulance." He paused. "She's pretty screwed up."

"Everybody's screwed up." Bobby shrugged. "Anyway, you need to leave. At six o'clock tonight, Click and Kate are going to be here." He hesitated. "I don't know whether to tell you this, or how to say it. But they're coming here for me to kill them."

Scott's heart popped hard against his sternum. He tried to sound calm. "They sound like unusually cooperative people."

The scarred young man made a gurgling sound deep in his chest that was supposed to be laughter. "Funny."

"Thanks a lot, but . . ."

"Leave here now and it'll all be over tonight. You'll be clear. I made a deal."

"A deal with whom?" Scott looked down at the stone walkway.

"With *whom*?" He made a gurgling chuckle. "I slipped away from Click last night a few hours after we got to the island. Then"—he chuckled—"surprise. While I was watching, the man who set up all this came to see him."

"Who?"

Bobby shook his head. "The man who worked everybody around so the Hunter woman would get murdered. Smart guy. Knows how to handle people. I walked in on him and Click. Had a talk. Pulled him outside for some privacy and got offered a deal."

"And this unnamed man just told you everything you wanted to know."

A thin grin spread across his face. "I had Click explain my . . . my motivations to him. Then I just had to hurt the guy a little, and he hollered like a cat bird."

Scott looked hard into Bobby's black eyes. "Why are you doing this?"

He shrugged. "What?"

"Putting yourself at risk? Locking Click in your trunk? Threatening some guy who you claim set me up for Patricia Hunter's murder?"

"I like it. I like . . . handling people." He paused. "And I like hurting people who need it."

"Why are you helping me?"

"You're my brother."

Scott examined his sibling's melted face. "It's that simple?"

"Everything's simple."

Scott turned to look off down the road. "Is this guy you made a deal with the 'him' you mentioned last night? What happened since last night when you were standing up there on the road? You said last night that you'd take us to 'him,' whoever the hell 'he' is."

"No, I didn't."

"Hell, yes, you did." Scott pointed over his shoulder. "Standing right back there on the road. You said, 'I know where he is,' and something like you'd take us to him."

"Wasn't me." Bobby paused for three beats and made the gurgling sound again. "Just fuckin' with you. See, I'm funny, too. Now." Bobby squared off in front of his brother. "You need to leave. I don't want to hurt you, but I will." He paused. "Now go."

Scott breathed deeply. He wanted to lash out. But what he wanted wouldn't help him or Natalie. So he turned and walked to the edge of the yard before turning back. "What if I call the cops?"

Bobby shrugged. It was his most consistent communication. All he said was "Call 'em."

"Or I could go see Charles Hunter. He's got security people here on the island."

Bobby froze and a veil seemed to drop over his waxy features.

"It's Hunter, isn't it?" Pieces of the puzzle that had never fit started to fall into place inside Scott's head. "You made a deal with Hunter."

Bobby didn't answer. He turned and walked back through the front door. The door shut, and Scott heard a dead bolt slide home.

The older Thomas brother stood at the stone wall for a long time and watched the house. When he couldn't think of anything useful to do there, he turned and started back to town. As he mounted the hill overlooking the town square, Scott saw a convertible Jeep heading toward him. He stepped aside as the tires skidded to a stop.

Captain Frank, the man who'd met Natalie and him on the mainland and brought them out to the island, jumped from the driver's seat. "Nothing serious, sir. But the lady's been in a minor accident."

"Natalie? Are you telling me that Natalie's hurt?"

"Like I said, nothing major. But she would like to see you." The bearded captain pointed at the Jeep. "Hop in. I'll have you there in nothing flat."

The doors had been removed. Scott jumped onto the passenger seat, the captain swung in beside him, and they roared off together down the hill. Scott was so upset that he didn't notice that the Jeep wasn't heading toward the medical offices in town or toward their guest cottage. No. Scott was less than a quarter mile from Charles Hunter's house when he figured out where he was.

He raised his voice over the wind and engine noise. "Why are we going to Mr. Hunter's house?" Captain

Frank's eyes were glazed over. It was a question he didn't want to answer. Scott saw two security guards in the driveway ahead, and he grabbed the edge of his door. "Answer me!"

The bearded man turned. "It's where she is. That's all I know." His eyes moved to check out Scott's grip on the door frame. "You jump and there's just gonna be two of you hurt. What're you gonna do, leave her there alone? Asking for you?"

By that time, the Jeep was only yards from the driveway. Frank braked, and Scott sprang from the passenger door. He stumbled; the sandy ground came up faster than he'd expected and knocked the wind out of him—a horrible punch in the gut, followed by uncoordinated somersaults through rocks and gravel and jagged seashells.

A basketball-size boulder pounded his right knee just as he got his feet under him. A jolt of pain shot through his leg, and he started to run. But start was all. The two big men in guard uniforms blocked his path. Each carried a sidearm, and each had placed a cautionary hand on the grip of his pistol.

Scott turned to see Captain Frank blocking his path from the rear.

One of the security guards spoke first. "Stop! Stop right there, Mr. Thomas. Nobody's going to hurt you. Your friend Ms. Friedman is inside." The guard held one hand in the air, palm down, and made an up-and-down "be calm" motion. His other hand, though, never left the grip of his handgun.

Scott stopped and bent over to catch his breath. "Okay."

The quieter of the two guards unhooked handcuffs from his utility belt and moved toward Scott. Scott held out his hand now. "Forget it. You aren't putting those on me."

Scott heard fast footsteps behind him. He dropped onto one hand and swept his leg behind him. His shin caught Captain Frank across the instep and sent the bearded man hurling into sand and gravel. Before Frank had stopped rolling, Scott was on his feet and backing away from the guards.

A deep voice came from the yard. "That's not necessary."

The guard with the cuffs turned to look at Charles Hunter. "But, sir. He's already tried to run away. And look what he did to the captain."

Hunter turned to Scott. "Will you come inside without the cuffs?"

"I really don't have a hell of a lot of choice, do I?"

"No." Hunter shook his head. "You really don't."

Scott shrugged, and the realization hit that his dismissive gesture was a mirror image of his brother's favorite communication. "Lead the way."

Natalie sat on a soft leather sofa beneath the vaulted ceiling of Hunter's living room. She didn't look hurt or frightened or overwhelmed. She looked furious.

As Scott stepped into the room with Hunter, Natalie said Scott's name then stood to walk to him.

Hunter hesitated in the doorway. "Sit down, Ms. Friedman."

Natalie never missed a step. "Fuck you, Mr. Hunter." She walked up to Scott, put her arms around his neck, and asked, "Are you all right?"

Scott hugged her, then leaned back to look into her face. "They said you were hurt."

Natalie shook her head. "Jeez. Bunch of idiots told me the same thing about you." She turned to Hunter. "Too much of a strain to make up two stories?"

"You're both here, aren't you?"

As Natalie and Hunter glared at each other, Scott scanned the room. He listened hard for other human sounds in the house. They seemed to be alone. He guided Natalie back to the sofa, where he and she sat down. Scott looked at Hunter. "I have some questions."

Hunter came farther into the room. "I would, too, in your position. But the answers are going to be a while coming, I'm afraid."

Scott leaned back against leather cushions. "I didn't kill your wife, Mr. Hunter."

The architect remained impassive.

Scott tried again. "What do you want?"

Again the older man didn't answer.

Scott felt anger boil up inside. "We're trying to be civilized and discuss this with you. And you're playing at being some kind of tough guy." He sat forward. "If I wanted to, I could break your back before those guards could get through the door. I'm not doing it, but I could."

Hunter walked to the bar and plinked ice cubes into a crystal glass. As he covered the ice with scotch, he said, "I know all about your wrestling days, Scott. I used to be a pretty good lacrosse player myself. But I've got twenty years on you, so . . ." He cocked his head to one side. "I guess you could hurt me pretty badly if you decided to do that." Hunter took in a mouthful of scotch. "But you won't. First of all, Scott, you're an intellectual, not a thug like your brother. And, second, if you hurt me . . ." He cocked his head to the side again. It was his version of a thoughtful shrug. "Well, if you were that foolish, you and Ms. Friedman might find the remainders of your lives brief and depressingly uncomfortable."

Natalie spoke up. "This is kidnapping. You can't keep something like this quiet."

Hunter crossed to a club chair and sat down. "I have no intention of keeping anything quiet." He raised his glass to Scott. "Your boyfriend here is the prime suspect in the murder of my wife. You." He turned to Natalie.

"You're the woman who helped a wanted man escape from the hospital by—and correct me if this isn't true—but I understand you two were halfway to knocking bottoms when the cops busted in."

Scott leaned forward. "There are things short of a broken back. Things that wouldn't bother an intellectual like me in the least."

Hunter chuckled. "Okay, okay. Sorry if I offended the lady's dignity. Anyway, the cops also know the two of you were there when Phil Reynolds was gunned down." He grinned. "Hell, all I've done is capture two criminals who've come here to do me harm and then call the cops."

"You've called the cops?"

He closed one eye. "Not quite yet."

Natalie patted Scott's leg and leaned over to kiss him. As her lips brushed his cheek, she whispered, "I'm scared."

CHAPTER 47

The afternoon sun threw long shadows across the yard outside Charles Hunter's living room windows. Scott looked out and tried to run the events of the past few weeks through his head. He nodded almost imperceptibly at Natalie. "Give me a minute to think." He leaned back and closed his eyes. He visualized a notepad in his head and began to make notes.

Timing

He could see the word floating there in black and white, the lettering in his own scratchy handwriting. The list grew.

Timing
Desire
Kate—Reynolds
Kate—Click
Kate—Charles Hunter

No, that was out of order. He mentally erased the page. Someone said his name, but he stayed inside his mind. The list was right, just out of order. He started over.

Kate—Click
Kate—Charles Hunter
Timing
Desire
Kate—Reynolds
and . . .
Kate—Scott Thomas

Scott heard his name again and opened his eyes. Natalie had a small smile on her face. Hunter was leaning forward in his chair. "What the hell's the matter with you? You need a nap or something?"

The most obvious answer is usually the right one.

Had Hunter provided the guiding hand, the motive, and the timing? Was that forty-something, whisky-soaked man really able to manipulate and corrupt so many people?

Scott cleared his throat. "Who was the first one who got seduced?"

Hunter had a small smile on his face now. "Depends on what you mean by seduced."

"Right." Scott tried hard to sound sure of what he was saying. "I understand that you seduced Kate with your life, with dreams of what her life could be. I just don't know whether you were sleeping with her at the same time she was sleeping with your wife."

Now the architect grew agitated. "Patricia would fuck anything that moved. Man, woman, or—"

"Or her own teenage stepson? Is that what you were going to say?"

Hunter looked out the window at the Atlantic Ocean.

Natalie interrupted. "How do you know that?"

"Kate told me," Scott said. "She said it was a rumor. Maybe she was trying to manipulate me into saying something derogatory about Patricia to Dr. Reynolds. I don't know. And I don't really know whether Kate and

Patricia were getting it on in the hospital. But Patricia didn't strike me as the kind of woman who enjoyed the company of prettier women half her age. There was . . . something between them.

"So." He turned back to Hunter. "You had Kate. And she had Patricia, in a matter of speaking. Now you needed a scapegoat, a . . ."

Hunter said, "A fool. Is that the word you're searching for?"

And there it was. Scott kept pressing. "Nope. Just someone with no support system. Someone who—if you made the evidence condemning enough and disgusting enough—there'd be no one to stand by him. Someone with a criminal history would've been perfect. Maybe a registered sex offender, someone like that. But the hospital did too good a job of screening personnel. So you ended up with me—after you sent somebody to Birmingham to check out my background."

Charles Hunter stood. "Either of you want a drink?"

Scott was still thinking things out and didn't answer. Natalie suggested that Hunter make a rearward insertion of his drink. The architect chuckled and poured another for himself. "Well"—he looked over at Scott—"is that it?"

"No. Reynolds comes in there somewhere. The poor bastard thought Kate was going to leave you and come back to him." Scott stood and began to pace.

"Come back over here beside me." Natalie held out her hand toward Scott, and he walked over and sat beside her. She squeezed his hand. "I've got a question." She took a breath. "What the hell are we waiting on?" Her eyes flickered toward Hunter. "Is he really going to call the cops, or is he going to kill us?"

"No, Natalie. No way. Too many people know we're on the island. Too many people saw us come in here under guard." Scott tried to sound more certain than he

was. "If we die now, acclaimed architect Charles Hunter
gets indicted for murder."

She was starting to look angry again. "Then what the
hell are we doing?"

Scott turned to Hunter. "Waiting for my brother to
kill Kate and Click."

Hunter went pale, but kept quiet. He set his fresh
drink on an end table, sloshing expensive whisky as glass
collided with wood. The architect stood and walked to
the window.

He still hadn't admitted anything.

Scott studied the older man's face. Charles Hunter
may have been an asshole, but he was a brilliant asshole.
If Scott was right, the man had managed to identify and
recruit a beautiful sociopath to plan and organize the
murder of his despised wife. He had set up a nearly flaw-
less frame of Scott for the murder. And when that had
started to fall apart, he'd managed to work out "a deal"
with poor Bobby to clean up his mess.

The architect turned to face them. "Do you know
where this murder is supposedly taking place? Tell me.
I'll go there myself."

And there it was.

No security guards would storm the Beckers' beach
house. No cops would save the day. Charles Hunter
would go himself, and, by the time the sun set on the
perfection of Spinnaker Island, he would have discovered the double murder of Kate and Click.

Scott stood. "I can show you."

Natalie's voice cracked. "No!" The look in her eyes
showed that she understood more than she was letting
on. At the very least, she'd figured out that accompany-
ing Hunter to a scene of violence was a deadly idea.

Charles looked from Natalie to Scott. "I'm not going
for a ride with the man who killed my wife."

Scott sat back down on the sofa. "Up to you" was all he said.

The tensions felt by each person in the room seemed to feed off each other until there was a palpable charge in the air. Scott waited as Charles paced. Finally, when the architect couldn't work out a decent alternative, he said, "Okay. Let's go."

"Natalie goes back to town."

The older man paused. "In the company of my guards."

Scott just wanted her around witnesses. "Not in some back room. Out in public. Take her to the restaurant."

Hunter looked at Natalie. "Will you behave?"

She cut her eyes at Scott. He nodded, and she answered, "I'll behave. Just bring this one"—pointing to Scott's chest—"back to me."

Hunter hobbled to the door, yanked it open, and called in the guards.

When everyone was loaded into the island Jeeps, Scott told Hunter to follow the guards.

"Is the place near town?"

"Just follow them until I tell you different." He didn't think Hunter would hurt them, but he wasn't going anywhere with Charles Hunter until Natalie was around other people.

Hunter understood what Scott was doing. He slowed to a crawl and then stopped a hundred yards outside the town square. "You can see from here." In the distance, the guards pulled up to the restaurant and gently guided Natalie inside. Hunter leaned toward Scott. "Okay?"

"Fine." Scott wondered how long the architect would keep up his ruse. Clearly, Hunter had put Click into the Becker house. He knew where Bobby was even better than Scott. "It must get complicated."

Hunter watched people move around his town. "What's that?"

"Remembering what you're supposed to know. Pretending not to know the thing that could be incriminating."

Hunter looked to the right, past Scott's face. "I don't know what you're talking about." His eyes changed. "What the hell is that?"

Scott's eyes only flicked right for a heartbeat, but that was long enough. Of course there was nothing—nothing but a tire iron across his cheekbone as he turned back toward Hunter. The world rocked from side to side. Hunter's form blurred. Only the iron stayed in perfect focus. Moving in slow motion, as if in a dream, the iron bar reached its pinnacle near the top of the windshield and bounced a little before beginning another downward arc toward his skull. Scott thought of yelling. He almost raised a hand to fight back, but he was hurt. He spun right, pushing hard with his legs.

A jolt of fire shot through his shoulder. Before he could even scream, the ground hit him full in the chest.

The only thought Scott had was "He's going to run over me." Scott rolled hard away from the Jeep. The tires spun, and Charles Hunter was gone.

Struggling to his hands and knees, Scott raised his head to see Hunter speeding away toward the northern end of the island. The young shrink sat back on his haunches and touched his face. The skin felt thick and numb. When he pulled his hand away, the fingers were coated with blood. Scott tried to stand. His legs wobbled but held. The shoulder throbbed but seemed to work.

Scott looked toward town. If he ran into town in that condition, he'd be arrested by Hunter's security force. He looked at the guards' parked vehicle down at the restaurant then turned to watch the receding Jeep of Charles Hunter.

He made the only decision available to him. Scott turned his back on the town and started to run.

CHAPTER 48

Charles Hunter's mind spun as fast as the wheels on his Jeep. He ran over future scenarios in his head, then rolled memory clips of every conversation he'd ever had with Kate, Click, and, now, Bobby Thomas. He was certain he'd never promised Kate anything, never asked her to harm anyone. He'd said even less to Click and Bobby. That wasn't how he worked. Charles Hunter had always been able to get people to do what he wanted—*whatever* he wanted—without asking.

Some people can play the piano. Some carry a football with grace and power and beauty and don't understand how or why they can do it. Charles Hunter's gift was more subtle. He had never asked anyone for anything. It just came when he wanted it.

The hill was just ahead now. Soon he would pull into the driveway of the Beckers' house and confront a horrible scene.

His wheels slid on the shell drive, and the door of the house swung open. Charles stepped out of the Jeep expecting to see Bobby's shining mask peeking out. But there was nothing. Just an open door.

Hunter had no intention of stepping inside that house, not without knowing exactly what had happened.

He would sooner climb back into the Jeep and deal with whatever scenario unfurled down the road.

"Who's there?"

No answer came. Hunter already had one foot in the Jeep when two figures appeared in the doorway. Bobby's plastic features shone over Kate's shoulder. Her face was drawn tight, her eyes round with fear. A knife was at her throat.

"Help me, Charles."

"Where's Click?"

Kate's voice was half an octave higher than usual. "He's dead."

"Who killed him?"

She didn't answer. Bobby said, "Come inside."

Hunter examined Bobby's face, then his eyes slid down and lingered on the tight ligaments along the back of Bobby's right hand—the one holding the knife. "Don't kill her. I don't know what she's done to Scott, but you don't want to commit murder to save him."

Bobby's blank eyes flickered over Hunter's face, and something that might have been a smile twisted the scarred slit that was his lips. His knife hand flicked hard across Kate's throat, and he spun her body onto the floor.

"I'm leaving."

Charles held his hands out to his sides, palms open toward Bobby. "I won't try to stop you."

Bobby turned to toss the knife inside the house, then he stepped out into the yard and continued to walk toward Hunter. "Yeah, I know you won't. I'm taking Scott's Cruiser."

"I don't think you should do that. If you get caught . . ."

Bobby climbed into the old Land Cruiser and cranked the engine. He dropped the transmission into reverse, backed up, and stopped next to Hunter. "You better pray I don't get caught."

"I—"

"Shut up." His black irises bored into Hunter's eyes. "You think I got nothing to tell. Maybe. Maybe not. But I'll still come see you. Might take a year. Might take ten years. But I'll come. And you can't handle what I'd do." Bobby paused. "Tell me you understand."

Hunter's mouth was too dry to answer. He nodded.

"Good. Now go inside. You got what you wanted. Go inside and figure out how to handle it. If it was me, I'd go with the 'Click cut Kate's throat after she shot him' story. But"—he gave his characteristic shrug—"that's up to you."

Bobby let out on the clutch and backed the old four-by-four out onto the roadway. Seconds later, the only trace that Bobby Thomas had ever been there—other than the bodies inside—were two parallel clouds of white dust hovering over the road.

Scott's legs ached and wobbled. His lungs burned, and each labored footfall sent hot acid rushing through his smashed shoulder. He could see the hill now. The Becker place was just beyond it, just beyond the spot where his brother had stood in the storm and called out to him.

The roar of an engine sounded ahead of him. Panic seized something deep inside Scott, as though a giant fist had reached into his chest and grabbed his heart. All he could think was that Charles Hunter was coming back to finish him.

His eyes frantically searched for a hiding place and, failing that, a weapon. *Any* weapon. Anything he could use to take Hunter's head off.

Glancing once more in the direction of the approaching roar, he turned and sprinted twenty yards to a tangle of driftwood. There was a thick trunk, half buried in sand and covered with a sun-bleached tangle of limbs intertwined like finger-thick snakes. Scott grabbed the tree and pulled. The smaller branches broke and tore at the skin on his fingers. He jumped over the trunk and almost landed on a limb three feet long and three or four inches in diameter. Scott wrung the limb out of the sand and hunkered down as best he could behind the other driftwood.

He waited only a second or two before his own vehicle crested the hill like some dream of rescue. Bobby was at the wheel.

Scott jumped up and ran for the roadside, waving his driftwood weapon in the air. Bobby slammed on brakes, skidded to a stop ten yards away, and stepped out to face Scott. "You gonna hit me with that?"

Scott looked at the limb in his hand. "I thought you were Hunter."

"He's back at the house."

"Did you kill them?"

Bobby cocked his head to one side, like a dog hearing a loud whistle. "You could say that. I'm going into town. Need a ride?"

"You need to get off the island. I'll call the police when I know you're safe." Scott began to walk toward the Land Cruiser. "If you ever need anything . . ."

Bobby nodded and interrupted his brother with that rusty hinge of a voice. "You remember the way it was?"

Scott stopped walking. "What?"

Bobby shrugged and climbed into the driver's seat.

Scott tossed away his makeshift weapon and got in beside him. His eyes stayed on the ground ahead. "I remember. I don't idolize it, though. The only good stuff . . . The good memories are about you and me."

Bobby nodded. "Not them."

"No," Scott said. "Not them."

Together, the two Thomas brothers drove to the

town square. Natalie spotted them from the restaurant and called out. Scott jumped out and ran to meet her as the two beefy security guards looked on.

"Oh, God. I was so worried." She stepped back to look at the bloody gash on his cheekbone. "What did that asshole do to you?"

"I'm fine. But everything else is pretty awful." Scott smiled because she was there, and it hurt. "We need to help Bobby. I know—"

"Where is he?"

Scott turned toward the Land Cruiser. "He's . . ." His eyes scanned the square. "He was right here."

Natalie put an arm around Scott's waist. "Bobby can take care of himself. We need to get your face looked at."

"I've got to call the police, Natalie. We need to call as soon as possible."

"Scott," she said, "that's the smartest thing you've said since I met you."

Charles Hunter ran scenarios through his head. It was time to bring in the mainland police. He reached into his pocket, flipped open his phone, and dialed 911. The emergency operator answered immediately.

"Hello? This is Charles Hunter out on Spinnaker Island. Oh, God, this is awful." His voice had suddenly grown hoarse and high-pitched—conveying the timbre of horrified disbelief overlaid with adrenaline. "Oh, God. Oh, God."

"What's happened, sir? Please give me your address and phone number."

"I'm at the Becker house out on Gull Way. Oh, my God. I came by to check on the house. The owners are out of town. I came by to check on the house, and . . . oh, my God. There are two bodies in there. One of them is my nanny. Her throat is cut. And there's a man. Oh, God. Oh, God."

"Stay away from the scene, sir. If you're alone, you should go to a safe location. Hold on, please." Hunter took the opportunity to scan the horizon for surprises. There were none. He was pretty sure that Scott Thomas was out of commission for a while. He smiled at how easy it had been. *Why, Officer, as soon as my security guards left with Ms. Friedman, this Thomas man just attacked me. I was lucky there was a tire iron handy there in the Jeep. You know, he's a lot younger . . .* "Sir? Are you still there?"

"I'm here."

"Sir. Please go to a safe location and wait. We'll have someone out there within twenty minutes. Do you understand?"

"Yes. I understand. But please—hurry."

The operator said, "Leave the scene, sir." And the line went dead.

Hunter grimaced at the thought of what came next. If you say you've discovered two bodies, he thought, there damn well better be evidence that you went into the house at least far enough to see them. He closed his flip phone and dropped it into his hip pocket.

A careful man by nature, Hunter approached the doorway cautiously. Kate's motionless body lay about five feet inside the house, where Bobby had tossed her. She was on her stomach. Her hair covered the side of her face. She looked finished. But if Bobby had missed the jugular . . . He had to be sure.

Hunter eased inside. The droning chords of ancient monastic chants floated in from a stereo somewhere in the house. He glanced toward the back of the room and then carefully positioned the toe of his cast above Kate's buttocks. With a flick of his knee, Hunter jabbed hard between her glutes to check for involuntary reflexes. Her buttocks tightened, and his breath caught up short.

Charles Hunter glanced at her head. *Oh, God.* There was no blood around her face or throat. He spun on his heels just as the front door slammed shut.

The famous architect managed to say one word— "Click"—before the knife ripped a hole in his stomach. Click stabbed again and again, pounding the blade into Hunter's gut in a series of vicious uppercuts.

Hunter fell to the floor, clawing at the bloody mess that had been his stomach. Beside him, he saw Kate jump to her feet. She looked down at him and spat. The room began to swivel on some wobbly axis, and bright colors turned gray. He stared up at Click's pale, smiling face, then let his gaze drift to the bloody right hand that still held the knife Bobby Thomas had used when he'd pretended to cut Kate's throat.

Muscle turned to mush, and Hunter's head flopped involuntarily to the side.

The last thing Charles Hunter saw on earth was the bandaged stump of Click's left wrist, where it looked for all the world as if someone had chopped off one of the hacker's strong, pale hands.

CHAPTER 49

Scott Thomas couldn't get warm.

Heated air hissed from a vent in the ceiling, but the concrete floor and gray walls radiated the wet-cold of March in New England. Even the metal chair seemed to push cold into his aching joints. The shoulder hurt. He'd been injured pretty badly in wrestling, but this was something else. The doctors in North Carolina had said that, sooner or later, he'd be looking at an operation, and Scott wondered if prison docs were like the ones in the movies—either noble and ill-equipped or sadistic and stupid.

The door opened and Assistant District Attorney Anne Foucher stepped into the interrogation room. She didn't speak. She simply spread out six stacks of papers on the table between them and then eased into a chair. Minutes passed before she spoke.

"You were a real ass at our first meeting, Dr. Thomas."

"Mr. or Scott. I'm not a doctor."

She looked up. "Right. In any event, you made me about as mad as . . . Well, let's just say that I don't usually let suspects get to me. But you—I have to give you credit, Scott. You really shoved a bug up . . . Sorry, I'm working on my language." Scott noticed for the first time that ADA Foucher had had something expensive done to her hair. And something else. She still wore a suit, but it was soft and forest green. Even her skin seemed to glow. Overall, the woman just looked . . . healthier. Foucher watched his eyes. "Don't flatter yourself. I had let myself go. You were just the first person rude enough to point it out. That doesn't make you what you said right or anything. It just proves that even a jerk can teach you something if you can bear his presence."

"You attacked my friend. You were nasty and condescending. I responded in kind."

"Seemed pretty unkind to me, but . . . whatever. Let's just say you gave me a reason to become personally interested in your case. Unfortunately, the harder I tried to bury you, the more complicated things got. You see, Scott, we have computer people, too. It was easy enough to figure out what you'd been doing messing around in the hospital's computer system." She picked up a stack of e-mails. "How long did it take you to break the code?"

"Natalie figured it out."

"Um. We got that right off. But it took a while to trace the IP address of the sender to a hacker named Darryl Simmons. After that, it was simple to see that this Simmons had been communicating through the hospital's e-mail system with Kate Billings, Phillip Reynolds, and Charles Hunter."

"Hunter?"

"Oh." Foucher grinned. "You didn't know that, did you? Hunter was assigned a temporary hospital e-mail address when he was in the process of designing the new children's wing. Apparently, he held on to it."

"It wasn't on anybody's official list."

"Right." Foucher pushed back from the table and crossed one knee over the other. "Tennessee Bureau of Investigation nabbed Simmons in some flea-bitten motel in Memphis. Mr. Simmons—"

"Click."

"Right. Click seems to be missing a hand. A recent loss. You wouldn't know anything about that, would you?"

Scott's eyes never left hers. "No. I wouldn't."

"Good." She laced her fingers together in her lap. "The night Dr. Reynolds got shot outside the hospital? Were you supposed to be meeting him there?"

"No. Not him. I got a message that Kate wanted to meet me outside the hospital parking deck. I guess Reynolds got the same message."

"Right. The shots came from a second deck across the street."

Scott's heart began to pound. "If you know all this, what are you charging me with?"

Anne Foucher grinned. "Charles Hunter is dead. We've got Click in custody, and, sooner or later, we'll find Kate Billings, if Click hasn't already left her in a dumpster somewhere. But as for you . . . Well, being a sap and a sometimes horse's ass aren't really against the law in this state."

Scott got to his feet. "So that's it?" The room seemed to tilt, and he couldn't get his breath. "I can just go back to school like none of this ever happened?"

She grimaced. "Of course, we notified the graduate school. Unfortunately"—Foucher pressed her lips together—"they do not want you back."

His breathing slowed to normal as something more—much more—than relief settled over him. He was surprised by his reaction. The weight of the world seemed to have been lifted from his . . . the word that came to mind was "soul." Scott smiled. There was a lightness he hadn't felt since he was a child. "I always hated hospitals."

She just looked at him.

"So," he said, "for me, not going to jail is as good as it's going to get."

"Sorry, but that's about size of it." Foucher gathered up her papers and tucked them inside a manila folder. "Ms. Friedman is waiting for you downstairs. That's something you didn't have before." She got to her feet. "Something that might keep you from *ever* working fourteen hours a day, walking around some bullshit office with a sour expression and frayed cuffs." The directness of her comments made Foucher blush. It was a surprisingly attractive sight. "There's, ah, something else you should know. Your friend Natalie made a deal with the Boston PD to monitor your movements. It's one of the reasons they let you and her go when you were in custody." Scott felt his heart sink. Foucher saw the hurt in his eyes. "She never did it, Scott. Never. All Natalie ever did was call the police from New York and tell them to forget the deal. I think her exact words were along the lines of telling our Lieutenant Cedris to go fuck himself." She examined his face. "She was completely faithful to you. Remember that. And remember that frightened people—people who've never even thought of being arrested—do and say things under intense pressure that they don't really mean. Look, Scott. Find another school next year if having a PhD is what you want. But, for now, take some time off. Take Natalie to the Bahamas. Rent a sailboat. Go see your mother."

His face flushed. "My mother's dead."

ADA Foucher dropped her folder on the table and flipped it open. Thumbing through various reports, she found a fax from a detective with the Homewood, Alabama, Police Department.

Scott asked, "What is it?"

Foucher held up a palm while she finished reading. Then she placed the report back into the folder and closed it. "I'm sorry, Scott. I didn't . . . understand about your mother."

As Anne Foucher stopped to hold the door for Scott,

he had to ask. "Are you saying that if I'd never gone to North Carolina, you'd have figured all this out anyhow?"

"Truth?" The assistant DA chuckled. "We'd have probably never gotten Charles Hunter. Whether your presence down there brought things to a head between him and the other two . . . Who knows? Maybe he'd be dead even if you'd never gone near him. Or maybe"—she looked hard into Scott's eyes—"Hunter just finally tried to manipulate the *wrong person*."

Scott thought back on the strange look on Bobby's misshapen face as he sat in the Land Cruiser that last day on the island. "Did you kill them?" he'd asked. Bobby had made that almost smile. "You could say that."

Unbelievable.

Scott had thought then that Hunter had manipulated his brother into committing a double murder. Now, for the first time, he understood that maybe he was not the smarter of the Thomas brothers.

CHAPTER 50

They sat in the downstairs café at the Madison Hotel. Across the teeming street, the grass in Central Park hinted at the deep green color to come. Trees showed wisps of bright new growth. Across the table, Cannonball sat next to Natalie, who seemed enthralled by the old bluesman.

"Think I finally earned my money." The old man sounded tired, but there was something like satisfaction in his voice. "I've got some good news for you." He paused, still conflicted about what he was about to say, or, more to the point, what he was not going to say. "We got an agreement with John Pastings at the bank. They're gonna replace all the money that Click and his bunch stole outta your account. Not only that . . ."

Scott hunched forward. "Why the hell would the bank do that?"

Cannonball lied. "Hell, boy. It was the bank's fault. Lettin' somebody with no rights just dip a hand into your money . . . they can't do that. Once I got Mr. Pastings pinned down, hell, there wasn't much else he could do."

Something felt wrong. "That's great, but what about the fire and the cops down there reopening the investigation?"

"I don't know what Pastings thought he was up to.

Truth is, Doc . . . And I'm sorry to be the one to tell you this, but your daddy was mixed up in some business deals that went bad. Everybody down there has known for a long time that he set fire to his own house—meaning all the time to get you and Bobby and your momma out. Everybody agrees on that, too." Cannonball paused. "Your daddy was a good man, Scott. But he was weak, and he messed up. Messed up about as bad as a man can, but there wasn't any evil in it toward you and your family." Cannonball took a sip of iced tea. "They don't make this right once you get outta the South." He smiled, but there was sadness. "What you got to live with is a fuck-up for a father. He wasn't no murderer, though. Just got in over his head and messed up everything. Can you live with that, Doc?"

Scott leaned back in his chair, a blank expression on his face. "I guess I'm going to have to."

Cannonball sighed. "Worse things in the world than not having a family. Lots of folks be glad to give theirs away."

Scott looked over at Natalie as he spoke to Cannonball. "So that's it? I've got my money back, and the authorities down there don't suspect me of anything."

A picture of Nancy Thomas—sitting in that wicker rocker with her hideous scars hidden beneath twisted turban and flowing dashiki—floated into Cannonball's mind, and he felt a wave of nausea wash over him. "That's it. Only you got a little more money than Mr. Pastings said. There was another account or somethin'." Cannonball didn't explain that the other account materialized after three hours of arm-twisting in Pastings's office. "By the time it's all worked out, you're gonna have a solid hundred grand to finish up your schoolwork. That includes what you took out just here recently, though."

Natalie smiled. "We're rich."

"*We*, huh?" Scott turned back to Cannonball. "I don't know how to thank you."

"You paid me for this, remember? We're good, you and me." He scratched at salt-and-pepper curls. The old bluesman was spinning a web of half-truths and it was wearing on him.

The waiter placed their orders on the table. When they were alone again, Scott asked, "Anything else?"

"Nope." The old bluesman sighed. Without thinking, he reached up to finger a thick document in his inside coat pocket, and he immediately felt better.

He and Pastings had worked on the document for most of one night.

Pastings had admitted nothing in writing—not that he had been Robert Thomas's partner in the embezzlement scheme, not that he'd screwed over his partner along with everyone else, not that he'd paid for Scott's education out of ill-gotten funds, and not even that he'd spearheaded the funds drive that had rebuilt Nancy Thomas's home. But the banker did agree, in writing, to keep up payments on Nancy's house, her nurse, and all other expenses for as long as Nancy Thomas lived.

Cannonball still did not know whether Pastings's acts of generosity toward the Thomas family had been born of fear, guilt, or kindness. All Cannonball Walker knew was that John Pastings had been the lesser of two fuck-ups fifteen years ago and he'd been paying for it ever since.

But that wasn't true, either. Cannonball knew one other thing—that poor, scarred, crazy Nancy Thomas still kept a thick stack of love letters tied with pink satin ribbon. The insane little woman was damned proud of those letters: she'd showed them happily after Cannonball had sung blues and gospel and picked his old guitar.

Mixed together, as if the two men had been interchangeable, were letters from both Robert Thomas and

John Pastings. Cannonball had read just enough to understand that Nancy Thomas had been a beauty and that Robert Thomas and John Pastings had loved her with equal and extraordinary intensity.

As his mind returned to the present, Cannonball picked up a knife and fork and cut a bite of steak. Scott excused himself from the table, and the old man turned to Natalie. "You in love with that boy?"

Her face colored. "Well . . . yeah, I guess I am."

He chewed his steak, swallowed, and drank some tea. "He don't ever need to go back to Birmingham. Don't tell him I said it. Just make sure it doesn't happen." He saw alarm in her face. "It ain't like he's gonna be arrested or anything. It'd just . . . I think it'd break his heart. We clear on that?"

"We're clear." There were tears in her eyes.

He nodded and cut more steak. Cannonball's mind was still back in Birmingham. He remembered, when it was all over, standing in Pastings's paneled executive office, studying the banker's Hitchcockian profile—trying to imagine that rotund man as the impetuous, passionate young lover who had romped with Robert Thomas's beautiful young wife and then written torrid letters that remained, fifteen years later, among his conquest's greatest treasures.

He couldn't see it.

Scott came back to the table. He glanced at Natalie. "What's the matter with you? You look like your puppy died."

Cannonball grinned. "Woman says she's in love with you." The old man looked at Scott. "You figured out which body chemicals account for a beautiful woman lovin' a nerd like you?"

Scott laughed. He thought back on what Natalie and Cannonball, even Bobby, had done for him. Then mental images of Kate and Click, Charles and Patricia

Hunter, Peter Budzik and Cindy Travers filled his mind, and his smile faded. Scott glanced up at Cannonball and saw the old man's eyes fill with hurt.

Scott cleared his throat. "You know what I'm feeling, don't you?"

"Some of it."

Scott looked at Natalie and turned back to study the lines and years that marked Cannonball Walker's face. "It's complicated."

Cannonball started eating again. "That's all I been tryin' to tell you, boy. That's all I been tryin' to tell you."

Inside a Boston skyscraper designed by her father, ten-year-old Sarah Hunter sat on a tufted leather sofa. Carol Petring reached over to straighten Sarah's dark blue dress. "Honey, this has got to be perfect. Your father named me as your guardian in his will, but . . ." She couldn't tell the child that everything her father had ever done was being picked apart by prosecutors and judges. "Just remember what I told you to say, Sarah. When this is over, we can go back to Spinnaker Island. We'll build everything your father and I dreamed about."

Sarah pushed a suffocating mass of hurt down deep in her stomach. She sat up straight and reviewed her lines in her head. Carol had said "Be perfect." It was the only way she would get to stay with Carol, and, Sarah was convinced, it was the only way to finally to stop it.

First her mother had died. Then Trey. Then that awful Patricia. Now her father was gone, too, and Carol was the only one left who loved her. Sarah swallowed hard and bit down on her lip. She wasn't sure why everyone around her always died. She'd never even heard of something like that happening to anyone else. All she knew was that she had loved them all—all except Patricia. Clearly, she'd done something wrong. Sarah didn't understand what, exactly. But there had to be something.

Carol reached over to squeeze Sarah's hand. Sarah squeezed back briefly, then pulled away and folded both hands in her lap. She straightened her spine. "I'll be perfect, Carol. Don't worry. From now on I promise to be perfect."

THE LAST CHAPTER

Scott stood outside the door of the brick Tudor on Roseland Drive in Homewood, Alabama. His heart raced. A coiled cable of nausea slowly unwound inside his stomach.

He rang the doorbell.

A fat black woman opened the door and glared into his eyes. She didn't speak, and he didn't seem able to form intelligent thought. She seemed on the verge of shutting the door in his face when something like recognition formed in her eyes. She swung the door wide.

Scott pulled open the screen door and stepped inside his secret nightmare. The house had been put back exactly the way it had looked before the fire, and then never changed again. He stopped and glanced to the left, where the same tuxedo sofa and oval coffee table from his childhood still squatted against the back wall. Of course, they weren't the same ones—just the same brands and colors and placement.

"You comin'?" The fat nurse's voice jolted Scott inside his skin.

Scott nodded. He turned to follow her into the back den.

And that's when he saw her.

Nancy Thomas sat in a wicker rocker. Her head

wrapped by a black turban, her tiny body draped inside a
silver dashiki—his mother looked like a sinister Vulcan
queen on *Star Trek*. As he entered the room she began to
bounce the balls of her feet against the floor, and he saw
that she wore metallic-silver slippers to match her gown.

His eyes moved back up to her grinning face.

He broke the silence. "I'm Scott."

"No shit. Sit in the chair where Canon sits. Sit in
the chair where he makes music." She waved impatiently at an old easy chair. "Go on! I told you to sit!"

Scott walked over and lowered himself into the
chair. He wanted to speak, but the whirlwind inside his
head kept blowing away the words as quickly as they
came. Half-finished thoughts and sentences disappeared into a thick miasma of smells, sights, and emotions from the last night he had spent in this place
fifteen years before. He smelled smoke that was not
there. He felt the heat of a blazing fire scorch the skin
on his face.

He cleared his throat. "You met Canon Walker?"

"What I said. You're sitting in *his* chair. Always will
be. Canon's chair—that's what I call it. Canon's chair.
It's his." She stopped chattering and let her eyes roam
over Scott's face. "Didn't tell you, did he? Supposed to
be a friend, and he didn't tell you he ever saw me. Liking
him better all the time. That's what I am. Liking him
better all the time."

"He's a good man."

She made a snorting sound. "Canon thought he
found me. Guess you didn't tell the 'good man' about
your barbecued mommy." She held shiny, curled fingers
up to her lips and made a shushing sound. "Shhhh.
Don't tell anyone about the crazy woman. Don't tell the
teachers. Don't tell the schools. Don't tell the preachers.
And don't tell the fools." She changed her voice to
mimic some doctor from the past. " 'Scott's normal. He

deserves a good life. He's the normal one.' " Her voice went back. "Got to protect Scotty from his crazy, burned-up family."

"They—the doctors who treated you—they told me to move on."

"You did it! Moved on. Moved away. Gone!" Her eyes narrowed. "You tell folks that Bobby and I are dead, don't you?"

"I thought Bobby *was* dead." He took a shaky breath. "And, fifteen years ago, your own psychiatrist told me that *my* mother was dead. He said the person who was left didn't care about me."

She laughed that cackling laugh. "Well, the dumbass got that much right. Take off, Lazarus! Take off to the stars. Forget about all of us. Forget about the scars."

Scott's ribs spasmed and gripped his lungs with suffocating force. He sucked hard but couldn't seem to get air past his collarbone. *Breathe. Please, God, let me breathe.* He closed his eyes and forced his mind to go blank. Seconds passed, and his chest filled with air again. He looked up. "I came here to ask about Bobby."

"Knew you didn't come to see me." Her grin widened. "Everybody wants to know about Bobby. First that man from Boston, then Canon, then the cops." Nancy caught a flicker of something in Scott's eyes and sat forward. "That's right. Cops been around. Looking here. Looking there. Looking everywhere. But they're not looking at the *right* there. Nope. Not looking at the *there* that's the *there* where he is."

"Someone else came around asking questions *before* Cannonball?"

"What I said. Sent Bobby off looking for his *beautiful big brother*." She spaced out the last three words with biting contempt. "That boy can smell trouble. Smell it like smoke on fire." She waved a shiny claw in the air. "Saved your ass, didn't he? Saved your ass, and now he's run to the *there* instead of the *here*. He's at the *there* that's safe from the lookers. He's at the *there* that's the *there* where no one is."

"Are you telling me Bobby's safe?"

Nancy Thomas cackled. "Safe? Safe at home. Sliding in. Called by the ump." She threw her bony hands up and screeched, "Safe!"

Scott didn't know whether Bobby was safe or his mother was just nuts. "That's all I wanted to know. Bobby helped me. I wanted to know he's okay." He paused. "Tell him if he ever needs help . . ."

"Help?" His mother cackled. "Help? How're you gonna help *him*? That boy is two of you. Always has been. Lucky you got a brother like Bobby, that's what I say." Something hard passed through her eyes. "Lucky you. Unlucky him."

"Well . . ." Scott's voice faded as the room closed in on him. "I thought I should see you. I'm not sure what . . . Tell Bobby I was here." He rose to his feet and struggled for something to say. "I know this is hard for both of us."

Nancy slumped back into the rocker and closed her eyes. Tears welled up along her lashes, spilled over, and cut paths through thick powder on her cheeks. Finally, she held up her burn-scarred hands so that Scott could see them. "Hard for *you*?" Her tone mocking him. "Poor baby. Poor, poor baby." Her face hardened. "You make me sick. *Poor* Scotty. *Lucky* Scotty. *Perfect* Scotty." She chanted the words. "Bunk and junk. Bunk and junk." Her eyes narrowed. "Do you even *know* what you are?"

Scott looked down at the tiny woman. "I know what I am. *And* I know what I did."

She rocked forward, her thin voice rising in pitch. "Do you?"

"Yeah," he replied, "I do. But one night isn't going to swallow my life. Not anymore."

Her voice dropped to a contemptuous whisper. "The *good* son." She made a *huh* sound full of air. "The good son *knows* everything and *accepts* everything, and now it's time to get back to his perfect life."

Scott nodded. His mother was more right than she knew.

He turned and walked out of his childhood home, down red-brick steps, and between rows of dark monkey grass that lined the front walk. Outside the yard and moving faster now, he turned down Roseland Drive—down the street where he had played hide-and-seek and cops-and-robbers with Bobby tagging along, the street where he'd ridden his bike so many times.

Two blocks down, he slowed and then stopped.

Scott breathed deeply, and all the horrors of fifteen years before poured over him, drowning him in smoke and fire and the overwhelming emotions of childhood.

He tried to clear his thoughts, but couldn't shake the presence of his father. Scott remembered wandering into the den from his bedroom that night after the unfamiliar scent of gasoline had pulled him out of a sound sleep. That was where he had found his father, bleary-eyed and smelling of gin, slumped in his favorite recliner. A galvanized gas can had hunkered between his heavy wingtip oxfords, as out of place as a snake in a nursery.

"Scotty." The deep voice had slurred his child's name. "I need you to help me with somethin'." Then his father had leaned forward and tapped the gas can with the toe of his banker's shoe. "Pour the rest of this out over by the television, there."

"That's gasoline." It had been all Scott could think to say.

His father had glared down at him—in Scott's memory, looking impossibly tall and strong. "Pick up the god-damn can and do what I say."

Scott didn't remember speaking. He knew he'd shaken his head no. And he was sure now that he had cried—he knew because of his father's words. "A cry-baby. I need help and I got a goddamn crybaby." He pointed between his shoes. "Pick up the goddamn can and do what I said."

It was his father. And, in the end, Scott had poured out gasoline in the den of the house where his mother and brother lay sleeping.

Standing on the street now—a cool springtime breeze ruffling his hair—nausea boiled inside Scott's gut. He leaned over and gripped his knees to stay up-right.

His father came floating back, overpowering his thoughts—telling him to run away. But it was a vague and confused command. Scott's mind tumbled back fif-teen years again, recalling gruff words chopped and con-fused by the sobs that racked his body. He felt the pain of his father's grip on his small arm. He had tried to fight, but it had been useless. Flung out the front door like a bag of trash, he'd felt the brick steps come up hard against his knees and shins.

His father had glared down from the doorway—his face red and swollen, his drunken voice bellowing. "You goddamn little girl. I said *run!*"

Scott had never seen his father drunk. He'd never heard that mix of rasp, slur, and stupidity in his voice. "I need to get Bobby."

Robert Thomas had simply shaken his head. "I'll get the little sonofabitch." He waved a drunken hand in the night air. "You haul ass now." His voice suddenly turned to a roar. "Goddammit! I . . . said . . . run!"

Scott could remember the ground spinning beneath his feet. He remembered the soft beat of bare feet hitting pavement. He remembered running until his lungs had burned and he'd feared his chest would burst.

And, in all the years since, he'd kept running.

Scott straightened up and breathed deeply. The scents of wisteria and freshly cut grass floated on the breeze. Across the street, a new mother jogged behind a stroller and an elderly couple walked hand in hand down the sidewalk.

Scott turned back to look once more at his childhood home on Roseland Drive, then he turned his back and walked away.

Natalie was waiting.

ABOUT THE AUTHOR

Birmingham attorney Mike Stewart is the author of three acclaimed mystery novels—*Sins of the Brother, Dog Island,* and *A Clean Kill.* A native of Vredenburgh, a small South Alabama sawmill town, he grew up exploring the woods, rivers, creeks, and seashores of the Deep South that now play a central role in his fiction. He is at work on his next novel of suspense, which Dell will publish in 2006.